CLIVILIUS

INTERCONNECTED STORIES. INFINITE POSSIBILITIES

© 2024 Nathan Cowdrey. All rights reserved.
First Edition, 26 April 2024
ISBN 978-1-4457-9616-1
Imprint: Lulu.com

Step into Clivilius, where creation meets infinity, and the essence of reality is yours to redefine. Here, existence weaves into a narrative where every decision has consequences, every action has an impact, and every moment counts. In this realm, shaped by the visionary AI CLIVE, inhabitants are not mere spectators but pivotal characters in an evolving drama where the lines between worlds blur.

Guardians traverse the realms of Clivilius and Earth, their journeys igniting events that challenge the balance between these interconnected universes. The quest for resources and the enigma of unexplained disappearances on Earth mirror the deeper conflicts and intricacies that define Clivilius—a world where reality responds to the collective will and individual choices of its Clivilians, revealing a complex interplay of creation, control, and consequence.

In the grand tapestry of Clivilius, the struggle for harmony and the dance of dichotomies play out across a cosmic stage. Here, every soul's journey contributes to the narrative, where the lines between utopia and dystopia, creator and observer, become increasingly fluid. Clivilius is not just a realm to be explored but a reality to be shaped.

Open your eyes. Expand your mind. Experience your new reality. Welcome to Clivilius, where the journey of discovery is not just about seeing a new world but about seeing your world anew.

Also in the Clivilius Series:

Luke Smith (4338.204.1 - 4338.209.2)

Luke Smith's world transforms with the discovery of a cryptic device, thrusting him into the guardianship of destiny itself. His charismatic charm and unpredictable decisions now carry weight beyond imagination, balancing on the razor's edge between salvation and destruction. Embracing his role as a Guardian, Luke faces the paradox of power: the very force that defends also threatens to annihilate. As shadows gather and the fabric of reality strains, Luke must navigate the consequences of his actions, unaware that a looming challenge will test the very core of his resolve.

Paul Smith (4338.204.1 - 4338.209.3)

In a harsh, new world, Paul Smith grapples with the remnants of a hostile marriage and the future of his two young children. Cast into the heart of an arid wasteland, his survival pushes him to the brink, challenging his every belief. Amidst the desolation, Paul faces a pivotal choice that will dictate where his true allegiance lies. In this tale of resilience and resolve, Paul's journey is a harrowing exploration of loyalty, family, and the boundless optimism required to forge hope in the bleakest of landscapes.

Beatrix Cramer (4338.205.1 - 4338.211.7)

Beatrix Cramer's life is a delicate balance of contradictions, her independence and keen intellect shadowed by her penchant for the forbidden. A master of acquisition, her love for antiques and the call of the wild drives her into the heart of danger, making her an indispensable ally yet an unpredictable force. When fate thrusts her into the clandestine world of Guardians, Beatrix must navigate a labyrinth of secrets and moral dilemmas. Caught in the crossfire of legacy and destiny, she faces choices that could redefine the boundaries of her world and her very identity.

Kain Jeffries (4338.207.1 - 4338.211.2)

Kain Jeffries' life takes an unimaginable turn when he's thrust into Clivilius, far from the Tasmanian life he knows and the fiancée carrying their unborn child. Torn between worlds, he grapples with decisions concerning his growing family. Haunted by Clivilius's whispering voice and faced with dire ultimatums, Kain's resolve is tested when shadowy predators threaten his new home. As he navigates this new landscape, the line between survival and surrender blurs, pushing Kain to confront what it truly means to fight for a future when every choice echoes through eternity.

Karl Jenkins (4338.209.1 - 4338.214.1)

Plunged into Tasmania's most chilling cases, Senior Detective Karl Jenkins confronts a string of disappearances that entangle with his clandestine affair with Detective Sarah Lahey. As a dangerous obsession emerges, every step toward the truth draws Karl perilously close to a precipice threatening their lives and careers. "Karl Jenkins" is a riveting tale of suspense, where past haunts bear a perilous future.

4338.210.1 - 4338.214.6

NOAH SMITH

CLIVILIUS
INTERCONNECTED STORIES. INFINITE POSSIBILITIES

"Faith is the compass that guides us through the storms of life, always pointing us towards the light of hope and love."

- Noah Smith

4338.210

(29 July 2018)

LEAD, KINDLY LIGHT

4338.210.1

In the quiet of Sunday's early hours, Greta and I nestled into the heart of our home, a cozy nook filled with memories of laughter and love. The fragrance of brewed hot chocolate mingled with the soft scent of freshly bought frangipanis, a delicate aroma that Greta adored. She, an early riser and always the soul of our home, had already prepared a tray with steaming mugs of hot chocolate. Each mug, cradled in our hands, felt like a promise of warmth in the crisp morning air.

As I breathed in the comforting scent of the cocoa, I couldn't help but smile. This simple ritual, this quiet moment shared between us, had become a cornerstone of our Sundays. It was a time to pause, to reflect, and to simply be together before the day's hustle and bustle began.

Greta's hand found mine, her fingers intertwining with my own as we sat side by side on the plush sofa. Her touch, as always, was a source of comfort and strength, a reminder of the unbreakable bond we shared. I turned to look at her, my heart swelling with love and admiration for the remarkable woman who had stood by my side for over three decades.

The winter sun cast a gentle, golden glow through the frost-kissed windows, bathing the room in a soft, ethereal light. It was as if the world outside had paused, granting us this moment of solace and peace.

As I gazed out of the window, my thoughts drifted to our children, our pride and joy. Each of them, unique and special in their own way, had brought countless moments of laughter, love, and even the occasional challenge to our lives. They were the threads that wove the tapestry of our family, the bright spots of colour that made our world vibrant and alive.

The morning unfolded with the rhythmic cadence of our family's Sunday routine, each moment a cherished memory in the making. From down the hallway, I could hear the muffled sounds of Jerome, our second youngest, still engrossed in his Sunday morning ritual of selecting the perfect tie. It was a habit he had picked up from me, a reflection of the meticulous nature I saw in myself at his age.

I chuckled softly, remembering the countless Sundays I had spent in front of the mirror, carefully knotting my own tie until it sat just right. It was a small thing, but it mattered to me, just as it mattered to Jerome now.

Suddenly, the sound of laughter echoed through the house, a bright, joyful sound that never failed to bring a smile to my face. It was Charles, the playful spirit of the family, no doubt teasing Jerome good-naturedly about his sartorial choices.

Greta, with her gentle laugh and a knowing look in her eyes, rose from the sofa, ready to ensure that the banter didn't escalate into a full-fledged sibling skirmish. Her presence, always a calming force, brought a sense of harmony to our home, a reminder that no matter what challenges we faced, we would always have each other.

As Greta made her way towards their rooms, I couldn't help but marvel at the woman she was. Strong, compassionate, and endlessly patient, she was the glue that held our family together, the beating heart of our home.

Before long, amidst the familial chatter, the aroma of pancakes, a tradition as old as our eldest son, wafted from the kitchen. The scent, warm and inviting, brought a smile to every face, a reminder of countless Sundays filled with joy and togetherness. It was a smell that evoked memories of sticky fingers, syrup-soaked plates, and the sound of laughter ringing through the house.

As I inhaled deeply, savouring the comforting scent, Greta's phone rang, its shrill tone cutting through the morning's tranquility. I reached for her mobile, a smile already forming on my lips as I saw the caller ID. It was Lisa, our only daughter among five brothers, calling in from Salt Lake City.

"Dad!" Lisa's voice, warm and familiar, filled the room as I put her on speakerphone. "Happy Sunday!"

I grinned, my heart swelling with love and pride at the sound of her voice. "Happy Sunday, sweetheart," I replied, my tone filled with affection. "How are you? How's Will? And Eli?"

As Lisa launched into a lively recounting of their week, her voice a comforting presence bridging the distance between us, I couldn't help but marvel at the wonders of technology. The screen flickered with images of Lisa, her husband Will, and Eli, one of her brothers who was visiting for a period of time on a work visa. Their faces, displayed in the warm glow of the screen, echoed the very essence of The Smith Clan, a name that held a resonance of family bonds and our shared faith.

I leaned against the kitchen bench, gazing out across the breakfast bar and into the living room where my eyes roamed over the photographs that adorned the walls. Each one, a frozen moment in time, told a story of love and laughter. From family vacations to backyard barbecues, from graduations to weddings, these images were a testament to the life we had built, the memories we had created.

As I sat there, immersed in the familiar chatter and laughter, a sense of gratitude washed over me. These moments, simple yet profound, were the pillars of my life. They were a reminder of the blessings we had, the love we shared, and the faith that had guided us through every storm.

I closed my eyes, offering a silent prayer of thanks for the incredible family I had been gifted with. For Greta, my rock and my soulmate, who had stood by my side through every joy and every sorrow. For our children, the lights of our lives, who had grown into remarkable individuals, each with their own unique talents and passions. And for the faith that had sustained us, the belief in a higher power that had given us strength and purpose even in the darkest of times.

As the morning stretched on, the sun climbing higher in the sky, I knew that this was just the beginning of another perfect Sunday. A day filled with love, laughter, and the simple joys of being together. A day to celebrate the blessings we had been given, and to look forward to the bright future that lay ahead.

Our home in Adelaide, a haven of warmth and shared moments, became the launching point for our Sunday pilgrimage to church. As I stepped out onto the porch, the early morning sun casting a golden glow across the front yard, I couldn't help but pause for a moment, my eyes taking in the sight of the house that had been the backdrop of our lives for so many years.

The weathered bricks and the slightly overgrown garden held countless memories, each one a precious gem in the treasure trove of our family history. I could almost hear the echoes of laughter and the patter of tiny feet, remnants of a time when all six of our children filled these walls with the vibrant energy of youth.

Paul, our eldest, had long since flown the nest, settling in Broken Hill with his own growing family. Luke, the second born, had found his path in Hobart, while Lisa, our only daughter, had followed her heart to Salt Lake City, where she now lived with her husband Will and her brother Eli, who was staying with them for a time.

And then there were Jerome and Charles, the two youngest, still at home with Greta and me. At seventeen, Charles was on the cusp of adulthood, his boyish charm slowly giving way to the man he would become. It was hard to believe that so much time had passed, that the tiny baby I had once cradled in my arms was now a young man, ready to take on the world.

As I stood there, lost in thought, Greta's gentle touch on my arm brought me back to the present. Her smile, as radiant as the morning sun, held a lifetime of love and understanding. Together, we had weathered the storms of life, our faith and our love for each other guiding us through every challenge.

With a nod, I followed her to the car, where Jerome and Charles were already waiting, their faces eager for the day ahead. As we filed into the ageing but reliable vehicle, a sense of ritual enveloped us, a comforting familiarity that spoke of countless Sundays past.

The car, much like our family, had seen better days, but it was filled with memories and a steadfast resilience that had carried us through the years. As I turned the key in the ignition, the engine roared to life, a sound as familiar to me as my own heartbeat.

The drive to church was a journey etched in my mind, each bend in the road holding a story, a moment frozen in time. As we wound our way through the quiet streets of Craigmore, the early morning stillness slowly gave way to the gentle stirrings of a Sunday beginning.

The eucalyptus trees that lined our path swayed in the breeze, their leaves whispering secrets of a world beyond our own. The scent of their oils, carried on the wind, filled the car with a fragrance that was uniquely Australian, a reminder of the land we called home.

As we drove, the silence was punctuated by the soft murmur of conversation, Jerome and Charles discussing the latest happenings in their lives, Greta offering a word of encouragement or a gentle reminder. It was in these moments, these small pockets of togetherness, that I felt the true strength of our family bond.

Memories of past drives flooded my mind, each one a cherished snapshot of a life well-lived. I could almost hear the laughter of a younger Paul and Luke, the excited chatter of Lisa as she spoke of her dreams for the future. Even now, with half of our children scattered across the country, and the world, these memories held a power to bind us together, to keep us connected despite the distance.

As the church building came into view, its modest spire reaching towards the heavens, a sense of reverence settled over the car. This was more than just a building; it was a symbol of our faith, a testament to the beliefs that had shaped our lives and guided our paths.

The car park was already buzzing with activity as we pulled in, families much like ours gathering for the weekly service. Children raced across the asphalt, their laughter ringing out like bells, while parents exchanged greetings and smiles, the bonds of community strong and unwavering.

As I stepped out of the car, the warm winter sun on my face, I couldn't help but feel a sense of gratitude wash over me. This was where I belonged, surrounded by the love of my family and the strength of my faith.

Jerome and Charles were quick to disappear into the crowd, their youthful energy carrying them towards their friends and peers. But Greta and I took our time, our hands clasped together as we made our way towards the chapel doors.

With each step, I could feel the weight of the world falling away, replaced by a sense of peace and purpose. Here, in this sacred space, I knew that I would find the guidance and the strength to face whatever challenges lay ahead.

As we crossed the threshold, the familiar scent of polished wood and old hymn books enveloping us, I couldn't help but pause for a moment, my eyes taking in the sight of the congregation gathered before us.

The chapel, with its modest yet dignified architecture, always served as a reminder of the solace and peace found in faith. Greta, with her artistic eyes that saw beauty in the simplest things, gazed around with admiration. She was captivated by the kaleidoscope of colours streaming through the stained glass windows that adorned the hall. I could almost hear her silent appreciation for the intricate craftsmanship. It was as if each beam of light, transformed into a tapestry of divine artistry, spoke to her soul. Her fingers lightly brushed against the cold, textured glass, a tactile connection to the sacred stories depicted in vibrant hues. The way she admired the windows, with a gentle yet profound appreciation, often made me see them anew, through her eyes.

My own attention, however, was drawn to the familiar faces that filled the pews. The Smith Clan, with its diverse branches, had become an integral part of this congregation. I felt a swell of pride and belonging as nods and smiles were exchanged with friends who had shared in the tapestry of our lives. These were not just acquaintances; they were companions in our journey of faith. Each face represented a story intertwined with ours — the laughter we shared, the challenges we faced together, the moments of solace we found in each other's company.

Walking through the aisles, I greeted many with a warm handshake or a pat on the back. Their responses, kind and genuine, were reminders of the strong bonds we had formed over the years. This church was not just a place of worship for us; it was a living chronicle of our collective journey. Each service, each gathering, was like adding another thread to the rich tapestry of our community's story.

As we made our way to our usual pew, I noticed Sister Baker approaching us, her warm smile radiating an inner joy that seemed to light up the room. She was a dear friend and kindred spirit to Greta, their shared passion for gardening having forged a deep bond between them over the years.

"Sister Smith," Sister Baker said with a twinkle in her eye, her voice filled with a playful enthusiasm that belied her age. "Have you tried planting those new tulip bulbs? They're simply divine."

Greta's face lit up at the mention of the tulips, her eyes sparkling with excitement as she launched into a lively discussion about soil quality and watering techniques. I couldn't help but smile as I watched them, their heads bent together in a conspiratorial whisper, their laughter ringing out like bells in the quiet of the chapel.

It was moments like these that reminded me of the true beauty of our church community — the way it brought people together, forging connections that ran deeper than mere acquaintance. These were the bonds that sustained us, that lifted us up in times of trouble and celebrated with us in times of joy.

As Greta and Sister Baker continued their conversation, I felt a gentle tap on my shoulder. Turning, I found myself face to face with Brother Evans, the local historian and a cherished member of our congregation. His eyes, bright with a quiet wisdom, seemed to hold the weight of a thousand stories.

"Brother Noah, Sister Greta," he said, his voice warm and rich, his handshake firm and reassuring. "A pleasure, as always. I was just perusing some old records in the church library. I didn't know that your great-grandparents were among the founding members of our congregation here in Adelaide."

I felt a flutter of pride at his words, a sense of connection to the past that ran deeper than I had ever realised. "I've always been fascinated by their stories," I replied, my voice filled with a quiet reverence. "It's a legacy we hold dear."

Brother Evans nodded, his eyes twinkling with a shared understanding. "I thought you and your parents were born in England and migrated here?" he asked, his head tilting slightly in curiosity.

"That's true," I replied, my mind drifting back to the stories my father had told me as a child, of the long journey across the sea and the promise of a new life in a new land. "My family came to Australia when I was a young boy. But my great-grandfather was an early church member in England and he spent several church missions over here. He was quite instrumental in getting the Lord's work started down here."

Brother Evans' face lit up with interest, his eyes widening with a newfound respect. "Indeed, Brother Noah, a legacy that continues to enrich us all. The roots of the Smith Clan do indeed run deep, intertwining with the narratives of every member here. It's a beautiful tapestry, isn't it?"

I nodded, feeling a lump rise in my throat at the emotion that welled up within me. It was a tapestry indeed, a rich and vibrant weaving of stories and lives, of joys and sorrows, of faith and love. And as I looked around the chapel, at the faces of those who had become like family to me, I knew that I was blessed beyond measure to be a part of it.

As the opening notes of the organ began to fill the air, a hush fell over the congregation. Greta and I took our seats, Jerome and Charles sliding in beside us, their faces filled with a quiet reverence that belied their youth.

The familiar cadence of the hymns washed over me, the words and melodies as comforting as a well-worn blanket. I closed my eyes, letting the music fill my soul, feeling the weight of the world fall away as I lost myself in the beauty of the moment.

And as I sat there, surrounded by the love and faith of my family and my community, I couldn't help but feel a deep sense of gratitude for all that I had been given. The journey of life was never an easy one, but with the strength of my convictions and the support of those who loved me, I knew that I could face whatever challenges came my way.

For in the end, it was moments like these that made it all worthwhile —" the quiet beauty of a Sunday morning, the warmth of a loving embrace, the joy of a shared laugh. These were the threads that wove the tapestry of a life well-lived, the moments that reminded us of the goodness and grace that surrounded us, even in the darkest of times.

As the final notes of the hymn faded away and the congregation settled in for the sermon, I felt a sense of peace wash over me, a deep and abiding calm that seemed to emanate from the very walls of the chapel. And as I looked over at Greta, her hand finding mine in a gentle squeeze, I knew that I was exactly where I was meant to be.

With a final, silent prayer of thanks, I settled back into the pew, ready to listen and learn, to grow and be nourished by the words of wisdom that would soon fill the air. And as the first speaker began their talk, her voice ringing out with a clarity and conviction that seemed to resonate in the very depths of my being, I knew that I was truly home.

The intermediate hymn, "Lead, Kindly Light," lingered in the air of the chapel like a benediction, its melody gentle yet profound. As Greta and I joined the congregation in this moment of collective devotion, our voices blending with those around us in a harmonious expression of faith, I felt a sense of unity and peace wash over me. The hymn, with its comforting words and serene tune, seemed to elevate the atmosphere, creating a sacred space where the worries of the world momentarily ceased. It was a poignant reminder of the strength and comfort found in our shared beliefs, a balm for the soul in times of uncertainty.

As the final notes of the hymn faded away and the congregation settled back into their seats, a hush fell over the chapel. The spirit of reverence that had settled upon us deepened, and I found myself leaning forward slightly, eager to absorb the wisdom and guidance that I knew would come from Bishop Hahn's words.

He rose to the pulpit, his presence commanding yet humble, his eyes scanning the congregation with a warmth and sincerity that I had always admired. "Brothers and sisters, dear members of the congregation," he began, his voice resonant and steady, "I am grateful for the sacred spirit that envelops us on this Sunday morning. As we joined our voices in the hymn 'Lead, Kindly Light,' the words and melody echoed the sentiments of our collective journey — a journey marked by faith, guided by a light that shines even in times of uncertainty."

I nodded in agreement, deeply moved by his words. The familiar strains of the hymn still resonated in my mind, echoing the sentiments he expressed. The journey of faith, like a pilgrimage guided by a kindly light, had indeed been a constant in my life, a guiding force through all seasons. At that moment, I felt Greta's hand find mine, her fingers intertwining with my own in a silent acknowledgment of the shared path we had traversed for over thirty years.

Bishop Hahn's voice carried through the chapel with a clarity that captured the congregation's attention, his words imbued with the worries of our current times. "We find ourselves at the crossroads of our faith today, contemplating the theme 'Enduring Faith in Times of Uncertainty,'" he said, his gaze seeming to meet each of ours in turn. "In a world that often feels tumultuous and unpredictable, the foundation of our faith becomes all the more crucial."

The hymn we had just sung, 'Lead, Kindly Light,' he noted, beautifully encapsulated the essence of our enduring journey. His description of the hymn, as a metaphor for our collective striving to follow the light that beckons us forward, resonated deeply with me.

I felt a stirring within me at his words, a sense of recognition and understanding. The world around us had indeed been feeling increasingly uncertain in recent times, with whispers of change and upheaval on the horizon. It was a feeling that had been nagging at the back of my mind, a sense that something momentous was about to happen, though I couldn't quite put my finger on what it was.

Bishop Hahn continued, speaking of the challenges and uncertainties shadowing our path. "As we navigate the labyrinth of life, the assurance that we are not alone, that a guiding light leads us through the darkness, becomes our source of hope and resilience." These words struck a chord within me, reminding me of the countless times I had leaned on my faith during moments of doubt and fear.

"It is fitting, then, that we delve into the scriptures and the teachings of our Saviour, Jesus Christ, seeking solace and wisdom as we grapple with uncertainties both personal and universal," Bishop Hahn said, his voice filled with conviction. "Our faith is not tested in times of ease, but in moments when the road ahead is shrouded in shadows. It is during these moments that our enduring faith shines brightest, illuminating the path for ourselves and those around us."

I glanced at Greta, feeling a shared sense of purpose and determination. We had faced our fair share of trials and tribulations over the years, but through it all, our faith had been the rock upon which we had built our lives. It was a foundation that had never failed us, even in the toughest of times.

Bishop Hahn then quoted the apostle Paul: "We walked by faith, not by sight" (2 Corinthians 5:7). This profound statement seemed to capture the essence of our journey. Our faith, like the kindly light, was not always visible to the naked eye, yet it guided us with unwavering certainty.

The profound simplicity of that statement struck a deep chord within me. The journey, a series of steps taken in faith, each one guided by an unseen hand, resonated with my own experience. It reminded me of the countless times I had moved forward, guided by faith, even when the path ahead was unclear. This moment of reflection, amidst the words of Bishop Hahn, strengthened my resolve to continue walking by faith, trusting in the light to lead me through times of uncertainty.

As Bishop Hahn spoke of Lehi and his family's journey through the wilderness in the Book of Mormon, a parallel with my own life's voyage emerged in my thoughts. "In their darkest hours, the Lord provided a Liahona – a compass of sorts – to guide them according to their faith and diligence," he said, his voice imbuing the ancient story with a sense of immediacy and relevance. The mention of this spiritual compass stirred memories of the many times my family had navigated through the vicissitudes of life. Just like Lehi's family, we had faced our share of uncertainties, but it was our faith, our own spiritual compass, that had always guided us through our personal wilderness.

As Bishop Hahn paused, I sensed a depth of emotion that resonated with my own experiences. His voice cracked unexpectedly, revealing a vulnerability that was both human and endearing. In that moment, I felt a connection to him that went beyond mere words, a sense of shared understanding and empathy.

"My dearest Brothers and Sisters," he continued, his voice now steady but still tinged with emotion. "We cannot know everything in this life, but I feel compelled by the spirit to share with you my knowledge that I know our Saviour lives." His words seemed to reach into the very core of my being, affirming my own faith and beliefs. "We are standing on the precipice of a new chapter. A divine calling awaits, and as we embark on this journey together, may our faith have endured, shining as a beacon of hope and light for all."

The atmosphere in the chapel shifted palpably at his words, a sense of anticipation and wonder hanging in the air. I felt a tingling sensation run down my spine, a sense that something momentous was about to unfold. Greta's hand tightened in mine, her eyes reflecting a mixture of curiosity and trust, a silent communication that spoke of our readiness to face whatever lay ahead.

As I looked around at the congregation, at the tapestry of diverse lives and experiences that made up our church family, I felt a sense of unity and purpose. We were all on this journey together, each of us facing our own uncertainties and challenges, but bound by a common faith and a shared destiny.

Bishop Hahn's final words, "May we, as a congregation, draw strength from our collective faith, trusting in the kindly light that leads us through the uncertainties of our mortal existence. In the name of Jesus Christ, amen," resonated deeply within me. As the word "amen" echoed through the chapel, I felt a sense of resolve settle over me, a determination to face whatever the future might hold with courage and conviction.

The kindly light, a symbol of unwavering faith, illuminated not just the path ahead but also the depths of our hearts. As Greta and I exchanged a knowing glance, a silent affirmation of our readiness to embrace the divine calling that lay ahead, I felt a sense of peace wash over me.

Our hearts, aligned with each other and our faith, were filled with a sense of assurance and readiness to face the unknown. And as the congregation began to rise, the rustle of clothing and the soft murmur of voices filling the air, I knew that whatever challenges lay ahead, we would face them together, guided by the light of our faith and the strength of our love.

For in that moment, I understood that the journey of faith was not about knowing what the future held, but about trusting in the One who held the future in His hands. It was about walking forward with courage and conviction, even when the path ahead was shrouded in shadows.

And so, with a heart full of hope and a soul filled with the light of faith, I stood tall and proud, ready to embrace the next chapter of our lives, whatever it might bring. For I knew that with Greta by my side and the love of our Heavenly Father guiding us, there was nothing we could not face, no challenge we could not overcome.

As the sacrament meeting drew to a close, I noticed Brother Johnson, a pillar of our congregation known for his discreet manner, making his way toward us. His approach was unobtrusive yet purposeful, a sign that something was amiss from the usual Sunday routine. There was a quiet intensity in his gaze, a sense of urgency that belied his calm demeanour.

"Brother Noah, Sister Greta," he said in a hushed tone that was almost inaudible amid the quiet murmurs of the departing congregation. "The Bishop would like to meet with both of you in his office after the Priesthood and Relief Society meeting."

A ripple of curiosity stirred within me as he spoke, my mind already racing with possibilities and questions. Greta's eyes met mine in the moment Brother Johnson relayed the message, her gaze holding a depth of understanding and a hint of curiosity that mirrored my own feelings. In that brief, silent exchange, a multitude of thoughts and emotions passed between us, a testament to the unspoken bond we shared.

"Any idea what this is about?" Greta whispered, her voice low but tinged with a note of excitement. I could see the wheels turning in her mind, the same sense of anticipation that I felt bubbling up inside me.

"I'm not sure," I responded, matching her quiet tone. "But it's not often we get a personal request from the Bishop."

And it was true. In all our years as members of this congregation, personal meetings with the Bishop were rare, usually reserved for matters of great importance or sensitivity. The fact that he had requested both of us only added to the sense of intrigue that hung in the air.

At the close of Sunday School, as we made our way to the combined Priesthood and Relief Society meeting, the familiar surroundings of the chapel took on a different light. The soothing colours and gentle hum of the congregation engaging in post-meeting conversations suddenly felt charged with a new energy, a subtle yet palpable shift in the atmosphere. It was as if the very walls of the building were holding their breath, waiting for the revelation that was to come.

I found myself lost in thought as we took our seats, my mind turning over the possibilities of what the Bishop might have to say. Could it be a new calling, a new responsibility that would challenge us and help us grow in our faith? Or was it something else entirely, a message from on high that would change the course of our lives in ways we couldn't even begin to imagine?

Greta's hand found mine, her fingers intertwining with my own in a gesture of comfort and support. "Do you think it's about a new calling?" she asked quietly, her voice barely above a whisper.

"It could be," I mused, my brow furrowing as I considered the possibilities. "Whatever it is, I'm sure it's important."

And it was. I could feel it in my bones, a sense of destiny that hung heavy in the air. Whatever the Bishop had to say, I knew that it would be a turning point in our lives, a moment that we would look back on as a defining chapter in our journey of faith.

As the meeting progressed, I found it harder and harder to concentrate on the words being spoken from the teacher. My mind was a whirlwind of thoughts and emotions, a maelstrom of anticipation and uncertainty that threatened to overwhelm me.

Greta and I moved through the motions of the meeting, our eyes meeting now and then in silent communication. Each glance was a reminder that we were in this together, that whatever challenges or opportunities lay ahead, we would face them as one. Our faith, our love, and our commitment to each other would be our guiding light, the foundation upon which we would build our future.

As the meeting drew to a close and the congregation began to disperse, I felt a sense of nervous energy coursing through my veins. This was it, the moment of truth that we had been waiting for. With a deep breath and a squeeze of Greta's hand, I rose to my feet.

Together, we made our way to the Bishop's office, our footsteps echoing in the emptying halls of the church. Each step was a reminder of the journey we had taken to get here, of the trials and triumphs that had shaped us into the people we were today. And as we stood before the closed door, our hearts pounding in unison, I knew that whatever happened next, we would face it with the strength and courage that had always defined us.

With a final, reassuring glance at Greta, I raised my hand and knocked on the door, the sound reverberating through the stillness of the building. There was a foreboding, deep within my soul, that this meeting was the beginning of a new chapter in our lives, a moment that would test our faith and our resolve in ways we had never been tested before.

DIVINE SUMMONS

4338.210.2

In the hushed ambiance of Bishop Hahn's office, Greta and I took our seats across from him, the leather chairs creaking softly beneath us. The room, usually a place of routine meetings and spiritual guidance, felt different this time, charged with a mixture of anticipation and trepidation. The walls, lined with books and religious texts, seemed to stand as silent witnesses to the solemnity of the moment, their spines bearing the weight of countless stories and teachings.

Bishop Hahn's eyes, kind and discerning, met ours with a depth that spoke of the seriousness of our meeting. There was a gravity in his gaze, a sense of purpose that went beyond the usual warmth and compassion I had come to know from him. "Brother Noah, Sister Greta," he began, his tone measured and infused with a sense of urgency, "I appreciate your dedication to the church and your unwavering faith." His words, though reassuring, carried an undercurrent of something significant about to unfold, like the distant rumble of thunder heralding an approaching storm.

He paused momentarily, his gaze shifting to a letter on his desk, the white envelope stark against the rich, dark wood. The action, simple yet deliberate, drew our attention immediately, our eyes fixed on the mysterious document that seemed to hold the key to our presence here. Bishop Hahn retrieved the letter, handling it with a reverence that suggested its importance, his fingers grazing the surface with a gentle touch that belied the weight of its contents.

As he pulled the letter from the envelope, the soft rustling of paper filling the silence, Greta's hand found mine under the table, her fingers intertwining with my own in a silent expression of our shared curiosity and the unspoken bond we had forged over years of facing life's challenges together. The physical connection provided a comforting sense of solidarity, a reminder that whatever lay ahead, we would face it as one, our love and faith guiding us through any uncertainty.

Bishop Hahn cleared his throat softly before continuing, the sound echoing in the stillness of the room. "I have received a letter from the Area President that goes beyond the ordinary path of our worship," he said, his words hanging in the air, heavy with implication. The mention of the Area President indicated the significance of the correspondence, hinting at a message that could potentially alter the course of our service within the church, a calling that went beyond the everyday duties and responsibilities we had grown accustomed to.

I felt a surge of curiosity, mingled with a sense of responsibility, as I awaited the Bishop's next words, my heart pounding in my chest with a mixture of excitement and apprehension. The usual calmness of the Bishop's office was replaced by a heightened sense of awareness, every detail - from the soft ticking of the clock on the wall to the Bishop's measured breathing - seeming to underscore the importance of this moment, a turning point in our spiritual journey.

As Bishop Hahn extended the letter towards me, his eyes meeting mine with a silent request, I accepted it with a sense of solemnity, the paper feeling heavy in my hands, a tangible symbol of the weighty message it carried. I unfolded it carefully, the soft rustling of the paper filling the silence once more, aware that what I was about to read aloud might herald a significant change in our lives, a divine calling that would test our faith and our resolve.

"To Bishop Greg Hahn," I began, my voice soft yet clear, each word spoken with the reverence it deserved, the formality of the greeting setting a serious tone for what was to come. I paused, glancing up at Bishop Hahn, seeking confirmation to proceed, my heart racing with anticipation. His discernible nod, a subtle gesture of encouragement, was all I needed to continue, the words on the page drawing me in like a compass pointing towards a new horizon.

"I extend my warm greetings to you and the members of the Playford Ward," I read, the words flowing from my lips like a sacred invocation, a blessing upon our congregation. "In light of recent revelations and promptings received by the First Presidency, we are compelled to initiate a significant and sacred gathering of devout members in our area." My heart started to beat a little faster, sensing the gravity of what was unfolding.

"Through prayerful consideration and seeking the guidance of the Spirit, we have received guided revelation that there are members within the Playford Ward that demonstrate unwavering faith in their Saviour, Jesus Christ, and complete commitment to the church." As I read these words, a sense of awe washed over me, the notion of being part of something divinely orchestrated both humbling and exhilarating, a testament to the power of our faith and the guiding hand of the Lord.

"I am entrusting you with the responsibility of selecting the most dedicated and faithful members within your ward to convene at the Adelaide Temple for a special meeting, on Sunday 31st July 2018." Greta's gasp, soft yet filled with surprise, punctuated the room, her hand tightening around mine in a mixture of shock and anticipation. "That's tonight," she whispered, her voice a blend of wonder and trepidation, the realisation of the immediacy of this sacred gathering settling upon us like a cloak of destiny.

Giving Greta a brief, reassuring look, a silent promise that we would face this together, I continued reading, the letter's words weaving a tapestry of mystery and anticipation, each sentence a thread in a larger pattern that we had yet to fully comprehend. "The purpose of this gathering is not disclosed at this time, but rest assured, it carries great importance in the ongoing work of the Lord," I read, the message clear yet enigmatic, cloaked in a veil of secrecy that added to the mystique of the situation, a divine plan unfolding before our very eyes.

"We encourage you to approach this task with the same diligence and devotion that has marked your service as a bishop. The Lord knows His chosen servants, and we have faith that you will prayerfully discern those who should be part of this sacred assembly." I could feel the suspense in the room thickening, the unspoken question hanging in the air like a tangible presence. Who would be chosen for this sacred assembly? The responsibility laid upon Bishop Hahn was immense, and the impact of this decision would, no doubt, ripple through our community, a stone cast into the still waters of our faith.

"I emphasise the confidentiality of this matter," I continued, the words resonating with the seriousness of the task at hand, a reminder of the sacred trust being placed in our hands. "We request that you disclose only to those whom you select for this gathering, and even then, encourage them to share this information with no one else." The weight of secrecy settled upon us, a cloak of confidentiality that would shield this divine calling from curious eyes and wagging tongues.

The letter concluded with words of gratitude and trust, leaving us with a sense of profound responsibility and anticipation, a call to rise to the occasion and embrace the unknown with faith and courage. "May the Spirit be your guide in this sacred task, and may the chosen members be prepared both spiritually and temporally for the significant work that lies ahead. Your devoted service is appreciated, Bishop Hahn. We look forward to the blessings that will unfold as a result of this divine calling."

As I finished reading, the room was enveloped in a reflective silence, the magnitude of the message sinking in like a stone in still water, rippling through our hearts and minds with a profound sense of purpose. The air was charged with a mix of excitement and solemnity, a feeling of standing on the threshold of something momentous, a divine calling that would shape our journey in ways we couldn't yet fathom, a path illuminated by the light of our faith.

"Brother Noah, Sister Greta," Bishop Hahn started, his voice breaking the prolonged silence that had enveloped the room, his words measured and filled with a quiet intensity that demanded our full attention. "You are both among the most devout members of our ward. Your commitment to the principles of our faith has not gone unnoticed." His words, spoken with a solemn sincerity, echoed in the stillness of his office, a testament to the depth of our devotion and the strength of our testimonies. The Bishop's discerning gaze met ours, conveying a deep respect and trust in our dedication, a recognition of the light that shone within us.

Greta's grip on my hand tightened, a silent affirmation of our shared sense of duty and devotion, a physical manifestation of the unbreakable bond we shared in our faith. Her touch was a reassuring presence, a tangible reminder of the strength we drew from each other, a wellspring of love and support that would sustain us through whatever lay ahead. I felt a surge of humility and pride, a swirling mix of emotions at being recognised for our dedication to our faith, a recognition that both honoured and humbled us.

"This is not a responsibility to be taken lightly," Bishop Hahn continued, his voice steady and earnest, his words carrying the weight of divine purpose. "The Lord's work is vast, and He calls upon His chosen servants to fulfil His purposes. I trust that you will approach this with the same dedication that has marked your journey thus far." His words were an affirmation of the path we had walked together in faith, a path marked by devotion and service, a journey that had led us to this very moment, a crossroads of spiritual significance.

"Thank you, Bishop," I managed to say, my voice betraying a quiver of emotion, the magnitude of the moment settling upon me like a mantle of responsibility. The weight of the invitation, of being chosen for such a sacred gathering, was not lost on me. It was a profound honour, yet with it came a deep sense of duty, a call to rise to the occasion and embrace the unknown with faith and courage.

"I know I have left you little time, but pray on it, seek the guidance of the Holy Spirit, and tonight, we will gather at the Temple as a chosen group," Bishop Hahn concluded, his words both an instruction and a blessing, a charge to prepare ourselves spiritually for the significant event that lay ahead. He reached out to take the letter from my trembling hands, his touch gentle yet firm, a symbol of the transfer of this sacred duty, a passing of the torch that would light our way forward.

As the meeting drew to a close, Bishop Hahn extended his hand in a gesture of support and solidarity, his grip strong and reassuring, a physical display of the spiritual bond we shared. "May the Lord bless and guide you, Brother Noah, Sister Greta, as you embark on this journey of faith," he said, his words a benediction upon our souls, a promise of divine guidance and protection as we stepped into the unknown.

Exiting the Bishop's office, as Greta and I stepped into the hallway, the reality of the divine calling began to deeply resonate within me, echoing through the chambers of my heart like a celestial symphony. The Adelaide Temple, a sanctuary of countless prayers and sacred moments, now beckoned us as a site of mystery and divine purpose, its spires reaching towards the heavens with a newfound significance, a beacon guiding us towards an unknown yet spiritually momentous experience.

Our ordinary Sunday, typically marked by familiar rituals and comfortable routines, had indeed transformed into something extraordinary, a day that would be etched into our memories as a turning point in our spiritual journey. It felt as if we were stepping into a new chapter of our lives, not just in the physical sense of travelling to the Temple, but also a spiritual odyssey into the realm of the unknown, a journey guided by a faith that transcended the usual confines of the familiar, pushing us into a realm of greater purpose and deeper commitment.

As Greta and I walked together, our steps in perfect unison, a sense of awe and contemplation enveloped us, the magnitude of the moment settling upon our shoulders like a mantle of responsibility. The air around us, once filled with the typical Sunday chatter and laughter of our congregation, now seemed to carry a hushed reverence, a sacred stillness that spoke of the weighty matters that lay ahead. Our footsteps, synchronised and purposeful, took us through the church grounds, each one seeming to echo with the consequences of the decision we had already made, a decision that would shape the course of our lives in ways we had yet to comprehend.

Looking at the faces of our fellow church members, their expressions filled with the usual warmth and camaraderie, I felt a bittersweet pang, a mixture of anticipation and longing. These were the people with whom we had shared so many Sundays, the joys and sorrows of our spiritual community, the bonds of faith that had sustained us through the years. Yet, in this moment, we were carrying a secret, a sacred duty that set us apart, a responsibility that we were honoured to bear, yet one that also felt isolating, knowing that we couldn't share it with those who had been our spiritual companions for so long.

As we made our way towards the carpark, the sun's rays casting a golden glow upon the asphalt, I couldn't help but feel a sense of trepidation mingling with the excitement that coursed through my veins. The Adelaide Temple, a place I had always associated with peace and spiritual solace, now seemed to hold a different allure, a sense of destiny that called to us from across the distance. It was as if the Temple itself was beckoning us to step into a larger plan, one that was orchestrated by divine hands, a plan that would unfold before us like a sacred scroll, revealing the mysteries of God's will.

The familiar path to the Temple, once tread for routine visits and quiet moments of reflection, now awaited our steps for a purpose that was shrouded in mystery, a purpose that would test our faith and challenge our understanding of the world we thought we knew. As we climbed into our car, the seats creaking beneath us, Greta squeezed my hand, her touch a silent expression of her shared feelings, a gesture of love and support that spoke volumes in the quietude of the moment.

There was excitement in this call to higher service, a sense of anticipation that set our hearts racing and our minds reeling with possibilities. But there was also a solemnity, a recognition of the uncertainty of what might lay ahead, a realisation that we were stepping into uncharted territory, a land where our faith would be our only compass and our love for each other our only anchor.

As I turned the key in the ignition, the engine roaring to life like a herald of the journey to come, I couldn't help but feel a sense of awe at the path that lay before us. We were stepping into the unknown, but we were doing it together, hand in hand, heart to heart, with a faith that had always been our guiding light, a faith that would sustain us through whatever trials and tribulations lay ahead.

Pulling out of the carpark, the church disappeared in the rearview mirror like a fading memory. I couldn't shake the feeling that we were embarking on a journey that would change the course of our lives forever. This was a journey not just of physical distance, but of spiritual depth, a pilgrimage that would lead us to a greater understanding of God's plan and a deeper connection to His love.

THE GATHERING

4338.210.3

The crunch of gravel beneath the tires echoed through the car park as Greta and I arrived at the Adelaide Temple, the sound reverberating through the stillness of the night like a solemn drumbeat, heralding the beginning of our sacred journey. The noise, usually mundane and easily overlooked, tonight seemed to carry a deeper resonance, as if it were a prelude to the profound experience that awaited us, a subtle reminder of the weight and significance of the moment.

The winter night held a quiet reverence, a stillness that seemed to envelop everything in a cloak of anticipation, wrapping us in its gentle embrace. As we stepped out of the car and into the chilly night, the air was crisp and cold, biting at my cheeks and stealing my breath, but it was more than just a physical sensation. The very atmosphere seemed to hum with a palpable sense of expectancy, as if the night itself was aware of the sacredness of our visit, holding its breath in hushed anticipation of the revelations to come.

The soft glow of the Temple's exterior lights cast a warm, almost ethereal aura around us, bathing us in its comforting radiance. The Temple, always a beacon of peace and spiritual reflection, now felt like a gateway to something much larger than ourselves, a portal to a realm of divine mystery and endless possibility. Greta's gloved hand found mine, her fingers intertwining with my own in a gesture of love and support, her touch a reassuring connection amidst the unknown that lay ahead. Despite the barrier of the gloves, I could feel the warmth and steadiness of her grip, a silent message of unity and shared purpose in this significant moment.

"Feels different tonight, doesn't it?" Greta's voice carried a mix of excitement and contemplation, echoing the tumultuous emotions that swirled within my own heart.

I nodded in response, the weight of the unknown pressing on my chest, a reminder of the magnitude of the journey we were about to embark upon. "It's like the air is charged with something sacred," I replied, my voice low but filled with awe, a reverent whisper that seemed to echo through the stillness of the night. There was a sense of entering into a realm that transcended our normal experiences at the Temple, a step into a deeper spiritual mystery that we had only glimpsed before.

We exchanged a glance that spoke of our shared curiosity and the weight of the sacredness that enveloped us, our eyes meeting in a moment of perfect understanding. In the depths of Greta's gaze, I saw reflections of my own faith, hope, and the winding journey that had brought us to this moment.

The Temple loomed ahead, its spires reaching towards the starlit sky like silent sentinels guarding the mysteries within, their white stone facades gleaming in the moonlight like beacons of purity and truth. Its familiar structure, which I had seen countless times before, now appeared as a majestic testament to the divine calling we were about to heed. The stars above seemed to twinkle with a special significance, as if they too were part of this sacred night, celestial witnesses to the unfolding of God's plan.

With each step towards the Temple, my heart beat with a mixture of reverence and anticipation, a heady cocktail of emotions that threatened to overwhelm me. This was not just another visit, not just a routine trip to a beloved place of worship. It was a journey into the very heart of our faith, a calling that held unknown implications but was guided by the unwavering light of our belief, a leap of faith into the arms of the divine. As Greta and I walked hand in hand towards the Temple's entrance, our footsteps falling in perfect unison, I felt a profound sense of purpose and a readiness to embrace whatever lay ahead in this unique and sacred gathering.

As we entered the Annexe, a hallowed silence enveloped us, its sacred stillness urging us into a contemplative state, a mindset of reverence and openness. The atmosphere felt charged, as if the very air was holding its breath in anticipation of the night's proceedings, a tangible presence that seemed to cling to our skin like a holy mist. The soft rustle of white fabric resonated in the room, a sound that was both familiar and yet, under these circumstances, filled with new meaning, a symphony of preparation and purification. Around us, faithful Saints, like ourselves, prepared for the upcoming gathering, their movements reverent and purposeful, a dance of devotion and readiness.

Greta's fingers gently brushed mine as we separated briefly to change into our white clothing, each touch a silent communication of support and unity, a reminder that we were in this together.

The white garments, symbols of purity and readiness, felt different tonight, imbued with a new significance that went beyond mere ritual. The familiar act of donning these clothes took on a new meaning, as if each fold and crease was a step further into the unknown. It was a transformation not just of attire but of spirit, preparing us for whatever revelations and challenges lay ahead.

Dressed in white, rejoining Greta, I felt a sense of unity and shared purpose with those around us, a bond that went beyond mere acquaintance. Around us, whispers hung in the air like incense, their muted tones carrying conversations filled with speculation and wonder about the nature of the evening, a buzzing undercurrent of excitement and anticipation. The speculation wasn't fearful; it was filled with a sense of awe and reverence, a shared feeling among all present that we were on the cusp of something truly extraordinary.

Sister Bennett, a longtime friend with a gentle demeanour, approached us with a warm smile that seemed to light up the room. "Noah, Greta, have you ever felt such anticipation before?" she asked, her voice barely above a whisper, yet carrying a depth of emotion that resonated within my very soul.

I smiled back, feeling a kinship in her words, a shared sense of the magnitude of the moment. "Not like this, Sister Bennett," I replied, my voice steady and filled with conviction. "Something very special is about to happen." My words were a statement of fact, a truth that I could feel in the very marrow of my bones, a certainty that transcended mere belief.

In the shared camaraderie of this sacred space, faces both familiar and unfamiliar exchanged knowing glances, a silent communication that spoke of a deep understanding and shared purpose. There was a sense of unspoken unity, a communal feeling of being part of something much larger than ourselves, a divine plan unfolding before our very eyes. A nod here, a smile there—we were a community bound by faith, each of us awaiting a revelation that stirred the very essence of our beings, a call to a higher purpose that we could not yet fully comprehend.

The air in the Annexe buzzed with excitement and speculation, each whisper and hushed conversation adding to the atmosphere of expectancy, a palpable energy that seemed to crackle and spark around us. This space, usually a haven for preparation, had become an incubator of anticipation, a sacred chamber where the veil between the earthly and the divine seemed to thin and shimmer. Each of us, in our white clothing, was not just preparing for a ceremony but for a journey into the spiritual unknown, a leap of faith that would test our resolve and deepen our connection to the eternal.

As we readied ourselves to move into the Temple, the sense of unity and purpose among us was inspiring, a testament to the power of faith to bring people together in a common cause. We were individuals brought together by a shared belief, standing on the brink of an experience that promised to deepen our understanding and connection to the divine, a sacred journey that would forever change the course of our lives. The Annexe, with its sacred stillness and whispered speculations, had set the stage for the mysteries that were about to unfold in the Temple beyond, a prelude to the revelations that awaited us in the holy sanctuary.

❖

At the front desk, Brother Davis, a familiar face who had become something akin to a gatekeeper to these sacred spaces, greeted us with his warm, inviting smile. His presence always brought a sense of comfort and familiarity, a reminder of the many times we had passed through these halls in pursuit of spiritual enlightenment, seeking the guidance and wisdom that could only be found within the hallowed walls of the Temple. As we handed over our Temple recommends, the weight of the laminated cards in my hand felt significant, like a tangible manifestation of our commitment and dedication—a physical representation of our worthiness to enter into the presence of the divine, a ticket to a revelation that awaited us this evening.

Brother Davis, with his ever-present warm and reassuring smile, acknowledged our worthiness with a simple yet profound nod, his eyes meeting ours with a depth of understanding that spoke of a shared faith and a common purpose. It was a gesture that spoke volumes, a silent affirmation of our faith and dedication, a recognition of the spiritual journey we had embarked upon and the sacred trust we had placed in the Lord's hands. As he handed back our recommends, his words carried a depth of sincerity that touched my very soul, "Noah, Greta, may this evening bring you blessings beyond measure."

"Thank you, Brother Davis," Greta responded, her voice imbued with a blend of gratitude and anticipation, a reflection of the complex emotions that swirled within us both. She then turned towards me, her eyes reflecting our shared reverence for the upcoming experience, a silent communication of the profound significance of this moment in our spiritual lives. With a soft squeeze of my hand, a gesture that always offered me strength and assurance, we moved forward. It felt as though invisible threads of excitement were weaving their way through the Temple corridors, guiding us towards our spiritual destination, a path illuminated by the light of our faith.

As we navigated the quiet expanse of the Temple, a comforting hush enveloped us, creating an atmosphere of introspection and reverence, a sacred stillness that seemed to permeate every corner of the building. It was in this serene setting, this haven of spiritual contemplation, that we encountered Sister Anderson, a seasoned temple worker known for her gentle spirit and comforting presence. She was the embodiment of warmth and kindness, qualities that always made our visits here more meaningful, a living testament to the love and compassion that were the very heart of our faith.

Sister Anderson, with her open-hearted approach to everyone she met, embraced Greta in a gesture that transcended the usual greetings, a hug that was filled with a depth of affection and understanding that could only be found among those who shared a common spiritual path. It was a hug that spoke of deep respect and genuine affection. "Sister Smith, it's always a joy to see you. Your presence adds an extra layer of peace to the Temple," she said, her words infusing the air with a sense of belonging and tranquility, a reminder of the sacred nature of this space and the people who filled it.

Greta returned the embrace with a serene smile, one that reflected a deep understanding and shared devotion. Her eyes, always so expressive, held a depth of emotion that spoke of our joint spiritual journey and the deep connections we had forged within this community, the relationships that had become an integral part of our lives and our faith.

Sister Anderson then spoke softly, her voice barely above a whisper, yet carrying a profound blessing that seemed to emanate from the very depths of her soul, "Greta, Noah, may the Lord's blessings be upon you tonight, and may your hearts be open to the revelations that await." Her words, filled with hope and faith, resonated deeply within me, echoing the desires of my own heart and the anticipation that had brought us to this sacred place.

As we continued toward the Endowment Room, the Temple corridors were alive with a soft murmur of prayers and exchanged greetings, a gentle hum of spiritual energy that seemed to fill the very air around us. These sounds, gentle yet filled with meaning, were like a gentle chorus of souls preparing for a sacred communion, a harmonious blend of voices united in their desire to draw closer to the divine. The air itself seemed to vibrate with a spiritual energy, each greeting and shared acknowledgment contributing to the tapestry of anticipation that enveloped us, a palpable sense of purpose and unity that could only be found within these sacred walls. This sense of collective preparation made the journey toward the sacred space even more profound, transforming each step into a part of a larger, communal act of devotion, a shared pilgrimage towards a higher understanding of our place in the grand design of the universe.

Approaching the room, I instinctively braced myself for the familiar division of men on one side and women on the other—a longstanding tradition in our temple rituals, a physical representation of the different but complementary roles we played in the grand scheme of God's plan. Yet, tonight was different, a departure from the norm that spoke of the special nature of this gathering. A whispered revelation echoed through the corridor, a gentle yet startling disruption of our usual practice—we could sit together, side by side, as couples united in faith and purpose.

Brother Stevens, a fellow temple-goer known for his kind demeanour and ready smile, shared the news with a twinkle in his eye, his voice filled with a quiet excitement that was impossible to ignore. "Noah, Greta, tonight's different. Unity is in the air." His words were simple yet they carried a depth of significance, hinting at the special nature of this gathering, a recognition of the importance of facing the mysteries of faith hand in hand, heart to heart.

The departure from tradition struck a chord deep within us, resonating with the very essence of our relationship and the sacred bonds of marriage that had brought us together. It was a symbol of the unity and shared purpose of the couples attending this sacred gathering, a physical manifestation of the spiritual journey we were all embarking upon together. Greta's eyes met mine, and in them, I saw my own astonishment and gratitude reflected, a silent communication of the profound significance of this moment.

This change emphasised the uniqueness of this occasion, a break from the routine that spoke of the special nature of the revelations that awaited us. It was as if the very structure of our worship was adapting to underscore the significance of what was to unfold, a recognition of the sacred nature of the bonds that tied us together as husbands and wives, as partners in faith and in life. The normal order of things had been gently shifted to create a space where unity, not just of individuals but of couples, was at the forefront, a powerful symbol of the strength and resilience that could be found in the sacred institution of marriage.

As we entered the Endowment Room, the sense of unity was a tangible presence that seemed to fill the very air around us. The room, usually marked by a respectful division, now presented a unified front, couples sitting side by side in preparation for the sacred experience, a sea of white clothing and expectant faces that spoke of the shared journey we were all embarking upon. It was a beautiful representation of partnership and support, a testament to the power of love and faith to bring us closer to each other and to the divine.

In the hallowed stillness of the Endowment Room, Greta and I found our seats in the front row, side by side, our hands instinctively seeking each other out in a gesture of comfort and unity. The soft padding of the seats felt comforting, almost as if they were imbued with the weight of countless stories and shared experiences of those who had sat here before us, a silent witness to the enduring nature of faith and the sacred bonds that tied us all together. We waited, hand in hand, for the arrival of other patrons, each of whom would be part of this unique spiritual journey.

Sister Henderson, a longtime friend from the ward, took her seat nearby, her presence a comforting reminder of the many Sundays and gatherings we had shared, the bonds of friendship and faith that had been forged over countless hours of worship and service. She nodded toward us with a soft smile, her eyes reflecting the same sense of wonder that I felt, a silent acknowledgment of the special nature of this gathering and the revelations that awaited us all. "Noah, Greta, isn't this something amazing?" she whispered, her voice barely audible yet carrying a weight of shared astonishment, a recognition of the profound significance of this moment in our spiritual lives.

I nodded back, feeling a deep resonance with her words, a connection that went beyond mere friendship and spoke of the sacred bonds that tied us all together as members of this faith community. "It truly is," I replied, my voice low but filled with emotion, a reflection of the profound sense of anticipation and reverence that had settled over the room like a sacred mantle. "I can feel that tonight holds something remarkable." The anticipation in the room was tangible, almost like a collective breath held in waiting, a communal readiness for the divine revelation that awaited, a shared sense of purpose and destiny that could only be found in moments like these.

As the Endowment Room slowly filled, the atmosphere became increasingly reverent, a hushed stillness that spoke of the sacred nature of the gathering. Familiar faces, along with revered figures from our church community, took their places, each arrival adding to the sense of solemnity and significance that permeated the room.

The air became dense with the presence of prominent church couples, their collective devotion palpable in the silent exchanges and nods of acknowledgment that filled the room, a powerful reminder of the strength and resilience that could be found in the sacred bonds of marriage and the enduring nature of faith.

The arrival of the Temple President, a figure deeply revered for his local spiritual authority, marked the commencement of what felt like a sacred procession, a solemn march towards the revelations to follow. His dignified entrance, slow and measured, set the tone for the evening, a powerful reminder of the sacred nature of the gathering. The aura of reverence that accompanied him seemed to fill the entire room, heightening the already palpable sense of solemnity, a tangible presence that could be felt in the very air around us. His eyes, which I always perceived as reservoirs of the wisdom accumulated through years of dedicated service, met ours briefly with a nod of acknowledgment, a silent blessing that seemed to emanate from the very depths of his soul. It was a simple gesture, but in that moment, it felt deeply affirming.

"Noah, Greta," he said softly, addressing us directly, his voice carrying the unmistakable weight of spiritual leadership and experience, a tone that commanded attention and respect. "May this gathering bring you the peace and understanding you seek." His words, imbued with a sense of hope and blessing, resonated within me, echoing the depth of our shared quest for spiritual enlightenment.

Following closely behind was the Area President, a figure whose presence carried the weight of broader spiritual oversight, a reminder of the far-reaching nature of our faith and the sacred responsibilities that came with leadership. His entrance was marked by an air of quiet authority, a testament to his role that extended beyond our local congregation, a powerful symbol of the unity and cohesion that bound us all together as members of this global faith community. As he stepped into the room, his gaze swept across the gathering, each of us touched by an unspoken blessing that seemed to extend from his very being, a silent acknowledgment of the sacred nature of the journey we were all embarking upon together.

The Temple President and Area President, standing together like pillars of faith, took their places at the front of the room. Their presence brought a sense of completeness to the gathering, as if their arrival had signalled the readiness for whatever was to unfold.

The profound silence that suddenly enveloped the Endowment Room announced the entrance of Mark Kimball, one of the Twelve Apostles, a figure whose presence carried the weight of divine authority and the sacred responsibilities that came with it. His presence, as he stepped into the space, was both imposing and comforting, embodying the essence of a living conduit between heaven and earth, a powerful reminder of the sacred nature of living revelation. My heart quickened with a mix of reverence and anticipation as he made his way to the front, a sacred aura perceptibly surrounding him, a tangible presence that seemed to fill the very air around us.

Greta's hand found mine, instinctively seeking the familiar comfort of our shared bond. Her touch was warm, a grounding force amidst the charged atmosphere that now filled the room, a reminder of the unbreakable bond we shared and the sacred journey we were embarking upon together. The realisation that we were about to receive words from an Apostle, a messenger of God, stirred a mix of awe and humility within me, a profound sense of the sacred responsibilities that came with being a member of this faith community. This was not just a meeting; it was a moment of spiritual significance, a rare opportunity to be in the presence of one so close to the divine, a chance to hear the words of God spoken through his chosen servant.

As we sat there, hand in hand, the Apostle took his place, seated at the front of the room. His presence commanded attention, not through demand, but through the sheer force of his spiritual calling, a quiet authority that seemed to emanate from the very depths of his soul. A hush fell over the room, a collective reverence that seemed to hold us all in a state of eager expectancy.

The quiet reverence of the gathering spoke to the spiritual hunger of every soul present, including my own, a deep yearning for the wisdom and guidance that could only be found in the words of God spoken through his chosen servants. It was as if each of us was seeking something, a piece of wisdom, a touch of divine insight, something to anchor our faith and guide our journey, a light to illuminate the path ahead and bring clarity to the challenges and uncertainties of life. The anticipation was not just individual; it was shared, a communal experience of seeking and yearning for spiritual nourishment, a recognition of the profound significance of this moment in our lives and in the life of our community.

THE UNVEILING

4338.210.4

The hallowed strains of a familiar hymn began to fill the Endowment Room, its melody resonating through the sacred space like a gentle caress, enveloping us in a cocoon of spiritual warmth and comfort. Each note seemed to echo off the walls and settle into the hearts of the gathered, creating a serene atmosphere that transcended the ordinary, a tangible reminder of the divine presence that permeated this holy place. The shared voices of the congregation created a harmonious backdrop to the unfolding revelation, uniting us in a singular, spiritual experience that seemed to transcend the boundaries of time and space.

Brother and Sister Fleming, seated beside us, were known in our community for their powerful testimony, a living embodiment of the strength and resilience that characterised our faith. Their voices joined the chorus, blending seamlessly with ours in a symphony of faith. It felt as though the hymn was not just a song, but a shared prayer, sung from the depths of our hearts, expressing our devotion and our readiness to receive divine wisdom, a collective outpouring of our love and trust in the Lord.

Following the hymn, a prayer was offered that seemed to transcend the confines of the room, rising up to the heavens like a sweet incense, carrying with it the hopes and dreams of all who were gathered here. The words, spoken with earnestness and reverence, were a petition for guidance and understanding, a humble request for the Lord's presence to be made manifest in our midst. They resonated within me, echoing my own desires. As the prayer unfolded, I felt a profound sense of being part of a vast, spiritual tapestry that stretched across the ages, connecting us to the pioneers who had gone before and the generations yet to come.

In the familiarity of the prayer, a ritual that had marked so many significant moments in my spiritual journey, I found solace, a sense of comfort and peace that seemed to wrap around me like a warm embrace. It was as if each word, each phrase, was a stepping stone leading me deeper into the heart of our faith, a path illuminated by the light of divine truth and the guiding hand of the Lord.

As the prayer concluded, the room was filled with a profound stillness, a moment of collective introspection and reverence that seemed to stretch out into eternity. It was as if the prayer had opened a gateway to a deeper spiritual understanding, preparing our hearts and minds for the revelations that were to come, a silent invitation to step into the presence of the divine. In that moment, the Endowment Room felt like a sanctuary, a sacred space where the divine and the earthly met, and where we, as seekers of truth, sat ready to receive the wisdom and blessings that awaited us, our souls open and receptive to the whisperings of the Spirit.

As the Apostle began to speak, his voice resonated through the Endowment Room, not merely as a sound but as a conduit for a profound spiritual awakening, a clarion call that seemed to pierce the very veil that separated heaven and earth. He narrated church history with a reverence that captivated every soul present, his words painting a vivid picture of the trials and triumphs that had shaped our faith. "In the early days of the Church," he began, his voice low and measured, each syllable imbued with the weight of centuries past, "our ancestors faced trials that tested the very fabric of their faith, challenges that would have broken lesser men and women." Each word seemed to echo with the struggles and resilience of those who came before us, a powerful reminder of the sacrifices that had been made to ensure the survival and growth of our beloved church.

His recounting of the pioneers who crossed vast plains and the saints who weathered persecution painted a vivid picture of our church's journey, a saga of faith and fortitude that had been etched into the annals of history. These stories, the foundation upon which we now stood, were not just historical accounts; they were reminders of the sacrifices made for the faith we now practiced freely, a testament to the enduring power of belief in the face of adversity.

Each word the Apostle spoke felt like a brushstroke in a grand mural, depicting scenes of faith, resilience, and divine guidance, a masterpiece that seemed to come to life before our very eyes. Brother and Sister Reynolds, longtime friends who had been pillars of support in our community, exchanged glances, their eyes glistening with tears of gratitude and awe, clearly moved by the power of the historical accounts that were being shared.

As the Apostle recounted tales of sacrifice and communities bound by shared devotion to the gospel, the room transformed into a living testament to the endurance of our faith through the ages, a sacred space where the past and the present converged in a moment of profound unity. I could almost see the images of these pioneers and saints, their faces marked by determination and hope, their eyes alight with the fire of unwavering belief, a vision that seemed to flicker and dance in the soft light of the Endowment Room.

"The struggles, the triumphs, the moments of divine intervention—all of them have led us to this pivotal point," the Apostle continued, his gaze sweeping across the assembled congregation, his eyes filled with the wisdom and compassion of years of service. His eyes, windows to a soul that had been touched by the hand of God, seemed to connect with each of us individually. "It is in understanding our past that we find the strength to face the challenges of our future. Today, we stand on the shoulders of giants, and the Lord, in His infinite wisdom, has deemed us worthy of a charge that echoes through the corridors of eternity, a sacred trust that will shape the destiny of our church and the world at large."

The air in the Endowment Room became electric with a sense of continuity, a palpable recognition that we were part of an ongoing saga, a story that had begun long before our birth and would continue long after we had returned to the dust from whence we came. Our faith's narrative was not static but a living, breathing journey, a river of testimony that flowed through the generations, connecting us to the past, present, and future. Each generation, including ours, played a crucial role in the unfolding of God's divine plan, a responsibility that filled me with a profound sense of purpose and humility.

As the Apostle's gaze swept across the room, there was an intensity in his eyes that seemed to reach into the very core of each person present, a piercing look that seemed to lay bare the depths of our souls. His gaze was probing, yet not intrusive, as if he were gently seeking the measure of our commitment and readiness, a silent assessment of our worthiness to receive the revelations that were about to be shared. "Brothers and sisters," he spoke with a measured solemnity that resonated in the quiet of the room, "before we proceed, I offer you a choice. The revelations you are about to hear carry profound implications, a weight of responsibility that will rest upon your shoulders from this day forward. If any among you feel that the weight of this calling is too much to bear, I extend to you the opportunity to leave now, with no judgment or condemnation."

His words, spoken with such sincerity, hung in the air, creating a pregnant pause that seemed to envelop us all, a moment of quiet introspection that seemed to stretch out into eternity. The gravity of his offer was clear, acknowledging that the path ahead was one of sacred weight and immense responsibility, a journey that would require the utmost dedication and sacrifice. It was an exit offered without judgment but with an understanding of the profound nature of what was to come, a final chance to step back from the precipice of divine revelation.

Around me, patrons exchanged glances, their expressions a mix of contemplation and resolve, a silent conversation that seemed to speak volumes about the depths of their faith and commitment. Sister Riley, a woman in our Stake known for her thoughtful insights and deep faith, shared a brief, yet meaningful look with her husband, a glance that seemed to encapsulate a lifetime of shared devotion and unity of purpose. It was a silent conversation that seemed to speak volumes of their shared resolve and commitment to stay, to see this journey through to the end.

Greta's eyes met mine in a silent exchange that communicated more than words ever could, a glance that seemed to reach into the very depths of my soul. In her gaze, I saw a reflection of my own feelings — a commitment to our faith that knew no bounds, a readiness to embrace whatever revelations were to be shared, no matter how difficult or challenging they might be.

The room, filled with faces both familiar and unfamiliar, seemed to collectively inhale, a shared moment of introspection as each person contemplated their choice, a decision that would shape the course of their lives and the lives of generations to come.

Yet, in the profound silence that followed the Apostle's offer, not a single soul stirred from their seat, a testament to the unwavering faith and dedication of those who had been called to this sacred gathering. The unity in purpose among us was palpable, a tangible affirmation that we, as a congregation, were committed to undertaking this sacred journey together. The weight of the revelation, the sense of being chosen for a divine purpose, seemed to anchor each member firmly in their place, a silent declaration of their willingness to bear the mantle of responsibility that would soon be placed upon their shoulders.

As the Apostle's gaze, laden with the knowledge of sacred trust, swept across the room once more, his eyes met each individual's, locking for a moment that seemed to peer into the depths of our souls, a silent acknowledgment of the sacred bond that had been forged in this holy place. "Brothers and sisters," his voice, resonating with both authority and compassion, filled the room, each word imbued with the weight of divine purpose, "what you are about to hear carries a weight of divine significance, a revelation that will shape the destiny of His people and the world at large. But with such a sacred charge comes an equally sacred responsibility, a burden that you must bear with the utmost reverence and dedication."

The room, transformed into a temple of collective anticipation, seemed to hold its breath. The air was thick with a sense of profound reverence and solemnity, a palpable presence that seemed to fill every corner of the Endowment Room. In the sacred hush that followed the Apostle's words, their gravity settled over us like a solemn benediction, filling the space with an almost tangible sense of purpose, a call to action that resonated in the depths of our souls.

"I ask of you a sacred commitment," he continued, his words deliberate and measured, each syllable piercing the silence with its significance, a clarion call to the faithful. "What transpires here is not to be taken lightly. The revelations about to be shared are a trust between you and the Lord, a sacred covenant that must be honoured and upheld. As His chosen, you are stewards of sacred knowledge, guardians of the divine plan, and the weight of this responsibility will rest upon your shoulders from this day forward." His message was clear: we were being entrusted with something far beyond ordinary understanding, a covenant of immense spiritual magnitude that would shape the course of our lives and the lives of generations to come.

The Apostle then requested a solemn oath of secrecy, his voice echoing through the hallowed space like a trumpet blast, a call to arms in the battle for the souls of men. "Raise your hand to the square," he instructed, his eyes unwavering and deep with expectation. As we raised our hands in the ancient gesture of covenant-making, a symbol of our willingness to enter into a sacred pact with the divine, it felt as if we were sealing a sacred promise, a bond that would endure through the ages. "By this act, you covenant with God to protect the sanctity of what you are about to learn. Let not the sacred charge be spoken of lightly or without purpose. The mysteries of His kingdom are to be guarded with the same dedication as the pioneers guarded the embers of faith in times of trial, a sacred trust that must be preserved at all costs."

As our hands were raised, heads bowed in reverence, a collective affirmation filled the room, a chorus of voices united in a single purpose. Each "yes" was a pledge, not merely spoken, but felt deeply within, a solemn agreement to carry the burden of this revelation with utmost fidelity, a promise to honour the sacred trust that had been placed in our hands.

This moment bound our hearts to a purpose greater than ourselves, a calling that transcended the boundaries of our individual lives and connected us to the eternal tapestry of

God's plan. The weight of this responsibility filled me with a sense of solemn pride and deep humility, a recognition of the immense trust that had been placed in our hands. We were, in that moment, entrusted as guardians of a holy truth, a role we accepted with the utmost reverence and commitment, a mantle that we would bear with honour and dedication for the rest of our lives.

The Apostle's voice, resonant and imbued with purpose, became a vessel for a revelation that felt destined to reshape the very fabric of our lives, a message that seemed to emanate from the very throne of God. As he spoke, high-level details of a divine plan unfolded before us, each revelation feeling like a stone laid in the construction of a monumental spiritual edifice, a temple of truth that was being built in the hearts and minds of the faithful. The room, thick with anticipation, seemed to lean in, each person absorbed as the Apostle's words wove a narrative deeply rooted in the annals of our church history, a story that was at once familiar and yet filled with new meaning and purpose.

"Brothers and sisters," he began, his voice steady and profound, each word weighted with the significance of the moment, "as we embark on this sacred journey, let us reflect on the early days of our church, the humble beginnings from which we have grown. The pioneers who, with unwavering faith, crossed plains and mountains to establish Zion, a city of God in the wilderness." His words conjured images of those early believers, their journeys marked by hardship and unshakeable faith, a testament to the power of belief in the face of adversity. "Today, you are called to be modern pioneers, forging a new chapter in the history of the restored gospel, a chapter that will be written in the annals of eternity."

The call to move to Salt Lake City, the epicentre of our faith, resonated powerfully through the room, a clarion call that seemed to echo through the centuries. The city, steeped in sacred history and imbued with spiritual significance, was now presented as the crucible where we, the chosen, would forge the beginnings of the New Jerusalem, a city of God that would stand as a beacon of light and truth in a world shrouded in darkness.

"As we look to the future," the Apostle continued, his voice a guiding light in the unfolding revelation, a beacon that seemed to illuminate the path ahead, "let the sacrifices of our pioneer forebears inspire and guide us. Their resilience, their willingness to heed the call, laid the foundation for the strong church we are today, a church that stands as a bastion of truth in a world of shifting sands." His words were a bridge connecting the past with our present, a reminder that the sacrifices of those early pioneers were not in vain, but rather a seed that had been planted in the fertile soil of faith, a seed that had grown into a mighty tree whose branches now reached to the heavens. "In your relocation, you carry the torch of their faith, becoming pioneers of a new era, a era of growth and expansion that will see the gospel spread to every corner of the earth."

As the details continued to unfold, a map of the future began taking shape in my mind, a vision of a world transformed by the power of the restored gospel. It was a tapestry woven with threads of faith, sacrifice, and shared purpose, a vision of a collective journey toward a profound spiritual objective, a destination that seemed to shimmer on the horizon like a city of gold.

Sister Phillips, seated nearby, nodded in understanding as the Apostle spoke, her eyes glistening with tears of joy and gratitude. Her years of dedication and deep knowledge of church history were evident in her expression, a living testament to the power of faith to transform lives and shape destinies. Her eyes, reflecting the deep well of her spiritual reservoir, seemed to beckon us to draw from its waters, to partake of the wisdom and strength that had sustained her through a lifetime of service and devotion. In them, I saw the reflection of our collective responsibility and the depth of the journey we were about to embark upon, a journey that would require every ounce of faith and fortitude we possessed.

The timeframe of our call to Salt Lake City remained deliberately undisclosed, veiling the immediacy of our journey in a shroud of mystery, a sacred secret that was not yet meant to be revealed. Yet, despite the uncertainty of timing, a palpable assurance filled the room, permeating the air with a sense of unity and support, a tangible reminder that we were not alone in this endeavour. It was a path we were to tread together, hand in hand, heart to heart, a pilgrimage of the soul that would test our resolve and strengthen our bonds.

"In the sacred space of the Temple," the Apostle continued, his voice imbued with a comforting certainty, a balm to the soul in the face of the unknown, "the church pledges its unwavering support. You are not alone in this endeavour, but rather part of a grand tapestry of faith and dedication." His words were a promise, a covenant of support and guidance that seemed to wrap around us like a warm embrace. "The practicalities of relocation, the intricacies of uprooting lives for a divine cause, will be met with the assurance that the church will stand as a steadfast ally, a beacon of light in the darkness. We are committed to your well-being, both spiritually and temporally, and will walk beside you every step of the way."

The weight of the revelation we had just received was now intertwined with a promise of support, a sacred trust that bound us together in a common purpose. As the Apostle spoke of assistance, it felt as if a mantle of comfort had settled over the room, a tangible reminder that the divine hand guiding this endeavour extended beyond celestial guidance and reached into the practicalities of our mortal existence.

"In this sacred work," the Apostle concluded, his voice resonating with a finality that seemed to encapsulate the gravity of his address, a benediction that sealed the covenant we had made, "may you find strength in each other, solace in your faith, and assurance in the knowledge that you are not alone. As you step forward into the unknown, may the pioneers of old walk beside you, and may the Lord's hand guide your every step, leading you to the promised land that awaits."

The room, which had been filled with the weight of revelation and the implications of our calling, now resonated with a collective commitment, a shared resolve to answer the call that had been placed upon us. Each of us, prepared to become a modern pioneer, felt the magnitude of the task ahead.

As the Apostle concluded his address, a sacred hush settled over the gathering, a moment of collective reflection and introspection. It was a pause to absorb and contemplate the uncharted path that awaited us, a moment to gather our strength and fortify our faith for the journey ahead. The Apostle's words lingered in the air, a final blessing before we dispersed, each of us now carrying the news of our new calling and the assurance of divine and communal support as we navigated this unprecedented journey, a journey that would forever change the course of our lives and the lives of generations to come.

A sense of finality settled over the room, a recognition that the sacred charge had been delivered and the covenant sealed. The weight of the moment hung in the air, a palpable presence that seemed to fill every corner of the Endowment Room. It was a weight of responsibility, yes, but also a weight of privilege, a sacred trust that had been placed in our hands by the very hand of God.

❖

The final notes of the hymn lingered in the air, a sacred melody that seemed to reverberate not just in the Endowment Room, but within the very walls of my soul. The harmonies, woven together by the voices of the faithful, created a tapestry of devotion and unity, each thread a testament to the shared purpose that had brought us together in this holy place.

As the collective voice of the chosen rose in unison in a closing prayer, there was a palpable sense of unity, a shared strength emanating from each voice, a power that seemed to transcend the boundaries of the physical world. This prayer was more than words; it was a petition for guidance, strength, and the fortitude to fulfil the sacred charge that had been entrusted to each one of us, a plea for the divine hand to guide us on the journey that lay ahead.

When the prayer concluded, a hushed reverence enveloped the room, a silence that was at once profound and intimate, a moment of collective introspection and communion with the divine. The Apostle rose from his place, his movements imbued with a sense of purpose and solemnity. His farewell was not just a routine parting but felt like a personal benediction, a spiritual embrace that continued to resonate even as he began to move through the room, greeting each person with a depth of love and understanding that seemed to emanate from his very being.

Sister Williams, a member known for her deep compassion and understanding, offered a heartfelt "thank you" as the Apostle clasped her hands, her voice thick with emotion and gratitude. His parting words to her, a blend of personal spiritual insight and gentle encouragement, visibly moved her, tears glistening in her eyes as she absorbed the weight of his message. It was clear that his words left an indelible mark on each recipient, a final touch of divine blessing and guidance that would stay with them long after this sacred gathering had ended.

Watching the Apostle move through the room, his presence a beacon of light and love, I felt a sense of anticipation building within me, a knowing that my own encounter with him would be a moment of profound significance. And then, suddenly, he was standing before me, his gaze holding mine with an intensity that seemed to reach beyond the temporal realm, touching something deep within me, a place of vulnerability and truth that I had never before revealed to another soul.

In his eyes, I saw a depth of understanding and wisdom that was both comforting and awe-inspiring, a reflection of the divine love that had brought me to this sacred place. His presence was a reminder of the connection between the divine and the earthly, a bridge across realms that seemed to blur the lines between the seen and the unseen, the known and the unknown.

His voice, though a mere whisper, carried the weight of ancient truths and future revelations, a sound that seemed to echo through the ages and resonate in the very depths of my being. It was a personal message that seemed to pierce directly to my heart and situation, a communication that was at once intimate and universal. The words he spoke, though meant only for me, felt as if they were echoing through time, carrying a significance far beyond this single moment, a message that had been ordained from the foundations of the world.

"Noah," he said, his words resonating like a celestial melody, each syllable imbued with a power and authority that could only come from the divine, "you are a cornerstone in the Lord's design, chosen with purpose and anointed for a sacred work." His statement filled me with a sense of destiny and responsibility, a weight of purpose that settled upon my shoulders like a mantle of divine calling. "As the architect of the New Jerusalem, the Lord has seen fit to entrust you with a sacred role, a mission that will require every ounce of faith and dedication you possess." The gravity of his words was not lost on me; they painted a vision of a spiritual journey that was both daunting and exhilarating, a path that would lead me to the very heart of God's plan for His children.

"In the crucible of change, let your faith be the anchor, your love be the guiding light, and your humility be the fertile ground for miracles," he continued, his counsel a beacon of hope and direction in the face of the unknown. "The path ahead is paved with challenges, but the Lord, in His wisdom, has equipped you with the strength to navigate them, the grace to overcome them, and the wisdom to learn from them. Stand as a beacon of faith, a light in the darkness, and the divine hand will guide you, step by step, toward the glorious future that awaits."

The Apostle's hand, warm and steadying, descended upon my shoulder, imparting a blessing that transcended the physical touch, a transference of spiritual power and authority that seemed to flow from his very being into mine. It was a gesture that seemed to infuse me with strength and assurance, a tangible reminder of the divine support that would sustain me through the trials and triumphs that lay ahead. His eyes, windows to eternity, held a glimpse of the sacred journey ahead—a journey uniquely tailored to my soul's evolution, a path of growth and enlightenment that would lead me closer to the heart of God.

The resonance of his prophecy echoed in the chambers of my heart, a guiding light for the road that lay before me, a promise of divine guidance and protection that would never fail. As he moved on to the next patron, his presence a lingering warmth in the space beside me, I stood in the quiet aftermath of his whispered words, feeling a deepened connection to my faith and calling, a renewed sense of purpose and determination that burned within me like a holy fire.

❖

In the reverent silence outside the Temple, the gathered patrons slowly dispersed, each soul carrying with them the residue of the sacred experience we had all shared. The crisp winter air felt almost cleansing as it brushed against my skin, rejuvenating in its chill, a tangible reminder of the spiritual renewal that had taken place within the hallowed walls of the Temple. I looked up, noticing how the stars above sparkled, their celestial light seeming to dance with a new intensity, as if they too bore witness to the divine covenant we had made, a silent testament to the sacred bonds that now united us all.

Greta and I walked hand in hand, our steps echoing softly in the stillness of the Temple grounds, a gentle rhythm that seemed to beat in time with the pulsing of our hearts. The spiritual messages we had received in the Endowment Room lingered in my mind, resonating like a gentle whisper that promised strength for the journey ahead, a constant reminder of the divine guidance that would light our path. The profound revelation we had been a part of seemed to infuse the very air around us, imbuing the familiar path back to our car with a newfound sense of purpose, a sacred charge that had been entrusted to us by the hand of God.

Our cars awaited us, humble vehicles that, in the vastness of the universe, seemed like small vessels ready to carry us back into the familiar yet forever changed landscape of our lives. They were no longer just modes of transportation, but sacred chariots that would bear us forth into the unknown, carrying the weight of our divine calling with every turn of the wheel.

As we walked, I felt the unspoken bond among the patrons we left behind, a connection that went beyond mere acquaintance or friendship. It was a bond forged in the crucible of shared revelation, a spiritual tie that knit our hearts together in a tapestry of collective strength and unity that I knew would accompany us far beyond the Temple gates, a constant source of support and encouragement in the days and years to come.

Once inside the car, the door closed with a soft click, cocooning us in the quiet solitude of the night, a sacred space that seemed to echo with the whispers of eternity. The familiar scent of the car's interior, a blend of worn leather and the faint traces of our daily lives, now seemed infused with a new essence, a reminder of the spiritual journey we had just embarked upon. I started the engine, feeling its subtle vibration beneath us, a gentle reminder of the journey back to our everyday lives, a return to the world we knew, yet one that would never be the same again.

As we pulled away from the Temple, the stillness within the car mirrored the reverence that lingered in my heart, a hushed awe that seemed to fill every corner of my being. The Temple, its spires rising majestically into the night sky, grew smaller in the rearview mirror, a physical representation of the sacred space I was leaving behind, yet one that would forever remain etched in my sous. The road ahead stretched out before me, a ribbon of asphalt that seemed to symbolise the path I had chosen, the journey of faith and obedience that would lead me to the very heart of God's plan.

Overwhelmed with the joy and the weight of the divine calling, tears began to flow freely down my cheeks. Each drop felt like it carried the essence of the sacred experience we had just been a part of, a liquid prayer that spoke of gratitude, humility, and an unwavering commitment to the path that lay ahead. They were tears of joy, of wonder, and of a deep, abiding love for the God who had seen fit to entrust us with such a sacred charge, a mission that would forever change the course of our lives and the lives of countless others.

Greta, my steadfast companion on this journey of faith, sat beside me in respectful silence, her presence a balm to my soul, a reminder of the unbreakable bond we shared. Her hand found mine, fingers intertwining in a gesture that spoke volumes without a single word, a tactile expression of the love and support that would sustain us through the challenges and triumphs that lay ahead. In the unity of our touch, we shared more than just a marital bond; we shared a connection forged by a covenant that now transcended the mortal realm, a sacred pact that had been sealed in the presence of God and angels. We were united, not just as husband and wife, but as partners in a divine undertaking that would reshape our lives and faith forever, a sacred mission that would require every ounce of our devotion and sacrifice.

In the silence of the car, broken only by the soft hum of the engine and the gentle whisper of our breathing, I offered a silent prayer of gratitude and supplication, a heartfelt plea for the strength and wisdom to fulfil the sacred trust that had been placed in my hands. I prayed for the faith to follow wherever the Lord might lead, for the courage to face the trials and tribulations that would surely come, and for the love to bind our hearts together as one, a united front against the forces of darkness that would seek to thwart our divine purpose.

4338.212

(31 July 2018)

GRETA'S STRUGGLE

4338.212.1

The last remnants of the late afternoon sun had vanished, and the cold evening was rapidly enveloping our home, casting long shadows across the kitchen and dining room. The usual comforting aromas of an almost cooked dinner seemed muted, overshadowed by the strained energy that had been building with each passing moment, a palpable tension that hung in the air like a gathering storm.

Greta had been unusually short with Charles all afternoon, her patience thinning like ice over a pond in spring, a testament to the weight of the revelations we had received and the secrecy we were bound to maintain. Sensing that the moment of inevitability had finally arrived, I braced myself for the storm that was brewing in our kitchen, a tempest of emotions and unspoken truths.

"I can't believe you're so careless, Charles! Can't you do anything right?" Greta's voice, usually calm and nurturing, carried a sharp edge as she plated the food, her movements jerky and abrupt. The irritation in her tone was uncharacteristic, hinting at deeper concerns than just the dinner table setting.

Charles, who was never one to shy away from a confrontation, especially with his mother, retorted with equal intensity, his voice rising to match Greta's. "Seriously, Mum? It's just us for dinner. What's the big deal?" His words, though spoken in defence, lacked the awareness of the emotional undercurrent that was at play, a testament to his youth and the innocence that still clung to him like a protective cloak.

Greta's response came swiftly, her words like arrows fired in rapid succession. "The big deal is that you never pay attention. I asked you to set the table properly, and what do I find? Utensils all over the place, not a single napkin folded properly. It's like living with a teenager who can't be bothered." Her frustration over the mundane task of setting the table became a vessel for the larger anxieties that had been brewing within her, a burden that seemed to grow heavier with each passing moment.

Jerome, seated in the living room, was seemingly oblivious to the escalating tension, his attention focused solely on the glowing screen before him. With his headphones on and eyes glued to the computer, he had tuned out the brewing conflict, a protective mechanism against the family's current state of stress. I could tell he was intentionally distancing himself from the tension, a survival tactic that had become all too familiar in recent days, a way to cope with the uncertainty that had taken hold of our household.

Feeling too weary to intervene or mediate, I slowly sat myself at the head of the table, a position that often felt more like that of a referee than the head of a family, a role that weighed heavily on my shoulders. The tension in the room was palpable, a sorry contrast to the usual warmth and laughter that filled our family dinners, a reminder of the simpler times that seemed to be slipping away.

As I sat there, watching my family navigate through this tense moment, I couldn't help but feel a deep concern, a worry that gnawed at the edges of my consciousness like a persistent ache. The revelation and the divine calling we had received were supposed to bring us closer, to unite us in faith and purpose, a sacred bond that would strengthen our family and guide us through the challenges ahead. Yet, here we were, grappling with the very human aspects of our existence, the everyday challenges that seemed magnified under the weight of our newfound responsibilities, a testament to the fragility of our mortal condition. I knew that we needed to find a way to come together, to support each other through this significant transition, but at that moment, I felt at a loss for how to bridge the growing divide, a chasm that seemed to be widening.

"Mum, seriously? You're making a big deal out of nothing," Charles scoffed, dismissing his mother's frustration with a wave of his hand. I could see the irritation in his stance matching Greta's growing exasperation, a dance of emotions that threatened to spiral out of control. I looked towards Greta, offering her a gentle smile in an attempt to diffuse the tension, a silent plea for understanding and patience. But my gesture seemed to only add fuel to the fire, inadvertently intensifying the emotional atmosphere in the room, a spark that ignited the tinder of our collective stress.

"No, Charles, I'm not making a big deal out of this. I'm making a big deal out of everything," Greta's voice, now strained with emotion, carried the weight of the unspoken truth that had been burdening her all day, a truth that she longed to share but was bound to keep hidden. "Can't you see that we're on the brink of something monumental, and all you care about is arguing over the table setting?" Her words echoed in the room, revealing the depth of her internal struggle, a battle between her sacred duty and her maternal instincts.

Charles, looking perplexed and still unaware of the impending revelation about our move to Salt Lake City, shot back with a mix of confusion and concern, his brow furrowed in a way that made him look far older than his years. "What are you talking about, Mum? You've been acting weird all day."

I sighed deeply, realising the difficult position we were in, a balancing act that required the utmost care and sensitivity.

Charles was right in his observation; the tension that had been building up was unusual and noticeable, a deviation from the norm that had once defined our family life. Yet, Greta's frustration was also understandable, given the monumental changes looming over our family, a future that had been shaped by divine intervention and human choice.

Undeterred by Charles's confusion, Greta quickly retaliated, her voice tinged with a mix of urgency and caution, a tone that spoke of the weight of the secrets she carried. "I'm talking about something much bigger than the table setting, Charles." The words hung in the air, a veiled hint at the larger revelation we were grappling with, a truth that threatened to spill out at any moment.

A tight knot twisted in my gut as I sent a rapid prayer to the heavens, hoping that Greta wouldn't break her oath of secrecy, at least not under the current strained circumstances, a plea for divine intervention in a moment of human weakness.

"But, of course, you wouldn't understand," Greta said, her voice a mix of frustration over both the mundane and the monumental, a reflection of the inner turmoil that had taken hold of her heart. Her words lingered in the air, heavy with unspoken implications, as she stormed out of the room, her footsteps echoing down the hallway like a drumbeat of discontent. Her departure left a palpable void, the tension she carried with her leaving an echo of unease, a reminder of the challenges that lay ahead.

Charles, looking genuinely bewildered by his mother's abrupt exit, turned to me for answers, his eyes searching mine for a glimmer of understanding in the midst of the confusion. He collected a plate of food from the kitchen bench, his movements slow, almost reflective, a contrast to the heated exchange that had just taken place. "What the heck is up with her?" he asked, pausing at the doorway of the dining room, his voice a mix of concern and frustration. His face bore a look of genuine worry, a sign of the love he held for his mother despite their recent conflicts.

I replied with a simple shrug, trying to mask the complexity of emotions and thoughts swirling within me. "She's just a little stressed," I said, trying to sound nonchalant, a façade that felt flimsy and transparent in the face of the truth. It felt like an understatement, a gross oversimplification of the monumental changes that loomed on the horizon, but I wasn't ready to delve into the deeper truths that were at play, a revelation that would forever alter the course of our lives.

Pouting, Charles seemed dissatisfied with my answer, his face a picture of teenage angst and frustration. He pivoted on his heel, a sign of his irritation and perhaps a reflection of his inability to deal with the unexplained tension that had taken hold of our household. "I'm going to eat in my bedroom," he announced, his voice carrying a hint of resignation as he walked away, his footsteps fading into the distance like a retreating storm.

Left in solitude, I sat at the head of the table, enveloped in the depths of my own thoughts, a sea of emotions and concerns that threatened to drown me in their intensity. My gaze settled on the empty table before me, an unsettling representation of the disjointed state of our family at that moment, a metaphor for the challenges we would face in the days ahead. The room, usually filled with the warmth and chatter of family dinners, now felt cold and silent, an unpleasant reminder of the changes that had already begun to take hold.

As I sat there, the weight of the revelation we had received at the Temple and the impending changes it would bring loomed large in my mind, a constant presence that seemed to overshadow every aspect of our lives. The challenge of balancing our sacred duty with the needs and emotions of our family felt more daunting than ever, a tightrope walk that required the utmost care and sensitivity. The responsibility of guiding my family through this transition, of maintaining unity in the face of such monumental change, weighed heavily on me, a burden that I carried with a mix of reverence and trepidation.

Greta's reaction, Charles's confusion, and Jerome's indifference were all signs of the underlying current of tension and uncertainty that had gripped our household, a reflection of the human struggles that lay beneath the surface of our divine calling. It was a tension that needed to be addressed, yet the path forward was unclear, a road that had yet to be fully mapped out. The revelation we were tasked with safeguarding was both a blessing and a burden, its implications reverberating through the very fabric of our daily lives.

Lost in contemplation, I knew that the journey ahead would require not just faith but also wisdom, understanding, and a delicate balancing act between our sacred obligations and the very human dynamics of our family life. It was a path we would need to navigate together, each step taken with care and guided by the divine hand that had led us to this point, a pilgrimage of the soul that would test our resolve and strengthen our bonds.

❖

The clunk of two plates being placed on the table signalled Greta's return, abruptly pulling me from the deep sea of my thoughts.

Neither of us spoke as we began to eat, the scrape of utensils against the plates the only sound that punctuated the heavy stillness. Each bite was an effort, a struggle against the steadily growing unease that seemed to envelop the room, a palpable presence that hung in the air like a gathering storm.

Greta, who was usually the heart and soul of our home, the one who brought warmth and laughter to even the most mundane of moments, pushed her food around her plate absentmindedly, her appetite seemingly lost to the turmoil that raged within her. Her gaze was distant, her thoughts seemingly a world away, caught up in the maelstrom of emotions like a tempest that threatened to sweep us all away.

Unable to bear the weight of the unspoken any longer, I set down my fork and looked at Greta directly, my eyes seeking hers in a silent plea for connection. "What's going on, Greta?" I asked, my voice breaking the oppressive silence, a question that seemed to hang in the air like a fragile lifeline, a bridge across the gulf that had opened up between us.

Greta sighed, a sound that seemed to carry the weight of the world. Her shoulders slumped as if releasing a heavy load. "Noah, it's just... the call we received in the Temple. It's tearing at me, tearing at us," she confessed, her voice laced with an aching vulnerability, a raw honesty that cut through the façade of normality we had been trying to maintain.

I reached across the table, placing my hand over hers in a gesture of support. "Greta, we're in this together. Whatever happens, we'll face it as a family," I reassured her, trying to offer some solace amidst the uncertainty, a glimmer of hope in the darkness that seemed to surround us.

"Noah," Greta's voice trembled as she spoke, revealing the depth of her anguish, a pain that seemed to emanate from the very core of her being, "Luke has been gone for years. We've known, deep down, that his choices had led him away from the Church. And now, with this call to gather, it feels like a stark reality. A reality that we might not have our family complete in the eternities."

Her words hung heavily in the air, a poignant expression of the pain of a mother's heart — the pain of potentially losing a child not just in this life but in what we believed to be the life hereafter, a sorrow that transcended the bounds of mortality. I squeezed her hand gently, offering what little comfort I could in the face of such a profound grief, a shared pain that had lurked in the shadows of our family life, now brought into sharp focus by the divine calling we had received.

"Greta," I began, my voice tempered with both concern and understanding, a delicate balance between the roles of husband and father, "we can't control the choices our children make. All we can do is love them, guide them, and hope that the seeds of faith we planted will someday bear fruit." It was a truth that we both knew, a fundamental principle of our belief in agency and free will, but in moments like these, it was particularly hard to accept, a bitter pill to swallow in the face of our deepest fears.

She nodded, the tears in her eyes reflecting the turmoil within, a mirror of the storm that raged in her soul. "But what if this tears our family apart, Noah? What if Luke's influence leads others away too?" Her voice trembled, betraying the deep-seated fear that had clearly been haunting her thoughts, a spectre that loomed over our family like a dark cloud.

The fear in her eyes was a mirror of my own internal struggles, a reflection of the doubts and concerns that had been gnawing at the edges of my consciousness since the moment we had received the revelation. We had both grappled with the uncertainty of our children's spiritual journeys, each in our own way, a private battle that we had fought in the depths of our hearts. I took a deep breath, trying to find the right words to offer some semblance of comfort, a balm to soothe the wounds that had been reopened by our current situation.

"We've always faced uncertainties as parents. Our love and commitment to the gospel have been constants. We can't predict the future, but we can trust in the foundation we've laid." I hoped to convey both reassurance and a sense of resilience, even as I grappled with my own doubts, a flicker of faith in the darkness that threatened to consume us.

Greta's shoulders slumped, a visible sign of the immense weight her fears were placing on her, a burden that seemed to press down on her very soul. "Noah, I've been so sick. The fear, the uncertainty—it's been overwhelming. I'm terrified that Paul, too, might not be Temple worthy. What if our family, the one we've tried so hard to keep together, is torn apart by this call?"

Her words struck deep into my heart, echoing the concerns that often kept me awake at night, the fears that lurked in the shadows of my mind. The vulnerability she displayed tore at me, a raw and honest glimpse into the depths of her pain, a pain that I shared but had tried to keep hidden beneath a veneer of strength and faith. The idea of our family, which we had nurtured and fought to keep together in faith, being torn apart by this divine calling was a thought too painful to contemplate, a possibility that felt far too real.

Without a word, I pulled Greta into a tight embrace, offering the only comfort I could in that moment, a physical reminder of the love and support that would always be there, no matter what the future might hold. Holding her close, I felt her body shudder as she allowed the dam of her emotions to break, a torrent of tears that had been held back for too long. It was a rare moment of complete vulnerability for her, a glimpse into the depths of her soul, and all I could do was provide a safe space for her to express her fears and sorrows, a sanctuary in the midst of the storm.

"Greta," I whispered, my voice a tender reassurance amidst the overwhelming emotions swirling around us. "We're facing the unknown, and the fear is natural. But our family is resilient. We've weathered storms before. We'll face this challenge with love, with unity, and with faith in the divine plan that binds us together." I spoke with conviction, trying to infuse both of us with a sense of hope and strength, even as my own heart wrestled with similar fears, a battle between faith and doubt that raged within me.

She clung to me, her body trembling with the force of her sobs, her tears soaking into the fabric of my shirt. I could feel the fragility of the moment, a poignant reminder that our journey was indeed about to take an unforeseen and potentially tumultuous turn. The room was filled with a palpable sense of vulnerability, a shared understanding that the road ahead would be fraught with challenges and obstacles, a test of our faith and our resilience.

As Greta's sobs began to subside, she looked up at me, her eyes brimming with a deep-seated fear, a terror that seemed to reach into the very depths of her soul. "Noah, what if we lose them? What if this call becomes the wedge that separates us forever?" Her words cut through me like a knife, echoing the unspoken fear that had taken root in my own heart.

Yet, even in the face of such a profound and terrifying possibility, I refused to succumb to despair, a flicker of faith that burned within me like a small but steady flame. "Greta, we won't lose them," I said firmly, trying to dispel the growing shadows of doubt, a declaration of hope in the midst of the darkness. "Our family is bound by more than mortal ties. Love will be our guide, and faith will be our anchor. We'll face whatever comes, together." I hoped my words would bring her some comfort, even as I grappled with my own concerns, a battle between the head and the heart that raged within me.

Greta's tears continued to flow, a river of sorrow and fear that seemed to have no end, but she seemed to find solace in my embrace, a momentary respite from the storm that raged within her. My arms wrapped tightly around her, offering her the strength and support she needed, a physical reminder of the love that would always be there, no matter what the future might hold. In our shared vulnerability, our love became a sanctuary, a refuge from the storm of uncertainty that threatened to engulf us, a beacon of hope in the darkness.

Despite the deep, internal feeling that Greta might be right —that this event could indeed split our family both here and now, and possibly in the eternities—I made a silent promise to myself, a vow that I would do everything in my power to keep our family together. Hand in hand, heart in heart, Greta and I would embrace the unknown, a journey into the uncharted waters of our faith and our love. I was determined to navigate the uncharted waters of this divine calling, even if it meant facing the deepest fears that lingered in the shadows of our souls, a battle that I was willing to fight for the sake of our family and our eternal destiny.

SPIRITUAL AMBIGUITY

4338.212.2

In the quiet solitude of my study, where the dim light cast elongated shadows across the walls, I sank to my knees, feeling both small and significant in the vast tapestry of the cosmos. The room was a place of rest and escape, a private space where I could lay bare the depths of my soul, a sanctuary from the turmoil that raged beyond its walls. The weight of the recent revelation from the Temple bore down on me with an almost tangible force, a burden that seemed to press upon my very being, and the uncertainty that clouded my understanding sought solace in the time-honoured sanctuary of prayer.

As I bowed my head, my hands clasped together in a gesture of reverence and supplication, I felt the sacredness of the moment enveloping me, a mantle of divine presence that settled upon my shoulders like a comforting embrace. It was a communion between the mortal and the divine, a bridge between my earthly concerns and the celestial guidance I sought, a moment of profound connection that transcended the bounds of the physical world. The quiet of the room amplified the sound of my own breathing, each inhale and exhale a rhythm of life amidst the storm of emotions and thoughts swirling within me, a reminder of the fragile nature of my existence in the face of the eternal.

With every word I uttered, each syllable a sacred offering laid upon the altar of faith, there was a profound sense of connection, a feeling that transcended the physical space I occupied. My prayer was not just a series of spoken words; it was a plea from the heart, a reaching out beyond the limitations of language, a desperate attempt to touch the divine and seek the guidance that I so desperately needed. I poured out my fears, my hopes, and my uncertainties, laying them at the feet of the divine, a humble supplicant seeking the wisdom and strength to navigate the path that lay ahead.

"Oh, Father," I whispered, my voice barely audible in the quiet of the room, the words a delicate melody woven with threads of desperation and yearning. "I stand at the crossroads of sacred duty and familial bonds, a humble servant seeking guidance in the face of uncertainty. The revelations from the Temple weigh on my soul, a burden that seems to grow heavier with each passing moment, and the path ahead seems shrouded in shadows, a journey into the unknown that fills my heart with trepidation."

The room resonated with the echoes of my plea, the walls seeming to absorb the weight of my words and reflect them back to me in a symphony of silent understanding. The flickering candlelight on the desk danced across the walls, casting a play of shadows that seemed to visually echo the internal struggle unfolding within me, a battle between faith and fear, hope and doubt. It was as if the light and dark were engaged in a silent ballet, mirroring the conflict that raged within my soul, a struggle that threatened to consume me.

"I seek not only clarity for myself but also wisdom to navigate the complexities that lay ahead," I continued, the words flowing out like a fragile offering laid at the feet of the divine, a plea for guidance and understanding in the face of the unknown. "My children, dear to my heart, are scattered along the spectrum of belief and understanding, each one a unique thread in the tapestry of our family, a precious soul entrusted to my care." The thought of my family, each member on their own spiritual journey, filled me with a deep sense of concern, a fear that the revelations we had received would create rifts and divisions that could tear us apart. "I fear discord, Father, the fractures that may appear in the unity of our familial fabric, the wounds that may be inflicted by the weight of the truths we now bear."

A profound silence enveloped the room as I paused, the sacredness of the moment palpable, a tangible presence that seemed to fill the very air around me. It felt as if the room itself was holding its breath, waiting in anticipation of some divine response, a sign or a whisper of guidance that would light the path ahead and ease the burden that weighed so heavily upon my soul. The plea in my heart expanded, reaching beyond my own personal burdens to encompass the collective destiny of my family, a recognition of the profound responsibility that had been placed upon my shoulders. I thought of each member—Greta, Charles, Jerome, Eli, Lisa, Luke, and Paul—and the intricate tapestry of our lives, interwoven with purpose and divine calling, a sacred trust that had been placed in my hands.

"Guide me, Father, as I stand on the precipice of revelation," I continued, my voice a hushed murmur in the stillness of the room, a plea for divine intervention in the face of the unknown. "Grant me strength to shoulder the weight of sacred secrets and discernment to know when and how to share this sacred charge with those bound to me by flesh and spirit, a wisdom that transcends my own limited understanding." Each word felt like an anchor, grounding me in my plea for divine guidance and support, a lifeline in the midst of the storm that raged within me.

The words flowed from me like a river, carrying with them the essence of my deepest fears, hopes, and aspirations, a torrent of emotion that poured out of me in a cathartic release of the burdens that had weighed so heavily upon my soul. In this moment of divine alchemy, prayer transcended mere words; it became a sacred conversation that defied the limitations of mortal understanding, a communion between the finite and the infinite, the temporal and the eternal. I felt as if I was reaching beyond the veil, touching something ethereal and profound, a connection to the divine that filled me with a sense of awe and reverence.

As the closing moments of that hallowed communion enveloped me, I found myself surrendering my will to a higher purpose, a recognition of the fact that my own understanding was but a small part of a much larger plan, a divine tapestry that stretched across the ages and encompassed the entirety of creation. It was an act of faith, trusting in the wisdom of a divine plan that was far greater than my own understanding, a leap into the unknown that required a level of trust and surrender that I had never before experienced. The flickering candlelight in the room stood as a silent witness to this sacred transaction—a soul laid bare in the presence of the Almighty, a humble supplicant seeking the guidance and strength to navigate the path that lay ahead.

As I rose from my knees, with a deep breath, I extinguished the candle, the room plunging into darkness save for the faint glow of the moonlight that filtered through the window, a reminder of the eternal light that shone beyond the veil of mortality.

❖

In the realm of dreams, where reality and imagination meld into a surreal tapestry, my nocturnal journey took an unexpected turn, a twist in the fabric of my subconscious that left me reeling with a mixture of awe and trepidation. This path, which my slumbering mind had conjured, was adorned with threads of fear, intricately woven into the fabric of celestial revelations that had been occupying my waking thoughts, a vivid reflection of the turmoil that had taken root in my soul.

Standing before my children in this ethereal sanctuary, a place born of my deepest anxieties and hopes, I felt the weight of my words as they hung in the air, each syllable a heavy burden upon my tongue. The room was thick with anticipation, a palpable presence that seemed to press in on me from all sides, a reflection of my longing for their acceptance and understanding of the divine calling that had been placed upon our family, a sacred charge that threatened to reshape the very foundations of our lives.

Yet, as I spoke, fear crept into the edges of my consciousness, a sinister presence that lurked in the shadows of my mind. It whispered doubts that echoed in the recesses of my being, casting shadows over the dream's surreal landscape, a darkening of the vibrant hues that had once painted this realm of my imagination. Would my children listen? Would they truly hear and understand the gravity of the divine calling that had been laid upon us? Would they willingly embark on this path laid before us, a path fraught with uncertainty and requiring unwavering faith, a journey that would test the very limits of our devotion?

The faces of my children, each a vivid representation of their individual personalities and beliefs, mirrored a spectrum of emotions, a kaleidoscope of reactions that seemed to shift and change with each passing moment. Some faces radiated with the glow of understanding, their features illuminated by a light that seemed to transcend the dream itself, a reflection of the divine spark that burned within their souls. These were the faces filled with faith and acceptance, ready to embrace the journey ahead with open hearts and willing spirits, a testament to the strength of their convictions.

Others, however, were clouded by the shadows of uncertainty and skepticism, their brows furrowed with doubt and their eyes filled with a hesitance that mirrored my own inner turmoil. These faces reflected the doubts and fears that I, too, harboured within me, a recognition of the monumental nature of the task that lay before us and the sacrifices it would require. The tapestry of our family unity, which I had always held so dear, now seemed frayed in this dreamscape, a once-vibrant weave that threatened to unravel under the strain of the revelations that had been thrust upon us. Threads of doubt and fear threatened to unravel the sacred charge we had been entrusted with, a warning of the fragility of our bonds in the face of the unknown.

In the dream, a figure emerged from the shadows, unexpected and enigmatic, a presence that seemed to fill the room with a palpable energy that crackled and sparked like a live wire. It was my second eldest son, Luke, once a stalwart pillar of the church, a young man whose faith had burned bright and unwavering. In this surreal landscape of my subconscious, he revealed himself as a leader, yet the aura that surrounded him was not what I had known, a shift in the very essence of his being that left me reeling with confusion and apprehension. He was engulfed in vibrant swirls of electrified colours, a spectacle that was both mesmerising and disconcerting, a visual representation of the tumultuous journey he had undertaken. The hues around him collided and sparked with an otherworldly energy, transcending the boundaries of my understanding and challenging the perceptions I held, a testament to the transformative power of the choices we make and the paths we choose to follow.

Luke, bathed in this kaleidoscope of brilliance, exuded a charisma that seemed to captivate his siblings, a magnetism that drew them in like moths to a flame. The dream cast him in a role that was both familiar and unfamiliar to me—a harbinger of change, an agent of uncertainty, a figure whose influence threatened to reshape the very fabric of our family.

The sparks that flew as the colours collided infused the dream with an intensity that mirrored the complexities of his journey in life, a journey that had taken him away from the path we had hoped he would follow, a divergence that had left a void in our hearts and a question mark on our future.

As the dream unfolded, my initial interpretation of Luke's presence veered into the realm of fear and suspicion, a gnawing sense of unease that settled in the pit of my stomach like a leaden weight. Was Luke an ally or an adversary in the divine calling that echoed through the corridors of my slumbering mind? The dream, like a cryptic riddle, left me grappling with questions that resisted easy answers, a labyrinth of uncertainty that seemed to stretch out before me with no end in sight. The ambiguity of Luke's role in the dream, surrounded by those electrified colours, made it difficult to discern his true intentions or the impact he might have on his siblings and our family's future, a murky water that threatened to pull us all under.

The fear that my children might be led astray by conflicting forces became a poignant undercurrent in the dream, a subtle thread that wove its way through the tapestry of my subconscious. This narrative, woven into the fabric of the dream, hinted at the complexities of familial bonds and divergent paths, a recognition of the delicate balance that must be maintained in the face of change and uncertainty. Luke, who I once perceived as a loyal follower of our faith, now stood as an enigma, a figure whose very presence seemed to challenge the foundations upon which our family had been built. The swirling tapestry of vibrant colours that surrounded him electrified the very essence of the dream, symbolising the dynamic and unpredictable nature of his influence, a force that could either illuminate or consume, depending on the choices he made.

As I navigated this dreamscape, the portrayal of Luke as both a beacon of change and a source of uncertainty reflected my deep-seated anxieties, a manifestation of the fears that had taken root in my heart. It was a vivid illustration of the internal conflict I felt - the struggle between my love for my son and my fears for the spiritual welfare of our family, a tug-of-war that threatened to tear me apart from the inside out. The dream, in its surreal and symbolic language, laid bare the depths of my concerns, a stark reminder of the challenges that lay ahead and the strength that would be required to face them head-on.

Waking from the dream, the remnants of fear clung to me like a ghost, haunting the corridors of my thoughts, a lingering presence that refused to be banished by the light of day. Lying in the dim light, I could still feel the vivid imagery and the intensity of the emotions from the dream, a residual echo that reverberated through my very being. The cryptic role assigned to Luke, the uncertain meaning behind his emergence as a leader, had transformed into a puzzle that now needed unravelling in the waking world, a challenge that would require all of my wisdom and discernment to navigate.

The dream, a vivid amalgamation of celestial visions and mortal anxieties, had thrust me into a realm of deep introspection, a journey of self-discovery that promised to be as transformative as it was daunting. I lay there, staring at the ceiling, feeling as if I were standing at a crossroads of interpretation, a fork in the road that would determine the course of our family's future. Each potential path seemed shrouded in uncertainty, a mist of doubt and apprehension that obscured the way forward. And the haunting spectre of familial disunity loomed over me, a shadow that threatened the unity and harmony I so deeply cherished in our family.

4338.213

(1 August 2018)

CHILDREN OF THE CLAN

4338.213.1

The soft glow of the computer screen cast a pale light across my face as I initiated the Skype call to Lisa and Will in Salt Lake City. I leaned forward, the weight of the monumental news from the Temple pressing upon me, a burden that seemed to grow heavier with each passing moment. Regardless of their individual reactions, I trusted both Lisa and Will enough to keep the information to themselves, a confidence born of the deep bonds of family and faith that had always been the bedrock of our relationship.

Ideally, Greta and I should have shared this opportunity together, a united front in the face of the unknown, but the warning from last night's dream echoed in my mind, urging me to act swiftly, a clarion call that could not be ignored. I felt a strong impression that time was not on our side, a sense of urgency that seemed to permeate every fibre of my being. The spirit seemed to whisper to me, nudging me to rally as many of my children as possible to our cause, a divine mandate that could not be denied. I especially believed that Lisa and Eli could be instrumental in persuading Luke to reconsider his current path and return to the fold, a prodigal son whose homecoming would be a balm to our troubled hearts.

"Hey, Dad!" Lisa's cheerful voice broke through the screen, a ray of sunshine in the midst of my troubled thoughts. But her eyes seemed distracted, fixated on something beyond the camera's reach, a reminder of the distance that separated us.

"Morning!" Will's voice chimed in, his presence felt rather than seen, a disembodied voice that seemed to float in the ether.

"Good morning, you two," I responded, a knot of anxiety forming in my stomach as I tried to gauge the right moment to bring up the Temple revelation, a secret that burned within me like a sacred flame. "I wanted to talk to you about something significant that happened recently."

But before I could delve into the details of our family's divine calling, a sacred charge that would forever alter the course of our lives, Lisa's attention wavered, her gaze shifting off-screen, a momentary distraction that seemed to shatter the fragile connection we had established. "Oh, hang on, Dad. Will, did you grab the sleeping bags from the closet?"

"Uh, yeah, I think they're in the trunk," Will responded, his voice carrying from somewhere in the background.

I paused, momentarily thrown off by the interruption, a jarring reminder of the mundane concerns that so often intruded upon the sacred. I realised then the delicate balance of blending the ordinary aspects of our daily lives with the extraordinary nature of our spiritual journey, a tightrope walk that required the utmost care and sensitivity.

As I waited for Lisa to refocus on our call, I contemplated how best to share the revelation, a message that had the power to reshape the very foundations of our family. The importance of conveying the message clearly and with the right sense of urgency weighed heavily on me, a burden that seemed to press down upon my very soul. In that brief pause, I gathered my thoughts, steeling myself for the conversation that would follow, a conversation that would set in motion a series of events that could redefine the future of our family, a destiny that had been written in the stars.

"Alright, Dad, sorry. What were you saying?" Lisa refocused on the screen, her attention returning to me after the brief distraction, a flicker of interest in her eyes that gave me hope for the message I was about to impart.

I took a deep breath, steeling myself to restart the conversation, the importance of the revelation weighing heavily on my mind. "I wanted to share something important that happened at the Temple the other night. There was a revelation—" I began, hoping to convey the significance of the message.

"Wait, Dad. Will, do you have the camping stove in the car?" Lisa interrupted again, her gaze drifting off-screen, drawn away by another concern, a mundane matter that seemed to pale in comparison to the eternal truths I longed to share.

"It's in the garage, I think," Will's voice floated in from a distance, somewhat muffled.

"Okay, Dad, sorry about that. Go on," Lisa urged, turning her attention back to me, a flicker of impatience in her eyes that sent a pang of disappointment through my heart.

As I resumed, poised to delve into the details of the revelation, yet another interruption followed. "Oh, hold on, Dad. Will, did you grab the marshmallows?"

I sighed heavily, the distractions continuing to chip away at my resolve, leaving me in a state of lighthearted surrender, a rueful acknowledgment of the challenges of communication in the modern age. The urgency of sharing the revelation from the Temple was overshadowed by the simplicity and immediacy of Lisa's present moment, a stark contrast that left me reeling with a sense of disorientation. "Maybe we can talk after your camping trip. You go and enjoy your hiking adventure," I conceded, a smile creeping onto my face despite the inner turmoil that raged within me, a mask that concealed the depths of my disappointment.

"Yeah, thanks Dad. We love you too," Lisa replied, her cheerful voice cutting through my disappointment like a knife, a bittersweet reminder of the love that bound us together, even in the midst of our differences. She blew a kiss from the palm of her hand towards the screen, a gesture of affection that was typical of her, a momentary balm to my troubled soul.

Feeling the conversation slipping away but not wanting to lose the opportunity to connect with another of my children, I interjected quickly, "Can I talk to Eli before you go?" There was a part of me that clung to the hope of sharing at least a part of what weighed on me, a desperate attempt to forge a connection in the face of the unknown.

"Yeah sure," Lisa answered casually. Then, turning away from the screen, she called out, "Eli! Dad's on Skype for you!"

Lisa waved a quick goodbye, her face disappearing from view as the screen transitioned from what I presumed to be Lisa and Will's bedroom to the guest bedroom where Eli was staying during his visit. The change of scenery on the screen was a telling reminder of the physical distance between us, yet it also represented a bridge of communication across that gap, a fragile connection that I clung to with all my might.

❖

As the room came into view, I prepared myself for a different kind of conversation with Eli, a son whose heart had always been open to the whisperings of the spirit. The dynamics with each of my children were unique, a complex tapestry of personalities and beliefs that required a delicate touch and a deep understanding. I wondered how Eli would receive or react to any part of the revelation I might share.

The anticipation of this new interaction brought a mix of hope and apprehension. My heart raced slightly as I waited for Eli to appear on the screen, each second stretching longer than the last, a moment suspended in time and space.

In that brief transition, I found myself reflecting on the intricate web of relationships within our family. As a father, my role was to guide, support, and love them, all the while navigating the complex terrain of our collective spiritual journey, a path that had been ordained from the foundations of the world. This moment of connection with Eli, though facilitated by technology, was an important link in maintaining the bonds that held our family together, especially in light of the significant changes that loomed on the horizon, a storm I feared, that threatened to tear us apart.

"Eli, how's it going?" I greeted him, offering a warm smile and hoping that this conversation would be more focused than the previous one, a chance to share the burden that weighed so heavily upon my soul.

"Hey, Dad! Sorry, Lisa and Will are getting ready for our camping trip. What's up?" Eli responded, his voice carrying a hint of distraction as he adjusted the laptop to get a better view. Despite the casual tone, I sensed an openness in him, a willingness to listen that I hadn't found with Lisa.

I seized the opportunity, eager to convey the message, a sacred charge that had been entrusted to me by the hand of God. "I wanted to talk to you about something significant that happened at the Temple the other night. There was a revelation," I began, my voice steady but filled with the importance of what I was about to reveal.

"Whoa, seriously? That sounds important," Eli said, his casual demeanour shifting to one of genuine interest, a flicker of understanding in his eyes that gave me hope for the message I was about to impart. His eyes widened slightly, indicating that he understood the seriousness of what I was saying.

A small smile tugged at the corner of my mouth, encouraged by his response. "Yes, it is," I affirmed, my brow creasing as I considered how best to explain the revelation. "An Apostle shared a vision about building the New Jerusalem, and we're called to prepare for a significant move to Salt Lake City," I explained, keeping my tone measured but earnest, a delicate balance between the urgency of the message and the need for sensitivity.

Eli's expression shifted, a clear sign of his engagement, as he leaned in closer to the screen. "That's huge, Dad. What does it mean for us?" His voice conveyed a mix of surprise and curiosity, which gave me a sense of relief that at least one of my children was ready to grasp the situation.

As I started explaining the profound nature of the revelation, emphasising that specific details were still rather unclear, a message that had been shrouded in mystery and symbolism, Eli's focus didn't waver, a testament to the depth of his faith and the openness of his heart. He absorbed the information, nodding at key points, showing an understanding that was both comforting and encouraging, a balm to my troubled soul. It felt like a small victory, a moment of connection in a time fraught with uncertainty and apprehension.

The conversation, however, was going well only until Lisa's voice echoed from the background. "Eli, we need your help with the tent. Can you come here for a sec?" Her request, though simple, felt like an abrupt interruption to the crucial discussion we were having.

Eli sighed, his gaze shifting to somewhere off-screen, a momentary distraction that threatened to break the spell of the moment. He glanced apologetically at the camera, a silent acknowledgment of the conflicting demands that pulled at him from all sides. "Sorry, Dad, duty calls. I'll get back to you on this, okay?" The regret in his voice was evident, but so was the necessity of his immediate attention elsewhere.

"Of course, Eli. Help your sister, and we'll talk more when you're free. Love you," I replied, my voice tinged with a mix of understanding and disappointment, a bittersweet acceptance of the realities of life in the modern age. As the screen went suddenly black, I was left staring at my own reflection on the blank monitor, a ghostly image that seemed to mock the depths of my longing.

I frowned, slumping back into the computer chair. A sense of disappointment lingered in the air, my attempt to share this profound experience with my children falling victim to the practicalities of camping preparations, a bitter irony that left a sour taste in my mouth. The news would have to wait, leaving me in a state of contemplation about the unfinished conversations.

❖

The brief moment of contemplation was interrupted by Jerome's sudden arrival. "Hold up!" he called out, his voice echoing through the hallway as his hands gripped the doorframe, almost stumbling into the room with haste, a whirlwind of energy and urgency that seemed to crackle in the air around him. His chest heaved with each breath, a sign of his exertion and the weight of the emotions that swirled within him.

As he regained his balance, Jerome's eyes darted to the laptop screen, his gaze searching for a connection that had already been severed. His expression fell as he realised that the call with Eli and Lisa had already ended, a flicker of disappointment that seemed to dim the light in his eyes.

"Quickly, call them back," Jerome urged me, his tone insistent, a plea that carried the weight of his own longing. But I couldn't bring myself to do it, a heavy resignation settling over me like a shroud. My brow furrowed with the weight of the knowledge that the moment had passed, a fleeting opportunity that had slipped through my fingers like grains of sand. Jerome noticed the expression on my face, his own features softening in response.

"What is it?" he asked, his voice gentler now, tinged with a hint of worry that belied his youth and the depth of his concern. There was a vulnerability in his tone that tugged at my heartstrings, a reminder of the tender soul that lay beneath the surface of his young adult bravado.

I took a deep breath, choosing my words carefully before replying, a delicate dance of truth and omission that had become all too familiar in recent days. "They're busy packing to go on this camping trip of theirs," I said, the words feeling heavy on my tongue, a bitter reminder of the distance that separated our family, both physical and emotional. The words felt like a betrayal, a confession of the cracks that had begun to form in the foundation of our once-unshakable bond.

Recognition flashed across Jerome's face, his eyes widening slightly as the pieces fell into place. "Of course. I forgot all about that," he said, a hint of envy creeping into his voice, a longing for the carefree adventures that seemed to belong to a different lifetime.

It was a feeling I knew all too well, the ache of watching our children grow and change, of knowing that the world beyond our walls held a siren song that we could never fully understand.

"Where are they going again?" Jerome asked, his gaze fixed on me.

I shrugged, answering honestly, a painful admission of my own limitations and the secrets that I had been forced to keep. "I don't remember," I said, the details lost amidst the swirling maelstrom of my own thoughts and fears. The revelation that had been burned into my soul seemed to eclipse all else, a consuming fire that left little room for the mundane concerns of the world outside.

Jerome waved his hand dismissively as he turned to leave the room, a gesture that spoke volumes about his own frustration. "I'll message Eli later," he said, his voice trailing off as he reached the doorway, a halfhearted promise that hung in the air like a question mark.

Something compelled me to call him back, a nagging sensation in the pit of my stomach that refused to be ignored. "Jerome?" I said, my voice cutting through the silence.

"Yeah?" Jerome responded, turning back around to face me, his eyes meeting mine with a flicker of hope and apprehension. As his gaze locked with my own, I could see a shiver run down his spine, a reflection of the seriousness that had undoubtedly seeped into my expression.

I opened my mouth to speak but then hesitated, the words caught in my throat, a jumble of thoughts and emotions that threatened to overwhelm me. Exhaling softly, I finally asked, "How's Millie?"

Jerome's brow knitted with concern, his eyes clouding over with a mixture of uncertainty and fear, a reflection of the love and worry that he carried for his beloved pet. "I've not heard yet. I'll contact the vet later this morning and see when I can collect her," he said, his voice strained with the effort of maintaining his composure, a valiant attempt to be strong in the face of the unknown.

I nodded, trying to reassure him, even as my own heart ached with the thought of the faithful dog in distress. "I'm sure she'll be fine. Mum's been praying for her," I said, hoping that the words would bring some measure of comfort, a balm to soothe the wounds that seemed to multiply with each passing day.

Jerome scoffed slightly, a soft chuckle escaping his lips. "And apparently all the Sisters in the Ward too," he added, a hint of amusement creeping into his voice.

I couldn't help but laugh, feeling a welcome smile break across my face, a momentary respite from the burdens that weighed so heavily upon my shoulders.

"Dad—" Jerome began, but he stopped himself short, his expression growing sombre once more, a flicker of hesitation that spoke volumes about the doubts and concerns that plagued his young mind.

Just as I was about to urge him to continue, to offer him the comfort and guidance that he so desperately needed, the heated voices of Greta and Charles erupted from the kitchen, their words muffled but the tension palpable. I sighed heavily, the weight of the situation pressing down on me like a cross that I had been called to bear.

Jerome, seeming to sense an opportunity to escape from voicing his unasked questions, gave me a half-smile and said, "You'd better sort them out." His words were a gentle push, a reminder of the responsibilities that rested upon my shoulders.

I nodded in agreement, although another reluctant sigh escaped my lips. As I stood up to head towards the kitchen, my mind raced with the various concerns that plagued our family, a tangled web of emotions and expectations that seemed to grow more complex with each passing day. The challenges that lay ahead seemed daunting, a mountain that loomed before us, its peak shrouded in mist and uncertainty. But as I stepped into the hallway, I silently prayed for the strength and wisdom to guide us through, to keep our family together, no matter what storms may come our way, a desperate plea for divine intervention in a world that seemed to be on the verge of spinning out of control.

Stepping into the kitchen, the familiar family chaos greeted me, though today it seemed more pronounced, a crescendo of emotions and tensions that threatened to boil over at any moment. Greta was engaged in a tug-of-war with Charles over some leftovers he had grabbed for breakfast, his playful antics starkly at odds with the solemnity of the morning, a jarring contrast that set my teeth on edge.

Charles, with a mischievous grin that seemed to light up the room, clearly irked Greta with his choice, a deliberate provocation that spoke volumes about the simmering resentments that lay beneath the surface of our family dynamics.

"I was saving that food for dinner tonight," Greta said, her blazing eyes meeting mine as I entered the room, a silent plea for support and understanding. Her voice carried a tone of frustration, a clear indication that this was more than just about leftovers, a symbol of the deeper issues that plagued our household.

"Charles, this is important. You can't be silly about your meals. Put the food back and have a proper breakfast," I chided, my voice a mix of authority and concern, a desperate attempt to restore some semblance of order and normality. I hoped to convey the importance of routine and respect, especially given the recent stresses we were under.

"As if this little bit of lasagna would feed us all," Charles scoffed, wedging the container between two others in the fridge in a way that was both dismissive and defiant.

"That's not the point," Greta continued, her scowl deepening. "I was going to put it with something else." Her frustration was palpable, a pressure cooker of emotions that threatened to explode at any moment.

Charles' eyes rolled obviously, his typical teenage response that did little to defuse the situation, a flippant dismissal of the concerns and needs of those around him.

"And besides that, you didn't ask!" Greta added, her tone laced with contempt.

"You didn't ask to eat my last piece of chocolate either," Charles retorted, his voice rising as he slammed the fridge closed, signalling the end of the argument.

There was a brief moment's pause, a fleeting hope that the morning's drama might be over. But Greta had one last comment. "You know it gives you eczema, anyway," she replied, a mixture of concern and exasperation in her voice.

Charles, having seemingly given up the fight, brushed past his mother and stepped into the hallway. "Where are you going?" Greta asked pointedly, her voice carrying no small hint of annoyance.

Charles didn't stop as he called back, "I've got seminary, remember," his voice trailing off as he continued up the hallway.

As the tension in the kitchen eased with Charles's departure, my thoughts turned to Paul, the next child on my list to talk to about the Temple revelation, a daunting task that loomed before me like a mountain to be climbed. The challenge of conveying the significance of this revelation persisted, a burden that seemed to grow heavier with each passing moment, a weight that threatened to crush me beneath its immensity. I couldn't shake the feeling that the day was far from over, a sense of foreboding that settled in the pit of my stomach like a leaden weight.

It was still early, barely six-thirty in the morning, and the events thus far seemed to hint at a day filled with more surprises and challenges, a gauntlet of emotions and expectations that would test the limits of my faith and my resolve. I took a moment to gather my thoughts, preparing myself for the next conversation, aware that each interaction with my children would require patience, understanding, and a delicate touch, a balancing act that would demand every ounce of my strength and wisdom.

❖

After several unsuccessful attempts to reach Paul, each call going straight to his voicemail, a realisation hit me. Greta had made several remarks over the last few days, asking if I'd heard from Paul. At the time, they seemed like passing comments, and I hadn't given them much thought. While Paul and I spoke regularly, it wasn't uncommon for us to go several weeks without contact, both of us caught up in the day-to-day demands of our lives. However, given the recent developments with our move to New Jerusalem and now the pressing need to discuss them with all the children, I felt a growing concern gnawing at the pit of my stomach. I decided the best course of action was to seek Greta's insight, hoping she might shed some light on Paul's uncharacteristic silence.

I made my way back to the kitchen. Greta stood at the counter, her hands wrapped around a steaming mug, her brow furrowed in thought. "Have you heard from Paul yet?" I asked, trying to keep my tone casual despite the worry creeping into my voice. "I just tried to call him but it's gone straight to his voicemail."

Greta shook her head, her expression one of slight annoyance mixed with concern. "No," she said bluntly, her lips pressing into a thin line. "Claire is still pestering me about him. You know how she gets. Keeps that annoying finger of hers on the dial button, calling at all hours. It's no wonder he's turned his phone off just to get some peace."

I raised an eyebrow, surprised by this new information. "Is he not in Broken Hill with her?" I inquired, trying to piece together Paul's whereabouts.

"Apparently not," Greta replied, her tone indicating there was more to the story than she was letting on. She took a sip of her drink, her eyes meeting mine over the rim of the mug.

I silently urged her to continue, my curiosity piqued by the enigmatic nature of her response. The situation with Paul was beginning to feel more complex than I had initially thought, and I found myself eager for any scrap of information that might shed light on his whereabouts and well-being.

Just then, Charles's booming voice cut through the air, "I'm off!" Moments later, the front door closed with a bang, the sound reverberating through the house and startling me out of my thoughts. I jumped slightly, my heart racing at the sudden noise.

Greta frowned, her irritation evident. "I'm surprised he doesn't wake the whole street up every morning with that racket. He's like a bull in a china shop, that one. No consideration for anyone else trying to have a peaceful morning."

Despite the seriousness of the situation with Paul, I couldn't help the playful smile tugging at the corner of my mouth. Greta's tendency to get easily stressed was well-known, and I often found a little humour in her melodramatics, even though I knew I shouldn't. It was one of the quirks of our relationship, a balance of stress and lightheartedness that had seen us through many challenges over the years.

Either unobservant of my faint amusement or simply choosing to ignore it, Greta resumed her explanation about Paul's whereabouts, her focus solely on the matter at hand. "According to Luke, Paul's gone to stay with him in Hobart for a few days. Some sort of impromptu brothers' retreat or something." She waved her hand dismissively, as if the very idea was absurd.

"I'm surprised he hasn't told us about it," I remarked, a twinge of concern threading through my words. It was unlike Paul to embark on such a trip without at least a brief mention to either of us. We had always maintained open lines of communication, even as the children grew older and more independent. The fact that he had seemingly vanished without a word left an unsettling feeling in the pit of my stomach.

Greta's expression shifted, her mouth tightening into her infamous you-should-know-better pout. "I'm sure there's plenty that son of yours doesn't tell you." Her tone was a blend of sarcasm and seriousness.

A twang of disappointment struck my gut at her words. I had always considered Paul and I to have a strong bond, a relationship built on mutual respect and open communication. The idea that he might be keeping things from me, important things that could impact his well-being or that of his children, was disconcerting to say the least. I pondered over what Greta knew that I didn't, though I still held onto the belief that Paul was more forthcoming with me than with his mother. Or so I had thought, until now.

"Any idea when he's planning to-" I began to ask, hoping for more clarity on the situation, but Greta cut me short with a wave of her hand.

"Actually, Luke said he was going to get Paul to call me, and that was more than a few days ago. I even spoke with the police, and she hasn't called me back either," Greta huffed out, her frustration evident in the tightness of her jaw and the slight tremor in her voice.

"The police?" I asked, incredulously, my eyes widening in shock. My concern for Paul's situation, and especially for the welfare of his two young children, rose sharply at this revelation. If the police were involved, it had to be serious. "Why didn't you tell me sooner?"

Greta's response came with a slight shrug, her shoulders slumping as if the weight of the world rested upon them. "I was going to, Noah, I really was. But then with the whole New Jerusalem thing, I guess it just...slipped my mind," she answered, her voice tinged with a mix of guilt and exhaustion.

I found myself momentarily speechless, my mouth opening but no words emerging. The revelation of our impending move to New Jerusalem had indeed been all-consuming, a seismic shift in our lives that had left little room for anything else. But the news about Paul, about Greta's contact with the police, was significant. Her oversight, while completely understandable given the tension of the last few days, added another layer of complexity to an already challenging situation.

A sharp knock at the front door instantly cut through our conversation, snapping us out of the heavy discussion about Paul and his whereabouts. "I'll get it," I told Greta, quickly pulling my dressing gown tighter around me as I made my way out of the kitchen. My sense of decorum left me feeling less than thrilled about having to answer the door so early in the morning, and in my current state of undress no less. But the urgency of the knock overruled any hesitation I might have had.

"It's probably just Charles forgetting something," Greta called out down the hallway, her voice trailing behind me as I hurried towards the front of the house. "That boy would forget his own head if it wasn't attached!"

As I reached the front door, the coldness of the doorknob was a stark contrast to the warmth of my hand, sending a shiver down my spine. I twisted it, pulling the door open, expecting to see my youngest son's sheepish grin on the other side as he retrieved whatever item he had left behind in his haste to leave for seminary.

But it wasn't Charles standing on the doorstep. "Luke!" The name escaped my lips in a gasp, my surprise rendering me momentarily speechless as I stared at my second eldest son, the one who was supposed to be in Hobart with Paul. My jaw dropped in disbelief, a million questions racing through my mind as I tried to process the unexpected sight before me. *Why was Luke here? Where was Paul? And what in the world was going on?*

FOLLOW THOU ME

4338.213.2

"What are you doing here?" The words escaped my mouth abruptly, an unfiltered reaction to the bewilderment of seeing Luke on my doorstep.

Luke responded with a chuckle, his tone light despite the surprise of my greeting. "I know it's been a few years, but that's hardly the warm welcome that I was expecting," he replied, his eyes twinkling with a hint of mischief. Despite the unexpectedness of his visit, it was clear that Luke's good-natured spirit remained intact.

"I'm sorry," I stammered, still reeling from the suddenness of his arrival. "I just wasn't expecting it to be you at the door." I was trying to regain my composure, to shift from the shock to the reality of having Luke standing right in front of me. It had been far too long since I'd seen him in person, and the weight of that realisation settled heavily on my chest.

"Is it Charles?" Greta's voice echoed from somewhere in the house.

"No, it's Luke," I called back, stepping aside to open the door wider, allowing Luke to enter. There was a rush of conflicting emotions as I watched him step into the familiar surroundings of our home - joy at seeing him after so long, concern over the reason for his unexpected visit, and a nagging sense that something was amiss.

"Thank you," Luke said as he walked inside, his demeanour calm and collected. He moved with a casual grace, his tall frame filling the entryway as he shrugged off his coat and hung it on the nearby rack.

The sound of hurried footsteps approached, and Greta appeared, her expression a mix of shock and joy. "Luke!" she cried out, running down the passageway to embrace her son. Her face was alight with happiness, the years melting away as she wrapped her arms around him. "Where's your brother?" she asked, the question laced with a mother's concern as she held him close.

"Ah," Luke replied, gently disengaging from her embrace. He turned his head towards me, his expression serious. "I need to talk to you in private," he said, his tone leaving no room for argument.

Greta's response was immediate, a mixture of curiosity and defensiveness. "Anything you need to say to your father, you can say to me too. You know we have no secrets in this family."

Caught off guard by Greta's assertive remark, a strange, involuntary gurgle escaped my lips. I shot Greta a look, signalling her to give us some space. "Come into the study with me," I told Luke, my tone firm yet inviting. I knew that whatever had brought Luke here, it was important enough to warrant a private conversation.

Greta, clearly displeased with being left out, huffed loudly and tromped back along the hallway. "So much for a happy return," she muttered to herself as she turned into the kitchen, her voice carrying a tinge of frustration. I made a mental note to smooth things over with her later, knowing that her reaction stemmed from a place of love and concern for our children.

I led Luke along the hallway, making the first left into the study. The room was bathed in the soft glow of the morning light, the bookshelves lining the walls casting long shadows across the floor. I closed the door behind us, the click of the latch sounding almost ominous in the stillness of the room.

As I turned to face Luke, I braced myself for the conversation that awaited. The sudden arrival of my son, his request for a private talk, and the tension in Greta's reaction, all hinted at the complexity of the situation unfolding. The study, a room typically associated with quiet reflection and work, was now the setting for what I sensed would be a significant and potentially challenging discussion.

❖

"What's going on, Luke?" I asked bluntly, my tone edged with a mix of concern and urgency. I pulled my robe tighter around me, suddenly self-conscious of exposing my sacred garments—a personal reminder of my faith and commitment. The early morning chill seemed to seep through the fabric, sending a shiver down my spine, but it was the intensity in Luke's eyes that truly unsettled me.

For what felt like an eternity, I held Luke's gaze. His eyes, once so familiar, now seemed to hold depths I hadn't seen before. The silence stretched between us, thick with unspoken words and emotions. I could feel the weight of the moment pressing down on me, a sense that whatever Luke was about to reveal would change everything.

Then, breaking the silence with a decisiveness that took me aback, Luke said, "I've had a vision."

My brow creased considerably at his words. "I thought they would have stopped by now," I replied, my voice tinged with a mixture of surprise and a hint of skepticism. A battle raged within me, torn between curiosity about the content of Luke's dream and the wistful hope that perhaps this vision might signify his return to the church. "It's been five years since the last vision reported in our family. Your grandfather was the last, only a few weeks before he passed. And even that came after the last one you spoke to me about, seven years prior."

My words trailed off, laden with the history and significance of our family's spiritual experiences. I remembered the awe and reverence I had felt when Luke had first confided in me about his visions, the sense of divine purpose that had filled my heart. But as the years had passed and Luke had drifted further from the church, I had begun to wonder if those visions had been nothing more than the imaginings of a young mind.

Luke shook his head, his response sending a ripple of surprise through me. "They never stopped."

"What was this vision about?" I asked, the question barely above a whisper. My heart thumped in my chest, a mix of apprehension and awe at the thought of God still speaking to Luke, the son I had always considered most spiritually attuned. I leaned forward slightly, my hands gripping the arms of my chair, as if bracing myself for the impact of his words.

A deep silence once again enveloped the room. I watched as Luke's eyes seemed to light up, as if he were reliving the vision in his mind. The intensity in his gaze was palpable, and I found myself leaning forward even further, eager yet apprehensive about what he might reveal.

"The building of a great new civilisation," Luke finally said, his voice filled with a quiet reverence that sent a shiver down my spine. The excitement in his tone was palpable, and I felt a warmth spreading through my chest, a sensation that was both unsettling and invigorating. His words echoed the revelation I had received at the Temple, yet they seemed to take on a different dimension coming from Luke. It was as if pieces of a larger puzzle were slowly coming together, each piece revealing a part of a divine plan that was larger and more complex than I had imagined.

I gasped softly, the revelation striking a chord deep within me. "The New Jerusalem," I whispered, my eyes widening with the realisation that my son was not yet lost. The words left my lips almost in a hush, reverberating with hope and a newfound understanding. I felt a wave of emotion washing over me, a mix of relief and gratitude that threatened to bring tears to my eyes.

"You could call it that," Luke said, his tone indicating a depth of knowledge and experience that was both intriguing and mysterious. He leaned back against the bookcase, his posture relaxed yet confident, as if he held the secrets of the universe within his grasp.

"So, God really is still speaking with you, then?" I asked, the question laced with hope and a deep yearning for it to be true. The possibility that Luke was still in communion with the divine, despite his apparent distance from the church, was both a relief and a revelation. I felt a flicker of excitement igniting in my chest, a sense that perhaps this was the moment I had been praying for, the moment when my wayward son would find his way back to the fold.

"I know you believe in miracles," Luke told me, his eyes locking with mine in a gaze that was both searching and profound. There was a hint of challenge in his voice, as if he were testing the depth of my faith, the strength of my convictions.

"Of course," I replied earnestly, my voice filled with a quiet intensity. The conversation was taking a turn I hadn't expected, and it filled me with a mixture of excitement and apprehension. "Luke, I have important news for you too," the words tumbled out of my mouth as I struggled to contain my excitement at the thought of my son returning to the fold. "At the Temple last-" I began, eager to share the revelation that had shaken me to my core.

But Luke interrupted me, his voice calm yet insistent. "I have a miracle to show you."

His words halted me in my tracks, and I felt a flicker of uncertainty. "You being here is a miracle enough for me," I replied, the joy in my heart radiating across my face. Luke's presence, his talk of visions and miracles, it all felt like a dramatic answer to prayers. I reached out, placing a hand on his arm, as if to reassure myself that he was really there, that this moment was not just another dream.

Luke began to move the computer desk away from the wall, his actions purposeful and deliberate. "Help me clear some space," he instructed, his voice indicating that whatever he was about to reveal required room. I hesitated for a moment, confusion and curiosity warring within me, but the earnestness in Luke's eyes compelled me to follow his lead.

I didn't understand what was happening, but I helped anyway, my curiosity piqued. Together, we shifted the desk and cleared the area, creating an open space in front of the wall. The study, a place of contemplation and order, was now transformed into a stage for whatever Luke was about to unveil. My heart raced with anticipation, a sense that I was standing on the precipice of something momentous.

When the entire wall was clear from furniture and books, Luke pulled some strange object from his pocket. It was small and rectangular, with intricate markings etched into its surface. I squinted, trying to make out the details, but before I could ask any questions, Luke pointed the object at the wall and pressed a small button.

With a swift motion, the wall lit up in a spectacle of bright, swirling colours. The swirls sent short sparks into the air whenever the colours of energy collided, creating a dazzling display that took my breath away. It was mesmerising, almost hypnotic, and I found myself drawn into the depths of the colours, as if they held the secrets of the universe.

It's exactly like my dream! The realisation hit me like a lightning bolt, and I gasped softly, unable to hold back my emotions. The vision that had haunted my sleep, the swirling colours and sparks of energy, was now playing out before my very eyes. I felt a rush of awe and wonder, a sense that I was witnessing something truly miraculous.

"I always knew you would be the one to lead our family to the New Jerusalem," I told Luke, pulling him into a tight embrace, overwhelmed by the realisation that the visions and dreams were intertwining in ways I couldn't have fathomed. Tears pricked at the corners of my eyes as I held my son close, feeling the warmth of his body against mine, the steady beat of his heart. In that moment, all the doubts and fears that had plagued me seemed to melt away, replaced by a sense of divine purpose and certainty.

Luke pulled himself away gently, his eyes searching mine. "Does this mean you'll follow me through?" he asked, his question carrying a weight of responsibility and expectation. There was a vulnerability in his voice, a hint of uncertainty that belied the confidence he had shown moments before.

"If you promise to lead our family in righteousness, of course we'll follow you to Salt Lake City," I replied without hesitation, my voice filled with a quiet conviction. My response was a testament to my trust in Luke's spiritual guidance and the divine plan unfolding before us. I knew in my heart that this was the path we were meant to take, that Luke was the one destined to lead us to the promised land.

The sudden squeak of the study door interrupted the profound moment between Luke and me. "Are you two done with your secret man's business yet?" Greta's voice, tinged with a mix of curiosity and impatience, filled the room. She stood in the doorway, hands on her hips, her eyes quickly drawn to the swirling, vibrant colours on the wall. I could see the confusion and wonder playing across her face, the same emotions that had overwhelmed me just moments before.

"The New Jerusalem is just beyond the Portal of colour," Luke said, his grip on my arm firm and insistent. "Will you and mum follow me through?" There was an urgency in his voice, a sense that time was of the essence, that we had to make a decision now.

Greta, stepping into the room, asked with a tone of bewilderment, "What is all this?" Her eyes were locked on the mesmerising display of colours, her initial irritation giving way to intrigue. I could see the wheels turning in her mind, trying to make sense of the strange and wondrous sight before her.

A still, small voice whispered in my mind, *Follow thou me.* The words, quiet yet clear, resonated with a sense of divine prompting. I felt a warmth spreading through my chest, a sense of peace and certainty that I had never experienced before. It was as if the voice was speaking directly to my soul, guiding me towards a destiny that had been written in the stars.

Finding Greta's hand, I squeezed it hard, searching for a way to convey the depth of what I believed. "Do you love me?" I asked her, my voice laden with emotion and a deep-seated need for her to understand. I looked into her eyes, willing her to see the truth that had taken root in my heart.

Greta's gaze shifted from the colours to my eyes, her expression softening. "You know I do," she replied, her voice gentle yet filled with an unspoken question. I could see the love and trust in her eyes, the same love and trust that had sustained us through all the trials and tribulations of our life together.

"Then we will follow Luke, and he will lead us to the New Jerusalem," I told her with a conviction that surprised even me. "We must follow him." The words came from a place deep within me, a place of unwavering faith and trust in the divine plan.

"But what about Salt Lake City?" Greta asked, her face contorting in confusion. The revelation at the Temple, the preparations for moving to Salt Lake City — all seemed to clash with this new, unexpected path. I could see the doubt and uncertainty in her eyes, the same doubt and uncertainty that had plagued me just moments before.

The soft voice beckoned again, *Follow thou me.* The words were a reassurance, a divine guidance amidst the confusion. I felt a sense of peace washing over me, a certainty that this was the path we were meant to take, no matter how unexpected or daunting it might seem.

"I don't understand everything, Greta. But this was in my dream last night. I know that God is calling his elect. We are his elect, Greta," I explained, trying to make sense of the overlapping revelations and my own tumultuous feelings. I squeezed her hand tighter, willing her to feel the same sense of purpose and destiny that had taken hold of my heart.

Tugging gently on her hand, I encouraged her to follow me. Hand in hand, together we walked into what I believed was God's merciful light.

As we stepped forward, energised tingles swept through my entire body. It was as if we were crossing a threshold into something extraordinary, something that defied explanation or understanding. Stepping into what seemed like bright daylight, I heard a voice. It wasn't audible in the traditional sense, but I could feel the words and the tone of the voice in my mind. *Welcome to Clivilius, Noah Smith,* the voice said, its tone warm and inviting.

I felt a rush of emotion, a sense of awe and wonder that threatened to overwhelm me. I looked at Greta, seeing the same emotions reflected in her eyes, and I knew that we had made the right decision.

❖

I stood there in awe, taking in the sight that surrounded me. Before us lay an endless expanse of rolling hills, painted in shades of brown and orange dust, a landscape unlike anything I had ever seen. A surge of exhilaration ran through me, a mix of excitement and wonder at this new world we had stepped into. Clivilius — a name I had never heard before, yet it echoed with significance. As I gazed at this alien yet strangely beautiful landscape, I realised that what we had experienced was far beyond the bounds of any ordinary journey.

The voice I had heard, welcoming me to Clivilius, still resonated in my mind. I wanted to attribute it to the still small whisperings of the Holy Spirit, but this felt different, more personal. It was as if I had heard and felt the very voice of God, resonating deep within me, speaking directly to my soul. The magnitude of the experience left me breathless, my heart pounding with a mix of reverence and anticipation.

"Dad! Mum!" a familiar voice called out, snapping me out of my reverie. Turning towards the sound, my eyes widened with surprise and gratitude as I saw Paul jogging towards us. My mind raced with questions — I was about to ask him what he was doing here, considering he was supposed to be in Hobart. Yet, here he was in Clivilius, and Luke, who had brought us here, wasn't in Hobart either. The situation was as puzzling as it was miraculous, a testament to the incredible ways in which God works.

But before I could voice any of my questions, I saw Jerome stepping through the swirling mass of colour behind us. My surprise turned into delight at the sight of another of my children joining us in this extraordinary place. It felt right that Jerome was here, that we were all beginning to gather here together. This event, this journey to the New Jerusalem, was something I had always envisioned experiencing as a family, united in our faith and purpose.

As Paul reached us, I embraced him warmly, my heart swelling with a mixture of relief and joy. His presence here, along with Jerome's, was a confirmation that this was indeed the path we were meant to take. In the excitement and surreal nature of the situation, I had completely forgotten about my attire — or rather, the lack thereof. Standing there in only my dressing gown and undergarments, a hint of self consciousness crept in. I quickly pulled my gown tighter around me, attempting to maintain some semblance of decorum in this extraordinary setting.

Greta, ever the protective mother, enveloped Paul in an almost suffocating embrace. As Paul gently broke free, she said in her characteristically blunt manner, "Claire's been looking for you." Greta's mention of Claire was typical. The relationship between Greta and Claire had always been strained, marked by a polite but unmistakable coolness. I couldn't help but think that few people really got along well with Claire. She was undeniably talented, but her personality often made her difficult to be around. For the sake of my own sanity and to keep the peace between her and Greta, I had always preferred to keep Claire at a distance.

As my eyes continued to survey our surroundings, I searched for any sign of other people or clues that we were indeed at the site for the New Jerusalem. The vastness of the rolling hills of brown and orange dust seemed to stretch infinitely, offering no immediate answers. Greta's mood, which had shifted back to grumpiness, barely registered in my mind, so overwhelmed was I by the magnitude of what we were experiencing.

In this moment, standing in Clivilius with my family, I felt an odd mix of elation and uncertainty. The concept of the

New Jerusalem, something I had always associated with spiritual metaphor and distant prophecy, was suddenly a tangible possibility. Yet, the landscape around us, while awe-inspiring, offered no clear indication of the prophesied city. Questions swirled in my mind - *where exactly were we? How had we come to be here? And most importantly, what was our role in this new world?*

The sudden appearance of Luke through the wall of colour brought me back to the present moment, cutting through the maze of thoughts swirling in my mind. "Where's Charles?" he asked, his voice direct and to the point. The question caught me off guard, a reminder of the practicalities we had left behind in our sudden transition to Clivilius.

Without hesitation, Greta, Jerome, and I responded in unison, "Seminary!" Our chorus-like reply highlighted the routine nature of Charles' commitment, even amidst the surreal circumstances we found ourselves in. It was a touch of normality in a situation that was anything but normal.

Paul chuckled at our synchronised answer, a light moment amidst the tension. However, Greta's mood quickly shifted as she turned to Luke, her expression morphing into a deep scowl. "Luke!" she screeched, her voice filled with a mix of anger and confusion. "What have you done!?" Her words echoed across the barren landscape, carrying the weight of a mother's concern and frustration.

Luke's response was surprisingly nonchalant, his demeanour calm as he shrugged and said, "I did what was necessary." His casual attitude seemed at odds with the gravity of the situation, and I couldn't help but feel a twinge of frustration at his lack of apparent concern for our abrupt transition to this place. It was as if he had expected us to simply accept this new reality without question, without any explanation of how or why we had come to be here.

Paul's remark was heavy with sarcasm. "You didn't think it was necessary to let them change out of their pyjamas first?" While I didn't think it was the most pressing issue at hand, I appreciated Paul's nod to practicality. The contrast between our state of dress and the landscape around us only added to the surreal nature of the situation.

"It didn't really cross my mind, to be honest," Luke replied dismissively, his focus clearly on matters beyond our immediate comfort. His words did little to ease the growing sense of unease that had begun to settle in the pit of my stomach.

Unable to hold back any longer, I voiced the question that had been gnawing at me since the moment we arrived in this peculiar place. "And where's the New Jerusalem?" The question tumbled out, my eyes still scanning the barren, yet strangely beautiful landscape before us, seeking any hint of the prophesied city. My heart raced with a mix of anticipation and trepidation, desperate for some sign that we were indeed in the right place, that this wasn't some elaborate misunderstanding.

Paul shot Luke a look of bewilderment, his expression mirroring my own growing anxiety. The uncertainty of our situation, the surreal environment, and Luke's enigmatic demeanour only added to the sense of unease. It was clear that Paul, too, had expected more concrete answers, more tangible evidence of the New Jerusalem's presence.

Unfazed by our reactions, Luke continued confidently, "It's just over the hill." His words were simple, yet they carried a weight that suggested a deeper meaning, a promise of something yet to be revealed. He gestured towards a distant rise in the landscape, his eyes alight with a certainty that I wished I could share.

Suddenly, my eyes lit up with a mixture of hope and expectation at Luke's announcement. The prospect of finally witnessing the New Jerusalem, a vision that had been so central to our faith and family discussions, was tantalising. I wanted to believe him, to trust in the assurances of the Spirit that had guided us to this place. Yet, a part of me couldn't help but wonder if we were chasing a dream, a figment of my own spiritual yearnings.

However, Paul's response, throwing his hands up in a somewhat defeated gesture, contradicted the excitement I felt. His action seemed to convey skepticism or frustration, perhaps a reaction to the ambiguity of our situation or Luke's vague guidance. It was suddenly apparent that not everyone shared the same level of faith or certainty in this moment.

"Paul will take you there," Luke announced abruptly, his gaze fixed on Paul with an intensity that left no room for argument. The suddenness of the statement caught me off guard, and I found myself looking between my two sons, trying to gauge their reactions.

"What!?" Paul's protest was immediate and forceful. He seemed as taken aback by Luke's declaration as I was. His eyes widened in surprise, his body language conveying a mix of confusion and resistance. It was clear that he had not expected to be thrust into the role of guide.

Luke's furrowed brow mirrored my own, a sign of the tension brewing between him and Paul. Before I could voice my own concerns, Luke responded, "I don't know why you're getting so worked up." His tone was dismissive, almost challenging. "I told you I would bring them here." The words hung in the air, a reminder of some previous conversation or agreement that I had not been privy to.

"Yeah, but I thought-" Paul tried to argue back, his voice rising in frustration. He lifted a laptop he had brought with him, as if it held some significance to his argument. The gesture only added to the confusion of the moment, leaving me wondering what role technology could possibly play in this new world.

I watched my sons cautiously, the tension between them palpable. Paul and Luke, the eldest two and close in age, had a history of finding themselves in challenging situations, and it seemed this instance was no exception. Their dynamic, a blend of brotherly love and rivalry, was playing out before us in these unusual circumstances. As their father, I knew I had to step in, to find a way to bridge the gap and bring us all together.

"Oh, plans changed," Luke interrupted Paul, his voice tinged with sarcasm and a hint of defiance. "Dad wanted to go to the New Jerusalem instead." His words struck me like a physical blow, a reminder of the weight of my own desires and expectations. *Had I unwittingly put this burden on my sons? Had my longing for the New Jerusalem overshadowed their own needs and concerns?*

I narrowed my eyes at Luke, ready to intervene and address the confusion and mounting tension. But before I could say anything, Jerome's voice cut through the exchange. "What is she doing?" he asked, his tone laced with confusion. He pointed towards a middle-aged woman who was navigating an assortment of supplies with a shopping trolley. She looked completely out of place in this barren landscape.

The woman's presence in Clivilius was as baffling as everything else we had encountered since our arrival. She moved with a purpose, seemingly oblivious to the surreal nature of her surroundings. My mind raced with questions: *Who was she? How did she come to be here? And what could her presence mean for us in this mysterious world?* Her appearance added another layer of complexity to an already bewildering situation.

As Luke called out to the woman named Karen with noticeable enthusiasm, my curiosity about her and this strange place only grew. Despite the distance between us, she heard Luke's call and stopped, turning to face us. Her body language, even from afar, spoke volumes. Her shoulders slumped in what seemed like frustration or exhaustion. "I'm busy, Luke," she shouted back, her tone conveying a mix of annoyance and weariness. It was clear that she had no desire to engage with us, her focus solely on the task at hand.

"It'll only take a few minutes!" Luke shouted back, his determination evident in his voice. He seemed intent on bringing Karen over to us, despite her evident reluctance. I couldn't help but wonder what his motivation was, why he was so keen on introducing us to this stranger in the midst of our own family's transition.

Karen, after a moment's hesitation, left her trolley and began trudging towards us. Her steps were slow, her reluctance clear in every movement. It was as if she was carrying a weight far greater than just the physical distance she had to cover. As she drew closer, I could see the lines etched on her face, the weariness in her eyes. She was a woman who had seen and experienced much, and I found myself both intrigued and wary of what her presence might mean for us.

"Karen, meet my parents, Noah and Greta," Luke introduced us when she finally reached us. "And this is my younger brother, Jerome," he added, gesturing towards Jerome with a grand flourish of his hand. The introduction felt oddly formal, a stark contrast to the casual manner in which Luke had been interacting with us thus far.

Greta, ever the embodiment of hospitality and warmth, immediately wrapped Karen in a tight embrace. "Lovely to meet you, Karen," she said, her voice filled with genuine warmth and welcome. It was a testament to Greta's nature, her ability to extend kindness and acceptance even in the most unusual of circumstances.

Karen, however, seemed caught off guard by Greta's enthusiastic greeting. She didn't reciprocate the gesture, her arms staying rigidly at her sides. "Likewise," she muttered, her response polite but lacking warmth. Her demeanour, guarded and distant, added another layer of mystery to this already bewildering place. I couldn't help but wonder what experiences had shaped her, what had brought her to this strange world.

Feeling increasingly out of place in my dressing gown in this warm environment, I found myself pulling it tighter around me. The gown, appropriate for a chilly morning back home, was becoming uncomfortably warm here. The obvious contrast between the cold winter we had left and the warmth of Clivilius was disorienting.

Luke, noticing my discomfort, remarked, "I suppose I'd better get you some clothes to change into." His nod in my direction was a tacit acknowledgment of my growing discomfort, a small gesture of consideration. It was a reminder that, despite the tensions and uncertainties, my son still cared about my well-being.

Jerome, his eyes fixed on the giant, rectangular screen that we had just walked through, voiced the question that, I suspected, was on all our minds. "Can't we just go home?" His words hung in the air, a poignant reminder of the reality we had left behind. The longing in his voice was palpable, a reflection of the fear and uncertainty that had begun to creep into my own heart.

But before I could respond, the soft voice of the Spirit spoke to my mind again, sending a tingling confirmation shiver down my spine. *This is your home now, Noah Smith.* The words were a balm to my troubled soul, a reassurance that we were exactly where we were meant to be. Yet, they also carried a weight of finality, a sense that our old life was truly behind us.

The realisation that Clivilius was now our home settled over me with a weight I couldn't quite describe. It was a mix of acceptance, resolve, and a deep sense of divine purpose. We were here for a reason, part of a plan far greater than ourselves, and it was our duty to embrace this new life, to find our place in Clivilius. With this understanding, I prepared myself to lead my family in this new world, guided by faith and the whispered assurances of the Spirit.

"Well," Karen said, finally breaking free from Greta's embrace. Her tone was matter-of-fact, yet there was a hint of weariness in her voice. "I guess that's my cue to keep moving. These garden supplies won't move themselves," she finished, gesturing towards the dozens of trolleys grouped near the one she had recently left behind.

I gave Karen a slight wave, feeling a mix of gratitude and curiosity towards this enigmatic woman. The encounter had been odd, but she seemed amiable enough, a potential ally in this unfamiliar place. A wave felt like an appropriate, albeit small, gesture of goodwill. As she walked off, I couldn't help but feel a mix of curiosity and confusion about her role in this place. The mention of garden supplies and her apparent task of moving them suggested a sense of order and purpose in Clivilius, yet so much remained unclear.

Jerome's question still hung in the air, lingering with a sense of urgency and confusion. Paul, sensing the need for some explanation, placed his arm around Jerome's shoulder. "It's not quite that simple," he said, his voice carrying a hint of empathy for Jerome's evident desire to return home. "How about I explain it on our way to camp?" he suggested, his tone suggesting that there was more to this place and our situation than met the eye. It was a promise of answers, of clarity in the midst of the unknown.

"Great idea, Paul," Luke quickly agreed, motioning for Greta and me to follow them. His eagerness to move forward, to delve deeper into this new world, was palpable.

As we began to move, Paul paused and turned back to Luke. "Oh, and Luke," he added, "bring their clothes to camp, would you? Don't leave them at the Drop Zone this time." His words were laced with an undercurrent of responsibility, perhaps a reminder of past lapses or oversights. It was a glimpse into the dynamics of this place, the roles and responsibilities that had already been established.

Luke's response, a simple "Of course," did little to alleviate my growing curiosity about what the Drop Zone was. My mind conjured images of a place where supplies or people might be left, possibly a central hub in Clivilius. *Perhaps, I mused, it was a location where items needed for the New Jerusalem were gathered.* The thought was both intriguing and daunting.

As we prepared to leave, the giant screen that had served as our portal to this world burst into colour again. Luke stepped through and vanished, the colours dissipating after him in a display that was both mesmerising and unsettling. I found myself staring at the spot where he had disappeared, my mind trying to grasp the reality of what I had just witnessed. It was a reminder that the rules of this world were different, that the boundaries between the physical and the spiritual were blurred in ways I had never imagined.

"Come on. Follow me," Paul urged, gently pulling me away from my contemplation of the portal. His nudge brought me back to the present, to the reality of our new existence in Clivilius. I found myself wondering why Greta and I couldn't simply follow Luke through the portal as well, a question that lingered in my mind as we set off to follow Paul. The walk to the camp, I sensed, would be filled with revelations and perhaps more questions about our new home and our role in it.

BIXBUS

4338.213.3

As we began to walk, I found myself marvelling at the landscape around us. The rolling hills of brown and orange dust stretched out before us, an endless expanse that seemed to defy the very notion of boundaries. The air was warm and dry, so different from the crisp chill of the winter morning we had left behind. Each step kicked up small clouds of dust, leaving a trail of our passage across this unfamiliar terrain.

Paul walked ahead of us, his strides purposeful and sure. I watched him, my heart swelling with a mix of pride and trepidation. My eldest son, now a man grown, was leading us into the unknown, into a future that was both exhilarating and terrifying. I couldn't help but wonder what experiences had shaped him, what had prepared him for this moment. There was so much I still didn't know, so many questions that burned in my mind.

Beside me, Greta walked in silence, her eyes fixed on the horizon. I could sense the turmoil within her, the struggle to reconcile her faith with the surreal nature of our circumstances. She had always been the practical one, the one who kept our family grounded in the realities of day-to-day life. Now, faced with a reality that defied all logic and reason, I could see the cracks in her composure, the uncertainty that lurked beneath the surface.

Jerome trailed behind us, his steps hesitant and unsure. I glanced back at him, my heart aching at the lost look on his face. He was still so young, still grappling with the complexities of faith and identity. To be thrust into this new world, to have his entire reality upended in a matter of moments, was a burden I wished I could lift from his shoulders. I made a silent promise to myself, to be there for him, to guide him through whatever challenges lay ahead.

The warm mix of sand and dust beneath my bare feet was a new sensation, one that brought a certain rawness to our journey across the small hills. With each step, I could feel the grains shifting and sinking under my weight, a constant reminder of the unfamiliar terrain we were traversing. Greta, Jerome, and I followed Paul, our steps falling into a rhythmic pattern as we made our way towards the distant encampment.

It wasn't long into our journey when Greta's grumblings had begun, her complaints about the heat and the ever-present dust filling the air. "This is ridiculous," she muttered, wiping a bead of sweat from her brow. "I feel like I'm breathing in more dust than air." Despite my initial optimism and determination to embrace this new reality, I had to concede that she had a point. The environment here was dustier than anything we had experienced during our years living in Broken Hill, a place known for its arid climate and red desert sands.

"This is how it is everywhere," Paul said, glancing back at us over his shoulder. There was a hint of impatience in his voice, a subtle indication that he had grown accustomed to the constant presence of dust and sand. It was clear he had adapted more quickly to this environment, or perhaps he knew something we didn't, some secret to navigating this foreign landscape with ease.

As we descended the slope, the gown I was wearing became increasingly uncomfortable in the warm climate. The fabric clung to my skin, damp with perspiration, and I found myself longing for the comfort of my usual attire. I pulled the gown tighter around me, a futile attempt at modesty in this vast, open land. The action felt almost absurd, given the circumstances, but old habits die hard, and the ingrained sense of propriety was hard to shake.

My thoughts drifted to the pioneers of old, those brave souls who had crossed vast plains with minimal possessions, driven by their faith and the promise of a better life. Their journeys, fuelled by faith and resilience, resonated deeply with me now. Here we were, on our own journey of faith, traversing the sands of sacrifice, following in the footsteps of those who had come before us. A faint smile crossed my face despite the hardship, a flicker of pride and purpose. I had heard the voice of the Lord, and in my heart, I trusted that He would bless us for our diligence and perseverance, just as He had blessed the pioneers of old.

Upon cresting the final hill, a small encampment came into view, its modest structures and tents dotting the landscape like a beacon of civilisation amidst the barren surroundings. It was far smaller than I had anticipated, a handful of shelters clustered together, a far cry from the grand vision of the New Jerusalem that had taken root in my mind. The simplicity of the camp made me wonder if we were among the first Saints to be gathered in this place, the vanguard of a greater migration yet to come. The thought was both exhilarating and daunting, a reminder of the weight of responsibility that rested on our shoulders. We were pioneers in our own right, embarking on a journey that was as spiritual as it was physical, blazing a trail for others to follow.

The sight of the large chain-link fence surrounding the small camp sparked a mix of curiosity and fear in Greta. "Why the large fence?" she asked Paul, her voice carrying an undertone of both intrigue and apprehension. The fence stood out in stark contrast to the open expanse of the surrounding landscape.

"For protection," Paul answered, his response succinct, offering no further details. His brevity suggested that there were underlying issues we were yet to understand, dangers that lurked beyond the confines of the camp. The thought sent a chill down my spine, a reminder that even in this promised land, we were not immune to the perils of the world.

It was Jerome who drew our attention to something more unsettling, a sight that made my blood run cold. He pointed to the head of a black panther-like creature impaled into the ground at the camp's entrance, its black eyes staring out at us like a macabre warning. "What is that?" he asked, his voice a mix of fascination and horror, the curiosity of youth tempered by the instinctive fear of the unknown.

My stomach churned at the sight, a wave of nausea rising in my throat. The skull was a stark and disturbing symbol, one that spoke of dangers I hadn't anticipated in this new world. The dried blood and razor-sharp teeth were a grim reminder that even in this place of spiritual significance, the threat of violence and death loomed large.

Greta clutched me tightly, her reaction one of revulsion and fear. "Noah, that's so disturbing, I can't look," she exclaimed, pressing her face into my chest, her words muffled against my gown but dripping with dread.

I stroked Greta's hair, trying to offer her some comfort in this unsettling moment, even as my own heart raced with a mixture of fear and uncertainty. Despite the warmth of the environment, a haunting chill ran through me, a primal response to the sight of death and danger.

"We were attacked a few nights ago," Paul explained, his tone serious, his eyes fixed on the skull as if reliving the memory of that fateful night. "It is a reminder that we need to remain vigilant to the dangers that surround us, even here in Bixbus." His words carried a weight of experience, a hard-earned wisdom that spoke of the realities of life in this new world.

My back stiffened at his words, a sense of unease settling over me like a heavy cloak. *Dangers?* The thought of facing such threats, of putting my family in harm's way, was almost too much to bear. A deep sense of foreboding settled over me, a gnawing fear that perhaps I had underestimated the challenges that lay ahead.

As I stood there, staring at the menacing skull, I reminded myself that the early pioneer Saints faced their own trials and tribulations, their own moments of fear and uncertainty. They endured tremendous suffering for their faith, with many paying the ultimate price, their blood watering the soil of the promised land. This thought, while sobering, fortified my resolve, a reminder that faith often requires sacrifice, that the path to salvation is rarely easy or without hardship. If they could persevere through their trials, then so could we, drawing strength from their example and from the knowledge that God had led us here for a reason. The skull, a haunting reminder of the reality of this new world, also served as a call to faith and vigilance, a reminder that we were in God's hands, and in that truth, I found a measure of comfort amidst the uncertainty.

As Paul led us through the rattling gate into the camp, I could feel the curious eyes of its inhabitants on us, their gazes a mixture of interest and wariness. The sight of three men preparing to depart caught our attention, their purposeful movements and determined expressions a contrast to the stillness of the camp. "We're off to get this shed finished," one of them, a sturdy man with calloused hands, announced as we neared them, his voice carrying a note of determination.

I was acutely aware of my inappropriate attire in this setting, my dressing gown a stark contrast to the practical, worn clothing of the men before us. I pulled the gown tighter around me, feeling somewhat out of place and hoping Luke would soon arrive with more suitable clothing, a small comfort in the face of the larger challenges that awaited us.

The youngest of the three men, leaning on crutches, chimed in with determination in his voice. "Hopefully get the second one finished, too," he said, his words a testament to his spirit and resilience, even in the face of physical limitations. His enthusiasm was commendable, a reminder that even in the face of adversity, the human spirit could rise above, finding purpose and meaning in the work of building and creating.

"That sounds great," Paul replied, his voice carrying a note of encouragement and support. His introductions were brief, but I managed to catch the names of these industrious individuals, these fellow travellers on the path to the New Jerusalem. The first man who spoke was Adrian, clearly an expert in construction, his hands bearing the marks of a lifetime of hard work and dedication. The young man on crutches was Kain, an apprentice construction worker whose story of building a house for himself and his fiancee back in Tasmania, and his abrupt transition to Clivilius, piqued my interest. However, his sudden change in demeanour when recalling his past life made Paul swiftly change the topic, a reminder that even in this place of new beginnings, the weight of the past could still linger. The third man was Nial, who ran a fence construction business in Hobart, his expertise and knowledge a valuable asset in this new world.

Their friendly demeanour was noticeable, a warmth and camaraderie that spoke of shared experiences and common goals. But so was their rough exterior, the marks of a life lived in the trenches, of hard work and hard truths. As they made their departure, their occasional cussing and off-handed remarks about our unusual appearance made it clear they weren't the kind of Saints I had envisioned encountering in this new world, not the polished, pious individuals I had imagined walking the streets of the New Jerusalem. But perhaps, I mused, that was the point, that the New Jerusalem was not a place of perfection, but a place of growth and transformation, where imperfect souls could come together to build something greater than themselves.

Standing near the front gate, I took in the settlement's modest features with a mix of intrigue and mild disappointment, my eyes scanning the landscape for signs of the grandeur and glory I had imagined. Paul pointed out the caravans and motorhomes that dotted the area, a row of large tents, and a bonfire that seemed to serve as a communal hub, the heart of this small but determined community. His description of a large river snaking its way behind the tents and a distant lagoon piqued my interest, a hint of the natural beauty that existed beyond the confines of the camp, yet it all seemed so... mundane, so different from what I had envisioned the New Jerusalem to be, a far cry from the shining city on a hill that had captured my imagination for so long.

Jerome's face lit up at the mention of the lagoon, a spark of youthful excitement in his eyes. Paul, perhaps sensing his growing interest, quickly diverted his attention back to the immediate surroundings, a subtle reminder that there was still much to learn and understand about this new world, that the path to the New Jerusalem was one of patience and perseverance.

"And there, you have it," Paul said, as if to conclude our brief tour, his voice carrying a mixture of pride and a hint of resignation, as if acknowledging the settlement's simplicity, the gap between the reality before us and the grand vision that had brought us here.

Confusion furrowed my brow, a sense of unease and uncertainty settling over me like a heavy cloak. "Is this it?" I found myself asking as we moved towards the low burning campfire, the question spilling out before I could filter it, driven by a mix of surprise and a slight sense of disillusionment.

"Yep. Welcome to Bixbus," Paul confirmed, his voice carrying a sense of finality, mixed with a subtle undercurrent of pride for what had been established here, despite the apparent modesty of the settlement. The name was unfamiliar, a far cry from the New Jerusalem I had envisioned, but there was a certain ring to it, a hint of the unique identity and character of this place.

Greta, ever direct, voiced the question that was lingering in all our minds, the elephant in the room that could no longer be ignored. "So, this isn't the New Jerusalem?" she asked, her tone a mix of curiosity and a tinge of disappointment, a reflection of the hopes and dreams that had brought us here, the expectations that now seemed to hang in the balance.

The atmosphere shifted palpably, becoming heavy with an almost tangible awkwardness, a tension that seemed to crackle in the air like static electricity. Karen's voice cut through the near-silent tension, her words coarse and blunt, a jarring contrast to the spiritual significance of the moment. "What the fuck's a New Jerusalem?" she mumbled, more to herself than anyone else, yet loud enough for us all to hear, her words an unfortunate reminder of the gulf that existed between our expectations and the reality before us.

I tugged nervously at the ends of my robe's tie, feeling increasingly out of place in my current attire and in this settlement that seemed so far removed from our expectations. The realisation that our journey was not leading to the grandiose vision of the New Jerusalem, but rather to this humble and pragmatic community called Bixbus, was a jarring shift in perspective, a challenge to everything I had believed and hoped for.

"Karen," Paul called out, his voice cutting through the tension that had settled over us like a thick fog. He gestured towards her, a request for assistance in his eyes, a plea for help in navigating this awkward and uncertain moment. "Do you happen to know where we might be able to find some temporary clothing for my parents?" he asked, his tone both hopeful and apologetic, a recognition of the discomfort and unease that hung in the air.

Karen paused, considering Paul's request, her eyes scanning us with a mixture of curiosity and something else, something harder to define. After a moment, she nodded, a simple gesture that carried a weight of significance. "Follow me," she said, her voice firm yet not unkind, a glimmer of understanding in her eyes. She motioned for Greta and me to follow her, and Paul encouraged us to do so with a reassuring nod, a silent promise that everything would be alright, that this was just another step on the path to the New Jerusalem, even if it looked different than I had imagined.

As Greta and I followed Karen, a thick tension hung in the air, the awkwardness of our situation leaving us all at a loss for words, the weight of our expectations and the reality before us a palpable presence. Paul and Jerome remained behind, watching us walk away, into the unknown and the uncertain, but also into the possibility of a new beginning, a fresh start in this strange and wondrous place.

❖

Entering Karen's caravan felt like an intrusion into her personal space, especially given the compact nature of her living quarters. As I stepped over the threshold, I was immediately struck by the confined dimensions of the interior, a jarring contrast to the spacious home I had left behind. The walls seemed to close in around me, and I found myself hunching my shoulders slightly, as if trying to make myself smaller, to take up less space in this unfamiliar environment.

Despite my discomfort, I couldn't help but feel a sense of intrigue about life in Bixbus, about how people adapted and made homes in such unconventional settings. My eyes roamed the interior of the caravan, taking in the small details that spoke of Karen's life and personality. The worn but clean surfaces, the carefully arranged belongings, the hints of colour and warmth that softened the edges of the utilitarian space — it all painted a picture of a woman who had learned to make the most of what she had, to find comfort and meaning in even the most challenging of circumstances.

My attention was immediately drawn to a terrarium on the table, a small glass enclosure that seemed to pulse with life. Curiosity piqued, I leaned in to get a better look, my eyes widening in surprise as I realised that the terrarium was filled with baby spiders, their tiny bodies scurrying and spinning in a complex dance of survival. Their species was unfamiliar to me, their markings and patterns unlike anything I had seen before, adding to the sense of mystery and wonder that seemed to permeate every aspect of this new world.

"Ah, don't mind those," Karen said nonchalantly, gesturing towards the terrarium with a casual wave of her hand. "They're just my little eight-legged roommates." Her voice carried a hint of amusement, as if she found my fascination with the spiders to be slightly endearing.

Her casual remark brought a soft chuckle out of me, the first genuine smile since our arrival in Clivilius. There was something about Karen's easy acceptance of the unusual and the unexpected that was both comforting and unsettling, a reminder that life in this new world would require a certain level of adaptability and open-mindedness.

Greta, however, was visibly less comfortable with the idea of sharing living space with arachnids. "Roommates?" she nearly shrieked, her expression a mix of disbelief and alarm, her eyes widening in horror at the thought of cohabitating with such creatures. "In the Bible, spiders are a symbol of-"

"Hard work and diligence," Karen cut in smoothly, her interjection stopping Greta mid-sentence, her voice carrying a hint of gentle reproach, as if she found Greta's reaction to be slightly overwrought. "They're not something to be feared or reviled, but rather admired for their tenacity and skill." Her words carried a weight of wisdom and experience, a reminder that even the smallest and most overlooked of God's creatures had a purpose and a place in the grand scheme of things.

I watched the exchange with interest, my mind racing to recall any specific mentions of spiders in the Bible. Despite my extensive knowledge of the scriptures, I couldn't recall any particular passages or stories that dealt with the symbolic meaning of arachnids.

"But let's focus on finding you some clothes," Karen continued, turning her attention to a small pile of clothing that lay folded on a nearby shelf. "I don't think Chris's clothes will fit Noah, but I have something for you, Greta."

Feeling out of place amidst the women's discussion and the close quarters of the caravan, I announced, "I'll wait outside," and made a hasty exit, the need for fresh air and open space suddenly overwhelming. As I stepped back out into the bright sunlight of Bixbus, I took a deep breath, feeling the warm air fill my lungs and the dust settle on my skin like a fine powder.

❖

Standing outside Karen's caravan, I found myself meandering near the entrance, my bare feet kicking up small clouds of dust with each step. The sensation of the warm, powdery earth between my toes was a stark reminder of how far removed I was from the comforts and conveniences of my previous life. Yet, despite the unfamiliarity of my surroundings, I couldn't help but feel a sense of awe and wonder at the vast expanse of land that stretched out before me.

My gaze was constantly drawn to the landscape around me, my eyes roaming over the rolling hills and jagged rock formations that seemed to go on forever. The dust was omnipresent, a constant companion that clung to every surface and filled the air with a hazy, almost dreamlike quality. It covered every inch of the ground, painting the scenery in muted earth tones that ranged from deep, rich browns and reds to pale, ashy greys. The colours seemed to shift and change with the light, creating an ever-evolving tapestry that was both beautiful and haunting.

In the distance, a mountain range loomed, its peaks rising up from the dusty plains like ancient sentinels keeping watch over the land. The sight of those mountains stirred something deep within me, a sense of curiosity and longing that I couldn't quite explain. *What lay beyond those peaks? Was it more of this endless, dusty terrain, stretching out into infinity? Or was there something else entirely, a hidden world waiting to be discovered?*

As I stood there, lost in thought, the faint sound of flowing water reached my ears, carried on the warm breeze that whispered through the settlement. It was a gentle, soothing sound, a reminder that even in this harsh and unforgiving landscape, there was still the promise of life and renewal. The river that Paul had mentioned, hidden from view by the rolling hills and uneven terrain of Bixbus, seemed to call out to me, beckoning me to come and explore its secrets.

The proximity of the river was a comfort, a reassurance that we were not entirely alone in this vast and empty land. Yet, its invisibility added to the sense of mystery that seemed to envelop this place.

Lost in my musings, the occasional clang of tools against materials echoed in the distance, a jarring reminder that life in Bixbus was not just about survival, but also about building and progress. The sound was a testament to the hard work and determination of those who had come before us, the pioneers who had laid the foundation for this community in the midst of the barren wilderness.

I thought of Kain, Nial, and Adrian, the three men we had met earlier, toiling away in the heat and the dust to construct their shed. They were contributing to the settlement's growth in their own way, building not just structures, but also a sense of community and shared purpose.

The sound of the caravan door opening behind me pulled me from my reverie. I turned to see Greta emerging from the cramped interior, her expression visibly disturbed and slightly agitated. The sight of her discomfort sent a pang of concern through me, and I hurried over to her side, eager to offer whatever support and comfort I could.

"Greta, are you alright?" I asked softly, my hand reaching out to take hers in a gentle, reassuring grip. "You look quite unsettled. What happened in there with Karen?"

But Greta simply shook her head, her lips pressing together in a tight line as she refused to divulge the details of her conversation with the enigmatic woman. I could see the tension in her shoulders, the way her eyes darted around as if searching for some unseen threat. It was clear that whatever had transpired between them had left her deeply shaken, and I felt a surge of protectiveness rising up within me.

Knowing Greta as I did, it didn't take much to unsettle her, and I could only imagine how Karen's directness and no-nonsense attitude might have been too much for her to handle. Greta was a woman who valued propriety and decorum above all else, and the rough-and-tumble world of Bixbus was a far cry from the genteel society she was accustomed to.

I sighed softly, acknowledging the small frictions that were bound to arise in such close quarters and under these unusual circumstances. It was only natural that there would be some adjustments to be made, some growing pains to be endured as we learned to navigate this new world and the people who inhabited it.

But as I looked at Greta, standing there in her new clothes, a small sense of relief washed over me. At least she was now properly attired, no longer forced to wander the settlement in her pyjamas. It was a small victory, but one that felt significant in the face of all the uncertainty and upheaval we had experienced.

"Come, my love," I said gently, my arm slipping around her waist in a comforting embrace. "Let's not dwell on the unknowns of your interaction with Karen. We have each other, and we have our family. That's what matters most."

Greta leaned into me, her head coming to rest on my shoulder as we began to make our way back towards the centre of the settlement.

❖

As we stood by the dulled campfire, the arrival of Luke marked a shift in the atmosphere, a palpable change in the energy that swirled around us. Paul's irritation was immediate, his frustration bubbling to the surface like a pot about to boil over. "What's taken you so long?" he demanded, his tone sharp and accusatory, his eyes narrowing as he fixed Luke with a penetrating stare. "We've been waiting ages for you!"

Luke's response was a mumbled "Sorry," his gaze darting away from Paul's intense scrutiny, as if he couldn't bear the weight of his brother's displeasure. It was clear he was uncomfortable under the spotlight, his body language screaming his desire to be anywhere else but here. His attention quickly shifted to Greta, a flicker of amusement dancing in his eyes as he noted her changed attire. "Whose clothes?" he inquired, a hint of mirth in his voice, as if the sight of his mother in borrowed garments was a source of private entertainment.

Karen, appearing almost out of nowhere, startled Luke, causing him to jump slightly, his eyes widening in surprise. Her presence was unexpected, a sudden intrusion into the tense family dynamic that had begun to unfold. But she seemed unfazed, her demeanour calm and collected, as if she had seen this kind of thing a thousand times before. "I've lent her some of mine, since you were taking so long," she said sternly to Luke, her tone indicating that she wasn't pleased with his tardiness, her eyes flashing with a hint of annoyance.

Luke, regaining his composure, offered a sheepish smile, his hand rubbing the back of his neck in a gesture of contrition. "Thanks, Karen. That's very kind of you," he said, acknowledging her help, his voice tinged with a mix of gratitude and embarrassment. It was clear that he was aware of his own shortcomings, of the way his actions had inconvenienced those around him.

But Karen wasn't done yet, her gaze shifting to Greta, her expression serious and direct. "I'm not sure that your mother agrees that it was a suitable conversation," she remarked, her words hanging in the air like a challenge, a gauntlet thrown down at Greta's feet. The sudden tension that filled the air was palpable, a heaviness that seemed to press down on us all.

I felt a twinge of annoyance at Karen's decision to raise the topic in front of everyone, my jaw clenching slightly as I tried to maintain my composure. Family matters, in my view, were to be kept private, a sacred trust between those who shared the bonds of blood and love. Grievances were to be resolved quietly, behind closed doors, without drawing others into the fray. The fact that I was still in the dark about what had transpired between Greta and Karen only added to my discomfort, a nagging sense of unease that gnawed at the edges of my mind.

I glanced at Greta, hoping to gauge her reaction, to read the secrets that lay hidden behind her eyes. But she remained stoically silent, her face an unreadable mask, a fortress that even I couldn't breach. The situation was delicate, and I knew that pressing her for details in this setting would only exacerbate the tension.

Paul's intervention came as a relief, a welcome reprieve from the suffocating atmosphere that had descended upon us. He took the suitcases from Luke and handed one to Greta and me, his movements efficient and purposeful. "We're expecting the first sheds to be completed today, so why don't you bring us some food storage from home?" he suggested to Luke, a practical proposal in light of our new situation, a way to focus our energies.

Karen, intrigued and somewhat baffled, asked, "Food storage?" Her eyebrows raised in a quizzical expression, as if the concept was entirely foreign to her.

Greta's expression lit up with satisfaction, a smile spreading across her face like the sun breaking through the clouds. "Our church leaders have always taught the diligent Saints to have twelve months of food storage," she explained, her voice filled with a quiet pride, a sense of accomplishment that came from years of careful planning and preparation. She glanced at me, her smile broadening, her eyes shining with a sense of vindication. "It's always been Noah's pride and joy. We've been ever so obedient." Her tone was a mix of pride and a subtle hint of triumph, as if our preparedness was a point of honour, a testament to our faith and dedication.

Karen's dubious look towards Greta revealed her skepticism, her eyes narrowing slightly as she processed this new information. The concept of such extensive food storage seemed foreign to her, perhaps even excessive in her eyes, a luxury that few could afford.

Jerome, eager to support Greta's claim, joined in, his voice filled with a youthful enthusiasm, a desire to prove himself in the eyes of his elders. "Seriously, she's not lying. There's literally an entire room dedicated just to food storage," he confirmed, his words echoing the seriousness of our family's commitment to preparedness, a commitment that had been instilled in us from a young age.

Feeling a swell of pride, I couldn't help but chime in about our family's efforts, my chest puffing out slightly as I spoke. "There are tins of vegetables, pasta varieties of almost every kind, containers of flour and sugar, and-" I began, ready to list the extensive inventory of our food storage, to paint a picture of the bounty that we had worked so hard to accumulate.

But Karen cut in, her grin reflecting genuine pleasure, a warmth that seemed to radiate from her very being. "Well, it looks as though that obedience of yours is about to actually pay off," she said, her words carrying a note of approval, a sense of respect for the dedication and foresight that we had shown. She cast a sideways glance at Luke, as if to reinforce Paul's suggestion that our food storage be brought to the settlement, a silent encouragement for him to take action.

Paul continued his briefing with Luke, his voice steady and matter-of-fact, a leader taking charge of the situation. "Karen's been busy emptying a lot of shopping trolleys from last night's raid. Could you take them back to Earth and fill them with food stuff?"

Luke's eyes sparkled, igniting with a fire that reflected a passion that seemed to burn within him like a flame. "Yeah, that should work," he replied, his voice tinged with a palpable eagerness, a readiness to leap into action at a moment's notice. His enthusiasm was infectious.

Yet, despite Luke's confident response, I felt a twinge of unease at the mention of 'Earth', a word that seemed to hang in the air like a question mark, a reminder of the strange and unfamiliar world that we now found ourselves in. The implication that we were no longer on the planet that we had called home for so long was jarring, a realisation that shook me to my very core.

Karen chimed in seamlessly, her voice cutting through my thoughts like a knife. "Jerome and I will collect the empty trolleys and bring them to the Portal for you," she offered, her tone efficient, her demeanour all business. It was clear that she was a woman of action, someone who knew how to get things done.

Jerome, in contrast, let out a loud sigh of reluctance, his body language screaming his lack of enthusiasm for the task. His shoulders slumped slightly, his eyes rolling in a gesture of teenage rebellion, a silent protest against the responsibilities that had been thrust upon him.

But Greta, with her sharp tongue and no-nonsense attitude, was quick to admonish him, her voice cracking like a whip in the stillness of the air. "Go and make yourself useful," she prodded, her words like a command, a reminder of the importance of contributing to the greater good, of putting aside personal desires for the sake of the community.

As Luke, Jerome, and Karen set off to execute the new plan, their figures receding into the distance like shadows against the harsh glare of the sun, the dynamic shifted once more. Now, it was just Greta, Paul, and me left behind, standing in the middle of the settlement like islands in a vast and uncharted sea.

A sense of isolation crept over me, a feeling of being adrift in a world that I didn't fully understand, a world that seemed to operate by rules that were entirely foreign to me. My mind drifted into thought, mulling over the host of new terms that Luke and Paul had casually tossed around during their exchange, words that seemed to carry a weight and significance that I couldn't quite grasp.

Portals, night raids, and the stark implication that we were no longer on Earth — these concepts swirled in my head, colliding with my beliefs and understandings like waves crashing against the shore. I loved to delve deep into the doctrines of the church, to wrestle with theological complexities and ponder the mysteries of the universe. But this... this was another realm entirely, a world that seemed to defy explanation, a world that challenged everything that I thought I knew.

It was mind-boggling, disorienting, and frankly, a little frightening, a realisation that sent a shiver down my spine, a chill that seemed to seep into my very bones. I felt like a man standing on the edge of a vast and unknown abyss, peering into the darkness and trying to make sense of the shapes and shadows that danced before my eyes.

Greta's voice, tinged with genuine curiosity and expectation, cut through my muddled thoughts like a beacon in the night. "Where's our house again?" Her question, innocent yet laden with the weight of our new reality, anchored me back to the present, a tether that kept me from drifting too far into the recesses of my own mind.

I stepped beside her, a gesture of solidarity in this bewildering world, a silent promise to face whatever challenges lay ahead together. Placing a reassuring hand on her shoulder, I found myself seeking the same answers that she was, my own curiosity and confusion mirroring her own.

My gaze fixed squarely on Paul, waiting, expecting, hoping for some kind of explanation, some kind of clarity in the midst of the uncertainty that swirled around us. But Paul's response, when it came, was far from the comfort that I had been seeking.

He let out a resigned sigh, his shoulders slumping slightly as if under the weight of some unseen burden. "What you see is what you get," he stated, his words frank, his tone final, a declaration that seemed to hang in the air like a pronouncement of doom.

My brow furrowed as I silently contemplated the implications of his words, the realisation that our new reality was far more stark and unforgiving than I had ever imagined. What did it mean, to be told that this was all there was, that the comforts and conveniences of our old life were now nothing more than a distant memory?

As I stood there, surrounded by the dusty landscape and the makeshift shelters of Bixbus, I couldn't help but feel a sense of profound loss, a sudden and unexpected grief for the life that we had left behind.

A NEW JERUSALEM

4338.213.4

The crisp freshness of the morning air stood in stark contrast to the emotional turmoil simmering around the campfire. Despite my attempts to offer comfort, Greta remained visibly unsettled, pacing back and forth like a caged animal. Her restlessness was tangible, a palpable presence that seemed to hang in the air like a heavy fog, seeping into every corner of the settlement.

As I watched her, my heart ached with empathy and concern. Greta's hands fidgeted with a small handkerchief, twisting and turning it as if it held the answers to the questions that plagued her mind. She carved a path through the dust that blanketed the ground, her footsteps leaving a trail of distress in their wake. The sight of her like this, so fraught with anxiety, tugged at the very core of my being, a reminder of the profound impact that our current situation was having on us all.

I found myself struggling to come to terms with the reality of our surroundings, my own mind grappling with the stark contrast between the world we had left behind and the one we now found ourselves in. The place we had been brought to was a far cry from the New Jerusalem I had envisioned, a promised land of divine revelation and spiritual fulfilment. Instead, we were in a makeshift settlement on an unfamiliar world, surrounded by dust and uncertainty, a landscape that seemed to stretch out before us like an endless sea of questions and doubts.

Sitting in silence, I grappled with a mix of worry and disappointment, my thoughts churning like a tempest within me. Questions assailed my mind, each one more pressing and urgent than the last. *How were we to build a life here, in this place that seemed so far removed from everything we had ever known? What was the purpose of this unexpected journey, this detour from the path we had believed was laid out before us? And most pressingly, where would we find shelter and rest when night fell, when the darkness closed in around us like a suffocating cloak?*

Paul's vague responses offered little reassurance, his words a flimsy balm that did little to soothe the ache of uncertainty that had taken root in my heart. I yearned for something more, for a clear sign or direction that would help us navigate this uncharted territory. But as I sat there, watching Greta's relentless pacing, I knew that my role as her partner and as the head of our family was to find a way through this uncertainty, to be the rock upon which she could lean in times of trouble.

It was my responsibility to provide stability and hope, to be the anchor in this storm of unfamiliarity. Yet, even as I sat there, trying to muster the strength to rise to the occasion, a part of me felt as lost as she did, as adrift in this sea of doubt and confusion. I prayed silently for guidance, for a sign or an indication of what our next steps should be. My faith had always been my compass, guiding me through life's challenges with a steady hand and an unwavering sense of purpose. Now, more than ever, I needed that faith to show me the way, to help me lead my family through this uncharted territory with the same strength and conviction that had always been my hallmark.

Paul's cautious approach interrupted my contemplation, drawing my attention to his tentative figure as he moved towards us with a hesitant step. "Mum, Dad. Can we talk?" he asked, his voice gentle, yet underlined with an unmistakable anxiety that resonated deeply with my own unsettled feelings. There was a vulnerability in his tone, a raw honesty that spoke to the weight of the moment.

As I looked up at him, a wave of empathy washed over me, a profound understanding of the burden that he carried. I could see the weight of responsibility in his eyes, the heavy mantle of decisions made and the consequences that were now unfolding around us like a tapestry of uncertainty and doubt. A part of me worried that he and Luke had become entangled in complexities far beyond their control, that they had stumbled into a web of intrigue and danger that threatened to consume us all. It pained me to think that my ability to guide and protect them in this unfamiliar environment might be limited, that I might be powerless to shield them from the storms that lay ahead.

Greta halted her pacing, her emotions spilling forth like a torrent, a tumult of feelings that had been simmering beneath her stern exterior for far too long. Her attention fixed on Paul, her eyes shimmering in the sunlight, reflecting the depth of her distress and the intensity of her pain. "Paul! How could you do this to us?" she exclaimed, her voice echoing with weariness and betrayal. "The New Jerusalem—it was all a lie!" The tremor in her voice, a blend of anger and a profound sense of betrayal, resonated through the air, amplifying the tension that crackled between us like an electrical current.

Hearing her words, a pang of pain struck deep within my heart, a searing ache that threatened to consume me whole. I had always harboured trust and faith in Paul and Luke, despite not always aligning with their decisions or agreeing with their life choices. The thought that they might have knowingly led us into a situation fraught with real danger was almost unbearable, a betrayal of the deepest kind. Yet, as my gaze once again fell upon the ghastly sight of the shadow panther's head, a symbol of the very real threats that surrounded us, doubts began to cloud my mind like a gathering storm.

The juxtaposition of Greta's palpable anguish and the stark reminder of the dangers that lurked in this new world left me wrestling with a maelstrom of emotions, a tempest of conflicting thoughts and feelings that threatened to tear me asunder. I struggled to reconcile my inherent trust in my sons with the harsh reality of our current situation, to find a way to bridge the gap between the love and loyalty I felt for them and the gnawing sense of unease that had taken root in my gut. *Could it be that their actions, however well-intentioned, had inadvertently placed us all in jeopardy? Could it be that their desire to do what they believed was right had led us down a path fraught with peril and uncertainty?*

I looked at Paul, searching for answers in his face, for any sign that might help me understand the choices that had led us here. It was crucial for me to grasp the full scope of what was at play, to comprehend the decisions that had shaped our path to this strange and perilous place. I needed to know the truth, to understand the motivations and the circumstances that had brought us to this point, so that I could find a way to lead my family through the challenges that lay ahead.

Paul's deep exhale resonated with the gravity of the moment, a tangible release of tension and regret that hung in the air between us. "I know, Mum, and I'm sorry. Luke— he thought he was doing the right thing," he said, his words heavy with the weight of responsibility and the burden of choices made. But there was a hesitation in his voice, a lack of conviction that sent a chill down my spine, as if even he was unsure of the path we had taken.

Meeting Paul's eyes, I tried to convey the tumult of disillusionment and confusion that raged within me. "We were prepared to leave everything behind, Paul," I began, my voice carrying the strength of my convictions, yet betraying the underlying anguish that tore at my heart. "For our faith. For our family. But this— I paused, momentarily overwhelmed, a small cough breaking the intensity of my speech. "This is not what we were promised." My words were a lament, a cry of despair that echoed through the stillness of the morning air, a testament to the depth of my disappointment and the intensity of my pain.

Paul moved to sit beside me, the bench creaking under our shared weight, a symbol of the shared burden that we now carried. His attempt to console us was palpable, a physical presence that sought to offer comfort in the midst of our distress. "I understand, and I'm sorry you were misled. But we're here now, and we need to make the best of it," he said, his words carrying a forced optimism, a desperate attempt to find a glimmer of hope in the darkness that surrounded us. But the uncertainty that laced his tone was unmistakable, a subtle undercurrent of doubt that belied his outward confidence.

In that moment, as I sat next to my son, a flood of conflicting emotions surged through me, a tidal wave of feeling that threatened to sweep me away. There was disappointment in the realisation that our leap of faith had brought us to a place so far removed from our expectations, a land that bore little resemblance to the promised paradise we had envisioned. There was a sense of betrayal, not just in the situation we found ourselves in, but in the notion that we had been led here under false pretences, that the trust we had placed in Paul and Luke had been misplaced.

Greta's agitated pacing resumed, her movements reflecting the turmoil that churned inside her like a raging tempest. "But we'll never go home again, will we?" she asked, her voice soaked in sadness, heavy with disbelief and despair, a poignant reminder of the magnitude of the sacrifice we had made. "I can't... I can't accept that." Her words were a plea, a desperate cry for reassurance in the face of an uncertain future, a future that seemed to stretch out before us like an endless expanse of questions and doubts.

As Paul reached out to take her hand gently, I observed a son trying to provide comfort in an uncomfortable truth, a truth that we all struggled to come to terms with. "Mum, I know this is hard," he said softly, his voice a soothing balm that sought to ease the ache of our collective pain. "It's hard for all of us."

I watched this exchange, feeling a swell of empathy for Paul, a profound understanding of the burden that he carried. As a father, it pained me to see any of my children in distress, regardless of the circumstances. Paul's struggles were as real as ours, a poignant reminder of how deeply interconnected our fates had become, how inextricably linked we were.

Paul continued with a sincerity that resonated with me, a depth of feeling that spoke to the strength of his character and the depth of his love for us all. "But we're together, and that's what matters. We'll build a new life here, a new home," he said, his words full of hope and determination, the kind of encouragement that I clung to in difficult times, the kind of assurance that I needed to hear in this moment of uncertainty and doubt.

However, Greta's reaction was telling, her body language rigid, a stark visual representation of the mental anguish that consumed her. Her sharp retort cut through the air like a knife, underscoring the pain that the thought of permanent separation from our past life brought her. "But we're not all together, are we!?" she snapped, her words laced with the anguish of our current fragmented reality, a reminder of the pieces of our family that were still missing, still lost to us.

Her response stung, a poignant reminder of the bigger picture that overshadowed our present predicament. It was true; we were not all together, not in the way that we had always been. The physical separation from several members of our family, from our church, and from the life we had known was like an open wound, a gaping hole in the fabric of our existence that threatened to unravel. Her words echoed in my mind, amplifying my own sense of loss and uncertainty.

In that moment, I realised the depth of the challenge before us, the magnitude of the task that we now faced. It wasn't just about adapting to a new environment or coming to terms with our unexpected journey. It was about reconciling with the loss of our former life, about finding a way to rebuild our sense of home and community in this new, landscape. It was about forging a new path forward, even as we mourned the one we had left behind.

Standing up, I felt a profound need to alleviate Greta's distress, to offer her some measure of comfort in the midst of her pain. Placing a firm, reassuring hand on her shoulder, I tried to offer her some solace, to be the rock that she needed in this moment. "He's right, Greta," I gently told her, my voice a soothing balm that sought to ease the ache of her soul. "We have each other, and that's more than many can say." My words were genuine, a heartfelt attempt to console her, but they seemed to barely scratch the surface of the deep-seated foreboding that enveloped us, the profound sense of unease that had taken root in our hearts.

Greta finally settled beside me on the bench, her body language exuding defeat, her breaths slow and heavy with the weight of her emotions. "I just miss our home, our church, our community," she confessed, her voice a soft lament that resonated with my own longing, a poignant reminder of all that we had left behind, all that we had sacrificed in the name of faith and family.

Paul's whisper broke through the thick air of nostalgia. "I miss them too," he said, his voice tinged with a raw honesty that revealed a vulnerability I hadn't seen before, a glimpse into the depths of his own struggle and the weight of the burden he carried. "But we have a chance to build something new here. Together," he added, his words attempting to infuse hope into our desolate situation.

Yet, despite Paul's intentions, his words only compounded the sense of isolation that gnawed at me, the profound feeling of disconnection from everything that we had once held dear. We were far from everything familiar, everything that we had known and loved. The concept of building something new, while hopeful, also felt daunting, a mountain that seemed impossible to climb in the face of our current circumstances. The familiarity of our old life, with its routines, its community, and its comforts, seemed like a distant memory, now replaced by the unknown challenges of Clivilius, a land that felt as foreign to me as the surface of the moon.

As I tightened my grip on Greta's shoulder, I felt the weight of our collective struggles resting heavily on me, a burden that threatened to crush me under its immense weight. I knew that I had to be the pillar of strength for Greta, to keep her from seeing the depth of my own doubts about our situation, the cracks in my own façade of confidence and faith. "Paul's right," I affirmed, my voice steady despite the internal battle to believe my own words, to find the strength to carry on in the face of overwhelming adversity. "We've always been a strong family. We can get through this, as long as we stick together." My words were a rallying cry, a call to arms in the face of an uncertain future.

Feeling Greta lean into me was a poignant reminder of the solace we found in each other's presence, the comfort that we drew from the warmth of our shared love and devotion. Her body language softened, and in that moment, her vulnerability was palpable, a glimpse into the depths of her own pain and the weight of the burden she carried. "I just need time, Noah. Time to adjust," she whispered, her voice a tender echo of our shared need for resilience in the face of adversity.

Paul, sensing the need to offer his support, moved closer and wrapped an arm around Greta, his touch a gentle reminder of the love that bound us all together. His gesture was a testament to the bond we shared as a family, a bond that had always been our anchor through every storm, our guiding light in the darkest of nights. "Take all the time you need, Mum," he reassured her gently. "We're here for you, always." His words were a promise, a vow of unwavering support and love.

In the midst of this solemn quietude, a faint smile found its way to my lips, a flicker of hope in the darkness that threatened to engulf us all. Despite the challenges we faced, there was comfort in knowing that our family's unity remained unbroken. Paul's words and actions were a gentle reminder of the love and support that bound us together, the glue that held us fast in the face of adversity. It was these very bonds that would help us navigate through the uncertainties of Clivilius, that would guide us through the storms that lay ahead and lead us to the promised land that we had always sought.

As the minutes ticked by, I could see Greta's anxiety mounting again. She resumed her pacing, each step mirroring the unrest that churned within her. The rhythmic pattern of her footsteps against the dusty ground created a soundtrack to the turmoil that enveloped her – a physical manifestation of her inner struggle.

Watching her, I felt a deep sense of helplessness. I wanted to ease her mind, to provide her with the comfort and security she so desperately sought. But I had no more options to give.

❖

As I sat there, the silence between Paul and me was finally broken by his hesitant voice, a tentative probe into the depths of my thoughts. "Dad?" he asked, his tone revealing an unease that mirrored my own.

I turned to him, my gaze meeting his, ready to listen with an open heart and an attentive ear. "Yes, Paul," I replied, ensuring my voice was steady, even though I could feel the seriousness of the conversation that was about to unfold.

Paul hesitated for a moment, as if gathering his thoughts, as if trying to find the right way to voice the questions that burned within him. Then the words came tumbling out in a rush, a torrent of emotion and curiosity that could no longer be contained. "I can't help it," he said, his words gaining momentum like a flood breaking through a dam, a force of nature that could not be denied. "I just have to know. What made you think that you were coming to the New Jerusalem here? Is Luke really that manipulative?" His questions were pointed, piercing, a direct challenge to the beliefs and assumptions that had brought us to this strange and unfamiliar place.

His question took me by surprise, a jolt of electricity that ran through my body like a current. I found myself struggling to suppress a smile, not out of amusement, but from the realisation of how I had been swept up in the fervour of our church's announcement about Salt Lake City, how I had allowed myself to be carried away by the tide of excitement and anticipation. Reflecting on our journey here, it dawned on me that Luke hadn't needed to exert much effort to spur me into action, that my own eagerness and anticipation for what I believed was a divine calling had blinded me to the possibility of misinterpretation or manipulation.

As I turned to face Paul, a cocktail of emotions swirled within me, each one vying for dominance, each one clamouring for attention. There was a heaviness in my chest, a mix of trepidation and an almost desperate need to unburden myself of the secret that had been weighing on me, the truth that had been gnawing at my soul like a hungry beast.

My gaze met Paul's, and in his eyes, I saw a reflection of my own turmoil, tinged with a child's trusting curiosity, a desire to understand and to make sense of things. "Paul, there's something I've wanted to tell you about what happened back home, well, before all of this," I said, my voice barely above a whisper, as if speaking louder might shatter the fragile moment, as if the words themselves were a delicate crystal that could be broken with the slightest breath.

Before I could gather my thoughts further, before I could find the words to express the depths of my own confusion and doubt, Greta cut in, her voice sharp like a blade slicing through the tense air, a jarring intrusion into the moment of vulnerability and honesty that Paul and I had been sharing.

Her frustration was as evident as the lines of worry etched on her face, a map of the trials and tribulations that had brought us to this point. "But we couldn't find you and you never answered your phone." Her words were laced with accusation, a pointed reminder of the distance that had grown between us, the gulf of silence and separation. I could sense the undercurrent of concern beneath her frustration, the love and fear that mingled together in a potent cocktail, but it didn't lessen the impact of her words, the sting of her reproach.

Paul's response, sombre and laden with unspoken understanding, served as a stark reminder of the ordeals he must have endured, the trials and tribulations that had brought him to this place. "Well, now you know why," he said, his voice a low echo of the pain and confusion he must have felt, a reflection of the turmoil that had gripped his own soul.

Meanwhile, Greta's continued huffing, punctuating the silence like a metronome, underscored her ongoing distress. It was a sound that revealed her struggle to grapple with the situation, her emotions a tumultuous sea in the quiet sands of Clivilius, a tempest that threatened to sweep us all away.

Leaning in, Paul's face was a canvas of concern and encouragement. "What is it, Dad?" he probed gently, his eyes searching mine for answers, for some glimmer of understanding in the midst of the confusion that swirled around us like a whirlwind. His question, simple yet loaded with significance, nudged me towards the precipice of revelation, towards the edge of a truth that I had been holding back for far too long.

I felt a surge of paternal protectiveness, mixed with the fear of how my words might alter the fabric of our relationship, how they might change the way my son saw me forever. Yet, there was also a sliver of hope, a faint glimmer that by sharing my truth, I might bridge the chasm that had unwittingly formed between us, that I might find a way to connect with him on a deeper level than ever before.

I took a deep breath, feeling the weight of the moment settle on my shoulders like a heavy cloak, a mantle of responsibility and truth that I could no longer avoid. My gaze drifted towards the distant horizon, a line where the earth seemed to meet the sky in a tranquil embrace, a point of convergence that seemed to hold the answers to all of life's mysteries. It was a view that often brought me peace, a sense of calm in the midst of the storms that raged within me, but now, it served as a reminder of the vast, uncharted territory of my own thoughts and feelings, a landscape that I had yet to fully explore. I wondered whether any of what I was about to reveal really mattered now, whether the truth of our past had any bearing on the reality of our present.

"Last Sunday," I began, my voice tinged with a hint of nostalgia, a familiar excitement resurgent as the words left my lips, as if the very act of speaking them aloud had transported me back to that moment in time. I could almost smell the incense and feel the solemnity of that day, the reverence and awe that had filled the air like a tangible presence. "Your mother and I were invited to a special meeting at the Temple by the Bishop. It was a sacred gathering, with selected members of the church and one of the Twelve Apostles." My eyes glimmered with the memory of the reverence and awe that had filled the air during that meeting, the joy of being among the chosen few, the sense of purpose and destiny that had gripped my soul like a vice.

Paul remained silent, his expression a still canvas, yet his eyes, attentive and deep, were listening intently, absorbing every word that fell from my lips like a sponge. I could see him processing each piece of information, trying to fit this new puzzle piece into the chaotic jigsaw of recent events, attempting to make sense of the revelations that were unfolding before him like a map to an unknown destination.

"They told us that the Lord was gathering His elect," I pressed on, my voice a blend of reverence and earnestness, a testament to the depth of my own faith and conviction. Each word I spoke was imbued with the fervour and conviction that had gripped me that day, a feeling that was both exhilarating and overwhelming, a rush of emotion that had left me breathless and dizzy with anticipation. "We were preparing to relocate to Salt Lake City soon, to join other Saints and start building the New Jerusalem." The vision of a new beginning, a utopian dream, flickered in my mind's eye, so vivid it was almost tangible, a promise of a brighter future that had filled my heart with hope and joy.

A light frown formed on Paul's weary face, etching lines of confusion and concern. "But Dad," he said, his voice tinged with a mix of incredulity and a desperate need to understand. His brows knitting together, a sign of his inner turmoil.

"Walking through a Portal? How did you reconcile that with your beliefs?" His question was pointed, a direct challenge to the very foundation of my faith, a probe into the depths of my own convictions and assumptions.

I chuckled, a short, soft sound that floated in the air between us. Paul had instantly hit the nail on the head, pinpointing the very essence of my dilemma with his keen insight, his ability to cut through the noise and get to the heart of the matter. As I self-reflected on my impulsiveness, a sense of irony tickled the edges of my mind, a reminder of the folly of human nature and the dangers of blind faith.

"I guess I saw it as a sign, an opportunity provided by the Lord." My words came out slowly, each one heavy with the weight of introspection, a testament to the depth of my own self-examination and doubt. I paused, my gaze drifting off into a distant point, as if searching for answers in the vast expanse of the universe, as if the very fabric of reality held the key to unlocking the mysteries that had brought me to this moment. There was a certain raw honesty in admitting this to myself, let alone to my son, a vulnerability that laid bare the depths of my own uncertainty and confusion.

"Maybe I stretched my belief a bit too far, but it felt right at the moment," I finished, my voice trailing off slightly, as if the words themselves were a fragile thread that threatened to unravel at any moment. The words hung in the air, a complex interplay of faith and doubt, a reminder of the delicate balance that we all must strike in the face of the unknown and the unknowable. I was unable to bring myself to accept that the Lord had completely abandoned us yet, and deep down, I clung to the belief that this was somehow all connected, that there was a larger purpose at work that we had yet to fully comprehend.

"It's hard to make sense of it all, isn't it?" Paul's voice broke through my thoughts, the reflection in his voice clear and penetrating, a mirror that reflected the depths of my own soul back at me.

My eyes met Paul's, and in that moment, they suddenly swelled with the energy of my unwavering faith that had guided me my whole life, a flame that had never been extinguished, no matter how dark the night had become. It was a faith that had been my compass, my anchor in stormy seas, a light that had illuminated the path before me, even when all else seemed lost.

"It is, Paul. But I have faith that we're here for a reason. Maybe this is our New Jerusalem, just not in the way we expected." As I spoke, my voice grew stronger, imbued with a conviction that transcended the uncertainties of our present circumstances, a belief in a grander design, a larger purpose that we were yet to understand, but that held the key to our ultimate salvation and redemption.

Paul smiled softly, a tender, understanding expression that seemed to acknowledge the depth of my faith, the strength of my convictions in the face of overwhelming adversity. He placed a hand on my shoulder, a gesture of comfort and solidarity.

"I admire your faith, Dad. You just walked through a Portal and yet you still believe. That's really something." His words, simple yet profound, were a balm to my soul, a reminder of the power of belief and the resilience of the human spirit. In his eyes, I saw not just the love of a son, but the respect of a young man who had witnessed his father grapple with the unthinkable, yet hold fast to his beliefs. It was a moment of connection, a bridge across generations, fortified by faith and love.

I reciprocated Paul's emotion with a warm smile of my own, the corners of my mouth lifting in a gentle expression of shared understanding, a reflection of the love and respect that flowed between us like a river. As I placed a hand atop his, I felt the warmth of our connection, a tangible link between father and son, a bond that could never be broken, no matter what trials and tribulations we faced.

"Faith is a powerful ally, son. When our actions reflect our convictions, we can do miracles," I told him, feeling a firm resolve swelling within me, a sense of purpose and destiny that had been rekindled by the flames of our shared belief. The words flowed from a place deep within, a reservoir of belief and strength that had long been my guide, a wellspring of hope and resilience that had sustained me through the darkest of nights and the most trying of times.

"Even building a New Jerusalem in the desert," I added, my voice carrying a hint of wistfulness, a dream that had not yet been extinguished, a vision of a better tomorrow that still lived within my heart. As I said this, I gestured towards the dusty expanse that surrounded us, the barren landscape stretching out like a blank canvas, awaiting transformation by hands guided by faith and purpose.

In the ensuing quiet that enveloped our contemplative state, the world around us seemed to pause, as if giving space for our thoughts to breathe, as if the very fabric of reality was bending to accommodate the depth of our introspection and reflection.

"Actually, it's called Bixbus," Paul said softly, yet matter-of-factly, breaking the silence with a gentle reminder of the reality that surrounded us, a grounding force that brought us back to the present moment, back to the challenges and opportunities that lay before us.

As our eyes met, we chuckled lightly.

Meanwhile, Greta, seemingly inconspicuous of our conversation, continued her pacing, her movements restless and agitated, her worries remained unabated, a storm that raged within her, threatening to consume her from the inside out. Each step she took seemed to echo her inner turmoil, a relentless rhythm of concern and anxiety, a drumbeat that pounded in my ears like a call to action.

The brief levity with Paul quickly faded, replaced by a tight knot forming in the pit of my stomach as I turned my attention to Greta, a sense of unease and concern that gnawed at my insides like a hungry beast. Observing her, I contemplated how to ease her inner conflict, a task that seemed as daunting as reshaping the barren desert into a promised land, a challenge that would require all of my strength and wisdom, all of my faith and conviction. Her worries, if left unchecked, threatened to consume not just her but all of us, a cancer that would eat away at the very fabric of our family, leaving us broken and lost in the wilderness of our own doubts and fears. It was a challenge that I knew we needed to address, for our unity and strength depended on it, for the future of our family and the destiny that lay before us hung in the balance, waiting for us to seize it with both hands and never let go.

ENGAGING CHARLES

4338.213.5

Unable to help myself, despite the glaring brightness of the day that rendered the act almost unnecessary, I had thrown several logs onto the dying embers of the campfire. Now, I found myself sitting, almost mesmerised, watching the flames eagerly devour them, their flickering tongues licking at the wood with a voracious appetite. There was something about the predictable nature of fire burning wood that provided me with the faintest glimmer of normality, a comforting constant in what had become a day filled with unpredictability. It was a small act, yet in that moment, it felt like anchoring myself to a reality I understood, one where cause and effect still held sway, where the laws of nature remained unchanged by the upheaval that had swept us into this new world.

Greta sat beside me, her eyes, lost in the flickering dance of the flames, seemed to gaze through them, perhaps searching for her own piece of tranquility or maybe just absorbed in thought, a brief respite from the turmoil that had gripped her soul. Paul, bless his heart, had made several attempts to soothe her, putting forth efforts that were both tender and persistent. Yet, they had been to no avail, his words and gestures seeming to bounce off the walls of worry and uncertainty that surrounded her like an impenetrable fortress. The weight of worry and uncertainty she carried seemed a heavy cloak, resistant to the balm of comforting words, a burden that she bore with a stoic determination that both awed and concerned me.

As we sat there, the distant hums of shed building by the others in our group faded into the background, their industrious noises dwindling until they seemed like a distant memory, a remnant of a world that had been left behind. This gradual quietude enveloped us in a somewhat pleasant state of quiet, a rare pause in the day's worries, a moment of stillness. It was as if the world around us had decided to take a brief respite, allowing us a moment of peace amid the upheaval, a chance to catch our breath and gather our thoughts before the next wave of uncertainty crashed over us.

In this tranquility, my thoughts wandered, meandering through the events that had led us here, the choices made, and the paths yet to be travelled, a labyrinth of decisions and consequences that seemed to stretch out before us like an endless maze.

The fire before me became a focal point, not just of physical warmth but of reflection, a place where I could sift through the tangled threads of our lives and try to make sense of the tapestry that had been woven around us. I found myself pondering the nature of faith and the role it had played in our journey, the way it had both guided and challenged us, leading us to this moment of reckoning in a strange and unfamiliar land.

Suddenly, the calm of our contemplative silence was shattered by the sound of urgent footsteps, a jarring intrusion into the peaceful bubble that had surrounded us. Jerome came bolting through the camp's gate, his legs propelling him straight towards us with a fervour that instantly piqued my curiosity, a sense of urgency and excitement that seemed to crackle in the air around him. The excitement was palpable in his every movement, his hands tightly clutching something that seemed to be the source of his rush, a treasure that he held close to his chest like a talisman.

"Paul, you won't believe this!" Jerome managed to gasp out between his laboured breaths as he neared us, his face flushed from exertion, his eyes wide with a mix of disbelief and elation. His words, ripe with anticipation, stirred a sense of intrigue within me, a curiosity that burned like a flame in my chest, demanding to be satisfied.

Out of the corner of my eye, I caught Greta's reaction; her startled look and wide, panicked eyes were impossible to ignore. Instinctively, I placed a comforting hand on her thigh, hoping to offer some semblance of reassurance amidst the sudden disruption, a silent reminder that we were in this together, no matter what lay ahead.

"What's going on, Jerome?" Paul asked, his tone mirroring the curiosity that had taken hold of me, a sense of urgency and concern that seemed to hang in the air between us like a tangible presence.

Jerome opened his hand to reveal the treasure he carried - bundles of clean Australian notes, their crisp edges and vibrant colours a stark contrast to the dusty surroundings of the camp. The sight was so out of place, so unexpected in our current setting, that it took me a moment to process what I was seeing, to reconcile the familiar with the unfamiliar in a way that made sense.

"Beatrix and this new Guardian, Jarod, they brought us all this cash!" Jerome announced, his excitement undimmed, his voice ringing out like a clarion call in the stillness of the afternoon.

My brow furrowed in confusion, a thousand questions swirling in my mind like leaves caught in a whirlwind. Stealing a quick glance around me, I pondered the implications, the meaning behind this sudden influx of currency in a place that seemed so far removed from the trappings of modern society. *Why would they bring cash here, of all places?* It hardly seemed like it would serve any practical purpose in our current circumstances, a world where survival and faith seemed to be the only currencies that mattered.

"Cash?" Paul echoed, his voice tinged with a mixture of concern and bewilderment. "Where did all this come from?" His question hung in the air, a plea for understanding in a situation that seemed to defy explanation.

Jerome's broad smile glimmered in his eyes, a beacon of his unwavering enthusiasm as he handed Paul and I several of the crisp notes, their texture and weight a strange comfort in the midst of the unfamiliar. "I don't know the full story. Beatrix was in a rush. Something about it being time-sensitive." His words carried a sense of urgency, a hint of something larger at play that we had yet to fully comprehend.

As I held the notes in my hand, the texture of the paper between my fingers felt oddly grounding, yet simultaneously surreal. The situation presented a paradox; the familiar tactile sensation of currency juxtaposed against the backdrop of our unfamiliar surroundings, a jarring contrast that left me feeling off-balance and unsure. My mind raced with questions, the foremost being the purpose behind this unexpected windfall and the implications it held for us, the way it might shape our future.

Paul, with his typical resolve, seemed ready to leap into action. "We need to find out what's going on," he declared, his voice carrying a determination that I had come to know well, a reminder of the strength and resilience that ran through our family like a current. It was a call to action, a reminder that we were not just passive observers in our fate, but active participants in the unfolding drama of our lives.

"Wait, the laptop," Jerome interjected, his words halting Paul in his tracks, a sudden shift in the conversation that caught us all off guard. He reached out, grasping Paul's arm with urgency, his eyes wide with a mix of excitement and trepidation. "Luke said we can talk to Charles with it." His suggestion was a beacon of hope, a potential lifeline to understanding and possibly influencing our rapidly evolving situation, a chance to reconnect with the world we had left behind and the loved ones we had been separated from.

At the mention of Charles, a spark of interest ignited within Greta, a flicker of life in the darkness that had seemed to envelop her since our arrival in Bixbus. Her reaction was instantaneous, her head snapping up as her attention, previously scattered, now honed in on Jerome's words like a laser beam. "Charles?" she repeated, her voice a mix of hope and urgency, a desperate plea for connection and reassurance. "Is he ready to come through?"

Jerome's response, accompanied by an infectious grin, seemed to light a fire under Greta, a spark of energy and purpose that had been missing since our arrival. "He should be home from school any minute now. Luke's waiting for him." His words were like a catalyst, propelling Greta into motion with a suddenness that took us all by surprise, a reminder of the fierce love and determination that had always been at the core of her being.

As Greta moved with purpose toward the gate, I found myself compelled to follow. The urgency of the moment pulled me to my feet, and I rushed after her, driven by a mix of concern, curiosity, and an unwavering commitment to our collective well-being, a need to be there for my family in whatever way I could. The possibility of communicating with Charles, of bridging the gap between our current reality and the life we knew, was a thread of hope in the tangled web of our circumstances, a reminder that even in the midst of the unknown, there were still ties that bound us together, still anchors that kept us grounded and connected.

As I followed Greta, my mind raced with possibilities and questions, a whirlwind of thoughts and emotions that threatened to overwhelm me. *What would we say to Charles? How would we explain the incredible journey that had brought us to this strange and unfamiliar place?* And most importantly, how would we convince him to join us, to take that leap of faith and step through the portal into a world that defied explanation and understanding?

❖

"Do you really think we should bring Charles here, too?" The words tumbled out of me, heavy with concern, as we made our ascent up the final sandy hill. The terrain was unforgiving. Each step was a struggle, my feet sinking into the shifting sands, the heat of the sun beating down on my back like a physical weight. It was a landscape that seemed to resist our every move, a silent challenge to our determination to press forward.

Greta halted, the urgency in her steps giving way to a moment of contemplation as she turned to face me. Her expression was resolute, etched with a determination that I had seen on rare occasions. It was the look of a mother bear protecting her cubs, fierce and unyielding, a force of nature that would not be denied. "I don't know where we are, and I don't really understand any of this," she confessed, her voice wavering not with uncertainty, but with a raw emotion that underscored the gravity of our situation. "But I'll be damned if I'm going to be separated from my children." The quiver in her voice belied a steely resolve, a testament to the depth of her maternal instinct, the unbreakable bond that tied her to our offspring.

I could only nod in solemn acknowledgment, my own emotions caught in my throat, a lump that threatened to choke off my words. Greta's choice of words, so uncharacteristic of her usual demeanour, spoke volumes. It was a rare glimpse into the depth of her resolve, a reminder that some bonds were unbreakable, transcending even the most extraordinary circumstances. In that moment, I understood that no logic or reasoning would deter her; her decision was made in the unspoken depths of a mother's love, a place where rationality held no sway.

We resumed our journey, the silence between us filled with an unspoken understanding, a shared commitment to the path we had chosen. As we climbed, the sand underfoot shifted treacherously. My foot slipped, and I found myself momentarily on my knees, the fine, hot sand infiltrating my shoes, a gritty reminder of our vulnerable position in this new and challenging landscape.

Pulling myself up, I brushed off the sand, a futile gesture against the pervasive grains that seemed to cling to every surface, a constant reminder of the harshness of our surroundings. Yet, it was a moment of clarity, a realisation that struck me with the force of a revelation. Greta's unwavering determination to reunite our family, against all odds, was a beacon of hope in the vast uncertainty that stretched out before us. In her resolve, I found my own strength solidifying, a commitment to face whatever this new world threw at us, together, as a family. We would not be broken, not by the sands of Bixbus or the trials that lay ahead.

As Greta came to an abrupt halt at the crest of the hill, she planted her hands firmly on her hips, a gesture of defiance against the unknown, a physical manifestation of her refusal to be cowed by the challenges that confronted us. "I don't think that was there before," she stated with a bluntness that cut through the desert air, her voice carrying a mix of surprise and apprehension.

"What wasn't?" My voice was breathless from the climb, my chest heaving as I finally reached her side, eager to see what had captured her attention so completely. I squinted against the glare of the sun, my hand shielding my eyes as I scanned the horizon, searching for the source of her concern.

"That," she said, extending an arm to point into the distance, her finger unwavering as it directed my gaze towards the unfamiliar sight that had stopped her in her tracks. My eyes trailed the line of her finger, and what I saw rooted me to the spot, a chill running down my spine despite the oppressive heat of the day. There, beside the original Portal, stood a second, much larger gateway. It loomed ominously, a silent sentinel that heralded unknown changes to our already uncertain world. The sight of it sent a visceral knot of anxiety twisting in my gut, a tangible manifestation of my utter bewilderment. *How could this have appeared so suddenly?* My mind raced, trying to piece together a puzzle for which I had no reference points, the burgeoning headache a testament to the futility of my attempts to understand a world that no longer adhered to any rules I knew.

"But where's Charles?" Greta's voice, tinged with a mix of confusion and concern, snapped me back to the immediate crisis, the reason for our frantic climb to the top of this sandy hill. Her face contorted with worry, a mirror to the turmoil I felt inside, the fear that gripped my heart at the thought of our son, alone and vulnerable in a world that seemed to shift and change with every passing moment.

Without another word, she turned and began her descent down the hill, each step deliberate, a physical manifestation of her resolve to find our son and bring him back to the safety of our family.

"Greta! Wait!" I called out after her, my voice laced with urgency, a plea for caution in the face of the unknown. But she was already moving, her figure growing smaller as she navigated the treacherous terrain with a speed and agility that belied her years.

I followed in her wake, more cautious now, the memory of my earlier stumble a reminder of the need to navigate this new world with care. Each step I took was measured, a balance between my instinctive desire to rush to her side and the practical need to ensure I remained upright. The sand shifted beneath my feet, a constant reminder of the instability that surrounded us, the sense that the ground could give way at any moment, leaving us floundering in a sea of uncertainty.

As I made my way down the hill, my mind raced with the implications of the new Portal, the questions that swirled in my head like the sand that danced around my ankles. *What did it mean? Where did it lead? And why had it appeared now, just as we were on the cusp of reuniting with our son?* The coincidence seemed too great to be chance, a sign that the forces at work in this strange new world were beyond our comprehension, beyond our control.

But even as these thoughts threatened to overwhelm me, I clung to the one thing that anchored me, the one constant in the midst of the chaos: my family. Greta's determination, her unwavering commitment to our children, was a beacon of hope in the darkness, a reminder that we were not alone in this struggle. And Charles, wherever he was, was a part of that family, a piece of the puzzle that we would not rest until we had found and brought back into the fold.

❖

As we approached the scene, the sight that unfolded before me was nothing short of surreal. There, amidst the dusty hills and barren landscape, stood a young woman whose presence seemed almost ethereal, a figure plucked from the pages of a fantasy novel and dropped into the harsh reality of Clivilius. Her long, flowing silver hair cascaded down her shoulders, catching the light in a way that made it seem like a living, shimmering entity, a river of molten metal that defied the laws of nature. The area around her was littered with stacks of money, crisp bills fluttering in the gentle breeze, creating a stark contrast against the natural backdrop, a jarring juxtaposition of the mundane and the extraordinary.

My mind raced to connect the dots, to make sense of the scene before me, and I quickly surmised that this must be Beatrix, the Guardian that Jerome had mentioned earlier, the mysterious figure who had brought this unexpected windfall to our doorstep.

"Quite the haul, huh?" Her voice, light and amused, cut through my astonishment like a knife through butter, a playful reminder of the absurdity of our situation. Her grin was wide, almost mischievously so, as if she was in on a secret that the rest of us were yet to discover, a private joke that only she was privy to.

I found myself momentarily lost for words, my mouth opening and closing in a silent stammer, a fish out of water in the face of this bizarre new reality. It was only when I noticed her gaze wasn't fixed on Greta or me that I turned, following her line of sight, my eyes landing on the approaching figures of Paul and Jerome. They were hurrying towards us, their expressions a mix of curiosity and concern.

"This one," Beatrix said, gesturing towards the larger Portal with a casual ease, as if it were nothing more than a door to a room in her house, "seems to be linked to me and Jarod." Her tone suggested a familiarity with the Portal that I couldn't begin to fathom, a level of understanding that seemed to defy the very laws of nature and reason.

Paul's response was measured, his brow furrowed as he took in the significance of her statement, the implications of her words sinking in like a lead weight. "How did you manage this?" His voice carried a weight of concern, reflecting the myriad of questions swirling in my own mind.

It was Jerome's voice that brought me back from my thoughts, his use of "Dad" pulling me sharply into the moment, a tether that grounded me in the here and now. I turned to him, his face alight with a hopeful excitement that felt like a balm to the surrealness of the day.

"What, son?" I asked, feeling a mix of apprehension and anticipation, a sense that the next words out of his mouth would hold the key to our future, to the path that lay ahead.

Jerome's smile was infectious. As he held up the laptop, his next words felt like a beacon of hope. "Let's talk to Charles," he said, his voice filled with a determination that belied his years, a strength that I couldn't help but admire.

I nodded, a gesture of silent gratitude towards Jerome for taking the lead, for being the rock that we all needed in this moment of uncertainty. The complexities of our situation had rendered me introspective, often lost in thought, a man adrift in a sea of questions and doubts.

Paul and Beatrix's conversation, important as it was, became a distant murmur against the backdrop of my immediate concern: the safety and well-being of our family, the need to bring us all together in the face of this new world. Greta and I, united in our apprehension and hope, trailed behind Jerome as he led us toward the first Portal—the very same vortex of colours that had served as our unexpected gateway to Clivilius, the doorway to a reality that we were still struggling to comprehend.

"Why do we need to talk to him with that?" Greta's question pierced the air, her confusion and desperation evident in her furrowed brow, the lines etched on her face like a map of the turmoil that raged within her. "Can't we just bring him straight here?" Her words were a plea, a desperate cry for the simplicity and comfort of the familiar, for the reassurance that our family would be whole once more.

I made an attempt to speak, to offer some words of comfort and explanation, but Jerome beat me to it, his voice tinged with a hint of sarcasm that belied the seriousness of the moment. "Do you really expect Charles to simply walk through a giant wall of swirling colours?" he asked, his eyebrows raised in a silent challenge.

A soft sigh escaped my lips, a quiet acknowledgment of our shared leap into the unknown, the journey that had brought us to this strange and unfamiliar place. "We did," I murmured, a reflection not just on our physical journey but the emotional and psychological leaps we had taken since arriving here, the way our lives had been turned upside down in the blink of an eye.

Jerome's curious gaze, imbued with a twinkle of mischief, held a silent question, a playful challenge that seemed to dance in his eyes. "I still haven't figured out quite how that all happened yet," he mused, his words a reminder of the mysteries that still surrounded us, the questions that lingered like ghosts in the shadows of our minds.

"I think we can save that conversation for later," Greta chimed in, clearly itching to make contact with Charles, to hear his voice and know that he was safe.

As the Portal before us burst into life, a kaleidoscope of colours swirling into a spectacular display, a dazzling array of hues that seemed to defy description, Luke stepped through this vibrant gateway, embodying our only link to understanding and possibly controlling these forces. "Ready to talk to Charles?" he inquired, his gaze settling on Jerome.

Without a moment's hesitation, Jerome affirmed, his actions mirroring his resolve, a determination that seemed to radiate from every fibre of his being. He positioned himself before the laptop, a bridge between worlds, with a focus that was almost reverent. As he connected the device to the network cable that ran through the Portal, a tangible link to the familiar, to the world we had left behind, Greta knelt beside him, her presence a silent support, her anticipation a mirror to my own.

My gaze wandered, momentarily catching on Paul and Beatrix, their conversation a background hum to the main event unfolding before us, a reminder of the practicalities that still needed to be addressed even in the face of the extraordinary. "We need to keep this cash safe. My motorhome?" Paul suggested, his practicality surfacing in the midst of our extraordinary circumstances.

Beatrix, her attention divided between the piles of cash and the screen where our future communications would unfold, nodded in agreement, her mind clearly working on multiple levels at once. "Sounds like a plan. I'll help you move it," she said, her decision marking a temporary diversion from the main narrative, her own detour on the road to reuniting our family.

"He's answering!" Jerome's voice, crackling with excitement, acted as a beacon, drawing our collective attention to the small, glowing screen, the window into a world that seemed both impossibly distant and tantalisingly close. The moment Charles's face materialised, his features familiar and yet somehow new in the context of our current situation, it was as though reality had folded upon itself, creating a bridge between the mundane and the extraordinary, a connection that defied the very laws of time and space.

My pulse quickened, a mix of anxiety and elation coursing through me, a heady cocktail of emotions that threatened to overwhelm me. Greta's earlier confession, her admission of not understanding any of this, echoed in my thoughts. I found myself in rare, complete agreement with her sentiment, a recognition of the sheer scope of the unknown that stretched out before us like an endless expanse.

Despite the confusion and the fear, the burgeoning excitement at the prospect of our family, our unit, being together in this unfathomable situation was undeniable. It was a reassurance, a silent vow that no matter the odds, our unity would be our strength, our bond the foundation upon which we would build our future.

"Hey, Charles!" Jerome's voice, laden with brotherly affection, cut through the tension, reaching out across the digital divide, a connection that transcended the barriers of space and time.

Charles's response, light-hearted and jovial, was a splash of normality in the sea of the unknown, a reminder of the simple joys and pleasures that had once been the hallmarks of our everyday lives. "Yo, Jerome! Where the heck are you? Looks kinda bright and dusty out there," he said, his cheerfulness a stark contrast to the oddity of our situation, the sheer absurdity of the scene unfolding before us. His words, so typical of a conversation one might have after a day at the beach or a hike, felt jarringly out of place given the backdrop of our current reality.

Greta's sudden movement, driven by a mother's desperate need to connect with her child, to reassure herself of his safety and well-being, brought a moment of chaos to the fragile connection, a reminder of the raw emotions that simmered beneath the surface of our carefully maintained composure. She leaned in, her action almost toppling the laptop from Jerome's grasp, her eagerness bordering on recklessness in the face of her overwhelming need to hear her son's voice, to know that he was still a part of our world even in the midst of this upheaval.

"Whoa, Mum! Hold on there!" Jerome's exclamation, a mix of surprise and admonishment, momentarily broke the spell, a reminder of the delicate balance that needed to be struck in this moment of reconnection. Charles's laughter, booming through the speakers, was a balm to our frayed nerves, a reminder of the joy and light that he brought into our lives.

"Hey, mum," Charles's voice, casual and warm, filled the air, sparking a visible wave of relief in Greta's posture, a physical manifestation of the weight that had been lifted from her shoulders at the sound of his voice. Her desperation to ensure his safety was palpable, her movements abrupt and filled with maternal concern, a reflection of the primal instinct that drove her every action in this moment. "Charles! Are you okay?" she asked, her voice laced with urgency, her hands nearly sending the laptop tumbling from Jerome's grasp once more. Charles's reply came through, somewhat muffled, lost amidst the shuffling and the slight chaos of the moment.

Jerome's eyes met mine, conveying a silent plea for intervention, a mutual understanding that Greta's overwhelming concern, though born from love, needed a gentle check for the conversation to proceed smoothly, for the reunion to unfold as it should. Recognising the delicacy of the situation, and knowing that persuading Greta to temper her maternal instincts was a Herculean task best left for later, I responded to Jerome's unspoken request with a soft, apologetic shrug, a silent acknowledgement of the complexities of family dynamics. He nodded, a silent acknowledgement of the understanding that passed between us, and refocused his attention on Charles.

As I placed a reassuring hand on Greta's shoulder, a gesture meant to offer comfort and support in the face of her overwhelming emotions, she jumped, startled by the sudden contact. It was a simple gesture, meant to ground her, to remind her of the support that surrounded her, even in this otherworldly situation.

"Charles," Jerome's voice, firm yet warm, cut through the tension as he steadied the laptop with deliberate care, his focus unwavering. "Come to Clivilius," he said, his words simple yet profound, a straightforwardness that left no room for ambiguity or misinterpretation.

Charles's laughter, loud and unburdened, echoed around us, a sound so familiar yet so surreal in this alien landscape, a reminder of the simple joys and pleasures that had once been the hallmarks of our everyday lives. "I dunno, I can have all the computer time I want if I stay here," he joked, his humour a welcome respite from the weight of our circumstances.

I found myself smiling, an involuntary reaction to Charles's jest. His humour, a defining trait of his personality, had always been a source of lightness in our family. Despite the gravity of our situation, his ability to inject levity into the conversation was a testament to his resilience and his spirit. Charles, with his jokes and his easy laughter, had a way of diffusing tension.

Jerome's posture shifted, leaning forward with a conspiratorial urgency as he addressed the laptop screen, his voice a blend of pleading and jest, a reflection of the complex web of emotions that swirled within us all. "Please, Charles," he hissed, a mock desperation in his tone, a playful attempt to sway his brother's decision. "Don't leave me here alone with mum!" The intimacy of the moment, a brother's playful plea for solidarity, was palpable.

Greta's response was swift and affectionate, a playful whack across the side of Jerome's head, a gesture familiar and filled with the unspoken language of family life, the shorthand of love and understanding that had been honed over years of shared experiences and challenges. It was a moment of light-hearted reprimand, echoing the countless times she had navigated the thin line between discipline and love.

Charles's laughter, booming through the laptop's speakers, served as a testament to the bond they shared, a family unafraid to find humour amidst uncertainty, a reminder of the resilience and strength that lay at the core of our unit.

Turning to Greta, I found her momentarily distracted by the exchange, her maternal instincts always on alert, her focus divided between the conversation unfolding before us and the myriad of concerns that swirled within her mind.

"Greta," I began, my voice aimed to draw her back from the brink of worry, my hand finding her arm, a touch meant to reassure and guide, to offer a measure of comfort. "Why don't we step away for a bit. Jerome knows what he is doing," I encouraged, hoping to ease the tension that clung to her like a shadow, to offer a moment of respite from the weight of her fears and concerns.

Her reaction, a solid pout, was both expected and deeply human, a visual sigh that spoke volumes about the depth of her emotions. Reluctantly, she nodded, allowing me to lead us a few steps aside, creating a physical and emotional space from the unfolding negotiation.

As we stood apart, Greta's vulnerability surfaced, her bottom lip trembling slightly. "Noah," she said, her voice a whisper of fear, a reflection of the uncertainties that plagued her every waking moment. "I don't like our family being separated like this." The weight of her words hung between us, a shared apprehension for the unknown.

In response, I pulled her close, an instinctual move to offer comfort and assurance. My arms wrapped around her, a cocoon of warmth and protection, a silent promise that we would weather this storm together. Planting a soft kiss atop her head, I whispered promises of reassurance, my voice a balm to her troubled soul. "It'll all be fine," I murmured, infusing my voice with as much conviction as I could muster, a reflection of the faith and hope that had always been our guiding light. "Charles is a smart kid. He's got Jerome and Luke helping him with the decision."

It was a moment of intimacy and vulnerability, standing in the shadow of a giant, swirling Portal, miles from home, yet bound by the unbreakable ties of family, the love and devotion that had always been our anchor in the midst of life's storms. In the vast uncertainty of Clivilius, it was our unity, our shared strength and love, that offered the most profound sense of security, a reminder that we were not alone in this journey, that we had each other to lean on and draw strength from.

Greta's gaze met mine, a silent conversation passing between us, a moment of connection that transcended words and spoke directly to the heart. In her eyes, I saw a flicker of hope.

"Perhaps we should say a prayer?" she suggested, her voice a mix of vulnerability and strength.

I nodded in agreement, "Okay," I said, my voice soft and filled with understanding, a recognition of the power of faith and the solace that could be found in the act of prayer.

Together, we clasped hands, a symbol of the unbreakable bond that held us together. The act of bowing our heads in prayer was a surrender, an acknowledgement of our reliance on something greater than ourselves, a recognition of the divine guidance and protection that had always been our compass. The silence that enveloped us was profound, filled with the unsaid prayers of our hearts, the hopes and fears that we laid bare before the God who had always been our rock and our refuge.

I glanced at Greta, caught off guard by the slight misunderstanding, a momentary lapse in communication that spoke to the depth of our emotions and the weight of the moment. "I thought you were going to say it," she admitted, her voice tinged with a soft humour that belied the seriousness of our situation.

Nodding silently, I took the lead, a responsibility that I had always taken seriously, a reflection of my role as the head of our family and the spiritual guide that I had always strived to be. With a deep breath, I sought to calm the storm of thoughts racing through my mind, searching for the words that could convey the depth of our fears and hopes, the prayers that lay heavy on our hearts.

"Dear Heavenly Father," I began, my voice low and steady, a beacon of strength and faith. The prayer that unfolded was simple yet heartfelt, a request for protection and guidance not only for Charles but for all our children, a plea for the strength and wisdom to navigate the challenges that lay ahead. The sincerity of our plea, seemed to fill the space around us, a tangible presence that wrapped us in a blanket of comfort and peace.

As I continued, I could hear Greta's soft sobs, a sound that tugged at my heart, a reminder of the depth of her love and the weight of her fears. I squeezed her hands tighter, a silent promise of my unwavering support and love, a physical reminder that she was not alone in this journey, that we would face whatever lay ahead together, hand in hand and heart to heart. Our prayer was a pledge of faith, an acceptance of the journey that lay before us, regardless of where it might lead, a recognition of the divine plan that had brought us to this moment and the trust that we placed in the hands of a loving God.

In that moment, with our heads bowed and hearts open, I felt a profound sense of peace, a stillness that settled over me like a gentle breeze, a reminder that even in the midst of the chaos and uncertainty that surrounded us, we could find solace and strength in the power of prayer and the love that bound us together. It was as if we had found a quiet centre, a reminder that we were not alone in our journey, that the God who had always been our guide and our protector was with us still, walking beside us every step of the way. Our prayer was a beacon of hope, a light in the darkness, guiding us forward with the assurance that, no matter what lay ahead, we would face it together, as a family, united in faith and love.

Jerome's exclamation, "He's ready!" pierced the solemn atmosphere like a beam of sunlight breaking through clouds, instantly drawing our collective attention back to the screen, a reminder of the momentous decision that lay before us.

Greta, her eyes wide with a mixture of hope and urgency, broke away from our embrace, her movements filled with a renewed sense of purpose and determination. She moved with a speed I hadn't seen in years, a testament to a mother's love, as she quickly made her way to Jerome's side, eager for any news of Charles, desperate to hear his voice and know that he was ready to take this leap of faith with us.

However, Jerome's quick correction, "Oh, wait. No he's not," sent a shockwave through the air, a moment of confusion and disappointment that threatened to shatter the fragile hope that had begun to take root in our hearts. I felt my heart drop, a heavy stone of dread sinking into my stomach.

Watching Greta, I could see the panic set in, her face a canvas of fear and confusion. Her voice trembled with concern as she questioned, "What do you mean, he's not? Has he decided not to come?" The words were a plea, a desperate cry for reassurance, a mother's heart laid bare in the face of the unthinkable.

Jerome attempted to pacify her, his voice calm yet firm, a reflection of the strength and maturity that he had shown throughout this entire ordeal. He leaned closer to the laptop, his focus unwavering even in the midst of the emotional upheaval. The moment was fraught with tension, a family on the edge of their seats, hanging on every word, desperate for any sign of hope or reassurance.

Then, Luke's voice, clear and unmistakable, cut through the tension. "Hey, Jerome, can you go and get me some empty shopping trolleys for me? I'll bring them in here and Charles can help me finish bringing all that food storage into Clivilius." His words were a balm to our frayed nerves, a reminder of the practicalities that still needed to be addressed even in the midst of the extraordinary, a sign that the wheels of progress were still turning.

Relief washed over me like a cool wave, easing the tight knot of anxiety that had formed in my chest. The relief was twofold: not only was Charles still coming, his delay merely a logistical hiccup in their grand plan, but also seeing Greta's demeanour shift from panic to relief was a balm to my own frayed nerves.

Luke's sudden appearance from the Portal, with his broad smile and casual demeanour, momentarily shifted the atmosphere, infusing it with a sense of purpose and immediacy. His question, simple yet filled with the anticipation of action, "Who's going to help me get the trolleys?" echoed the pragmatic concerns of our new reality in Clivilius.

Greta's directive to Jerome, "Of you go, Jerome," her voice tinged with a mix of maternal authority and encouragement, was a seamless transition from worry to action, a reflection of the strength and resilience that had always been the hallmark of her character. It was moments like these that reminded me of the adaptability and resilience of our family, the way we could shift gears and rise to meet any challenge, no matter how daunting or unexpected.

I couldn't help but notice Jerome's cunning as he slyly pocketed a stack of money notes, a momentary flash of mischief that spoke to his resourceful nature and quick thinking. The sight sparked a mixture of amusement and admiration within me, a recognition of the clever strategy he employed to incentivise Charles's move to Clivilius, a reminder of the unique talents and perspectives that each member of our family brought to the table. Instead of voicing my thoughts, I let out a chuckle, appreciating the moment of lightheartedness amidst the uncertainty.

As Jerome rose, readiness etched into his posture, I felt an impulse to join him, to be part of this small yet significant mission, a chance to contribute in some small way to the reunification of our family. "I'll help you, Jerome," I offered, my voice steady with resolve, a reflection of the determination and purpose that had always been my guiding light. He nodded, a silent acknowledgment of my support as we prepared to venture together, a father and son united in a common goal.

Jerome shared a bit of reconnaissance with me, "There's a few empty, or almost empty ones at the Drop Zone." His knowledge of the terrain and its resources was a testament to his adaptability and awareness, qualities that made me quietly proud, a reminder of the strength and resilience that lay within him, waiting to be tapped and nurtured.

As we began our walk towards the Drop Zone, I reached out, placing my arm around Jerome's shoulder, a gesture laden with affection and a silent communication of my support, my love, and my unwavering belief in him. The weight of the day, the worries for our family, and the uncertainties of our situation seemed to momentarily lighten with this simple connection.

"I'm proud of you, son," I confessed, allowing my heart to speak through my words, a moment of vulnerability and honesty that felt both raw and necessary. It was more than just pride in his actions today; it was a recognition of his growth, his strength, and the invaluable role he played within our family, a testament to the man he was becoming and the bright future that lay ahead of him.

Jerome's response was brief, but within those two words, "Thanks, Dad," I heard layers of appreciation, understanding, and mutual respect, a reflection of the depth of our relationship and the journey we had embarked upon together. It was a simple exchange, yet it encapsulated the essence of our bond, the unspoken promise of support and love that had always been the foundation of our family.

As we walked together, side by side, I felt a sense of hope and determination settling over me, a quiet confidence in the strength of our family and the power of our love to overcome any obstacle, to weather any storm.

FOOD STORAGE

4338.213.6

The task at hand, Charles loading shopping trolleys back at our house on Earth, and Luke transporting them through the Portal, took on a rhythm that was both methodical and utterly bizarre. As I watched the trolleys emerge from the Portal, each laden with cans and packages of food, the surreal nature of our situation struck me anew, a realisation that hit me with the force of a tidal wave. The vast, barren landscape of Clivilius stretched out around us, a stark contrast to the domestic scene of shopping trolleys being wheeled across its surface. It felt like a scene plucked from a dream, the kind that leaves you questioning the line between reality and fantasy even after you've awoken, a sense of disorientation that lingered like a fog in the recesses of my mind.

My initial bewilderment gradually gave way to a growing concern for the practicalities of our situation—specifically, the preservation of our food supplies. The food, though non-perishable in nature, still required proper storage conditions to ensure its longevity, a fact that weighed heavily on my mind as I surveyed the scene before me. Back home, a cool, dry storage room was sufficient, a simple solution to a simple problem. But here in Clivilius, the options seemed severely limited, a realisation that sent a chill down my spine despite the heat of the day.

I had heard in passing of Adrian and Nial's efforts to construct several small sheds, which under normal circumstances would have been a commendable initiative. However, from what I remembered of our makeshift settlement, with its handful of tents and motorhomes, the realisation dawned on me that none of these would provide the necessary conditions for our food storage, a fact that filled me with a sense of dread and unease. Even a rudimentary shed, I feared, would succumb to the harshness of Clivilius' climate, becoming more of an oven than a pantry under the relentless sun, a thought that made my stomach churn with anxiety.

The irony of our predicament was not lost on me, a bitter twist of fate that seemed to mock our best efforts at survival. Here we were, in a world that defied explanation, relying on portals and magic to solve logistical problems, yet it was the simple, fundamental challenge of food storage that threatened to undermine our efforts, a reminder of the fragility of our existence in this new land. The juxtaposition of the fantastical and the mundane lent an additional layer of complexity to our survival strategy, highlighting the adaptability and resourcefulness required to navigate this new world, a challenge that seemed to loom larger with each passing moment.

Watching Paul in action, orchestrating the work into something resembling order, was a sight to behold. His project management skills, honed over years of experience, seemed to come alive in this unusual setting, a talent that was both impressive and reassuring in equal measure. He moved with purpose, his instructions clear and decisive, ensuring every task was assigned and every effort was directed efficiently, a conductor of a symphony of survival that played out before my eyes.

As I observed him, a pang of familial longing struck me, a sudden and intense yearning for the life we had left behind. Paul's life back in Broken Hill, along with Claire and their two children, Mack and Rose, felt worlds away from our current predicament, a reality that seemed to belong to another lifetime entirely. Their absence was a constant undercurrent of worry, a gnawing ache that never quite went away, and the thought of them being so far from us, especially now, tugged at my heartstrings with a force that threatened to overwhelm me. The notion of whether Paul had considered bringing his family to Clivilius flickered through my mind, a question laden with implications about safety, stability, and the unknown future we were all navigating, a question that I couldn't bring myself to ask aloud.

Yet, as quickly as the thought emerged, I pushed it aside, a conscious effort to focus on the task at hand. There were immediate concerns to address, and dwelling on what-ifs could wait. My focus shifted back to the task at hand—Paul's leadership in managing our current situation, a role that he had taken on with a sense of purpose and determination that filled me with a quiet pride. Despite my growing apprehension about the practicality of storing our food supplies, I found myself hesitating to voice my concerns, a reluctance born of a desire to support my son in his efforts to keep us all safe and provided for.

In that moment, I chose to trust in Paul's abilities, to believe that he had a plan for the food storage that he had not yet disclosed, a faith that was born of a lifetime of watching him rise to every challenge that had been placed before him. It was a silent pact I made with myself, to give him the benefit of the doubt, to have faith in his foresight and planning, a decision that filled me with a sense of hope and determination despite the uncertainty that surrounded us. After all, if there was anyone among us who could navigate the complexities of setting up a semblance of normality in Clivilius, it was Paul, a fact that I clung to like a lifeline.

"Dad," Jerome's voice, calling out to me, served as an anchor, pulling me back from the sea of my thoughts into the present moment, a reminder of the reality that demanded my attention. I lifted my gaze to meet his, my eyes silently urging him to go on, while Greta, ever vigilant when it came to matters concerning our family, closed the distance with her characteristic briskness, a sense of urgency that was palpable in the air around us. "What is it?" she interjected, the undercurrent of worry for Charles in her tone. "Is it Charles? Is he ready to come through the Portal?"

Her question hung in the air, a moment of breathless anticipation that seemed to stretch on for an eternity. For a fleeting second, I marvelled at how the extraordinary had become our new normal, a realisation that struck me with a force that left me reeling. The word 'Portal' slipped from her lips as if discussing the weather, not a phenomenon that had upended our very existence, a casual acceptance of the impossible that spoke volumes about the adaptability of the human spirit. It was a testament to human resilience, I supposed, how quickly we could acclimate to even the most fantastical elements when necessity demanded it, a survival instinct that ran deep within us all.

Jerome's response, "Not yet," seemed to deflate the tension slightly. Yet, almost immediately, the tension was rekindled by Greta's audible expression of frustration.

Turning back to me, Jerome shifted the focus of the conversation. "Luke and Charles are going to bring through those large barrels of wheat and rice that are in the garage," he informed me, his tone matter-of-fact, a simple statement of intent that carried with it a world of implications.

At his words, my initial reaction was one of approval for the foresight to secure such vital supplies, a sense of pride in the resourcefulness and preparedness of my sons. Yet, almost instantly, practical concerns overshadowed my optimism, a realisation of the challenges that lay ahead hitting me like a ton of bricks. The barrels he spoke of were not only substantial in size but also in weight, a fact that sent a shiver of apprehension down my spine. The logistics of manoeuvring them through the Portal, with just Luke and Charles on the task, seemed daunting, a challenge that threatened to test the limits of their strength and endurance. My mind raced through the scenarios, the potential risks and challenges they might face, a kaleidoscope of worst-case scenarios that played out in vivid detail behind my eyes.

It wasn't just the physical strain of transporting the barrels that concerned me; it was the symbolic weight they carried, a burden that seemed to rest heavily on my shoulders. Those barrels, filled with essentials for our survival, underscored the gravity of our situation, a stark reminder of the lengths to which we'd have to go to ensure our sustenance in this unfamiliar world.

"I'm not sure that Charles and Luke will be able to manage with just the two of them," I admitted, voicing my concern aloud, a moment of vulnerability that felt both necessary and terrifying in equal measure. It was a moment of realisation, the acknowledgment of the countless hurdles we had yet to face, a daunting prospect that threatened to overwhelm me with its sheer magnitude. Yet, within that acknowledgment lay a silent vow—a commitment to overcome, to adapt, and to persevere, together as a family, no matter the odds, a promise that I made to myself and to those I loved most in the world.

Greta's frustration was palpable, her voice tinged with anxiety and impatience. "Do they really have to do this now?" she asked, the strain of the situation evident in every word, a plea for respite from the relentless demands of our new reality. "Can't Charles just come here already?" Her words echoed the sentiment we all harboured—a desperate wish for our family to be reunited, for the uncertainty to end, a longing that was as powerful as it was painful.

I caught Jerome's eye, searching for some semblance of agreement or an alternative solution, but found none, a realisation that filled me with a sense of helplessness and despair. Turning back to Greta, I weighed my words carefully, understanding her need for action, yet also recognising the limits of our current circumstances, a balancing act that required both empathy and pragmatism in equal measure.

"Why don't you go back to the camp and I'll bring Charles as soon as he arrives," I suggested, hoping to offer a compromise that would alleviate her distress, even if just slightly, a temporary respite from the anxiety that had become her constant companion.

Greta's response was a nervous fidgeting of her hands, a silent plea for comfort and reassurance that tore at my heart.

Jerome chimed in, supporting the suggestion with his pragmatic viewpoint. "It's probably the best thing to do," he said, echoing my thoughts, a validation of the course of action that I had proposed. "There's not really much you can do here besides wait."

Her retort was sharp, a snap born of frustration and helplessness, a reflection of the toll that this situation was taking on her mental and emotional well-being. "And what am I supposed to do at the camp?" Greta's voice cracked slightly, underscoring the depth of her concern and the weariness of waiting without purpose, a burden that seemed to weigh heavily on her shoulders.

I found myself at a loss, shrugging in response, a silent admission of my own uncertainty and lack of solutions, a moment of vulnerability that felt uncomfortable.

"What about that lanky Karen woman?" Jerome posited, with a hint of optimism. "I'm sure she'll have something that you can help with." His words, intended to provide a solution, sparked an immediate reaction from Greta, whose expression quickly soured at the mention of Karen, a grimace that spoke volumes about her opinion of the other woman.

"I don't know where the camp is," Greta mumbled, almost as if grasping at straws to avoid the option, a last-ditch effort to find an excuse to stay by my side.

"It's just over the few small hills," I found myself saying, pointing in the general direction of the camp, trying to smooth over her concerns with a practical solution, a gesture of support and reassurance that felt both necessary and inadequate in equal measure. Yet, the persistence of her pout told me everything I needed to know—Greta was silently requesting, or rather insisting, that I accompany her, a plea for comfort and companionship that I couldn't ignore.

The sigh I released was heavy with resignation, carefully masked to hide my frustration from Greta, a moment of weakness that I couldn't afford to show in the face of her distress. "I'll come with you," I conceded, my words laced with a reluctance I hoped Jerome would understand, a silent apology for the inconvenience and delay that my absence would cause. The sideways glance I threw him was meant to communicate a myriad of things—apology, exasperation, and a silent plea for understanding, a recognition of the competing demands that pulled me in different directions.

Jerome's parting words, "Don't be too long, Dad," carried with them an undercurrent of concern for the tasks that lay ahead, a reminder of their urgency. "I could really use your help here with those barrels when they arrive," he added, emphasising the importance of my return, a subtle plea for my support and assistance.

"No problem," I assured him, though the promise felt hollow given the unpredictability of Greta's willingness to expedite our journey to the camp, an uncertainty that gnawed at the edges of my mind like a persistent itch. The dichotomy of my responsibilities—to my wife's emotional needs and to the logistical necessities of our situation—weighed heavily on me as we set off, a burden that seemed to grow heavier with each passing step. The balance between supporting Greta and fulfilling my duties within this new community was a tightrope walk, one that required patience, understanding, and a keen sense of timing, a delicate dance that I feared I might stumble in at any moment.

❖

The journey back to camp with Greta, our hands intertwined, was a silent pilgrimage marked by a complex tapestry of emotions. Her silence, borne out of an anxious anticipation for Charles's safe arrival, enveloped us like a cocoon, preserving her fragile state of hope and concern, a delicate balance that threatened to shatter at any moment. I respected this quietude, finding in it a space to immerse myself in my own whirlwind of thoughts, the quiet acting as a backdrop to the internal dialogue that played in my mind, a constant stream of worries and what-ifs that refused to be silenced.

As we approached the camp, its tranquility struck me—a stark contrast to the flurry of activity that was occurring at the Portal, a jarring juxtaposition that only served to heighten the sense of unreality that had become our constant companion. The distant sounds of construction, the rhythmic hammering, served as a reminder of the community's ongoing efforts to carve out a semblance of normality in this foreign landscape. It was a sound that, under different circumstances, might have been comforting, a sign of progress and human resilience, a beacon of hope in the midst of the unknown. Yet, in that moment, it underscored the surreal nature of our existence here in Clivilius, a reminder of the strange and unfamiliar world that we now called home.

Karen, engaged in what appeared to be an earnest discussion with a group of settlers, was a short distance away, their figures small but distinct against the backdrop of the camp. Their focus was intense, absorbed in their conversation, as they wielded folders that seemed to contain plans or important documents. They pointed and gestured with purpose, mapping out unseen visions in the air between them, a silent language of progress and possibility that spoke volumes about the determination and resolve of those who had been brought to this place. These settlers, strangers to me, were part of the fabric of this new world we were trying to weave ourselves into—a world where every settler's contribution was a thread in the larger tapestry of our collective survival, a reminder of the interconnectedness of our fates.

Observing them from a distance, I felt an odd mixture of detachment and yearning—a desire to be part of this communal effort, yet feeling distinctly on the periphery, an outsider looking in, a stranger in a strange land. This duality, this sense of being both a participant and an observer in our new reality, was disconcerting, a constant push and pull that left me feeling unmoored and adrift in a sea of uncertainty. Yet, it also provided a moment of reflection on the resilience of human spirit, our innate drive to build, to plan, to create something enduring, even in the most unfathomable of circumstances.

The decision to take a brief detour to the river was as much about finding a moment of tranquility as it was about grappling with the new reality that surrounded us, a chance to process the events of the past few hours and the implications they held for our future. The gentle flow of the water, a stark contrast to the chaotic influx of change we had been thrust into, offered a semblance of peace, a temporary reprieve from the relentless pace of adaptation required in Clivilius, a moment of stillness.

Greta, her anxiety palpable in the tight grip of her hand in mine, seemed to draw a measure of calm from the river's steady presence. It was there, amidst the soft murmur of flowing water, that I broached the idea of staying behind for a while. "Why don't you stay here and contemplate? Get some peace," I suggested, hoping to offer her a moment of solace, a brief escape from the weight of her worries, a chance to find some measure of equilibrium.

The look she gave me was one of understanding mingled with resignation, a silent acknowledgment of the different ways in which we processed challenges. Greta knew all too well my need to stay in motion, to occupy myself with tasks as a way of navigating through my own tumult of thoughts and concerns, a coping mechanism that had served me well throughout our years together. There was an unspoken acknowledgment between us that keeping busy was my way of coping, of maintaining a semblance of control in a situation that was anything but predictable, a way to anchor myself in the face of the unknown and the unknowable.

With a promise that carried the weight of my every intention, I assured her, "I will come back with Charles as soon as he arrives in Clivilius," a vow that served as a lifeline for both of us. It was a promise that I intended to keep, no matter what obstacles lay in my path.

As I turned to make my way back to the Portal, leaving Greta to her contemplation by the river, the heaviness in my chest lightened slightly with each step. The knowledge that she would be there, finding a moment of peace, provided a small comfort. Yet, the pull of my responsibilities, the need to assist with the food storage and to fulfil my promise of bringing Charles back, propelled me forward, a sense of purpose that drove me onward despite the weariness that settled deep in my bones.

❖

Returning to the Portal, the sight that greeted me was nothing short of remarkable. Three large barrels filled with rice had made their journey from our previous world into Clivilius, their white casings marred by the ochre dust of this new world.

Jerome's explanation caught me off guard, his words cutting through the haze of amazement that had settled over me. "They've been rolling them through," he said, noting my evident surprise, a hint of pride in his voice at the ingenuity and determination of his brothers. The simplicity of the method, yet the effort it must have taken to execute, left me momentarily speechless, a rare occurrence for a man who prided himself on his ability to find the right words for any situation.

"I'm impressed," I admitted, the understatement masking a whirlwind of admiration and relief, a feeling of gratitude and awe. Luke and Charles had not only tackled the logistical nightmare but had succeeded with what could only be described as sheer determination and ingenuity.

However, as I took in the scene, Jerome's solitary figure among the barrels raised a question, a niggling sense of unease that refused to be silenced. "Where's Paul?" I inquired, scanning the area for any sign of him, my eyes searching for the familiar figure of my eldest son. His absence was notable, especially given the scale of the task at hand, a realisation that sent a chill down my spine despite the heat of the day.

Jerome brushed off the clinging dust from his trousers. "He's gone to collect Adrian and Nial," he informed me, outlining Paul's plan to enlist further help, a strategic move that spoke to his leadership and foresight. "He's hoping that they can help us load the barrels onto the ute and drive them back to camp."

As I pondered over Paul's decision to use the ute for transporting the barrels, skepticism clouded my thoughts, a nagging doubt that refused to be silenced despite my best efforts to push it aside. The image of the vehicle, struggling to navigate through the dense, ochre dust of Clivilius with the heavy barrels in tow, seemed implausible to me, a feat of engineering and determination that bordered on the impossible. The practicality of moving such cumbersome objects in a landscape that was anything but accommodating was questionable at best, a realisation that filled me with a sense of unease. Yet, I chose to keep these doubts to myself, recognising that now was a time for action, not pessimism, a moment to rally behind the plan and put our faith in the strength and ingenuity of those around us.

Jerome and I then turned our attention to the immediate task of trying to stand one of the barrels upright, a seemingly simple goal that quickly proved to be anything but. It quickly became apparent that our efforts, though earnest, were somewhat futile, a realisation that sent a wave of frustration and despair washing over me like a tidal wave. The barrel, stubborn in its roundness, offered nothing but resistance, turning our attempts into a comedic dance of sorts, punctuated by our grunts and groans, a symphony of exertion and determination that echoed across the barren landscape.

The realisation hit me squarely—this was a task beyond the capabilities of just the two of us, a challenge that would require the strength and cooperation of many if we were to have any hope of success.

As we continued our struggle, a moment of levity broke through the frustration. "I'm even more surprised now, that Luke and Charles managed to bring even a single one of these here," I remarked, trying to catch my breath from the exertion, a wry smile tugging at the corners of my mouth.

Jerome's laughter in response was a welcome sound, breaking the tension that had begun to build. "I'm pretty sure they're much easier to move once they're tipped over," he observed, stating what had become painfully obvious to us both.

I couldn't help but chuckle in agreement, my own laughter mingling with Jerome's in a moment of shared understanding. Jerome's comment, simple as it was, shed light on the situation with a clarity that I had momentarily lost sight of.

The arrival of the ute, heralded by clouds of dust that danced and swirled in the air like a living entity, was a welcome interruption to our fruitless efforts with the barrels.

As the vehicle came to a halt, Paul emerged, flanked by Adrian and Nial, whose faces were familiar yet not entirely known to me. Our initial meeting had been brief, a whirlwind of introductions upon our arriving in Bixbus, leaving little room for any meaningful interaction, a fact that weighed heavily on my mind as I watched them approach.

Their greetings, though polite, carried an undertone of reservation, a subtle acknowledgment of the invisible line that seemed to separate my family from the established settlers of Bixbus, a divide that would need to be bridged if we were to have any hope of building a future in this place. I responded in kind, my greeting cautious yet friendly, aware of the delicate balance of our newcomer status in this tight-knit community.

The realisation that Adrian and Nial viewed us as outsiders did not unsettle me; if anything, it was a familiar feeling, a reminder of the challenges that we had faced throughout our lives. Outside the obligations of my church, socialising had never been my forte, a trait that perhaps made the notion of being an outsider less daunting, a shield against any uncertainties and insecurities.

Paul's directive snapped us all back to the task at hand, dispelling any lingering awkwardness. "Alright, let's figure out how to get these onto the ute," he said, his tone all business, a clear indication of his readiness to tackle the challenge before us.

I felt a wave of relief wash over me at his words, a sense of gratitude and pride in the strength and resilience of my son. Small talk had never been my strong suit, and it seemed Adrian and Nial shared my sentiment, their eagerness to address the task at hand mirroring my own. There was a certain comfort in the shared understanding that now was not the time for pleasantries but for action.

The focus shifted to the practicalities of loading the barrels onto the ute, a task that required cooperation and perhaps offered an opportunity to bridge the gap between us, however slight it may be, a chance to find common ground.

As we stood there, sizing up the barrels, a collective sense of apprehension seemed to hang in the air. The task before us was daunting, a challenge that seemed to defy the very laws of reason, and as I voiced my concerns about the logistics of lifting them onto the ute, I could sense a shared uncertainty among the group, a flicker of doubt that threatened to extinguish the flame of Paul's determination.

"I'm not sure how we're going to get these onto the back of the ute. Not to mention the weight of them," I admitted, the reality of our challenge becoming all the more tangible as the words left my mouth.

Nial's suggestion, delivered with a mix of humour and pragmatism, sparked a momentary lightness in our deliberation. "It'd be easier if we could roll them onto the back," he said, the idea seemingly absurd yet not without merit, a testament to the power of creative thinking and the willingness to look beyond the obvious solutions. "But I'm not sure that we have anything stable or strong enough to act as a base." His follow-up grounded us back in the reality of our limited resources.

"We could just tie a rope around them and drag them back to camp," Adrian quipped, his words a playful jab. His joke, though facetious, touched on what seemed increasingly like a viable, albeit last-ditch, strategy given the barrels' formidable weight.

Paul's call to action, however, redirected our focus. "Let's give lifting them a try first," he proposed, an air of determination in his voice. Despite my reservations, and the evident skepticism from Adrian and Nial, there was no disputing the unspoken rule of rallying behind a plan once decided, no matter how doubtful its success.

As we positioned ourselves around the first barrel, a mix of resolve and resignation among us, Paul's countdown served as the signal to unite our efforts, a rallying cry that echoed across the barren landscape. "On three," he instructed, and at his mark, "One, two, three!" we lifted, our muscles straining and our hearts pounding as we struggled to hoist the massive weight of the barrel onto the back of the ute. The strain was immediate, the barrel's weight testing our collective strength as much as our will.

Our bodies protested with every inch gained, a symphony of grunts and groans that filled the air like a primal chorus. Yet, through the sweat and the strain, the ute's protesting creaks and the dust that clung to our skin, we achieved our goal, a moment of triumph that seemed to defy the very odds that had been stacked against us.

Nial's exhausted declaration, "One down," punctuated by his laboured breath and the sweat that glistened on his brow, was a stark reminder of the effort required and the daunting realisation that this was only the beginning.

The sight of the ute's back wheels, already betraying their struggle against the soft, betraying dust of Clivilius, did little to ease my growing concern, a visual confirmation of the doubts that had been simmering in my mind, doubts about the practicality of our current approach and the feasibility of our plan.

Adrian's attempt at reassurance, "She'll be right, mate," accompanied by a friendly clap on the shoulder, was well-intentioned, a gesture of camaraderie. However, his confidence, though comforting in another context, couldn't fully dispel the unease that had taken root within me, a nagging sense of doubt that refused to be silenced. My attempt at a smile, in response, was a poor façade, morphing instead into a grimace that more accurately reflected my skepticism.

As we prepared to tackle the second barrel, the arrival of Luke and, importantly, Charles, shifted the atmosphere, a moment of reunion and relief that seemed to cut through the tension and strain of the day. Jerome's immediate departure from our task to greet his brother was a scene that momentarily paused the weight of our endeavours.

"Good to see you, lil' bro," Jerome's affectionate welcome, marked with a playful slap on Charles's shoulder, was a moment of normality amidst the abnormal, a glimpse of the life we had left behind.

Compelled by the same familial bond, I excused myself from the immediate task at hand, ensuring first that the barrel was securely placed to avoid any potential accidents.

Joining Jerome and Charles, I felt a surge of mixed emotions, a heady cocktail of joy and concern. The sight of Charles, another of my children now present in this uncertain new world, triggered both relief and a renewed sense of responsibility.

"Stuck together as a family forever in this bizarre place," I greeted him, my words laced with the dry humour that often served as my shield against the uncertainties of life, a defence mechanism that had served me well over the years.

Their simultaneous eye rolls, a typical response to my brand of humour, sparked a brief flicker of warmth within me. It was a welcome moment of levity.

"Let's take a short break," Paul's declaration cut through the air, a welcome reprieve that echoed in the collective sighs of relief from everyone involved.

In that moment of pause, I drew Charles closer for a casual embrace, my hand instinctively ruffling his slightly unkempt hair, a gesture of affection that spoke to the depth of my love and concern for my son.

Paul's observant eye caught a minor injury on Luke, "You've cut yourself," he noted, pointing out a small cut on Luke's elbow.

As their conversation unfolded, I found myself tuning out, my focus narrowing on Charles, a tunnel vision that blocked out the distractions and the demands of the world around us. The presence of the barrels, the ongoing tasks, and the looming promise I had made to Greta swirled in my mind, a kaleidoscope of concerns and responsibilities that threatened to overwhelm me in the face of this long-awaited reunion.

Yet, in that moment, it was clear that those barrels, stubbornly anchored in the Clivilius dust, weren't going anywhere anytime soon, a realisation that allowed me to shift my focus to the more pressing matter at hand. They would wait, as all inanimate challenges do, for my return, a silent acknowledgment of my priorities.

"Come on, let's get you to the camp," I urged Charles, aiming to shift his attention from the chaotic backdrop of our current setting, a desire to shield him from the harsh realities of our new world, if only for a moment. "Mum will be wanting to interrogate you," I added, a hint of humour threading through my words, hoping to lighten the mood and ease the tension that hung heavy in the air between us.

Paul's quick endorsement of the plan was a reassurance, an acknowledgment of the importance of reuniting Charles with Greta.

With Charles's nod of agreement, we set off toward the camp, our strides carrying us away from the immediate concerns of the barrels and towards a different kind of reunion.

After a few steps, I paused, casting a glance back to see if Jerome was following. His wave off, a signal of his decision to stay behind and engage further with Paul and Luke, was met with a moment of parental calculation. Recognising Jerome's autonomy, his capability to make his own choices, I turned back to Charles, draping an arm across his shoulders in a protective, guiding gesture as we continued our journey to the camp.

❖

The silence that accompanied us on our walk back to camp wasn't uncomfortable; rather, it felt like a mutual agreement to let the dust of our thoughts settle. The landscape of Clivilius sprawled endlessly around us, a constant reminder of the vast unknown we now inhabited. It was a sight that never failed to take my breath away, the sheer scale and grandeur of this unfamiliar land.

As we walked, the crunch of the ochre dust beneath our feet provided a steady rhythm, a metronome that seemed to mark the passage of time in this timeless place. The sun beat down upon us, its heat a physical presence that seemed to seep into our very bones. Yet, despite the discomfort, there was a strange beauty to the desolation that surrounded us, a wild and untamed beauty that spoke to the resilience of the human spirit and the depths of our own determination.

It was during this contemplative march that a practical concern nudged its way into my mind, a nagging thought that refused to be silenced. I glanced over at Charles, taking in his appearance with a critical eye.

"Did you bring any clothes with you?" The question broke the silence, directed towards Charles, whose immediate future seemed uncertain without the basic necessities one seldom thinks to grab in moments of unexpected transition.

His reaction was immediate, a mix of surprise and resignation that flashed across his face like a lightning bolt. "Nope. Didn't even think of it," Charles admitted, his response underscoring the abruptness of his situation, a reminder of the way in which our lives had been upended in the blink of an eye. It was a lapse so typical of Charles, a reflection of his carefree nature and his tendency to live in the moment.

I couldn't suppress the soft sigh that escaped me, a sound that carried with it a mixture of exasperation and affection. It was a sigh that spoke to the countless times I had witnessed Charles's impulsiveness, his tendency to leap before looking, a trait that had both endeared him to me and caused me no end of worry over the years. Yet, even as the sigh left my lips, I quickly masked it with reassurance, a desire to alleviate the anxiety that I could see creeping into Charles's eyes.

"Not to worry," I comforted him, my mind already ticking through solutions, a mental checklist of the steps that needed to be taken to ensure his comfort and well-being. "I'm sure Luke will bring you some before nightfall." It was a promise I hoped could be kept, relying on the continuity of our makeshift supply line through the Portal, a lifeline that seemed as fragile as the tenuous grip we held on our own sanity in the face of the impossible.

Charles's grin, irrepressible and bright, lit up his face, dimples and all, a sight that never failed to lift my spirits. "It feels like summer here compared to the winter we've just come from. I can always run around in my underwear," he quipped, his humour a welcome respite from the tension of adaptation.

His words sparked a flood of memories, vignettes of Charles's childhood where his love for freedom and disdain for clothing often led to moments both heartwarming and hilariously awkward. I could see him now, a toddler streaking through the house with abandon, his laughter echoing off the walls as he evaded capture and revelled in his own mischief. It was a memory that brought a smile to my face, a reminder of the simple joys that had once filled our lives.

"You can do that in your own space," I retorted, my voice tinged with a mix of amusement and resignation, a acknowledgement of Charles's irrepressible spirit and the way in which he had always marched to the beat of his own drum. It was a trait that I had always admired in him, even as it had caused me no end of consternation over the years, a reminder of the unique challenges and joys that came with being a parent.

As we continued our journey towards the camp, the conversation shifted the weight of our predicament, if only slightly.

DISHEVELLED GRETA

4338.213.7

As Charles and I arrived at the small camp, the sun's golden rays danced across the dusty landscape, casting long shadows that stretched towards the distant horizon. The air was thick with the scent of dried earth and the faint aroma of campfire smoke, a reminder of the sparse comforts this new world offered. My eyes scanned the makeshift shelters and tents scattered around the area, searching for any sign of Greta, but she was nowhere to be seen, a realisation that sent a shiver of unease down my spine.

My heart skipped a beat, a flicker of worry igniting in my chest. I took a deep breath, reminding myself that Greta was probably just down by the river, seeking solace in the gentle flow of the water, a moment of peace. Turning to Charles, I gave him a reassuring smile, masking my own unease, a façade of strength and calm that belied the turmoil that raged within me.

"Come on. Let's go find your mum," I said, my voice steady despite the trepidation that lurked beneath the surface, a false bravado that I clung to like a lifeline in the face of the unknown.

We headed towards the river, our footsteps crunching against the parched earth. The landscape stretched out before us, a vast expanse of muted colours, a tapestry of browns and reds that seemed to swallow us whole. As we neared the water's edge, I called out, "Greta!", my voice echoing through the stillness, carried by the gentle breeze, a desperate plea for a response. But there was no response, just the soft rustling of the shifting sands, a sound that seemed to mock our efforts and our hopes.

The flicker of worry in my chest grew into a steady flame, a raging inferno that threatened to consume me from the inside out. But I pushed it aside, reminding myself of Greta's strength and resilience, a force of nature that had always been the bedrock of our family. She was a force to be reckoned with, a woman who could handle herself in the face of adversity, a pillar of strength that had sustained us through countless trials and tribulations. Still, a twinge of guilt niggled at the back of my mind, a silent reproach for not being by her side when she needed me most.

With heavy hearts, Charles and I made our way back to camp, the sun's warmth bearing down upon our backs. As we approached the supply tent, its weathered canvas fluttering in the breeze, I spotted Karen, her friendly face a welcome sight amidst the unfamiliarity of our surroundings.

"Karen," I called out, waving her over, my voice laced with a hint of desperation. "Have you seen Greta?"

Karen nodded, her eyes sparkling with recognition, a knowing smile playing on her lips. "There's a small lagoon a little downstream. I suggested to her that she go and take a look."

Relief washed over me like a soothing balm, temporarily quelling the anxiety that had taken root in my heart. "Thank you, Karen," I replied, my gratitude evident in my tone.

Charles perked up, his curiosity piqued by the mention of the lagoon, a spark of excitement that lit up his face like a beacon in the darkness. "Is it far?" he asked, his young face alight with a sense of adventure.

Karen shook her head, her gaze fixed on Charles, a warmth emanating from her eyes. "Only a ten to fifteen minute walk."

It was then that I realised I'd forgotten my manners, so caught up in my own worries that I'd neglected to introduce my son, a lapse in etiquette that made me cringe with embarrassment. "Karen, this is Charles, our youngest," I said, beaming with pride as Karen extended her hand towards him.

"I'm Karen," she said, her smile warm and inviting. She glanced over her shoulder, her eyes searching the horizon, a hint of concern creeping into her expression. "And my husband, Chris, is out there somewhere."

Charles's brow furrowed slightly, his inquisitive nature shining through, a trait that had always been both a blessing and a curse. "What are they doing out there?"

"He was with Grant and Sarah. They're scouting a suitable location for the Orchard," Karen explained, her voice carrying a hint of expectation, a glimmer of hope that seemed to defy the harsh realities of our surroundings.

My eyes widened, surprise etched across my features, a reaction that I couldn't quite control. "We've got an orchard?" I asked, the words tumbling from my lips before I could stop them. As soon as the question left my mouth, I realised the absurdity of it, a moment of clarity that hit me like a ton of bricks. Of course, they didn't have an orchard yet, not in this barren landscape, a fact that seemed to mock my own naivety and ignorance.

Karen shook her head, a flicker of amusement dancing in her eyes. "Not yet. But Chris is eager to try and establish one."

I let out a low whistle, my gaze sweeping over the desolate terrain that stretched out before us, a landscape that seemed to defy all attempts at cultivation and growth. "I'd be surprised if he can get anything to grow out here," I mused, a twinge of doubt colouring my words, a reflection of the skepticism that had begun to take root.

Karen paused, a spark of realisation igniting in her eyes, a moment of clarity that seemed to bring the world into sharper focus. "You've not seen the coriander plants yet, have you?"

I shook my head, my brow knitting together as I tried to comprehend the significance of coriander plants in this unforgiving environment. "No," I replied, my curiosity piqued, a hunger for knowledge that refused to be satisfied.

Karen took a deep breath, preparing to share her knowledge, her voice filled with a quiet reverence. "The soil seems to have some unique properties," she began, but her words trailed off as something caught her attention, her gaze fixed on a point beyond my shoulder, a sudden shift in the atmosphere that sent a chill down my spine.

I turned, following her line of sight, and felt my heart lurch in my chest, as fear and concern gripped me like a vice. "Greta?" I mumbled, my voice a mix of awe and concern, barely above a whisper, a prayer and a plea all rolled into one.

There she was, my beautiful wife, wandering into camp like a lost soul, a spectre of the vibrant woman I knew and loved. She was soaked to the bone, her clothes clinging to her skin, a layer of dust caking her like a second skin. Her eyes, once bright and full of life, now held a haunted look, a window into the depths of her soul that threatened to shatter my heart into a million pieces.

Charles was already moving, his legs carrying him towards his mother, propelled by the urgent need to comfort her, a instinct that seemed to come as naturally to him as breathing. "Mum!" he called out, his young voice laced with worry, a plea for reassurance, a cry for help that pierced the very heavens.

I followed close behind, my own steps heavy with the weight of my own fears, a burden that seemed to grow heavier with each passing moment. We reached Greta just as she collapsed to her knees in the dust, a sight that tore at my very soul. A harrowing scream tore from her throat, a cry of anguish and despair that seemed to echo across the ages.

I knelt before her, gathering her into my arms, holding her close as she clung to me, her face buried in my chest. Her tears soaked through my shirt, a tangible reminder of the pain she carried within, a burden that I would have given anything to shoulder in her stead. I pressed a gentle kiss to the top of her head, silently willing her to draw strength from my presence, to know that she was not alone in her suffering, that I would always be there to catch her when she fell.

Glancing back at Karen, I saw the concern etched into her features, her eyes filled with a deep understanding of the struggles we faced. She stood a respectful distance away, a silent guardian, ready to offer support when needed.

Charles looked to me, his eyes wide and fearful, silently pleading for answers I didn't have, a desperation that tore at my heart like a knife. The pain that twisted in my gut was mirrored in his young face, a reflection of the helplessness that consumed me, a reminder of the responsibilities that weighed heavily upon my shoulders. As a husband and a father, it was my duty to protect my family, to shield them from harm, a sacred trust that I had sworn to uphold with every fibre of my being. But in this moment, as I held my broken wife in my arms, I couldn't help but question the choices that had led us to this point, the decisions that had brought us to this strange and unforgiving land.

Had I made a terrible mistake in following Luke through the Portal? Had I condemned my family to a life of hardship and suffering in pursuit of a dream that already seemed like a distant memory? The doubts swirled in my mind, a maelstrom of guilt and uncertainty, a tempest that threatened to sweep me away in its wake.

But I pushed them aside, focusing on the present, on the woman in my arms who needed me now more than ever.

After what felt like an eternity, Greta's sobs subsided, her body stilling in my embrace. She pulled back, her eyes red-rimmed and haunted, a window into the depths of her sorrow, a reflection of the pain that had taken hold of her.

"Are you okay? What happened?" I asked gently, my voice barely above a whisper, as if speaking too loudly might shatter the fragile moment, a delicate balance that could be upset at any moment.

Greta bit her trembling lip, shaking her head, a gesture that spoke volumes of whatever it was that she had witnessed and experienced. "I don't want to talk about it," she said, her voice raw with emotion, a hint of bitterness creeping into her tone as she shot Karen a fleeting glare, a momentary lapse in the mask of composure that she had always worn so well.

She turned to Charles, her expression softening, a flicker of love breaking through the darkness. "I'm glad we're together now," she said, brushing a tear from his cheek with a gentle touch.

The words rang true, a glimmer of hope amidst the despair. But I could sense the unspoken struggle behind them, the weight of Greta's unhappiness about being in Clivilius, a burden that seemed to grow heavier with each passing moment. Given her current dishevelled appearance, I couldn't blame her for her reservations.

As I helped Greta to her feet, Karen stepped forward, her voice gentle and understanding. "You've got your suitcase of clothes now. Why don't you come back to my motorhome and you can get yourself cleaned up and changed there?"

Greta hesitated, her eyes searching mine for reassurance, a silent plea for guidance. As much as I wanted to be there for her, to shoulder the burden of her pain, I knew that sometimes, she needed space to process her emotions, a chance to find her own way. And if I was being honest with myself, I wasn't sure I had the emotional strength to weather the storm with her, not in this moment, a realisation that filled me with a sense of guilt and shame.

"I'll even cover up the terrarium with the huntsman's, if that'll make you feel more comfortable," Karen offered, a small smile playing on her lips, a gesture of kindness in the face of our turmoil.

Charles's eyes lit up at the mention of the huntsman's, his curiosity piqued, a spark of excitement that seemed to defy the seriousness of the situation. But a stern look from Greta silenced any comment he might have made, a reminder of the need for tact and sensitivity in the face of her suffering.

Finally, Greta nodded, her voice soft and resigned, a whisper of acquiescence. "Okay."

I gave her hand a gentle squeeze, a silent promise of support. "You'll feel better once you've dried off and in clean clothes," I assured her, encouraging her towards Karen, entrusting her to the care of this kind-hearted stranger.

As the two women walked away, their figures receding into the distance, I felt a wave of gratitude wash over me, a sense of relief and appreciation for the kindness and compassion that Karen had offered Greta in her time of need. Karen was a godsend, a beacon of compassion in this unforgiving world, a reminder of the goodness that still existed even in the darkest of times.

Charles's voice pulled me from my thoughts, his words laced with concern. "Will Mum be okay?"

I nodded, mustering a smile, a façade of strength for my son's sake, a mask that I had worn so many times before in the face of adversity and challenge. "Your mother will be fine," I said, as much to reassure myself as him, a mantra that I repeated over and over again in my mind. "She's a strong woman, your mum. She's been through a lot, but she always comes out the other side, shining like a diamond."

I wrapped an arm around Charles's shoulders, drawing him close, feeling the warmth of his presence. "And you know what? We're going to be just fine, too. This place, Clivilius, it's a new beginning for us. It might not be easy, but we've got each other, and we've got our faith. As long as we stick together and trust in the Lord, we can face anything."

Charles rested his hand on my shoulder, an anchor in the midst of the storm, a reminder of the strength and resilience that lay within him. "I love you, Dad," he whispered, his words a balm to my battered soul.

"I love you too, son," I replied, my heart swelling with affection, a fierce protectiveness surging through my veins. Come what may, I would do everything in my power to keep my family safe, to guide them through the trials and tribulations that undoubtedly lay ahead.

POTLUCK IDEA

4338.213.8

The afternoon sun beat down upon the makeshift camp, its bright rays illuminating the sparse surroundings and casting deep shadows across the dusty ground. Charles and I found ourselves hovering near the campfire, mostly in silence as we waited for Greta's return, the crackling of the dying coals and the occasional pop of sparks the only sounds that broke the stillness of the warm afternoon air. The heat was oppressive, a tangible presence that seemed to wrap around us like a suffocating blanket, but we remained rooted to the spot, lost in our own thoughts and worries.

Charles, his face a mask of concentration, poked at the last of the glowing embers with a long stick, stirring up a flurry of sparks that danced and twirled in the sunlight like tiny fireflies. I watched him, a small smile tugging at the corners of my mouth, tempted to tell him to be careful, to stop before he accidentally burned himself. But the thought made me chuckle softly, a rueful sound that spoke of the difference in parenting styles between Greta and myself.

I realised that I was heading into the domain that belonged primarily to Greta, the realm of overprotectiveness and constant warnings. She was the one who was always cautioning the kids to be careful, about everything from crossing the street to handling sharp objects, her voice filled with a mixture of love and fear that I had come to know so well over the years. I, on the other hand, preferred to take a more general approach to parenting, establishing clear guidelines and trusting my children to make their own choices within those boundaries, a philosophy that had served us well thus far.

As long as they adhered to the guidelines, I wasn't going to monitor or condemn their individual decisions, a stance that had sometimes put me at odds with Greta's more hands-on approach. I had always felt it was important for them to learn about life in their own way, even if that meant sometimes learning the hard way, a belief that had been tested time and time again over the years.

Although I would never allow my children to cause themselves serious injury, I believed that it was crucial for them to explore and experiment, and if that meant minor incidental accidents, then so be it. It all created valuable learning opportunities, moments of growth and self-discovery that would shape them into the adults they were meant to become.

Even though I didn't always agree with the directions that my children had taken, I was proud of the people they had become, each of them unique and special in their own way. They were all independent, curious, and considerate individuals, each with their own strengths and quirks, a testament to the love and guidance that Greta and I had poured into them over the years.

As I watched Charles continue to poke at the embers, lost in his own world, I couldn't help but feel a surge of love and pride for the young man he was becoming, for the spark of curiosity and mischief that still shone in his eyes.

Glancing at the dwindling flames, I realised that it was drifting towards late in the afternoon, and it would be wise not to let the fire diminish completely, a practical concern that brought me back to the present moment. "You can throw another log or two on the fire," I told Charles, my voice breaking the contemplative silence that had settled between us.

Charles happily obliged, his face lighting up at the prospect of tending to the fire, a simple pleasure that seemed to bring him a measure of joy and purpose. He made his way to the considerable stack of firewood nearby. Grabbing a large chunk of wood, he carefully placed it into the fire pit, the flames eagerly licking at the new fuel, a burst of energy that seemed to mirror the excitement that was building within him.

As I watched him work, my peripheral vision caught someone approaching the camp, a figure that seemed to materialise out of the shimmering heat like a mirage. Lifting my gaze, I saw that it was Jerome, and thankfully, he still appeared to be in high spirits, his stride confident and his face beaming with excitement, a stark contrast to the weariness and uncertainty that had settled over the camp like a heavy blanket.

"You're in a good mood," Charles commented to Jerome before I got the chance to say anything, his tone light and teasing, a hint of curiosity lurking beneath the surface. I was sure that Charles tried to be subtle with the gaze of intrigue that accompanied his probing question, but subtlety had never been one of Charles's strong suits, a fact that I found both endearing and exasperating in equal measure. I found it amusing that he didn't seem to realise this character flaw, but if it meant that I was going to learn more about situations by observing his body language, then I wasn't about to let him know about it, a secret that I kept close to my chest.

With a quick shake of his head, a subtle gesture that hinted at a hidden secret or communication between them, almost as if it were a warning for Charles not to raise whatever topic held their attention, Jerome quickly moved the conversation along, his voice filled with a barely contained excitement that seemed to bubble up from within him. "We're having a celebration tonight," he blurted out, a wild grin spreading across his face, his eyes sparkling with anticipation.

Charles's face instantly broke into a matching grin, his excitement palpable in the way he bounced on the balls of his feet, eager to hear more about this unexpected development, a burst of energy that seemed to crackle in the air between them like electricity.

Curious, I raised an eyebrow and asked, "A celebration for what?", my mind racing with possibilities, trying to understand what could have prompted such a sudden desire for festivities in our current situation. It seemed like an odd thing to suggest, given the circumstances we found ourselves in, but I was willing to hear them out, to see where this unexpected turn of events might lead.

"For us," Jerome answered bluntly, his tone suggesting that it should have been obvious, a hint of exasperation creeping into his voice at my apparent lack of understanding. "To welcome us to Bixbus," he eventually extrapolated, seemingly in response to the puzzled looks on Charles's and my faces, a moment of clarity that seemed to dawn on him like a revelation.

I glanced around us, taking in the limited resources that we seemed to have at our disposal, the meagre supplies and makeshift shelters that dotted the camp like a patchwork quilt. The camp was sparse, and the supplies we had were a far cry from the bounty that would be needed to throw a proper celebration.

"I'm not sure that a celebration is a good idea," I told Jerome and Charles, cautiously trying not to completely burst their bubble of excitement that was rapidly expanding with each passing moment, a delicate balancing act that required both tact and sensitivity. It wasn't that I was opposed to the idea of a celebration in principle, but rather that I was concerned about the practicalities of pulling it off, given our limited resources.

"Yeah, it is," Jerome replied quickly, his enthusiasm undiminished by my reservations, a determination that seemed to radiate from every fibre of his being. "Paul and Luke are both on board with it. Luke's going to tell Beatrix too," he explained, making it clear that the decision had already been made, regardless of my opinion on the matter, a fait accompli that left me feeling slightly unsettled and out of the loop.

Charles let out a yelp of excitement, his face a picture of pure joy at the prospect of a celebration, a sound that seemed to echo across the barren landscape like a clarion call. But then, just as quickly, his expression fell into one of deep contemplation, his brow furrowing as a thought occurred to him, a moment of realisation that seemed to hit him like a ton of bricks. "But how are we going to have a celebration?" he asked, gesturing around at the nothingness that surrounded us, the barren landscape stretching out in every direction.

"Luke and Beatrix are going to bring us whatever we want," Jerome exclaimed, his voice rising with excitement, his eyes wide with the possibilities that now seemed within reach, a promise of abundance and plenty that seemed to defy the harsh realities of our surroundings. It was a bold claim, one that I found hard to believe, given what I had seen of Clivilius so far, but I couldn't help but be swept up in their enthusiasm, in the hope and optimism that seemed to radiate from them.

I shrugged nonchalantly, realising that there was little point in resisting the idea any further, a surrender to the inevitable that felt both liberating and terrifying. The boys' enthusiasm was infectious, and despite my initial hesitance, I found myself warming to the idea of a celebration, of a moment of normality, a chance to come together as a community and forge the bonds that would sustain us in the days and weeks to come. "I guess we could make it work," I suggested, a small smile tugging at the corners of my mouth, a flicker of hope and determination that seemed to mirror their own.

"Are you thinking something like a potluck dinner?" Charles asked, his mind already racing with ideas for the event, his face a mask of concentration as he considered the logistics, a problem-solver at heart who thrived on the challenge of making the impossible possible. It was a suggestion that made sense, given our limited resources and the need to pull together as a community, a way to make the most of what we had and create something greater than the sum of its parts.

Jerome nodded, a thoughtful expression on his face, his eyes distant as he mulled over the possibilities, a strategist at work. "I wasn't, but that's a great idea," he agreed, his eyes lighting up at the prospect of a communal meal, of everyone coming together to share in the celebration, a moment of unity and togetherness that seemed more important now than ever before.

I stood there, silently observing the two youngest Smiths as they began to devise their plan, their voices rising and falling with each new idea, their faces animated with excitement, a tableau of youthful exuberance and hope that filled my heart with a bittersweet mixture of joy and sorrow.

Jerome spoke of Luke's revelation of plenty of supplies already at the Drop Zone from the store raid they had conducted a few nights ago, a tantalising hint of the resources that lay hidden just beyond our sight, waiting to be claimed and put to use. For a moment, it almost felt as though we were back at home, planning a family gathering or a church social barbecue, and not stranded in a desolate foreign wasteland, a fleeting glimpse of the life we had left behind that brought a lump to my throat and a sting to my eyes.

"Dad," Jerome said loudly, his voice cutting through my wandering thoughts, pulling me back to the present with a jolt. I looked at him, my eyes widening as I realised that I had lost track of their conversation, my mind drifting to memories of different times.

"Is everything okay, Dad?" Charles asked, his brow furrowing in a rare display of seriousness, concern etched into the lines of his young face, a glimpse of the man he was becoming, the caregiver and protector that lay just beneath the surface of his carefree exterior.

"Of course," I answered, cutting my response short of delving into my ruminations, a half-truth that felt heavy on my tongue. Reminding the boys, in their moment of excitement, about what they had left behind didn't seem like the most appropriate thing to do, a burden that I would bear alone, at least for now. It was my job to protect them, to shield them from the harsh realities of our situation, even if it meant carrying the weight of my own doubts and fears in silence.

"What do you need me to do?" I found myself asking them, a small smile tugging at the corners of my mouth. It was another common question, another familiarity, another reminder of home, of the roles and responsibilities that had defined our lives for so long. The kids had always been better at organising these social gatherings than me, a fact that I had come to accept with a mixture of pride and bemusement, and I was happy for them to take the lead on this one too, to step up and take charge in a way that filled me with a sense of hope and possibility.

Jerome's face crinkled as he thought, his mind working through the various tasks that needed to be done, a general marshalling his troops for battle. "Can you and Mum do the cooking?" he asked, his tone hopeful, his eyes searching mine for confirmation, a plea for help and support that tugged at my heartstrings and filled me with a sense of purpose and resolve.

"Of course," I replied, grateful to be included and especially grateful to be assigned a task that I was comfortable with, a role that I could step into with confidence and ease. Cooking had always been a source of joy for me, a way to bring the family together and create lasting memories, a skill that I had honed over years of practice and experimentation. It was a way to contribute, to feel useful and needed.

"Where is Mum, by the way?" came Jerome's quick follow-up question, his gaze darting around the camp, searching for any sign of Greta, a hint of concern creeping into his voice.

"She's getting changed," I answered, keeping the explanation brief, given that I wasn't exactly sure myself what had happened to get her so distressed, a mystery that gnawed at the edges of my mind like a persistent itch, a question that I knew I would need to confront sooner or later, but not now, not in this moment of fragile peace and possibility.

"Again?" Jerome asked, his face somewhat concerned, his brow furrowing as he tried to make sense of the situation, a puzzle that seemed to defy explanation or understanding.

"She went for a swim," Charles added with a chuckle, his eyes sparkling with mirth at the thought of their mother taking an impromptu dip in the nearby lagoon.

Jerome, taken by surprise, turned to Charles, his eyebrows raised in disbelief, his mouth hanging open in a comical expression of shock and awe. "Really?" he asked, his tone a mixture of confusion and amusement, a question that seemed to encapsulate the strangeness and unpredictability of our new world, the way in which even the most mundane actions could take on a sense of the surreal and the absurd.

"I think it's a little more complicated than that, but—" I began, but the sound of women's voices distracted me from finishing the thought, a sudden intrusion into the quiet contemplation of the moment. Our heads turned in unison towards the direction of Karen's motorhome, and there, walking towards us, were Karen and Greta, their faces alight with smiles and laughter, a sight that filled my heart with relief.

Watching them approach, I found my muscles tensing as I strained to review Greta's features for signs of lingering stress, my mind racing with worry about her well-being, a concern that never seemed to fade, no matter how many times she proved her strength and resilience in the face of adversity. Thankfully, her time with Karen seemed to have calmed her, and she seemed to be carrying a genuine smile, her eyes crinkling at the corners as she laughed at something Karen had said, a moment of connection and camaraderie that warmed my heart and eased the knot of tension that had settled in the pit of my stomach. They even shared a brief chuckle between them as they walked, hinting at some inside joke that had formed during their time together.

Relief washed over me like a soothing balm, the tension in my shoulders easing as I realised that Greta was in a better state of mind, that whatever had troubled her earlier seemed to have been pushed aside, at least for the moment, a respite from the storms that raged within her, a momentary peace that filled me with a sense of gratitude and hope.

"You three look like you're conspiring," Greta said when they neared us, her tone light and teasing, her eyes sparkling with a newfound sense of ease, a playfulness that I had missed more than I realised.

"Always," Charles replied with a cheeky grin, his face a picture of mischief and innocence all at once, a boyish charm that never failed to bring a smile to my face.

"Dad's just volunteered you and him to do the cooking for our potluck dinner celebration tonight," Jerome said, getting right to the point, his excitement barely contained as he shared the news with Greta.

Both Greta and Karen seemed to be taken by surprise by the revelation, their eyebrows raising in unison, their mouths falling open slightly, a moment of shock and disbelief that quickly gave way to a sense of excitement and anticipation. Greta cast me a questioning look, her eyes searching mine for an explanation, for some insight into how this decision had been made.

"We'll keep it simple," I told her, my voice reassuring, my hand reaching out to give hers a gentle squeeze. I knew that Greta might have reservations about taking on such a task so soon after our arrival, but I also knew that she thrived on being needed, on having a purpose and a role to play in our family and our community, a sense of belonging that had always been so important to her.

"Are you cooking for everyone in the camp?" Karen asked, her tone a mixture of surprise and concern, her eyes widening as she considered the scale of the undertaking, the logistics and practicalities that would need to be worked out if we were to pull off such a feat.

"Yeah, I think so," Jerome answered, his voice confident, his eyes shining with the promise of a grand celebration, a moment of unity and togetherness that would bind us all together in a way that nothing else could. It was a vision that I found myself getting swept up in, a dream of a better tomorrow that seemed to beckon from just beyond the horizon, a future that was ours for the taking if we had the courage and the determination to reach for it.

"There's quite a lot of us now. That's a fair amount of work for just two people," Karen reasoned, her gaze shifting between Jerome and Charles, her expression making it clear that she questioned the logic of having a celebration so soon after our arrival, a practical concern that I couldn't help but share on some level. "Especially since you've only just arrived today," she added, her tone gentle but firm.

"We all have to eat, anyway," I found myself defending the boys, my voice steady and assured, a conviction that seemed to come from somewhere deep within me. The idea of a celebration, of a moment of normality and togetherness, had taken root in my mind, and I was prepared to see it through, to do whatever it took to make it a reality, even if it meant pushing myself beyond my comfort zone and taking on more than I would normally have thought achievable.

The crackle of the growing fire as it began to take hold of the fresh wood that Charles had thrown on earlier caught my gaze, the dancing flames sparking a fresh idea in my mind, a sudden burst of inspiration that seemed to come out of nowhere. I looked to Jerome as I spoke, my eyes alight with excitement, my voice rising with each word, a crescendo of possibility and potential. "If Luke can bring us some meat, I can cook us a barbecue," I told him, my mind already racing with ideas for marinades and rubs, for the perfect combination of flavours and textures that would tantalise the taste buds and bring us all together in a moment of shared pleasure and delight.

Jerome nodded enthusiastically, his face breaking into a wide grin, his eyes sparkling with the promise of a feast fit for kings, a celebration that would be talked about for years to come. "Yeah, I can ask him," he said, his voice eager, his feet already shifting as if he were ready to take off at a moment's notice, to track down Luke and make the request that would set the wheels in motion, the first step towards making our lofty aspiration a reality.

I turned to Greta, my eyes softening as I met her gaze. "Perhaps you could make some salads? Or maybe see what else is amongst our food storage that we've got here?" I suggested, my tone gentle, my hand still resting on hers.

Greta hesitated for a moment, her eyes searching mine, a flicker of uncertainty passing across her features, a momentary lapse in the mask of strength and resilience that she wore so well. But then, as quickly as it had appeared, it was gone, replaced by a soft smile and a determined nod, a silent acknowledgement of the task that lay before us and the role that she would play in making it happen. "I think it's a good idea," she replied, her voice steady, her eyes shining with a newfound sense of purpose, a glimmer of hope and possibility that seemed to light her up from within.

Karen's brow creased as she thought pensively. After a moment, she spoke, her voice firm but kind. "I'll help you prepare some food, Greta," she told her, her hand reaching out to give Greta's arm a gentle squeeze.

Greta took hold of Karen's arm, her eyes brimming with gratitude, her voice thick with emotion as she spoke, the words heavy with meaning and significance. "Thank you, Karen," she said, the simple phrase carrying the weight of a thousand unsaid thing.

Karen turned to me, her face set with determination, her eyes blazing with a fierce intensity that took my breath away. "When I see Chris, I'll tell him to come and help you," she said, her tone leaving no room for argument, her words a promise and a vow all rolled into one.

I shook my head, a small smile playing at the corners of my mouth, a flicker of amusement and appreciation dancing in my eyes. "That's okay. I don't mind cooking," I told her, my voice sincere, my mind already racing with ideas for the feast that lay ahead, the flavours and aromas that would fill the air and bring us all together in a moment of shared joy and celebration.

But Karen's face tightened, her expression reminiscent of Greta's when she had made up her mind about something and there was no persuading her otherwise, a stubbornness and determination that I had come to know and love over the years. "Don't be silly. Chris will help," Karen replied, her voice firm, her eyes brooking no argument, a reminder of the strength and resilience that seemed to run through her very veins.

I nodded, albeit reluctantly, realising that there was no point in resisting Karen's offer of assistance. "Thanks," I said simply, my voice genuine, my heart swelling with gratitude and appreciation.

Jerome and Charles, their excitement reaching a fever pitch, returned to their playful jibing and poking at each other, their laughter ringing out across the camp, a welcome sound amidst the stillness of the late afternoon air. "We'll go and see what's at the Drop Zone," Jerome said, eagerly tugging on Charles's arm to get him into motion, his feet already carrying him towards the camp's exit.

"And ask Luke for meat," I called out to them as they turned and broke into a light jog.

Pausing briefly, Charles turned, his face alight with mischief, his voice carrying across the distance between us. "Yeah, we'll get you a lot of meat," he called out in reply, his tone teasing, his eyes sparkling with the promise of a grand feast.

And then, with a final wave and a burst of laughter, the two boys passed through the camp's gate, their figures disappearing into the distance, leaving Greta, Karen, and me standing in the warm glow of the campfire, our hearts full of hope and excitement for the celebration to come.

SCHEMING

4338.213.9

Greta immediately began talking to Karen about what they might be able to cook, their voices rising with excitement as they traded ideas and suggestions, a flurry of creativity and inspiration that seemed to crackle in the air between them like electricity.

"What about some kind of pasta salad?" Greta suggested, her eyes bright with enthusiasm, her mind already racing with possibilities. "We could use some of the canned vegetables from the food storage, maybe add in some herbs and spices to give it a little kick."

Karen nodded thoughtfully, her brow furrowed in concentration as she considered the idea, her own culinary instincts kicking into high gear. "That could work," she said slowly, her voice tinged with a hint of excitement. "And maybe we could do a big batch of rice and beans, too. It's filling, and it'll go a long way to feed everyone."

Greta's face lit up at the suggestion, her eyes sparkling with the promise of a feast. "Oh, that's perfect!" she exclaimed, clapping her hands together in delight.

As I listened to their excited chatter, I couldn't help but feel a sense of pride and admiration for these two remarkable women, their strength and resilience shining through in every word and gesture.

Karen turned to Greta, her expression thoughtful, her voice low and conspiratorial as she leaned in closer, as if sharing a secret of great importance. "You know," she said softly, her eyes darting around the camp as if to make sure no one else was listening, "we could probably cook everything in my motorhome. It's got a pretty decent kitchen setup, and it would give us a little more privacy to work without everyone hovering around."

Greta's eyes widened at the suggestion, a flicker of excitement and gratitude dancing across her features, a silent acknowledgement of the kindness and generosity that Karen was offering. "That would be amazing," she breathed, her voice barely above a whisper, as if afraid to jinx the moment by speaking too loudly. "But what about Noah? He'll need somewhere to cook too."

Karen waved a hand dismissively, a small smile playing at the corners of her mouth, a hint of mischief and amusement in her eyes. "Oh, he can cook outside using the fire," she said breezily, as if it were the most natural thing in the world. "There's plenty of camping cooking equipment around, and I'm sure he'll be able to whip up something delicious with whatever meat the boys bring back."

Greta hesitated for a moment, her eyes flickering to mine, a silent question hanging in the air between us, a momentary uncertainty that seemed to vanish as quickly as it had appeared. "Are you sure you don't mind, Noah?" she asked softly, her voice tinged with a hint of concern.

I smiled reassuringly. "Of course not," I said gently, my hand reaching out to give hers a gentle squeeze. "I'm happy to cook outside. It'll give me a chance to enjoy the fresh air."

Greta's face softened at my words, a flicker of relief and gratitude dancing in her eyes. "Thank you," she murmured, her voice thick with emotion, her hand tightening around mine.

As Greta and Karen turned back to their conversation, their voices rising and falling with each new idea and suggestion, I found myself suddenly alone, left to my own thoughts and preparations. It was a strange feeling, being on the periphery of their excitement, watching from the sidelines as they planned and plotted, their minds whirring with possibilities and potential.

But even as I stood there, my eyes fixed on the dancing flames of the campfire, my mind racing with thoughts of the feast that lay ahead, I couldn't shake the feeling of being somehow disconnected, of being an outsider looking in on a world that I didn't quite understand. It was a feeling that had been growing steadily since our arrival in Bixbus, a sense of being adrift in a sea of unfamiliarity, of being a stranger in a strange land.

And yet, even as those thoughts swirled in my mind, I felt a flicker of something else, a glimmer of hope and possibility that seemed to dance just beyond the edges of my consciousness, a promise of something better, something brighter waiting just around the corner. It was a feeling that I clung to like a lifeline, a reminder that even in the darkest of times, there was always a light to guide us home, always a path forward if we had the courage to take it.

❖

Having thrown another few logs on the campfire, and taken a look at the camping supplies at the camp, I decided to go and check in with Jerome and Charles, to see how their food request was going. It would also be a good opportunity to see if there might be anything else useful at the Drop Zone, a chance to gather any additional resources that might help make our celebration a success.

As I approached the Portals and the Drop Zone, I could see that Jerome and Charles were with Beatrix, huddled over a small collection of shopping trolleys, seemingly engrossed in deep concentration. The sight of them working together brought a smile to my face, a welcome moment of normality amidst the strangeness of our new surroundings.

"Have you asked Luke for the meat yet?" I asked, my voice cutting through their focused silence, catching them all by surprise. I could see the startled expressions on their faces, the way their heads snapped up at the sound of my voice, a momentary flicker of confusion and surprise that quickly gave way to recognition and warmth.

Jerome shook his head, his brow furrowing slightly, a hint of disappointment and frustration creeping into his voice as he replied. "Nope. We haven't seen him yet," he said, his tone apologetic, as if he felt somehow responsible for the delay in securing the necessary provisions for our celebration.

I could feel my own brow creasing with concern as I cast a glance towards the sun in the distance, its golden rays painting the sky in shades of orange and pink, a reminder of the passage of time and the urgency of our task. Time was slipping away, and I knew that if we wanted to have this celebration, we needed to get things moving, to put our plans into action before the opportunity slipped through our fingers.

"I can get it for you, if you like?" Beatrix offered, her words catching me off guard, my eyebrows rising in surprise at the unexpected gesture of kindness. I could see the sincerity in her eyes, the genuine desire to help and support us in any way she could.

I stammered slightly, my mind racing to find the right words, to express my gratitude and appreciation for her offer while still maintaining a sense of propriety and responsibility. "It's okay. Luke can do it. It might cost a bit to get enough for all of us. I wouldn't want you to have to worry about that," I tried to explain, my hands gesturing awkwardly as I spoke, a physical manifestation of the uncertainty and discomfort that I felt at the thought of imposing on Beatrix's kindness.

To my surprise, Beatrix and Jerome chuckled in unison, a shared moment of amusement that only served to deepen the blush of embarrassment that crept across my cheeks. I could feel the heat rising in my face, a reminder of the awkwardness and self-consciousness that I often felt in social situations, a trait that had always been a part of my personality. Jerome, however, beat Beatrix to the retort, a mischievous glint in his eye as he spoke, a hint of playfulness and humour in his voice.

"I don't think she'll be using her own money," he said, extracting one of the hundred dollar notes from his pocket, a reminder of the earlier money heist that had taken place, a moment of confusion that seemed like a lifetime ago now. I could see the crisp edges of the note, the way it fluttered slightly in the breeze, a tangible symbol of the new reality that we found ourselves in, a world where the old rules and norms no longer seemed to apply.

I could feel the heat rising in my face as Beatrix quickly affirmed that Jerome was indeed correct, her laughter ringing out across the Drop Zone, a sound of pure joy and amusement that seemed to lift the spirits of everyone around her. "I don't think I'll ever need to use any of my own money again," Beatrix replied, her eyes sparkling with mirth, a hint of mischief and playfulness in her voice that made it clear she was enjoying this moment of levity and camaraderie.

Charles, his face alight with excitement, made a grab for the note in Jerome's hand, his fingers stretching out to snatch it from his brother's grasp, only to have it whisked away at the last moment, a playful game of keep-away that brought a smile to my face. "Can I have some too?" he asked, his voice hopeful, his eyes wide with anticipation.

I could feel my brow furrowing once more, mirroring Jerome's expression. "What do you need money for?" I asked, my tone a mixture of curiosity and concern, a desire to understand what was driving Charles's request, to ensure that he was making wise and responsible choices.

"Doesn't everybody need money these days," Charles jested playfully, his face a picture of innocence, his eyes twinkling with mischief, a reminder of the quick wit and humour that had always been a part of his personality. It was a trait that I had always admired in him, the ability to bring a smile to the faces of those around him with a well-timed quip or a playful jab.

Beatrix let out a soft giggle, her hand reaching out to ruffle Charles's hair affectionately, a gesture of warmth and affection that spoke to the bonds that had already begun to form between them. "Don't worry. There's plenty to go around. Perhaps you can be Bixbus's first banker," she joked, her voice light and teasing.

"Nah," replied Charles, his face stoic, his tone deadpan, a moment of seriousness that belied the playful nature of the conversation. "I wanna be the bank itself." His words elicited a round of chuckles from Beatrix, Jerome, and myself, the tension of the moment dissipating in the face of his playful wit.

"You're an idiot, Charles," Jerome joked, his voice filled with affection, his arm draping across his brother's shoulders in a gesture of camaraderie, a show of the love and loyalty that had always been the hallmark of their relationship.

I cleared my throat, bringing the conversation back to the matter at hand. "If you don't mind getting the meat, Beatrix, that'd be great," I told her, my voice sincere, my eyes meeting hers in a silent plea, a recognition of her willingness to go above and beyond to help.

"Sure. It's no problem at all," Beatrix answered, her smile warm and reassuring. "What do you want?" she asked, her voice filled with a sense of purpose and determination, a readiness to tackle the task head-on.

I paused for a moment, considering the options, my mind racing with the possibilities and potential of the feast. "I'll cook a barbecue, so I guess just a lot of sausages and steaks would probably suffice," I reasoned, my voice tinged with a hint of excitement and anticipation.

"Easy done," Beatrix confirmed, her tone confident, her eyes shining with enthusiasm.

I nodded, a sense of relief washing over me, a feeling of gratitude and appreciation. I paused in thought, my mind working through the logistics of the celebration, the tasks that still needed to be completed and the resources that would need to be gathered. "I'll come back in an hour or so, then?" I asked tentatively, my voice tinged with uncertainty, a recognition of the fluidity and unpredictability of our current situation.

Beatrix chuckled, her head shaking slightly, a hint of amusement and disbelief in her eyes. "It won't take me that long," she replied, her brows creasing as she turned her attention to Charles, her eyes narrowing in thought, a moment of concentration and focus that spoke to the depth of her knowledge and understanding of this new world. "You and Luke came through the Portal at a supermarket, didn't you?" she asked, her voice curious, her tone filled with a sense of excitement and possibility.

Charles nodded enthusiastically. "Yeah. It's across the road from our house," he replied, his words tumbling out in a rush of excitement.

"And I assume there'll be a place I can buy meat from there?" Beatrix asked, her gaze shifting between Charles and myself.

Charles shrugged, his face a picture of uncertainty.

"Charles only buys junk food," Jerome answered for him, his tone teasing, his eyes sparkling with mirth, a playful jab at his brother's eating habits and preferences that brought a smile to my face.

Beatrix chuckled, while Charles pouted, his face a mask of indignation, a moment of playful banter and sibling rivalry.

"There's a butcher, as well as a standard supermarket," I answered, my mind conjuring up images of the familiar shops and stores that had once been a part of our daily lives, a reminder of the world that we had left behind.

"Perfect!" Beatrix exclaimed, her face alight with excitement. "Give me fifteen minutes and I'll be back," she said, her words filled with a sense of urgency and importance.

The three of us gazed at Beatrix in awe, our mouths hanging open slightly, our minds struggling to comprehend the ease with which she spoke of traversing between worlds, her casual confidence and self-assurance.

"How can you do it so quickly?" Charles was the first to ask the question that was on all of our lips, his voice filled with wonder, his eyes wide with curiosity.

Beatrix grinned widely, her hand reaching into her pocket and extracting her Portal Key, holding it out for us to see, a small device that seemed to hold the power and potential of the universe within its sleek and shimmering surface. We looked at it in fascination, our eyes wide with wonder and amazement.

"Wherever Luke and I open the Portal on Earth, it seems to somehow record the location," Beatrix began to explain, her face scrunching up in concentration as she tried to put the complex mechanics and inner workings of the device into words that we could understand, a task that seemed to tax even her considerable knowledge and expertise.

"What does that mean?" Jerome asked, his brow furrowed, his mind working to make sense of the concept, to wrap his head around the incredible technology that seemed to defy all logic and reason.

"It means that Luke and Beatrix can come and go from any of those locations," Charles replied, his eyes turning to Beatrix for confirmation, his voice filled with a sense of understanding and clarity that belied his deceptive joviality, a reminder of the keen intellect that lay beneath the surface of his playful exterior.

"Bingo," Beatrix declared, her face lighting up with pride at Charles's quick grasp of the situation. "So, because you and Luke recorded the location at the shops, I can walk through the Portal here and exit right there," she explained, her excitement palpable, her words tumbling out in a rush of enthusiasm and energy.

"Hang on," Jerome interrupted, his hand held up in a gesture of pause, his face a mask of concentration. He pointed towards me as he continued to speak, his words slow and deliberate. "We came through the Portal at our house. Does that mean that you can go back to our house?" he asked Beatrix, his voice tinged with a mix of hope and trepidation.

"Sure does," Beatrix replied, her tone matter-of-fact, her eyes shining with the possibilities that this revelation presented, a reminder of the incredible power and potential that lay within the small device that she held in her hand.

I felt a knot form in the pit of my stomach, a sense of unease washing over me. "I don't think that's a very good idea," I said, my words cutting through the excitement and enthusiasm that hung in the air like a tangible presence, my tone serious and firm.

The three of them looked at me curiously, their faces a mix of confusion and concern, a silent communication of the questions and doubts that swirled within their minds, the desire to understand and make sense of what I was suggesting.

"The police might still be there," I explained, my mind conjuring up images of the chaos and confusion that had surrounded the sudden departure of Luke and Charles, the potential dangers and risks that might still be lurking at our family home, and the need to proceed with caution and care in the face of the unknown.

Jerome's brow creased, realisation dawning on his face as he considered my words, a recognition of the gravity and importance of the situation that we found ourselves in, the need to think carefully and strategically about our next steps and decisions. Charles frowned too, his excitement dimming somewhat in the face of this new information.

"What do you want to go back to our house for, anyway?" I asked, my gaze shifting between my sons, my voice tinged with a mix of curiosity and concern, a desire to understand their motivations and intentions.

Jerome shrugged, his face a picture of uncertainty, his eyes avoiding mine, a silent communication of the doubts and fears that swirled within his mind, the desire to hold onto the familiar and the known even in the face of the unknown and the uncertain.

"I'll go and get that meat for you," Beatrix interrupted, her voice cutting through the tension and uncertainty that hung in the air, her eyes filled with understanding and compassion.

"That'd be great," I answered, my voice filled with gratitude, my eyes meeting hers in a silent thank you, a recognition of the incredible gift that she was giving us.

And with that, the Portal burst to life, a swirling vortex of energy that crackled and hummed with power. We watched in awe as Beatrix stepped forward, her figure disappearing into the shimmering light, the Portal closing behind her in silence.

I stood there for a moment, my mind reeling with the events of the past few minutes, my heart filled with a mix of emotions that I couldn't quite put into words. Pride at the way my sons had handled themselves, amazement at the incredible technology that had brought us to this place, and a sense of unease at the thought of the life we had left behind.

But as I looked at Jerome and Charles, their faces filled with excitement and wonder, I knew that whatever challenges lay ahead, whatever obstacles we might face, we would face them together, as a family. And with the help of Guardians like Beatrix and Luke, with the strength of our faith in the Lord, and the power of our love, I knew that we would find a way to make this new life work, to build a future that was filled with hope and possibility.

❖

In Beatrix's absence, Charles and Jerome eagerly showed me the goods they had found at the Drop Zone, their faces alight with excitement and pride as they revealed their treasures. They had managed to procure several sets of stainless steel cooking utensils, gleaming in the sunlight like precious metals, along with colourful tablecloths and matching napkins that seemed to burst with festive cheer. Their excitement was palpable, a tangible energy that seemed to crackle in the air around them as they proudly displayed their findings, their faces beaming with a sense of accomplishment and satisfaction.

As I fumbled with folding one of the tablecloths, my fingers clumsy and awkward in the face of such domestic tasks, a thought suddenly occurred to me, a realisation that sent a chill down my spine and made my stomach clench with worry. "I don't think we have any tables," I interrupted their show and tell, my brow furrowing with concern, my voice tinged with a hint of desperation. "Not to mention the lack of chairs," I added, my mind already working through the logistics of hosting a proper potluck dinner in our current circumstances, the challenges and obstacles that seemed to loom larger with each passing moment.

Charles and Jerome's faces fell, the disappointment evident in their expressions as they realised the implications of my words, the wind taken out of their sails by the harsh reality of our situation. I could see their enthusiasm deflating, their grand plans for the celebration suddenly seeming less achievable, a dream that was slipping through their fingers like sand. It broke my heart to see them so crestfallen, to watch the light in their eyes dim and the smiles fade from their faces, but I knew that we had to be realistic, that we had to face the facts head-on if we were to have any hope of making this celebration a success.

Sensing their disheartened state, I quickly sought to offer a solution, my mind racing with possibilities and ideas, a desperate attempt to reignite their excitement and keep their spirits high. "Just keep it simple, like one of our church potluck dinners," I suggested, my voice filled with a forced cheerfulness that belied the uncertainty and doubt that gnawed at my insides. It was a familiar concept, a tradition that we had all grown up with, and I hoped that the familiarity would bring some comfort and reassurance to my sons.

At the mention of the church potlucks, Charles' and Jerome's eyes lit up instantly, their faces breaking into wide grins, a spark of recognition and excitement that seemed to banish the shadows of disappointment that had settled over them just moments before. "The chapel," they both echoed in unison, their voices filled with a renewed sense of possibility, a glimmer of hope that seemed to shine like a beacon in the darkness.

I frowned, clearly seeing where their minds were heading, a sense of unease settling over me like a heavy blanket. I knew that they were imagining the convenience of having Beatrix infiltrate our church building and bring back some of the fold-up tables and stackable chairs to Clivilius, a solution that seemed so simple and straightforward on the surface.

While the idea of having proper seating and tables for our celebration was appealing, a luxury that we had taken for granted in our old life, I couldn't help but feel a sense of unease at the thought of sending Beatrix on such a risky mission. Given our current situation, I knew that we had to be cautious and mindful of the potential consequences of our actions, that we couldn't afford to take unnecessary risks or draw unwanted attention to ourselves.

"Wouldn't that be amazing," Jerome turned to Charles and said, his voice filled with wistful longing, a dreamy expression settling over his features as he imagined the possibilities, the comforts and conveniences that seemed so tantalisingly close, yet so far out of reach.

Attempting to dispel their idea before it could take root, before it could grow into a full-fledged plan that would be impossible to stop, I interjected, my voice firm and unyielding. "I don't have my keys," I said, hoping that the practicality of the situation would be enough to dissuade them, to bring them back down to earth and remind them of the limitations and challenges that we faced. But I could see from the determined looks on their faces that they were having none of it, that they were not willing to let go of their dream so easily.

"Beatrix could get your keys," Charles suggested, his eyes sparkling with mischief, his mind already working on a plan to make their vision a reality, a scheme that seemed to dance just beyond the edges of my comprehension. I could see the wheels turning in his head, the gears shifting and clicking into place as he plotted and planned, a master strategist in the making.

I shook my head firmly, my face stern as I sought to put an end to their scheming, to nip this idea in the bud before it could grow into something uncontrollable. "Not tonight, Charles," I said, my tone leaving no room for argument.

But Jerome was not ready to give up so easily, his determination and stubbornness a match for my own. "Oh, come on," he pleaded, his voice taking on a wheedling tone, a hint of desperation creeping into his words as he sought to persuade me, to wear down my resistance with the sheer force of his enthusiasm. "It won't be a proper potluck if we have to sit in the dirt," he argued, his eyes wide and imploring, a look that I had seen countless times before, a look that never failed to tug at my heartstrings and make me question my resolve.

I felt my resolve wavering in the face of their earnest pleas, their heartfelt desire to make this celebration something special, something memorable. But I knew that I had to stand firm, that I had to be the voice of reason and responsibility in this situation, no matter how much it pained me to disappoint them. "We don't need tables," I said, my voice firm and unyielding, a reminder of the sacrifices and compromises that we would all have to make in this new world, a world that was so different from the one we had left behind.

Just then, the Portal burst to life, a swirling vortex of energy and light that seemed to fill the air with a crackling intensity, a reminder of the incredible technology and power that lay at our fingertips. Beatrix returned, her arms laden with bags of meat, a triumphant smile on her face as she handed them over to me, a gesture of generosity and kindness that warmed my heart and made me feel a surge of gratitude. "Hopefully this is enough," she said, her voice filled with a sense of accomplishment.

I peered into the bags, my eyes widening with satisfaction as I took in the generous amount of sausages and steaks that she had procured, a bounty that seemed almost too good to be true. "This is plenty. Thank you, Beatrix," I told her warmly, my gratitude evident in my voice.

Out of the corner of my eye, I caught Charles and Jerome exchanging a glance, a silent communication that spoke volumes about their intentions, their determination to see their plan through to the end. I knew that they were planning to ask Beatrix about getting my keys from our house, a request that filled me with a sense of dread and unease, a fear of the unknown and the unpredictable.

I moved quickly to intervene, to redirect their attention and steer the conversation in a different direction. "Can the two of you help bring—" I began, my words tumbling out in a rush, a desperate attempt to change the subject before it could even be raised.

But Charles cut me off, his determination overriding my attempt to redirect their attention, his voice filled with a mixture of hope and pleading, a desperation that seemed to pour out of him like a torrent. "Beatrix, can you get Dad's keys from our house?" he asked, his eyes wide and imploring.

"Charles!" I scolded, my frustration rising at his blatant disregard for my wishes, my voice sharp and stern, a reminder of the boundaries and limitations that we all had to respect, even in this new world. "I said no."

But Charles merely shrugged, seemingly unperturbed by my insistence, his focus unwavering as he maintained his gaze on Beatrix, his eyes wide and imploring, a silent plea for her to take his side, to help make his dream a reality.

Beatrix hesitated for a moment, her voice uncertain as she replied, a hint of confusion and uncertainty in her tone. "I guess. What do you need them for?" she asked, her brow furrowing slightly, a look of curiosity and concern settling over her features.

Before I had a chance to intervene, to explain the situation and dissuade her from getting involved, Jerome was quick to back up Charles, his words rushing out in a torrent of excitement and enthusiasm, a flood of information that seemed to sweep Beatrix along in its wake. "Dad has a key to the chapel. There's heaps of fold up tables and stackable plastic chairs," he said, his face alight with the prospect of making their dream potluck a reality, a vision that seemed to dance before his eyes like a mirage.

Beatrix's eyes lit up with recognition, a broad smile spreading across her face, a look of understanding and excitement that made my heart sink with dread. "Got it," she said, her voice filled with a sense of purpose and determination.

I tried one last time to dissuade them, my concern for Beatrix's safety overriding my desire to please my sons, my fear of the unknown and the unpredictable a weight that seemed to press down on my shoulders like a physical burden. "But the police—" I began, my words trailing off as Beatrix cut me off with a dismissive wave of her hand, a gesture that seemed to brush aside my concerns like so much dust in the wind.

"I'll be fine," she said, her voice filled with a confidence that I found both admirable and worrying, a self-assurance that seemed to border on recklessness. "They're not looking for me," she added, as if that would make her presence at our family home any less suspicious if she were to be caught, a logic that seemed flawed and dangerous to my worried mind.

I sighed loudly, recognising the futility of trying to argue with the combined determination of Beatrix and my sons, a force that seemed unstoppable in the face of their shared enthusiasm and excitement. "They're likely in the top drawer of my bedside table," I told her, my voice heavy with resignation, a defeat that seemed to settle over me like a shroud.

Charles and Jerome couldn't contain their grins, their faces splitting into wide smiles of victory, a sense of triumph that seemed to radiate from every pore. "Yes!" Charles cried out, his voice filled with a sense of elation and excitement, a joy that seemed to bubble up from deep within him.

Beatrix pulled her phone from her pocket, her fingers poised to type, a look of concentration settling over her features as she prepared to input the necessary information. "What's the address?" she asked, her eyes fixed on the screen, a focus that seemed to block out everything else around her.

Jerome eyed her curiously, his brow furrowing in confusion, a look of puzzlement that seemed to mirror my own. "I thought you could go straight to our house from the Portal?" he asked, his voice tinged with a hint of doubt.

Charles laughed loudly, his amusement at his brother's misunderstanding evident in his voice. "She means the church building, stupid," he told Jerome, his tone teasing and affectionate.

I watched as Jerome's face flushed a deep red, embarrassment colouring his features as he realised his mistake, a look of shame and discomfort that made my heart ache with sympathy and understanding.

"He's right," Beatrix confirmed, her voice gentle and reassuring, even as Jerome's face turned an even deeper shade of crimson, a blush that seemed to spread from his cheeks to the tips of his ears.

As I gave Beatrix the address, my voice shaking slightly with a mixture of fear and resignation, she typed the details into her phone, her fingers flying across the screen with practiced ease, a dexterity that seemed almost superhuman in its speed and accuracy. "I'm not sure whether anybody will be there tonight, but the keys will give you full access to the property and the building," I told her, my mind already running through the various scenarios that could unfold, the dangers and risks that seemed to lurk around every corner.

Charles and Jerome continued to let out cheers of success and excitement, their voices rising in a cacophony of joy and anticipation.

"I still don't think this is a good idea," I voiced my opinion, my tone heavy with concern and apprehension, a sense of unease that seemed to settle in the pit of my stomach like a lead weight.

But Beatrix merely grinned, a sly smile spreading across her face, a look of mischief and excitement that made my heart race with a mixture of fear and anticipation. "It'll be fun," she said, her voice filled with a sense of adventure and daring, a willingness to take risks and push boundaries that both thrilled and terrified me.

I could feel a slight grimace crossing my face, my mind torn between the desire to indulge my sons' wishes and the need to adhere to the rules and boundaries that had always governed our lives, the principles and values that had been instilled in us from a young age. I had always been a stickler for following the proper channels, for respecting authority and tradition, a belief that had served me well throughout my life. But here, in this new world, those rules seemed to hold less sway, a realisation that made me feel adrift and uncertain, like a ship without a rudder.

"I wish we had Portal Keys, too," Charles said, a forlorn look settling over his features as he contemplated the freedom and possibilities that such a device would afford, the power and control that seemed to be just out of reach.

Beatrix turned to him, her expression softening with understanding, a look of empathy and compassion that made my heart swell with gratitude and affection. "Your role here is just as important," she told him, her voice filled with a gentle reassurance. "And it can be just as fun and adventurous," she added, her eyes sparkling with a hint of mischief, a promise of excitement and wonder that seemed to dance just beyond the horizon.

But Charles remained unconvinced, his pout deepening as he crossed his arms over his chest, a gesture of defiance and disappointment that made my heart ache with sympathy and understanding.

Sensing that the conversation was veering off course, that we were getting bogged down in the details and losing sight of the bigger picture, I quickly interjected, my voice filled with a sense of urgency and purpose. "We need to get this meat back to camp," I said, my mind already racing with the preparations that needed to be made. "I need to start cooking soon."

Jerome turned his attention back to Beatrix, his voice filled with a mixture of hope and expectation, a sense of anticipation that seemed to crackle in the air around him like static electricity. "We'll meet you back here later?" he said, his words half question, half statement of agreement.

Beatrix nodded, her face breaking into a cheerful grin, a look of enthusiasm and excitement that seemed to light up the world around her. "Deal," she said, giving us a playful salute before activating her Portal and stepping into the swirling, colourful vortex, a dazzling display of light and energy that seemed to defy all laws of physics.

As the Portal closed behind her, I turned to my sons, my voice filled with a mixture of resignation and determination, a sense of purpose and responsibility that seemed to settle over me. "Come on, you two," I said, already making my way towards the camp, the bags of meat heavy in my arms.

With heavy sighs, they fell into step behind me, their footsteps crunching against the dry, dusty ground as we made our way back to the heart of our new community, a journey that seemed to stretch out before us like a winding road.

❖

As we approached the campfire, our arms laden with the meat, colourful tablecloths, gleaming utensils, and matching napkins the boys had collected from the Drop Zone, a sudden realisation hit me, a jolt of frustration and self-reproach that made my face fall and my brow furrow with disappointment.

"I forgot to check for any additional camping supplies," I said, my voice heavy with self-reproach, a sigh of frustration escaping my lips as I mentally kicked myself for the oversight. It was a simple task, one that should have been at the forefront of my mind, but in the excitement and drama of the moment, it had slipped through the cracks, leaving me feeling like a failure as a father and a leader.

Jerome and Charles exchanged a glance, a silent communication passing between them, a flicker of disappointment and impatience that danced in their eyes like a flame. I could see the unspoken desire to forge ahead with their plans without delay, to seize the moment and make the most of the opportunity that lay before them, even if it meant leaving some tasks unfinished.

Jerome set the collection of celebration goods down near the campfire, his movements careful and deliberate. Charles followed suit, his actions quick and purposeful, as if he couldn't wait to be on his way, to escape the confines of the camp and embark on the next phase of their grand adventure.

"We'll head back to the Portals to meet with Beatrix," Jerome said, his voice carefully neutral, his eyes searching mine for a reaction, a hint of the approval or permission that he so desperately sought. There was a pleading quality to his tone.

But my response seemed to catch them both off guard, a bombshell that shattered their hopes and dreams like a hammer striking glass. "I'll come with you," I said, my tone firm and unyielding.

Jerome's shoulders sagged, a groan of dismay threatening to escape his lips, a physical manifestation of the disappointment and frustration that seemed to well up within him like a tidal wave. Charles, on the other hand, let out a loud, vocal groan, his frustration echoing across the camp, a sound that seemed to pierce the very heavens and rend the air with its intensity.

I sighed wearily, my eyes flickering between my sons with a mix of understanding and exasperation, a recognition of the conflicting emotions that warred within them, the desire for independence and adventure that clashed with the need for guidance and protection. I knew that they were eager to move forward with their plans, to revel in the excitement of the upcoming celebration, to bask in the glow of their own accomplishments and triumphs. But as their father, I couldn't shake the sense of responsibility that weighed heavily upon my shoulders, the need to ensure their safety and well-being, even if it meant putting my own desires and wishes aside.

Just as I was about to reinforce that I would accompany them, to drive home the point and leave no room for misinterpretation or negotiation, a voice called out from behind us, cutting through the stillness of the camp, a sudden intrusion that shattered the moment.

"Noah," the voice called again, the sound drawing my attention away from my sons, a summons that I couldn't ignore, even if I wanted to. There was a familiarity to the tone, a hint of recognition that tugged at the edges of my memory, a sense that I had heard this voice before, even if I couldn't quite place it.

Jerome and Charles turned in the direction of the approaching man, their eyes widening with curiosity, a flicker of interest and excitement that danced across their features like a flame.

"I think it might be Chris," Charles leaned in and whispered to Jerome, his voice barely audible over the crackling of the campfire.

Jerome eyed him curiously, his expression signalling that the name still meant nothing to him, a blank slate that seemed to reflect the confusion and uncertainty that swirled within his mind. It was a reminder of the gaps in our knowledge, the pieces of the puzzle that we had yet to assemble.

"Karen's husband," Charles explained, his tone patient and understanding. There was a hint of pride in his voice, a sense of accomplishment and satisfaction that seemed to radiate from his face.

"How do you know that?" Jerome asked, surprise colouring his voice, a hint of admiration and respect that seemed to shine through the confusion and uncertainty that clouded his features. I couldn't help but wonder the same thing, marvelling at how quickly Charles seemed to be adapting to our new surroundings, a testament to his resilience and adaptability, his ability to thrive and flourish even in the face of such drastic change.

Charles shrugged, a playful, boastful smile tugging at the edges of his lips, as if he was relishing the fact that he knew something his brother didn't, a moment of triumph and achievement that seemed to fill him with a sense of pride and satisfaction. It was a reminder of the competitive spirit that had always existed between them, the desire to outdo and outshine each other.

As the man approached, I extended my hand towards him, a gesture of greeting and welcome. "Chris," I said, my voice warm and friendly.

As we shook hands, I caught sight of Charles nudging Jerome with his elbow, indicating that it was the opportunity for them to depart, a chance to escape the watchful eye of their father and embark on their own adventure, free from any constraints and limitations. It was a moment of rebellion and defiance, a reminder of their fierce independence and determination.

Without another word, Jerome and Charles spun on their heels and walked briskly away, their steps hurried and purposeful, a sense of urgency and excitement that seemed to propel them forward like a rocket, a force of nature that could not be denied or contained.

"Jerome! Charles!" Greta's voice echoed from behind them, her tone a mixture of concern and exasperation.

Ignoring their mother, Jerome and Charles broke into a light jog, their feet pounding against the dusty ground as they tried to put some distance between themselves and Greta, a desperate attempt to escape the weight of responsibility and expectation.

But they had barely taken more than a few steps when my voice boomed across the short distance, beckoning them to stop, a command that could not be ignored or denied. "Jerome! Charles! Come back here!" I called out, my tone leaving no room for argument or debate, a reminder of the authority and respect that I demanded as their father and leader.

Realising that ignorance had become futile, Jerome and Charles ground to an abrupt halt, their shoulders slumping in defeat. Slowly, they turned towards Greta, who was now hurrying towards them, her face a mask of concern and worry.

As Greta approached the boys, I turned my attention back to Chris. "It's good to finally meet you," I said to him as we shook hands, his grip firm and reassuring.

Chris smiled warmly, his eyes crinkling at the corners. "Likewise, Noah. Karen has told me a lot about you and your family."

For a moment, we both stood there in silence, the weight of our newfound circumstances hanging in the air between us. It wasn't an awkward or uncomfortable silence, but rather a shared understanding of the challenges and uncertainties that lay ahead.

It was Chris who finally broke the silence, taking a deep breath before he spoke. "Well, shall we get this cooking underway, then?" he asked, giving me a gentle clap on the shoulder.

I felt a smile tug at the corners of my mouth, a sense of gratitude and appreciation washing over me. "Yeah," I replied, nodding my head in agreement. "Let's get to it."

Together, Chris and I reached for the bags of meat, our hands working in unison as we began to unpack the supplies. As we worked, the occasional sounds of laughter from Karen and Greta filled the air, a reminder of the community that we were building, one meal and one moment at a time. And as the savoury aroma of grilling meat began to waft through the air, I couldn't help but feel a sense of hope and optimism for the future.

LIGHT THE FIRE

4338.213.10

The night unfurled like a vibrant tapestry under the dark Clivilius sky, the bonfire celebration at its heart reaching a euphoric crescendo. Flames danced wildly, casting a warm golden glow on the faces of settlers seated around the campfire. Their features flickered in the light, a living mosaic of joy, nostalgia, and camaraderie.

We were a motley crew of dreamers and doers, each with our own stories, yet bound together by the fire's shared warmth and our collective hopes for this new world we were building. The air filled with laughter and the scent of burning wood, hints of sweet spiced beverages drifting on the breeze.

My newfound family gathered close, voices merging into a harmonious symphony. Funny tales and heartfelt anecdotes wove together, each one adding colour to the rich communal life emerging around us. Amidst the convivial din, my gaze drifted to Greta.

Her laughter was music, weaving through the fire's crackle and the murmuring conversations. I reached out and grasped her hand, feeling the warmth of her skin against mine. She turned, eyes reflecting the fire's glow, and a radiant smile bloomed on her lips, lighting up the night even more than the flames.

"You've outdone yourself," I whispered to her, the words floating between us, carrying with them my admiration and the unspoken feelings that had been growing stronger within me. The bonfire's crackle seemed to pause, waiting for her response, as if the night itself hushed in anticipation.

Greta's hand tightened around mine, a silent communication more potent than words. Her smile widened, and she took a leisurely sip of her hot chocolate, the steam curling up into the cool night air, mingling with the warmth between us. Her simple gesture, a squeeze of the hand, conveyed volumes—recognition, gratitude, and perhaps a hint of something deeper.

The flickering firelight painted our surroundings with a surreal hue, transforming the ordinary into the extraordinary. As I glanced around, the uniqueness of our situation struck me — this motley assembly around the fire wasn't just a gathering; it was a testament to our resilience and unity. My heart swelled with a mix of pride and gratitude as I noticed four of my six children blending seamlessly into this unconventional tapestry of our new life.

Jerome and Charles, my youngest, stood out amidst the crowd. Despite their youth and the scarcity of peers in this fledgling settlement, they exuded an infectious enthusiasm that seemed to defy our unusual circumstances. Jerome, at twenty-one, was on the cusp of manhood, his eyes alight with an adventurous spirit. Next to him, Charles's laughter rang out, a clear, joyful sound that resonated with the crackling of the fire, reminding everyone around that happiness finds a way, even in the most unlikely places.

I couldn't help but feel a twinge of fatherly concern for them. The settlement, with its sparse young population, offered limited companionship for someone their age. Yet, here they were, mingling, laughing, and carving out a place for themselves among this eclectic group of settlers. It was a comforting reminder of their adaptability and resilience.

My eyes then wandered to Kain, a young man in his mid-twenties who was the closest in age to Jerome. Though I couldn't recall his exact age, it was clear he was slightly older, perhaps by a handful of years. A hope began to emerge that he might somewhat act as a bridge between the adults and the younger ones like Jerome and Charles, helping them to feel more comfortable in this strange, new environment.

The atmosphere around the bonfire took a spirited turn as Charles, with his innate flair for drama and humour, stepped into the limelight. Known within our family as the master jokester and storyteller, he had a unique talent for capturing an audience, and tonight was no exception. As he embarked on his exaggerated retelling of our family's arrival in Clivilius, I watched, a mix of amusement and apprehension stirring within me.

Charles's storytelling painted our journey with broad, colourful strokes of chaos and surprise, turning our real-life experiences into a captivating saga. His voice, rich with animation, echoed around the fire, drawing laughter and gasps from our fellow settlers. The way he described our initial moments in Clivilius, you'd think we had stepped into a slapstick comedy rather than a new world.

However, as he delved into the more personal aspects of our story, my amusement began to wane, replaced by a growing discomfort. When he touched upon our Mormon heritage and its influence on my decision to venture through the Portal, I felt a twinge of unease. These were intimate details, beliefs that guided not just our journey, but our very lives. I appreciated humour, but the sanctity of our faith and the profound convictions behind our decisions were not subjects I took lightly.

As Charles's narrative teetered on the brink of jesting about Greta's and my belief in finding the New Jerusalem in this land, my discomfort intensified. It was one thing to poke fun at our misadventures, but to make light of our spiritual journey felt like a step too far.

Sensing my unease, and perhaps sharing it, Greta intervened with a subtle, yet effective gesture. A short, stern look from her was all it took to steer Charles away from the delicate topic. It was a look that carried the weight of a thousand words, a silent reminder of the respect we owed to the beliefs that had, unwittingly, guided us here.

As Charles's narrative meandered, it took an unexpected detour into a tale about our family's food storage and a rather daring escapade involving him and Luke. The story, filled with twists and turns, depicted their last-minute ingenuity to outwit the police during a raid at our home. It was a story that straddled the line between audacity and recklessness, a tale I was only partially aware of, having been informed about it in mere fragments by Charles himself.

Disappointment twined around my heart as the details unfolded. Neither Luke nor Paul had seen fit to discuss the incident with me directly, leaving an uncomfortable pang in my chest. As a father, I longed for open communication with my children, for them to feel they could share their troubles and triumphs with me. And yet, here I was, learning about their exploits secondhand, in the same manner as the rest of the settlement, through Charles's animated recounting.

I had previously extracted a promise from Charles to keep this episode from his mother, hoping to spare her the worry and the stress. But as he spun the tale with his characteristic zeal, it became painfully evident that my request had slipped through the cracks of his selective memory. Classic Charles—intelligent, charismatic, but occasionally heedless of the promises he made.

Despite my mixed feelings, I couldn't deny the captivating effect of his storytelling. The settlers hung on his every word, expressions shifting between disbelief and amusement. His ability to bring a story to life, to infuse humour and excitement into the fabric of our daily existence, was undeniable. Even as I wrestled with my personal reactions, I couldn't help but admire his skill, the way he could command attention and lift the spirits of those around him.

As the story reached its climax, with Charles and Luke narrowly evading capture in a comically exaggerated finale, the crowd erupted in laughter and applause. I managed a smile, recognising the value of these shared moments of levity, especially in a world as uncertain as ours. The bonfire crackled in agreement, its warm glow a comforting presence in the cool night.

Greta's eyes met mine across the flickering flames, her gaze laden with concern and unspoken questions. Her expression, a silent inquiry into the veracity of Charles's tale, tugged at my conscience. I mustered a smile, aiming to be the beacon of reassurance she sought, despite the whirlpool of emotions churning inside me.

"It's not really anything serious," I said, my voice laced with a calm I didn't quite feel. I leaned on the knowledge of Charles's penchant for embellishment, hoping to downplay the situation. "I'll tell you about it later," I promised, locking eyes with her in a silent pledge of transparency.

Greta's response was a brief pout, a subtle display of her initial discontent, yet it faded as she seemed to accept my words, turning her attention back to the steaming mug cradled in her hands and the ongoing saga of Charles's narration. I watched her for a moment, her figure illuminated by the campfire's glow, a symbol of the stability and comfort I so valued.

With Greta's concern momentarily assuaged, I allowed myself a moment to breathe, the air cool and crisp against my skin. Yet, the relief was short-lived, overshadowed by a burgeoning resolve to seek clarity from Luke or Paul. The need to understand the full scope of what had transpired at our family home gnawed at me, a reminder of the unresolved threads of our past life, that continued to seep into our new one.

As I sat there, the laughter and warmth of the gathering swirling around me, a sudden wave of sadness enveloped me. The realisation that our family home, a repository of memories and milestones, was now a part of our irrevocable past, struck a chord deep within. I had always considered myself somewhat detached from material possessions, valuing experiences and relationships over physical objects. Yet, the stark reality of losing every tangible link to my past life, the abrupt severance from all I had known, stirred a sense of loss I hadn't anticipated.

Jerome's voice, tinged with a playful lilt, cut through the tapestry of my introspective thoughts, yanking me back to the vibrant reality of our campfire gathering. "Speaking of toilet rolls," he announced, his words laced with an impish mischief that promised a tale both amusing and potentially embarrassing.

Paul's reaction was immediate, his grin wide and knowing, as if the mere mention of toilet rolls had triggered a cascade of amusing recollections. "Is this that time in Broken Hill with the Clarke's?" he inquired, his smile betraying a shared history of inside jokes and past escapades.

I found myself momentarily adrift, my mind scrambling to connect the dots, to unearth the memory that seemed to amuse Jerome and Paul so much. Despite my efforts, the reference eluded me, leaving a blank space where a shared chuckle should have been. This wasn't unusual in our large, boisterous family, where individual adventures sometimes became communal lore before everyone had a chance to live them.

Jerome beamed with the delight of a storyteller holding a captive audience. "Yep, that one," he confirmed, his broad smile setting the stage for what was sure to be an entertaining recounting. His enthusiasm was infectious, and despite my initial disconnect, I found myself leaning in, eager to be swept up in the narrative.

"Is this really something that I want to know?" Greta's question, tinged with a note of disapproval, floated through the air, momentarily casting a shadow over the burgeoning excitement around the campfire. Her voice, laced with the familiar timbre of maternal concern, reminded me of the countless times she had tried to steer our children away from mischief, her vigilant eyes always watching over their youthful escapades.

I couldn't help but chuckle softly. Over the years, I had come to accept the inevitability of our children's mischievous undertakings. Despite Greta's diligent attempts at oversight, the kids, like all children, found their ways into harmless trouble, their adventures unfolding beyond the watchful gaze of parenthood. These instances, I believed, were part of growing up, essential stitches in the fabric of their childhood. Nothing they did ever struck me as alarmingly serious, just the usual antics that would later fuel family stories, much like the one Jerome was about to share.

Kain's enthusiastic interjection, "Oh, come on! You have to tell us now," mirrored my own curiosity. His eagerness to dive into the tale added a ripple of anticipation that spread through the group, igniting a collective intrigue.

Jerome, now the centre of attention, seemed almost overwhelmed by his own mirth, struggling to contain the laughter threatening to erupt. Watching him, I felt a surge of affection for these moments of shared joy, for the ties that bound us together through laughter and stories.

I found myself leaning forward, drawn in by the gravitational pull of the narrative about to unfold. There was something about the promise of a shared laugh, of a tale that would soon become another thread in the tapestry of our family's history, that was irresistibly captivating.

As Jerome launched into his narrative, the flicker of the campfire seemed to synchronise with the unfolding of his words, casting dancing shadows that mimicked the rhythm of his storytelling. "It was when we were living in Broken Hill. I was quite young, but Paul and Luke let me come along," he recounted, his voice imbued with a nostalgic reverence for a past adventure.

While Jerome wove the fabric of his tale, my mind wandered momentarily to Lisa and Eli, the absent siblings in this particular escapade. I pondered their whereabouts during the shenanigans that Jerome was now recounting. Lisa and Eli, the industrious heart of our family, often charted a different course from their more mischievous siblings.

I envisioned Lisa, even then, consumed by her budding talent for event organisation, likely orchestrating some church function with her characteristic zeal and flair. Her events, though grandiose for the modest outback branch of our church, were always met with enthusiasm and admiration. She had a unique ability to galvanise the community, to transform mundane gatherings into memorable occasions that resonated with warmth and unity.

And where Lisa went, Eli often followed. As the younger brother closest in age to her, he was invariably her steadfast collaborator, her right-hand man in these communal endeavours. I imagined him, even back then, lending his support, perhaps a tad begrudgingly but always loyally, to Lisa's ambitious projects.

Lost in the labyrinth of my memories, the vivid recollections of our past, I momentarily drifted away from the narrative thread that Jerome was spinning. The laughter and chatter around the fire seemed like distant echoes until Paul's voice, clear and insistent, sliced through my reverie, anchoring me back to the circle of warmth and flickering light.

"Forget all the irrelevant stuff. We t-pee'd the Clarke's house, and then—" Paul declared, his voice carrying a mix of mischief and pride over their youthful antics. His interruption jolted me, a sudden realisation that this story was veering into uncharted territories of my children's past misadventures.

Nial's interjection, innocent and curious, "Hang on! What's t-peeing?" momentarily lightened the atmosphere. His lack of familiarity with the term was a gentle reminder of the diverse backgrounds and experiences that enriched our little community.

Greta's explanation, delivered with a distinct lack of amusement, painted a clear picture of the event. "It means they threw toilet paper all over their house in the middle of the night," she elucidated, her voice tinged with disapproval. Her expression, a blend of resignation and mild annoyance, was one I had come to recognise well over the years.

Nial's reaction, a chuckle and a lighthearted acknowledgment of the act's mischievous appeal, "Oh, that actually sounds like a bit of fun," brought a reluctant smile to my face. His words served as a gentle reminder of the innocence and frivolity of youth, of the universal urge to rebel in small, harmless ways.

Jerome's playful hint at a climax in their tale rekindled the group's curiosity, his words acting like a magnet, drawing everyone's attention back to the unfolding narrative. His struggle to articulate the story through fits of giggles only added to the suspense, heightening our collective anticipation.

Luke's intervention, with a grin that spoke volumes of the fond memories attached to this escapade, painted the next stroke of the picture. "Paul and I sent Jerome to knock on their front door while we went into hiding just over the small garden fence." His words conjured a scene so vivid, I could almost see the young versions of them, hearts pounding with adrenaline, stifling their laughter as they executed their plan.

"I knock on the door, and..." Jerome's attempt to continue was a battle against his own amusement, a testament to the joyous absurdity of their youthful antics. Paul's commentary, "And then you just stood there!" brought a clearer image to mind, depicting Jerome, momentarily paralysed by the audacity of his own action, a deer in the headlights of his own making.

I couldn't help but chuckle inwardly. The scenario was quintessentially Jerome, a blend of boldness and comedic timing, even if unintentional. It was a moment that encapsulated the spirit of childhood and adolescence—brave yet foolish, a story of innocence and mischief.

Luke's admission, "Paul and I thought we were done for," resonated with the tangible fear of potential discovery that must have pulsed through them at that moment, a feeling so palpable even now around the fire.

Sarah's question, laced with eagerness, "And what happened? Did Jerome get caught?" mirrored my own growing curiosity.

Paul's recounting, "No, I had to sprint to the front door to grab him and drag him behind the fence. He nearly tripped me up on the way," evoked a scene filled with frantic action, a desperate scramble to evade detection, their youthful agility and quick thinking on full display. The group's chuckles served as a chorus to the unfolding drama, a shared amusement at the image of Paul and Jerome's near-comical escape.

Luke's addition, "And then the front door opens," was like a drumroll, heightening the suspense, while Paul's revelation, "And the family comes out and finds that their house has been t'peed," brought a climax to the scene, their successful prank laid bare in the confusion of the Clarke family.

Luke's "They came so close to finding us behind the fence," added a layer of thrill to the adventure, a near-miss that undoubtedly fuelled the adrenaline of the moment and the humour of the retelling.

Jerome, finally mastering his laughter, added a delightful twist. "But then one of their kids was like, I know who it was," he shared, pausing to let the suspense build, his giggle punctuating the air. The campfire crowd leaned in, collectively holding their breath for the grand reveal.

"And he was like, 'it must be the Smith's. They use home brand'," Jerome delivered the punchline with comedic timing, evoking a wave of laughter and relief that rippled through the group. It was the perfect end to their caper, a twist that sealed the story with a blend of irony and humour.

The laughter that erupted around the campfire was infectious, a shared release that bonded us further in the joy of the moment. Even Greta, whose earlier expression had been a blend of concern and maternal disapproval, couldn't hold back a chuckle. Her stern façade cracked, replaced by the warm glow of amusement, a testament to the light-heartedness of the tale and its happy conclusion.

The story, while a simple recounting of a childhood prank, held deeper layers for me. It was a snapshot of the innocence and mischief of youth, a time when the most pressing concerns were the execution of harmless pranks and the anticipation of their outcomes. The fact that these antics were interwoven with acts of kindness, like the baking of cupcakes —a tradition often spearheaded by the girls, with Lisa invariably at the helm—spoke volumes about the community we had nurtured back then, a balance of playfulness and care that defined our collective experience.

I found myself reflecting on the duality of those times, the way the pranks and the kindnesses, the laughter and the camaraderie, all wove together to create a tapestry of community life. It was a balance that underscored our human need for connection, for the shared experiences that shape us, and for the stories that we would carry with us, like torches, illuminating our paths forward.

The shift in the atmosphere was palpable as Paul introduced a gesture entirely foreign to our shared experiences, placing three fingers against his right temple and declaring, "Light the fire." The sudden solemnity of the moment sent a shiver down my spine, a stark contrast to the laughter and light-heartedness that had just filled the air. This unfamiliar ritual piqued my curiosity and, judging by the hushed silence that followed, I wasn't alone in my bemusement.

My eyes scanned the faces around the fire, all mirroring my own confusion and curiosity. When Luke and Beatrix, almost conspiratorially, shared a glance and then mirrored Paul's gesture—this time placing three fingers against their left temples—their synchronised action, "Share the light," added a layer of mystery and intrigue to the gathering.

This coordinated display, new and unknown, seemed to hold a deeper meaning, a significance that went beyond simple words and gestures. The collective pause that enveloped the group was a testament to the impact of this unexpected ritualistic exchange.

When Paul repeated his initial gesture with increased vigour, "Light the fire!" his voice resonating with a newfound authority, it felt as though we were on the cusp of uncovering some profound truth or tradition, perhaps a remnant of the world we'd left behind or a harbinger of the new world we were building together.

The group's response, led by Luke and Beatrix, "Share the Light!" reverberated through the air, a chorus that seemed to weave us all into a shared tapestry of momentary unity and purpose. The collective echo of their voices, in such stark unison, sent a wave of goosebumps cascading over my skin.

Despite the initial wave of uncertainty that washed over me, there was something compelling about the collective gesture and chant that enveloped the group. It was as if the very act of participating, of syncing with the others in this peculiar ritual, carried its own form of silent communication, a unifying force that momentarily eclipsed my hesitations. Thus, I found myself, somewhat unexpectedly, joining in, my voice melding with the others as we sent our chorus soaring into the night sky of Clivilius.

However, as my gaze wandered to Greta, I noticed her detachment from the ritual. She sat there, an island of solitude amidst the sea of communal participation, her expression unreadable in the firelight's flicker. The realisation that she had chosen not to partake in the gesture intensified the knot of worry already forming in my gut. Greta's struggle to adapt to our new environment, her yearning for the familiar comforts of home and the spiritual community we had left behind, was a silent undercurrent I could feel even amidst the night's revelry.

Our first day in Clivilius had been a whirlwind of emotion and adjustment, and I could sense that the evening's events, however benign or well-intentioned, might be weighing heavily on her. The stark contrast between my inadvertent involvement in the group's chant and her silent refusal underscored the chasm of discomfort she might be feeling, a chasm I felt ill-equipped to bridge in that moment.

Torn between my role as a participant in this new community's burgeoning traditions and my duty to offer solace to my wife, I found myself at a loss. Words of comfort seemed inadequate, perhaps even intrusive, in the face of her silent introspection. Thus, I chose to remain silent, a silent observer rather than an active comforter, hoping that the evening could unfold without further emphasising the sense of displacement that Greta—and, admittedly, I—were grappling with.

BEACON OF KINDNESS

4338.213.11

The bonfire's warm glow, casting dancing shadows upon our faces, had become a backdrop for a night filled with laughter and camaraderie. Luke, Paul, and I shared in the evening's merriment, a moment of respite amidst the whirlwind of our new life in Clivilius. Yet, despite the apparent joviality, a part of me remained on edge, attuned to the undercurrent of alcohol-fuelled revelry that seemed to grow as the night wore on.

When Greta approached, her presence seemed to alter the atmosphere around us. Her furrowed brow and the pronounced lines of concern etching her face spoke volumes before she even uttered a word. Her soft whisper, carrying my name, was a harbinger of the unease that had been building within her.

The tension in my stomach knotted further as she voiced her concerns. "I'm getting a bit worried about all the drinking. It's too much, and I don't like it," she declared with a conviction that resonated with her deep-seated values and beliefs. Her discomfort was palpable, a stark contrast to the carefree spirits surrounding us.

My gaze swept over our companions, taking in the scene with a renewed perspective. To me, the gathering seemed harmless, a collective letting go of the day's pressures and uncertainties. But through Greta's eyes, I could see how the scene might appear daunting, even threatening. Her life had always been anchored by the values and community of our church, a sanctuary from the worldly indulgences she so staunchly opposed.

Greta's difficulty in navigating these social waters was a poignant reminder of the challenges we faced in this new world. Her reluctance to engage with practices so distant from her own beliefs highlighted the isolation she must be feeling, amplified by the unfamiliarity of our surroundings.

My face mirrored the concern that Greta's words had ignited within me, a visible testament to the internal struggle I was grappling with. As I sought some semblance of guidance or reassurance from Luke and Paul, their expressions offered no immediate solution. "I don't really like it either," I admitted, aligning myself with Greta's discomfort, which was as much about solidarity with her as it was a reflection of my own preferences.

The admission wasn't just lip service; I genuinely shared her disquiet about the alcohol, recognising its potential to unsettle the delicate balance of our evening. "But I don't think there's a lot we can do about it," I conceded, voicing my sense of helplessness in influencing the collective behaviour of our new community.

Greta's determination, however, seemed to harden in the face of my resignation. "I think we should leave now. Will you get the kids?" she instructed, her tone brooking no argument, yet laced with an anxiety that tugged at my heartstrings. Her request wasn't just about removing herself from an uncomfortable situation; it was a protective instinct, a maternal shield poised to safeguard our children from an environment she deemed unsuitable—despite the fact that Charles and Jerome were old enough to make their own decisions, without our input or approval.

"Are you sure that's necessary?" I found myself questioning her decision, not out of defiance but from a place of hope that perhaps the situation wasn't as dire as she perceived. My gaze momentarily drifted to Jerome and Charles, their laughter and engagement with the group painting a starkly different picture of the night's festivities.

As I processed our exchange, Luke's subtle retreat from the conversation didn't escape my notice. It was a physical manifestation of the awkwardness that discussions of departure or disapproval can elicit, especially in the context of social gatherings where consensus is often the glue that holds the merriment together.

Observing Luke's subtle retreat from the impending discord was like watching a familiar play unfold, where his actions, so characteristic of his usual behaviour, offered a strange blend of comfort and consternation. It was almost amusing, this predictable pattern of avoidance that Luke exhibited, a trait that, in less fraught moments, might have drawn a chuckle or a shake of the head from me. Yet, beneath the humour, there was an undercurrent of disappointment, a faint sense of betrayal that he was stepping back, leaving Paul and me to navigate Greta's concerns on our own.

This behaviour wasn't just a quirk of Luke's personality; it was a reflection of the deeper undercurrents that rippled through our family dynamics. Luke's relationship with Greta had always been taut, a thread stretched thin by disagreements and differing perspectives. His decision to move states away wasn't just a search for new horizons but a retreat from the tension that seemed to find its epicentre in their interactions. While we never openly discussed this rift, its presence was an unspoken truth that lingered in the backdrop of our family narrative, colouring our interactions with a palette of complex emotions.

As Luke made his quiet exit from the scene, a part of me envied his ability to simply walk away, to detach himself from the discomfort. Yet, another part of me knew that such detachment came at a cost, a sacrifice of intimacy for the sake of peace. In that moment, as I stood at the crossroads of allegiance and understanding, I felt the weight of my role not just as Greta's partner but as a father navigating the intricate web of relationships that defined our family.

As Jerome and Sarah joined our small gathering, I couldn't help but observe the ease of their interaction, a stark contrast to the tension that was slowly enveloping our familial group. Throughout the night, their engaged discussions, punctuated by genuine laughter and nods of mutual understanding, had caught my attention. It seemed natural that their shared passion for the natural world—Jerome with his zoology studies and Sarah with her background in wildlife conservation—had drawn them together, creating a small pocket of shared interest amidst the broader festivities.

Yet, as they approached and caught the undercurrents of Greta's growing distress, I watched Jerome's expression morph from relaxed engagement to one of concern. He, better than anyone, could recognise the telltale signs of Greta's unease, her 'not impressed' mood that often acted as a precursor to more intense displays of discomfort.

The situation escalated quickly. Greta's panic, manifesting physically, was painful to witness. Her laboured breathing and the fluttering hands to her chest were telltale signs of her overwhelming anxiety. Her wide, fear-filled eyes scanning the lively surroundings, were a silent scream for escape, for a return to the familiar, the safe.

"Noah, please, I can't stay here," Greta's plea, laced with desperation, cut through the noise and laughter surrounding us, anchoring me back to the immediate reality of her distress.

My forehead furrowed deeply as I observed Greta's escalating distress, her anxiety manifesting in unmistakable physical tremors. My heart was heavy with concern for her, yet I couldn't help but acknowledge a familiar pattern in her reaction to situations she found disagreeable or unsettling. This wasn't just about the present discomfort; it was a recurring theme whenever we faced circumstances that didn't align with her expectations or preferences.

Taking Greta's trembling hands in mine, I sought to offer comfort, to ground her in the reality that we were now a part of this new community, for better or worse. "Greta, we can't just leave. This is our home now, and the kids are here. We can't run away just because we don't like something," I said, my voice a blend of firmness and compassion. The words were as much a reminder to myself as they were an appeal to her, an attempt to reconcile our need for stability with the inevitable challenges of adapting to our new life.

The unexpected collision of Greta's gesturing hand with Sarah's drink broke the tense dialogue, sending the cup clattering to the ground. Sarah's quick response, her calm demeanour as she stooped to retrieve her cup, was a welcoming contrast to the turmoil swirling around us.

Greta's stuttering apology, fraught with embarrassment and continuing anxiety, only added to the palpable tension. Sarah's gentle reassurance, "It's alright, Greta. Don't worry about the drink. Let's focus on helping you feel better," was a balm to the chaotic moment. Her words, imbued with an innate kindness and understanding, offered not just solace to Greta but a momentary reprieve to me as well.

In the midst of this unexpected turmoil, Sarah's composed and empathetic reaction highlighted her natural ability to soothe and reassure, qualities undoubtedly beneficial in her work with wildlife. Her presence, calming and stable, was a welcome counterbalance to the evening's upheaval, providing a glimpse of the compassionate, supportive community we were striving to build here in Clivilius.

Paul's soft sigh was a prelude to his generous offer. "Look since there's no spare motorhomes, why don't you take mine for the night?" he suggested, willing to exchange his comfortable space for a tent, a gesture not lost on me.

My hesitation was instinctual, a reluctance to inconvenience Paul, yet I couldn't ignore the palpable sense of relief that washed over Greta at the prospect of an escape. "That's really not necessary," I tried to assure him, grappling with the dilemma of accepting kindness at the expense of his comfort.

"What about the motorhome that Beatrix delivered late this afternoon?" Jerome chimed in, an idea that seemed to illuminate a path forward.

Paul's uncertainty, mirrored in his furrowed brow, highlighted the chaos of our day—so many arrivals and adjustments that a motorhome could arrive unnoticed. "I don't recall seeing it," Paul confessed. "It must be still near the Portal."

Opting for pragmatism, a trait that had often served me well, I embraced Jerome's suggestion. "That's okay. We can take that one for the night," I decided, feeling a sense of resolve. The darkness beyond the campfire's reach did not deter me; rather, it beckoned as a peaceful retreat from the night's earlier turmoil.

A walk under the night sky, though dark and uncertain, seemed a fitting metaphor for our current journey— venturing into the unknown for the promise of solace and stability. The prospect of finding that motorhome, a haven for Greta away from the revelry that had so unsettled her, felt like a step toward reclaiming a sense of control and comfort in this new world.

"No," Jerome's interjection cut through the uncertainty like a beacon. "I brought it back to camp. It's just over there," he informed us, pointing into the nebulous darkness beyond the camp's periphery.

Before Greta or I could process this new information, Sarah stepped in with her characteristic kindness, offering to guide us through the dark to the sanctuary of the motorhome. "I can walk you there," she said, her voice imbued with the gentle firmness that had already proven soothing. "I need to be getting home anyway."

Greta's expression, momentarily brightening with the prospect of a peaceful retreat, was a relief to witness. Her inquiry about Sarah's accommodations, "Oh, which one is yours?" revealed a flicker of curiosity amid her distress, a promising sign of her engaging with the moment rather than being consumed by her anxieties.

Sarah's response, accompanied by a nervous chuckle, hinted at a shared vulnerability, a reminder that we were all navigating this new existence with its mix of challenges and camaraderie. "My brother and I stay in a motorhome just over there," she indicated, her gesture pointing to another shadowed area of our nascent community.

Sensing Greta's lingering distress, I drew her close, offering a silent promise of support through a comforting embrace and a gentle kiss atop her head. It was a small gesture, but one laden with the commitment to see her through this moment of turmoil.

Sarah's gentle nudge, "Come on, let's walk you to the motorhome," was the cue we needed to move forward, literally and metaphorically, towards a space where Greta could find some semblance of peace.

Paul's well-meaning offer to join us was gently declined. The quiet understanding that Greta's comfort was paramount in this moment guided my insistence that we proceed with just Sarah's company. "It's fine," I assured Paul, hoping to convey that our immediate need was for tranquility and simplicity, not for a larger escort.

The unexpected voice of Jerome, offering to accompany us, introduced a brief ripple of disruption to the plan. "I'll come too," he stated, his words carrying an undertone of genuine concern or perhaps a hint of his own unease about the night ahead. The simultaneous and firm "No" from both Paul and Sarah piqued my curiosity. Their exchanged glances, laden with unspoken communication, hinted at dynamics or concerns beyond my immediate understanding.

Paul's quick reassurance to Jerome, "There's plenty of room in my motorhome for you," seemed to settle the matter, albeit with Jerome's reluctant acquiescence. The undercurrents of their interactions, while intriguing, were secondary to the pressing need to address Greta's distress.

Sarah and I, armed with fire torches lit from the campfire's enduring flames, prepared to navigate the dark path to the motorhome. The flickering lights in our hands cast dancing shadows around us, their warm glow a small comfort against the enveloping darkness of the night.

As we reached the security gate, a boundary between the camp's lively heart and the quiet outskirts where respite awaited, Paul's farewell was brief yet laden with genuine concern for our well-being. The simple exchange of goodnights and wishes for safety felt like a closing chapter to the day's tumultuous narrative.

Walking alongside Sarah, with Greta close by, the torches illuminating our way, I felt a blend of gratitude and weariness. Gratitude for the kindness and support of our new companions and weariness from the day's emotional and physical tolls. The night's journey to the motorhome symbolised more than just a physical transition; it was a step toward finding peace and stability in this new, uncharted chapter of our lives.

FIRST NIGHT

4338.213.12

As we trudged through the barren, dusty landscape, the silhouette of the motorhome loomed ahead, an oasis of hope in a world that seemed increasingly desolate. Sarah, with her brisk stride, reached the vehicle before Greta and I, her figure cutting a determined path through the dim glow of the fire torches. Her voice broke the heavy silence. "Looks like the keys have been left in the door, waiting for you," she remarked, her fingers deftly plucking the keys from their precarious perch in the lock before extending them towards me.

The weight of the day's journey lingered in my limbs, and my steps felt unusually heavy as I moved to accept her offering. Yet, before my fingers could graze the cool metal of the keys, Greta, ever the enigmatic presence, swept in with a fluidity that belied her usual stoicism. The keys, a symbol of progress and potential, slipped from Sarah's hand to Greta's with an ease that left me momentarily adrift in their dynamic.

There I stood, a silent observer, clutching the fire torch—a beacon in the encroaching night. Its flickering light cast dancing shadows over Greta's features as she leaned in to examine the motorhome's lock. The world seemed to shrink to this singular moment, the clinking of the keys, the hiss of the torch, and the soft rustle of our breaths merging with the night's stillness.

Despite the physical closeness, a chasm of unspoken thoughts and unacknowledged tensions yawned between us.

As Greta's fingers found their mark and the door creaked open, a surge of conflicting emotions wrestled within me. Relief at finding shelter clashed with a gnawing sense of displacement, a reminder of the transient nature of our existence in this fragmented world.

In that instant, as Greta crossed the threshold into the shadowed interior of the motorhome, a part of me longed for the simplicity of a past life, where keys were just keys, and doors led to familiar, welcoming spaces. Yet, as the cool night air brushed against my skin, I knew that those days were as distant as the sparks of fire that danced into the night sky, their light reaching us from a world forever altered.

The interior of the motorhome greeted us with an oppressive cloak of darkness, a stark contrast to the dim yet open expanse we had navigated just moments before. Greta's abrupt exclamation, "Damn it," sliced through the silence as she collided with an unseen obstacle, her frustration palpable in the tightness of her voice.

Outside, under the night's watchful eye, Sarah and I exchanged a look of shared unease. Her grimace, a silent echo of my own discomfort, spoke volumes in the quiet of the night. My response was a mere light shrug, a feeble attempt to diffuse the tension that hung between us like the heavy desert air.

"She'll be fine," I whispered to Sarah, my voice a low murmur intended only for her ears. The assurance was as much for myself as it was for her, a mantra to ward off the growing disquiet within me.

Sarah, ever helpful, suggested a practical solution. "The light switch should be just inside the door," she advised, her voice calm and steady as she stepped closer to assist.

The world around us transformed in an instant when the switch clicked, a flood of soft, welcoming light enveloping Sarah and me. The sudden brightness felt like a balm, chasing away the shadows and the uncertainty they harboured.

Greta's appearance at the doorway, albeit brief, offered a glimpse into her ongoing state of mind. "Thank you, Sarah," she expressed, her smile faint, her gratitude tinged with an underlying exhaustion. Despite her words of appreciation, there was a palpable tension in her demeanour, a subtle tightness that hinted at the turmoil swirling beneath her composed exterior.

As I stood there, bathed in the gentle glow of the outdoor light, a sigh escaped my lips, soft and laden with empathy. I knew that beneath Greta's polite façade lay a maelstrom of anxiety and fatigue, a tempest concealed just beneath the surface.

I lingered for a moment in the soft light that spilled out from the motorhome, turning to Sarah with a sense of gratitude swelling within me. "Thanks for walking us back," I said, infusing my voice with warmth, trying to convey the depth of my appreciation through a smile that I hoped would reach my eyes.

"Not a problem at all," she responded, her voice smooth and even, yet I sensed a layer of complexity behind her straightforward words. My gaze lingered on her, curious and slightly probing. There was an unmistakable sincerity in her offer of assistance, yet it seemed interwoven with an additional, unspoken thread. It was as if Sarah harboured a question or a thought perched on the edge of her tongue, waiting for the right moment or the right push to take flight into the open.

The air between us filled with a quiet tension, the kind that speaks louder than words, as we found ourselves caught in a web of unspoken communication. The silence stretched, a tangible entity, until Sarah finally broke it. "I'd better be finding Grant," she announced, her voice slicing through the stillness, albeit a touch too casually. "Don't want him getting lost out here in the dark."

I acknowledged her departure with a nod, the word "Goodnight, Sarah" escaping my lips in a gentle exhale, a subtle attempt to bridge the gap that silence had widened.

"Goodnight Noah," she echoed, her steps carrying her back toward the doorway, a lingering presence in the night. "Hope you get some good rest out here, Greta," she called out, her voice carrying a blend of concern and farewell.

Greta's response, a succinct "You too," floated from within the motorhome, devoid of any intent to emerge or engage further. The brevity and impersonality of her reply drew a suppressed chuckle from me, a soft ripple in the night's calm.

As the interior of the motorhome began to awaken with the gentle hum of several lights flickering to life, the abrupt extinguishing of the outdoor light plunged my surroundings back into a cloak of darkness. The unexpectedness momentarily disoriented me, like the sudden drop of a curtain at the end of a performance.

Sarah, her presence now just a silhouette against the dimly lit backdrop of the motorhome's interior, offered me a silent nod—a wordless goodbye that hung in the cool night air between us. With a quiet grace, she turned and vanished into the night, her departure leaving a subtle imprint on the canvas of the evening.

Left alone, with only the soft crackle of the fire torch for company, I found myself momentarily adrift in the sudden solitude. The torch, its flames dancing with a life of their own, seemed almost too lively a companion for the stillness of the night. I pondered its fate, feeling its warmth in my hands, aware of its potential hazard if left too close to the motorhome.

With deliberate steps, I navigated the dark, uneven terrain, my eyes adjusting to the night's embrace, seeking a spot where the torch could fulfil its purpose without threat. The ground beneath my feet whispered stories of the day's heat in soft puffs of thick dust as I made my way.

Finding what felt like a safe distance, I gently pressed the torch into the earth, its base sinking into the soft, forgiving dust. The flames continued their dance, casting a warm, flickering light that cut through the darkness, a solitary sentinel in the vast, silent landscape.

It can stay here for the night as a silent beacon, I mused internally, a smile creeping across my face as I admired the torch's steadfast glow. It stood there, a symbol of endurance and light amidst the uncertainties of our journey, its flames a silent testament to the resilience within us all. With a lingering glance at the torch's unwavering light, I turned back toward the motorhome, comforted by the small yet significant mark of our presence in the vast, whispering desert.

Stepping into the motorhome, I pulled the door shut with a soft click, sealing us inside this new sanctuary. The interior greeted me with an air of pristine freshness, the kind that speaks of untouched spaces and new beginnings. The scent of newness was unmistakable, filling my nostrils with the promise of uncharted territory. It was a sharp contrast to the rugged world outside, and for a moment, I allowed myself to be enveloped in the sensation of stepping into a different realm.

"The kitchen seems a decent space," I observed aloud, my voice carrying a note of approval as I took in the clean lines and orderly arrangement of the kitchen area. It was compact yet inviting, a small haven for culinary creativity within the confines of our mobile abode.

Greta's response, "It is a reasonable space," came with a measured tone, and I sensed a hesitation in her words, a prelude to a caveat. My instincts were proven right when she abruptly added, "Apart from there being no crockery, or utensils, or anything at all!" Her voice carried a mix of surprise and frustration.

I cast a more scrutinising glance around, my eyes now seeking out the details I had initially overlooked. Greta's observation hit home—while the motorhome boasted new furniture and an air of readiness, it was devoid of the essentials that would make it truly liveable. It struck me then, the odd juxtaposition of this well-appointed shell against the absence of life's basic necessities.

As we ventured further, inspecting each nook and cranny, the reality became increasingly apparent. Our personal items were nowhere to be found; the kitchen lacked the basic accessories one would expect; there was no bedding to promise a comfortable rest, nor towels to offer the comfort of cleanliness. With each discovery, the motorhome felt less like a refuge and more like a façade, a display model set up to tantalise but not to satisfy.

The realisation settled over me like a heavy blanket, a mix of disappointment and resolve. This motorhome, while offering a veneer of sanctuary, was just the beginning of another chapter of challenges. It underscored our journey's transient nature, a reminder that comfort was a luxury not easily found in our current existence. Yet, within this empty vessel of promise, there lay the potential for us to carve out a space of our own, to imbue this hollow display with the essence of our resilience and ingenuity.

Greta's demeanour shifted tangibly, her words cutting through the haze of my contemplation like a sharp breeze. "We can't even undress," she mumbled, her voice laced with a blend of frustration and resignation that pulled me abruptly back to our less-than-ideal reality.

Caught in the act of shedding my top, I paused, the fabric halfway up my torso, as her words resonated with the starkness of our predicament. With a reluctant sigh, I let the shirt fall back into place, the fabric settling heavily against my skin. "I'm not even sure what happened to our suitcases," I admitted, directing my words to Greta, though they were more an expression of my internal bewilderment.

"They're back at the camp," she huffed, her tone tinged with exasperation as she settled herself onto the edge of the large, uninviting bed, its bareness a reminder of our journey's new beginning.

An internal groan echoed through me, the weight of the situation pressing down. With a tentative hope, I broached the idea of postponing our problem-solving until daylight. "Can I sort it all out in the morning?" My question hung in the air, laden with a silent plea for understanding.

Greta's response was not verbal but no less eloquent. Her eyes, narrowed and piercing, fixed on me with an intensity that conveyed volumes. Her silent glare was a clear signal of her expectations, an unspoken but unmistakable insistence that the issue be addressed immediately, not deferred.

Yet, as she held her silence, I grasped at the slender thread of plausible deniability, choosing to interpret her wordless communication in a way that favoured a night's reprieve. Deliberately misunderstanding her, I proceeded to remove my shirt, folding it with a care that belied my internal turmoil, and placed it aside.

"It's not a particularly cold night, anyway," I ventured, attempting to inject a note of optimism into the thick air of our cramped quarters. Seizing her hand in mine, I sought to bridge the gap of comfort and convenience with a touch of human connection. "Besides," I added, hoping to kindle a spark of camaraderie in the face of adversity, "we have each other to keep ourselves warm."

In that moment, with our hands intertwined, I endeavoured to offer more than mere words—a gesture of solidarity, a silent vow to face the challenges together, to find warmth not just in the physical sense, but in the shared resolve to navigate the uncertainties that lay ahead.

Greta's gaze met mine, her eyes a clear window to her soul, brimming with the kind of vulnerability that only unshed tears can convey. It was a moment that tugged at the very fabric of my heart, seeing her so affected by our circumstances.

"I'm sorry this isn't the New Jerusalem," I whispered to her, my words floating between us, laden with empathy and a shared yearning for a place that promised peace and certainty.

Watching Greta's bottom lip quiver was like witnessing the physical manifestation of her inner turmoil. Her actions spoke volumes as she flickered the bedside lights to life only to extinguish the others, perhaps in an effort to create a semblance of sanctuary in our small, makeshift world.

Her return to the bedside was swift, her movements almost ritualistic as she knelt, an action so familiar yet so poignant in that moment. Instinctively, I mirrored her, our knees touching the cold, hard floor, an act of solidarity in our shared vulnerability.

As we clasped hands, the warmth of her skin against mine served as a silent reminder of our connection, of the shared path we walked, however treacherous it might seem. Greta's nod was a silent plea, her voice barely more than a whisper, "Can you say it?" It was a request laden with trust, with the need for the comfort found in shared rituals.

"Sure," I responded, feeling the weight and the honour of her request. As we bowed our heads and closed our eyes, the world beyond our small circle faded away. The prayer that flowed from me was more than a string of words; it was an outpouring of hope, of gratitude, and a plea for guidance. I spoke of our family, the safety we'd found, however fleeting, and the new bonds formed in Bixbus, each word weaving a tapestry of our current existence, grounding us in the belief that there was still much to be thankful for.

The sound of Greta's soft sobs punctuated the sacred silence, a poignant reminder of the rawness of our situation. As the prayer drew to a close, I felt an instinctive pull to provide comfort, to be a pillar of support in our shared uncertainty. Wrapping an arm around her, I drew her close, offering my presence as a sanctuary, a silent vow to weather the storm together. In that embrace, amidst the turmoil of our journey, there was a fleeting sense of peace, a momentary assurance that, despite everything, we were not alone.

Greta's question, "Is there really no going back?" resonated with a profound sense of finality, her voice muffled yet laden with emotion as she spoke into my chest.

I took a moment, letting the weight of her inquiry sink in, feeling the tangle of my own thoughts and emotions. "I don't think so," I finally responded, my voice a mixture of resignation and an undefined ache for the familiar and the lost.

Her silence that followed was telling, a quiet acceptance or perhaps an internalisation of our situation. Greta's movement away from me, as she climbed atop the mattress, felt like a physical manifestation of the distance we were all navigating in this new world.

Compelled by a shared need for comfort, I joined her on the surprisingly forgiving mattress. "It's surprisingly comfortable," I whispered, trying to inject a lightness into the heavy cloak of night with a soft chuckle.

Greta's response was non-verbal, a simple yet significant action as her hand reached out, finding and then turning off the bedside light. The motorhome plunged into near total darkness, a tangible symbol of our journey into the unknown.

In the enveloping blackness, my hands instinctively sought out Greta, finding her body and drawing her close with an arm wrapped securely around her. It was more than a search for physical closeness; it was an unspoken plea for connection, for the assurance of her presence in a world that felt completely alien.

With my eyes closed, the events of the day cascaded through my mind, each memory adding to the weight that pressed down upon me. In the quiet solidarity of our shared space, I found myself silently imploring the night to hasten its passage, yearning for the reprieve, however brief, that a new day might bring. Yet, even in the quest for sleep's escape, the reality of our circumstances lingered at the edges of my consciousness, a persistent reminder of the journey that lay ahead.

4338.214

(2 August 2018)

GUARDIANS

4338.214.1

Despite the absence of bedding, a testament to the hasty entrance into Clivilius that we had made, and the surreal, almost dreamlike quality of the events that had unfolded throughout the day, sleep had enveloped me with surprising swiftness. The comforting embrace of unconsciousness, however, was short-lived. As the first rays of dawn began to seep through the windows of the motorhome, painting the cramped interior with a soft, golden hue, my eyes fluttered open, and I was abruptly pulled back into reality.

Awakening at the break of dawn was not an anomaly for me in Clivilius; it was my routine, a part of the rhythm of my life that seemed to have always existed. Yet, this morning felt different. There was a peculiar stillness in the air, a sense of calm before the storm, perhaps. As Greta began to show signs of life beside me, I felt a surge of affection. Leaning over, I gently pressed a kiss to her cheek, a silent message of reassurance, before carefully extricating myself from the mattress.

The absence of a blanket had not gone unnoticed. Throughout the night, the cool air had been a relentless companion, seeping into the motorhome and wrapping its chilly fingers around me. Now, as I stood, I became acutely aware of the toll it had taken on my body. A dull ache throbbed in my lower back, a nagging reminder of the night's discomfort. With a grimace, I arched my back, stretching the tight muscles, feeling the stiffness start to dissipate with each movement.

As the light of dawn grew stronger, casting long shadows across the motorhome's modest interior, I took a moment to gather my thoughts. The events of the previous day replayed in my mind, a chaotic whirlwind of memories that seemed almost too fantastical to be real. Yet the reality of my situation was undeniable, tangible in the cool air, the sparse surroundings, and the weight of responsibility that rested on my shoulders.

As the morning light cascaded through the windows, the motorhome's interior was unveiled in a new clarity, the sparse furnishings standing stark against the early sunlight. Greta's observations from the previous night echoed in my mind – the space was indeed just a skeleton of what one might call a home. My gaze swept over the minimalistic setup, the lack of personal touches making the space feel impersonal and cold, a far cry from the warmth of our previous family home.

My thoughts wandered to Bixbus and the unknown plans that Paul and Luke had in motion. How they intended to procure the supplies we desperately needed was beyond my comprehension. Yet, Luke's ability to navigate through the Portal and retrieve bits and pieces of our former life sparked a flicker of hope within me. Perhaps he could bridge the gap between this sparse existence and the comfort of our past lives, bringing over more personal belongings to fill the void in this metallic shell.

Lost in these thoughts, I hadn't noticed Greta's gaze upon me. Her eyes, reflective and thoughtful, followed my every move, a silent observer to my morning contemplations. The realisation that she was awake and attentive brought a pause to my internal musings.

Feeling the need to break the morning's stillness, I reached for yesterday's shirt, its fabric a tangible reminder of our abrupt departure and the remnants of our past life left behind. Slipping it over my head, the familiar scent of the fabric momentarily transported me to a time before Luke had upended our lives.

Determined to inject a sense of normality into our surreal existence, I turned to Greta with a resolve. "I'll go and find our suitcases," I declared, my voice carrying a hopeful undertone. The smile I offered her was not just a gesture of reassurance but also a silent promise of efforts to reclaim pieces of our disrupted lives.

Her response, though muffled by lingering traces of sleep, was a gentle nod to reality. "That would be a good idea," she murmured.

Pushing the door open, I was greeted by the crisp, invigorating air of the Clivilian morning. My feet, clad in worn shoes, sank slightly into the unique, powdery dust of Clivilius as I stepped outside, each grain whispering tales of this alien land under my weight. The world outside was a stark contrast to the confined space of the motorhome, its vastness both liberating and daunting.

I trudged towards the remnants of last night's fire torch, its once vigorous flame now reduced to cold, lifeless ashes. Lifting the torch, I felt its weight, a silent testament to the night's ephemeral light and warmth. Carrying it back to the camp, the security gate loomed before me, its rattling echoes disturbing the morning's tranquility as I wrestled it open. Its base scraped against the thick layer of Clivilian dust that had gathered overnight, a gritty resistance against the gate's movement.

As I navigated through the camp, my attention was momentarily captured by the sight of Paul stepping out of his motorhome. His appearance was almost jarring against the desolate backdrop – bare-chested, clad in shorts, his skin stark against the muted colours of our surroundings. His presence was fleeting, though, as he quickly retreated back into the shelter of his motorhome

Following Paul's brief appearance, Lois, the golden retriever under his temporary care, caught my eye. The dog's presence added a touch of domestic normality to our otherwise stark existence. Lois, I knew, belonged to Glenda, the camp's doctor, whose absence hung over me with a shroud of mystery. The reasons behind her departure were unknown to me, sparking a swirl of curiosity and concern. It seemed counterintuitive for a place so in need of medical expertise to be without its sole healthcare provider. I couldn't help but speculate about the gravity of the circumstances that necessitated her absence, surmising that wherever she was, her actions were driven by a cause of significant importance.

Lois, embodying a zest for life that felt almost foreign in this desolate setting, darted around the perimeter fence with boundless energy. Her joyous romps around Paul's motorhome, which sat incongruously within the camp's protective barrier, sparked a moment of contemplation within me. The peculiar placement of Paul's abode, shielded within the fence while others lay outside, seemed to hint at underlying logistical decisions, perhaps dictated by scarce resources or unseen hierarchies within our makeshift community.

As I stood there, the remnants of last night's campfire caught my eye, its embers barely clinging to life. The sight triggered a sensory flashback to the previous evening's feast, the rich aromas and flavours still vivid in my mind, stirring a hearty grumble from my stomach in response to the memory.

It wasn't long before Paul reappeared, this time fully clothed. His casual observation about my early riser habits broke the morning's stillness. "You're up early," he noted, his voice tinged with the grogginess of a man freshly woken, as he joined me in the communal space we shared.

His comment elicited a reflective response from me. "I'm always up early," I admitted, my voice carrying a hint of nostalgia, perhaps longing for a time when the simplicity of a sunrise held different meanings. "Can't sleep once the sun begins to rise." My gaze drifted across the camp, taking in the quiet stillness, wondering if any of our companions were also on the cusp of greeting the new day.

Paul's understanding nod bridged the gap between us, a mutual recognition of the unspoken realities we faced in our daily lives within this camp. A silent acknowledgment passed between us, a shared understanding that, in this world, each morning was more than just a new day; it was a continuation of our collective struggle for normality.

As my eyes scanned the row of tents, a mental exercise began to unfold in my mind, an attempt to recall the temporary resting places we had chosen for our belongings amidst the suddenness of our arrival. The question of who might currently be nestled within those fabric walls added a layer of complexity to my morning quest. If my memory served correctly, and everyone had indeed found shelter within the caravans and motorhomes, the tents would be vacant, allowing me to search without the risk of disturbing someone's slumber.

Lost in this maze of thought, Paul's voice pierced my concentration with a question rooted in genuine concern. "Did you sleep alright?" His inquiry momentarily redirected my focus from the logistical to the personal.

Our eyes locked, and I felt a momentary hesitation, weighing the impact of my words. "Alright enough," I responded, opting for a response that bridged honesty with discretion. Acknowledging my own relatively fortunate circumstances, I was mindful of the collective spirit that had to be maintained in these trying times. Paul, already burdened with responsibilities and worries, didn't need the weight of my minor discomforts. "It took a while to get your mum settled, though," I noted.

Paul's reaction was a soft chuckle accompanied by a knowing smile. "Yeah, I can imagine," he agreed.

My curiosity piqued, I seized the opportunity to shift our dialogue to a phenomenon that had intrigued me during the night. "What was with all the glowing lights last night?" The question hung in the cool morning air, a striking departure from our previous exchange.

Paul's expression morphed into one of puzzlement, his brows knitting together in confusion. "What glowing lights?" he echoed.

I elaborated, gesturing towards the distant horizon where the Portals lay hidden from view. "The ones way out there," I clarified. My mind drifted back to the brief moment in the night when, half-awake, I had peered through the curtains. The sight of an odd, colourful glow casting a surreal light over the dunes had momentarily captured my attention, a mysterious luminescence in the deep of the night that now fuelled my curiosity.

Paul's face lit up with recognition. "Oh, those lights," he acknowledged, his tone shifting as he connected the dots. "That would have been the Guardians activating their Portals. Probably causing some sort of mayhem, as usual," he explained, his casual demeanour suggesting a familiarity with the phenomenon that was entirely new to me.

"Guardians?" I echoed, my intrigue deepening.

Paul's nod confirmed my suspicion. "It's what we call people like Luke, Beatrix, and Jarod, who can come and go through the Portals as they please." His explanation provided a glimpse into the hierarchical structure that governed our existence here, delineating a clear distinction between us and those with the power to traverse the mysterious Portals.

Absorbing this revelation, I felt a mix of awe and a touch of envy. The idea that some could navigate these gateways at will while the rest of us remained bound to this place sparked a flurry of questions. "So, how come they, the Guardians, can come and go, but we can't?" I inquired, my curiosity now fully ignited, seeking to understand the rules of this new reality and our place within it.

Paul paused, his demeanour shifting to one of contemplation, seemingly preparing to delve into the complexities of the Guardians and their Portals. Meanwhile, Lois, embodying the boundless energy typical of her breed, completed her circuit around the camp's perimeter and decided it was time to grace us with her presence. With a joyful trot, she approached, nudging Paul's thigh with her nose, a silent plea for attention that Paul readily obliged with a gentle pat and a scratch behind her ears. Her tail wagged with satisfaction before she resumed her enthusiastic exploration of the camp.

Watching Lois's simple joy and her quest for affection stirred a warm chuckle from within me. Her actions brought a rush of memories of Millie, our own canine companion, whose absence now cast a shadow over my heart. Millie, a rescue dog with her own set of quirks, was supposed to have been a temporary fixture in our lives, yet she had quickly become a cherished member of our family. The thought of her spending the night alone at the vet's, a situation that had been overshadowed by our abrupt departure to Clivilius, sparked a twinge of guilt and concern.

I made a mental note to speak with Jerome about Millie. The responsibility of her well-being primarily fell on him, given that it was his idea to bring her into our lives. Yet, as I stood there in the crisp morning air, watching Lois revel in the simple pleasures of life, I couldn't help but feel a surge of responsibility for Millie's situation. The reminder of our life before Clivilius, our routines, and the beings who depended on us, brought a sobering layer of reality to the surrealness of our new existence.

Paul's response to my inquiry about the Guardians' ability to traverse the Portal snapped me back to the present, his words tinged with uncertainty. "I'm not sure," he confessed, his voice reflecting a hint of the mystery that shrouded our understanding of the Portal's workings. "I think it has something to do with their Portal Keys. You should ask Luke to show you his when you get a chance," he proposed, offering a pathway to unravel some of the enigma that enveloped my new reality.

I nodded, my expression morphing into a contemplative visage as the weight of my ignorance settled upon me. The realisation struck that there was a vast expanse of knowledge and understanding about this world and our situation that I was yet to uncover. Coupled with the immediate concerns that needed addressing – Millie's wellbeing, locating our suitcases, and securing the essentials for our motorhome life – a sense of being overwhelmed crept upon me. The tasks ahead seemed daunting, a mountain of responsibilities and mysteries to unravel.

Paul's next suggestion offered a slight diversion from the burgeoning stress. "Speaking of Guardians, why don't we take a walk to the Drop Zone? We can see what chaos the Guardians have left us last night," he proposed, his tone light but carrying an undercurrent of curiosity about the aftermath of the Guardians' nocturnal activities.

Motivated by Paul's suggestion and feeling a need to step away from my spiralling thoughts, I pushed myself up to my feet. The prospect of visiting the Drop Zone, of witnessing firsthand the impact of the Guardians' actions, presented an opportunity to engage more directly with this world's peculiar dynamics. It was a chance to step beyond the confines of our immediate surroundings, to gather information, and perhaps, to find some direction in the midst of our tumultuous new life.

As Paul made to leave, a sudden sense of urgency gripped me, anchoring me momentarily to the spot. "I need to grab our suitcases first," I blurted out, my gaze darting back to the collection of tents. My voice betrayed a hint of the disarray within me, a mix of responsibility and confusion. "Although I'm not sure where they are," I added, the last words tinged with a touch of helplessness.

Paul's response came swiftly, laced with a nonchalance that contrasted sharply with my growing anxiety. "Mum can deal with those," he remarked dismissively, as if to swat away a minor inconvenience. His words, meant to reassure, instead tightened the knot of unease in my stomach.

In that moment, a silent debate waged within me. Paul was right; Greta was more than capable of handling the task. She had a knack for creating order out of chaos, and perhaps the act of unpacking would provide her with a sense of normality amidst our upheaval. Yet, relinquishing this small piece of control, entrusting another with a task I felt compelled to complete, stirred a measure of reluctance within me.

Choosing to set aside my hesitations, I realigned my focus towards the mysteries awaiting at the Drop Zone. The allure of uncovering what the Guardians had orchestrated under the veil of night tugged at my curiosity, urging me forward.

With a silent nod to Paul, I stepped through the camp's gate, our movements measured to avoid disturbing the tranquil dawn. Lois, however, brimmed with unrestrained enthusiasm, her presence a stark contrast to the quietude, as she bounded ahead toward our destination.

The crispness of the morning air bit at my skin, as a blanket of serene silence enveloped us. Side by side, yet ensconced in our respective solitudes, Paul and I treaded the path to the Drop Zone, each step carrying us closer to the unknown machinations of the Guardians, our thoughts our only companions in the still, dawn-lit landscape.

❖

The landscape that unfolded before us as we neared the two Portals was nothing short of staggering. My eyes took in the scene with a mix of disbelief and wonder, my heart pounding a rapid rhythm against my ribs. There, splayed across the Clivilian dust, was an incongruous collection of our worldly possessions. Items that once filled the rooms of our family home were now oddly juxtaposed against the barren backdrop of this new world.

Navigating this bizarre tableau, I felt as if I had stepped into a disjointed dream, where the familiar trappings of our past life were scattered like leaves in the wind. Each step took me past a different chapter of our lives: the couch where we gathered for movie nights, the dining table that hosted our discussions and debates, even the inconsequential knick-knacks that I never thought held much significance until now.

Paul's expression mirrored my own astonishment as he wove his way through this labyrinth of our past existence. The sight of him, moving amidst our scattered belongings, added an extra layer of surrealism to the whole experience.

Unable to contain my bewilderment, I let out a low, incredulous mutter, "What the heck?" My eyes settled on the computer, which sat atop its desk with an air of nonchalance, as if it had always belonged in this strange, dusty terrain. The sight of such a familiar object in this context was jarring, throwing into sharp relief the bizarre reality of our situation. Here, surrounded by the detritus of our old life, I was starkly reminded of the bridge between our past and our present, a tangible link to the world we had left behind.

The already bewildering scene took on an even more absurd quality when my eyes landed on Beatrix, Jarod, and Luke, who had inexplicably found respite amidst the chaos, dozing in our very own beds. The sight of Beatrix and Jarod, entwined in what was supposed to be Greta's and my sanctuary, tucked snugly under our duck-feathered blanket, was almost too much to process. The thought of Greta's reaction to this invasion of our personal space flickered through my mind, a mix of humour and disbelief tinged the edges of that mental image.

Paul and I, drawn together by the sheer absurdity of our surroundings, stood side by side in silent camaraderie, taking in the vast sprawl of our upended lives. It felt as if we were witnesses to the aftermath of some bizarre tempest, our belongings and the Guardians themselves caught and frozen mid-whirl.

Feeling a protective instinct rise within me, I reached out, my hand finding Paul's shoulder, holding him back from advancing towards the sleeping figures. The Guardians, so deeply ensconced in their slumber, remained blissfully unaware of our presence and the turmoil their actions had wrought. While a part of me clamoured for explanations, for some semblance of order to be restored, another, more rational voice counselled patience.

Let them sleep, it urged. There would be time enough to seek answers, to untangle the web of confusion and hold them accountable for the disarray. But for now, in the stillness of this surreal tableau, it seemed best to pause, to take a breath, and to prepare for the conversations and decisions that lay ahead.

As Paul and I meandered through the surreal landscape, the extent of the Guardians' intervention became increasingly apparent. The curtains from our home, once a symbol of domesticity, were now incongruously draped over the dusty terrain, fluttering slightly in the gentle Clivilius breeze. My eyes caught sight of a roll of carpet, awkwardly leaning against a makeshift wall of furniture, seemingly plucked from our living room and deposited here.

A chuckle escaped me, tinged with irony. The Guardians' efforts were nothing if not comprehensive, their actions a peculiar blend of chaos and meticulousness. But as a pang of melancholy nudged at the edges of my amusement, the reality of the situation settled in. The home that Greta and I had cherished was now a scattered memory, its elements dispersed across this foreign landscape.

Paul's voice pulled me from my reverie, his tone a mixture of disbelief and humour. "Carpet!? Seriously?" He looked at me, his expression a mirror of confusion and curiosity, as if I held some secret blueprint for making sense of the absurdity. "What the heck are we going to do with this?" he questioned, gesturing to the out-of-place carpet.

In that moment, a sense of resolve washed over me, a readiness to confront the absurd with pragmatism. My face settled into a determined calm, and a wry smile hinted at the blend of humour and resolve that defined my life's philosophy. "Build a house," I responded, my voice carrying a mix of jest and earnest. The suggestion was a nod to the need for adaptability, a recognition that while our surroundings were undeniably bizarre, they also offered a canvas for reinvention and resilience. In this odd conglomeration of our past life and our current reality, we were tasked with constructing not just a physical dwelling but a new sense of home, however unconventional it might be.

Paul's growing bewilderment crystallised into a palpable frustration, breaking through his typically composed exterior. "It's all too much," he grumbled, his intense gaze locked with mine, conveying a depth of emotion that words alone could not express.

"What is?" I inquired, seeking clarity on the root of his distress.

"All of it!" he exploded, his arms flailing in a gesture that encompassed the entire bewildering scene before us.

Indeed, the sight of our personal effects strewn about in was disconcerting. It was as if our life back on Earth had been fragmented, each piece now a puzzle part of an unfamiliar picture.

Paul didn't pause, his frustrations spilling out in a torrent. "It was bad enough when it was just Luke, but now there are three of them!" he exclaimed, referencing the trio of Guardians whose actions had so drastically altered our surroundings. "How am I supposed to keep up with all of the supplies and random crap they bring through the Portals, as well as manage the ongoing development of our settlement?"

His rapid-fire delivery, a cascade of concerns and responsibilities, elicited a soft chuckle from me, not out of amusement at his plight, but in recognition of his earnestness and dedication. I reached out, placing a comforting hand on his shoulder, acknowledging the weight he carried. Managing the Drop Zone as well as trying to oversee the entire development of a growing settlement, was a lot for one person to shoulder alone.

Paul's predicament echoed the tales of early pioneers, stories of individuals and communities who banded together to forge new lives in uncharted territories. They, too, faced daunting challenges, working collectively to build from the ground up under uncertain and often precarious conditions.

In that moment, the parallels between our situation and those historical narratives of resilience and community became strikingly clear. Just as those pioneers leaned on one another to transform the wilderness into habitable settlements, so too would we need to rely on our collective strengths and ingenuity to navigate this new world

The moment of inspiration hit me with sudden clarity amidst our conversation. "Why don't you leave me to manage the Drop Zone and the..." My voice trailed off as the reality of what I was proposing began to dawn on me. My gaze drifted across the scattered remnants of our past life, as I grappled with the scope of the responsibility I was about to assume. After a brief pause, I found the word I was seeking. "Guardians," I concluded, committing to the task at hand.

Paul's reaction was immediate, his eyes reflecting a mix of surprise and relief. "Are you sure?" he inquired, his question sounding more like a formality, perhaps out of politeness or a brief flicker of concern, rather than a genuine deterrent.

"I'm positive," I responded, my smile conveying confidence and resolve. There was a part of me that knew this was more than just an offer of assistance; it was a necessary step for my own well-being in this new world.

Paul exhaled deeply, a visible sign of the stress being alleviated. "Okay," he acquiesced with a nod, his voice carrying a tone of gratitude. "The gig's all yours."

Observing the tension dissipate from Paul's posture was gratifying. The decision to take on this role was not just about alleviating his burden; it was also a strategic move for my own mental health. In this unpredictable and disorienting environment, having a purpose, a focus, could be the anchor I needed.

My contemplation went deeper, acknowledging my physical limitations and preferences. While I didn't shy away from manual labour, my expertise and comfort lay more in strategy and oversight. The thought of being more involved in planning and coordination, rather than engaging in the physical rigours of construction, suited me. It played to my strengths and accommodated my back, which demanded consideration.

In this decision, I saw a dual opportunity: to support Paul and contribute meaningfully to our community's development while also carving out a role that resonated with my skills and interests. The satisfaction of finding a path that felt right in this new world was a small yet significant victory, a glimmer of order in the midst of upheaval.

DROP ZONE MANAGER

4338.214.2

Wandering amidst the remnants of our previous life, I felt a wave of determination mixed with a hint of bewilderment. The task at hand was akin to solving a complex puzzle with no clear starting point. With no sudden epiphanies to guide me, I resorted to the basics—sorting and categorising. It struck me how the Guardians' method, or rather the absence of one, had jumbled our belongings without regard. The kitchen items were entwined with laundry essentials, living room decorations were interspersed with bathroom utilities, and bedroom pieces were scattered throughout the mix.

The process of sifting through the chaos was grounding, yet the absurdity of finding a toaster next to a towel or a bookshelf beside a lawn mower was not lost on me. It was a physical manifestation of our upheaved lives, each item a fragment of a past normality now tossed into a new reality.

Paul's return interrupted my sorting endeavour, his presence a reminder of the shared burden of adaptation. "Dad, are you sure you're comfortable with this?" he inquired, his voice laced with a mix of concern and relinquishment. His question, genuine and considerate, sparked a wry smile on my face. I recognised his internal struggle, the challenge of handing over the reins of a project you've been deeply involved in, regardless of the associated stresses.

Facing Paul, I held my favourite photo of the Adelaide Temple, a symbol of structure amidst the disorder. My voice carried a blend of assurance and a burgeoning sense of responsibility. "Paul, I've managed bigger projects back on

Earth," I reminded him, the words as much for my own reaffirmation as they were for his comfort. "I can handle this." The confidence in my tone was genuine, yet beneath it lay a burgeoning realisation of the logistical puzzle that awaited me. The motorhome's limited space loomed in my mind, especially with the potential addition of Jerome and Charles. The mere thought of their cohabitation with Greta sent a wave of apprehension through me, anticipating the tension that was almost certain to arise.

Paul's acknowledgment came with a cautionary note, drawing my attention to the unpredictable nature of the Guardians. His gesture towards their slumbering forms, amidst the jumble of our earthly possessions, served as a tangible reminder of the challenges ahead. "Just remember, the Guardians can be unpredictable. Keep an eye out for them," he advised, his voice laced with a touch of irony as he added, "Case in point."

His words elicited a hearty laugh from me. The irony of his statement, juxtaposed with the task at hand, was not lost on me. "I've dealt with my fair share of unpredictable folks in my time. Don't you worry," I responded, my mind briefly wandering to the days of raising six spirited children, each with their own unique quirks and surprises. Those memories, a testament to my resilience and adaptability, bolstered my confidence. They served as a reminder that while the context had drastically changed, the core skills I'd honed over a lifetime—patience, organisation, and a touch of humour—would be invaluable in navigating this new chapter.

With the air seemingly cleared and our roles tentatively defined, I redirected my focus to the task at hand, the physical embodiment of our disrupted lives laid out before me. My hands methodically sorted through the jumbled assortment, each item a thread in the tapestry of our past existence.

Out of the corner of my eye, I could sense Paul's lingering presence, his form static, enveloped in a veil of contemplation. It struck me that while our logistical challenges were daunting, the emotional toll of our circumstances on each of us could be just as significant.

"Paul," I called out, my voice cutting through his introspection, tethering him back to the present. "Why don't you focus on that Project Management role of yours? You've got a knack for it," I suggested, aiming to anchor him in his strengths, to remind him of his value and capability within our community.

His response, accompanied by a tentative smile, betrayed a flicker of uncertainty, a subtle discord between his outward agreement and his inner turmoil. "Yeah," he acknowledged, his smile not quite masking the complexity of his emotions, "I suppose it's where I'm needed most now."

His tone, slightly deflated, tugged at my awareness, prompting a momentary pause in my sorting. It was a reminder of the fragile human element amidst our endeavours to adapt and rebuild. While I chose to focus on the immediate, tangible tasks, I recognised that our emotional resilience would be equally critical.

Silently, I resolved to keep a closer watch on Paul, understanding that our roles were not just about managing resources or organising chaos, but also about supporting each other, acknowledging the unseen struggles that each of us faced.

As I continued my efforts to bring some order to the mayhem around me, Paul's demeanour caught my attention. His slow, contemplative walk back toward the camp seemed to reflect a deeper internal struggle, perhaps a sense of redundancy in the face of our reassigned roles. This observation stirred a paternal instinct within me, a desire to uplift and remind him of his intrinsic worth to our collective endeavour.

"Paul," I called out, quickening my pace to catch up with him, a burgeoning idea igniting a spark of enthusiasm within me. As he stopped and turned, I wore an encouraging smile, hoping to inject a dose of optimism into our interaction.

"I know what's here," I gestured towards the scattered remnants of our former life, acknowledging the familiarity yet overwhelming nature of the task. "But why don't you give me more of a tour of the Drop Zone?" I suggested, pointing towards the area that had become Paul's domain. "I'm not familiar with what you've done with that."

The suggestion seemed to ignite a spark in Paul, his expression brightening at the opportunity to showcase his contributions. "Yeah, I can do that," he responded, his voice carrying a newfound enthusiasm. The timing was impeccable as a loud rumble from his stomach punctuated the moment, prompting a shared moment of laughter, a welcome reprieve from the weight of our conversations.

"Let me go back to camp and get us some food first," Paul proposed, a practical and caring gesture that I welcomed. It also conveniently delayed my inevitable confrontation with Greta over the uncollected suitcases—a task I was not eager to face head-on just yet.

"Nothing heavy though," I quipped, patting my stomach in a light-hearted manner. "Mum says I need to watch my figure."

Paul's joyous reaction was heartening, and as his smile spread across his face, a wave of paternal pride washed over me. Despite the myriad paths my children had taken, diverging from each other and from their upbringing, their happiness and resilience were my ultimate consolation.

❖

As the Guardians began to rouse from their deep sleep, I found myself drawn towards them, a concoction of curiosity, amusement, and a touch of paternal sternness brewing within me. I approached with a demeanour that balanced the line between light-heartedness and the impending seriousness of their actions last night.

"You three look like you've had a busy night," I commented, my tone laced with a hint of jest, yet underscored by an imminent sense of responsibility I felt they needed to acknowledge. Observing their bewildered awakening, I couldn't suppress a flicker of amusement at the peculiar situation—the nocturnal adventure that had led to our belongings being scattered across the landscape. There was a whimsical part of me that entertained the idea of joining such a caper, yet the reality of our situation, the need to establish order and normality, anchored me back to my sense of duty.

Luke's response was drowsy and disoriented, his mind still foggy from sleep. "Yeah," he muttered, rubbing the remnants of rest from his eyes, his voice tinged with confusion. "Is Paul here?" he inquired, his question perhaps indicative of their usual reliance on Paul's presence and leadership in the Drop Zone.

"No," I replied with a measured calmness, seizing the opportunity to inform them of the new changes. "We decided that I'll take charge of the Drop Zone management from now on." My statement was clear and deliberate, signalling a shift in our small community's dynamics and my active role in it.

Luke's reaction was one of mild surprise, a hint of perplexity crossing his features as he processed the change. It seemed the idea of Paul stepping back from a role he had embodied with such dedication was unexpected. This shift, a minor upheaval in our camp's microcosm, mirrored the broader sense of adaptation and transformation we were all undergoing. In this new world, roles shifted, responsibilities changed, and we all had to find our footing again, navigating the unfamiliar terrain of our altered lives together.

With a deliberate effort to maintain a neutral tone for added impact, I found it challenging to suppress the smirk eager to break free as I delivered my line. "He took one look at all of this and decided he couldn't handle you anymore," I quipped, the edges of my mouth betraying my amusement despite my intent to remain stern. The comment elicited a chuckle from me, the situation's absurdity too potent to ignore.

Luke's reaction was a stark contrast to my own, his frown indicating a failure to see the humour in my words. It was a clear signal to adjust my approach, to ensure the seriousness of the situation wasn't lost amid my attempts at levity.

Adopting a more serious demeanour, my gaze locked onto Luke's, the fatherly authority in my voice unmistakable. "You three may have pulled off a spectacular vanishing act, but we can't afford such recklessness," I stated, my arms sweeping around to indicate the disarray surrounding us. It was then that my eyes landed on the hens perched atop a bookcase, an incongruous sight that underscored the extent of the chaos. A silent sigh of resignation passed through me as I mentally noted the additional cleanup required.

Continuing my admonishment, I aimed to strike a balance between firmness and understanding, recognising the need to establish boundaries while acknowledging the Guardians' unique contributions. "Going forward, there will be more stringent controls," I declared, setting the expectation for a more organised and considerate approach to their interventions.

The collective groan from the trio was somewhat expected, a natural response to the imposition of stricter guidelines.

Yet, it was crucial for them to understand that their actions had repercussions, impacting not just the physical environment but the communal dynamics of our fledgling society. In this new world, where every action reverberated with amplified significance, it was essential for us all to act with a heightened sense of responsibility and cooperation.

Luke's attempt at reassurance, "It won't happen again," carried a note of fragility, his voice wobbling slightly, betraying the uncertainty behind his words. It was a promise that felt more like an optimistic aspiration than a solid commitment, a sentiment that Jarod's interjection only solidified.

"I'm not sure you can promise that," Jarod chimed in, his laughter cutting through the tension, while casting a complicit glance at Beatrix. Her response was a nonchalant shrug, her expression a canvas of both mischief and fatigue. It was clear that the trio shared a dynamic that thrived on spontaneity and perhaps a touch of rebelliousness.

This interaction offered me a poignant insight into the challenges Paul faced and now the ones I was about to embrace. Understanding Luke had always been a journey; his strong-willed nature, so reminiscent of his grandmother, meant that he approached life with a staunch determination and a desire to carve his own path. Now, recognising that Beatrix and Jarod likely shared similar traits, I braced myself for the task ahead.

Yet, within this realisation, there was no sense of dread, only a recognition of the need for adaptability and strategic guidance. My experience as a father of six had honed a skill set that I was now ready to apply in this new context. I knew that if I could harness their energies, channel their creativity and drive towards constructive ends, the chaos could be transformed into a force of positive change.

Embracing this new role, I saw an opportunity not just for leadership but for collaboration. It was about guiding these strong personalities, blending their distinct talents and visions with the collective needs and aspirations of our community. If navigated wisely, their dynamism could be the catalyst for our settlement's growth and success, turning potential turbulence into a wellspring of innovation and progress. In this newfound responsibility, I found a mission, a challenge that ignited a spark of anticipation for what lay ahead.

Luke's concession, "He's right, I really can't promise that this won't happen again," resonated with a certain honesty that drew me back into the gravity of our dialogue.

In response, I instinctively adopted the expression of disappointment, a look that had become a powerful tool in my parental arsenal over the years. It wasn't about instilling fear or asserting dominance; it was about evoking a sense of self-reflection and responsibility. My children had often remarked that this expression of mine was far more impactful than any display of anger.

As expected, this silent communication had its effect on Luke. His body language shifted, a subtle but noticeable acknowledgment of the weight my disappointment carried. "But I can make sure that you are better prepared and equipped to deal with it when it does," he offered, a compromise that hinted at a willingness to mitigate the potential fallout of their unpredictable actions.

Maintaining the intensity of my gaze, I ensured Luke understood the seriousness of this moment. It wasn't just about acknowledging the potential for future incidents; it was about establishing a mutual understanding, an unspoken agreement to strive for better. My look was not just a display of disappointment but a silent invocation of his deeper sense of duty and respect for the collective well-being of our community.

This moment was crucial, not just for Luke but for the dynamic of our group as a whole. My influence over Beatrix and Jarod was uncertain, their personalities still enigmas to me. Yet, through Luke, I hoped to extend a semblance of guidance and expectation. If he could embody and advocate for a sense of responsibility, perhaps it would ripple out to influence them as well.

As Luke extricated himself from Charles's bed, stretching and shaking off the remnants of sleep, our environment was pierced by an unexpected voice. It was Kain, making his way towards us with a determination that seemed to overshadow his reliance on crutches. His approach was swift, his use of the crutches more an accompaniment than a necessity, which piqued my curiosity and concern simultaneously.

I exchanged a glance with Luke, my eyebrow arched in silent inquiry about this unforeseen interruption. Luke's response, a noncommittal shrug, signalled that he was as taken aback by Kain's abrupt presence as I was.

When Kain reached us, there was a palpable urgency in his demeanour, his breath slightly laboured from the effort of his approach. "Luke, we need to talk," he stated, positioning himself with a deliberate intent that left no room for ambiguity. His presence and tone severed the thread of conversation between Luke and me, introducing a new layer of immediacy to the unfolding morning.

The young man's insistence on privacy further intrigued me. "In private," he added, an assertion that brooked no argument, marking the seriousness of whatever issue lay at hand. Luke's acquiescence, a simple "Sure," underscored his recognition of the significance Kain attributed to their discussion.

As they moved away, distancing themselves from the rest of us, a multitude of questions swirled in my mind. The nature of Kain's urgency, the implications of their private discussion, and how this might intersect with the already complex web of our community's dynamics—all these considerations lingered as I watched them retreat.

A PLACE OF LEARNING

4338.214.3

As I sifted through the disarray that once constituted the comforts of our family home, my focus honed in on a particularly precious quest: locating the large collection of folders brimming with family photos and journals. These weren't just documents; they were the tapestry of our shared history, each image and entry a thread in the fabric of our collective memory, meticulously compiled over the years.

The chaos wrought by the Guardians' actions had scattered these treasures haphazardly, making my search frustratingly piecemeal. So far, I'd managed to reclaim only two folders from the muddle, a small victory in the sea of disarray.

Amid my focused task, the dynamics around me continued to evolve. Beatrix and Jarod's conversation, tinged with intensity, caught my peripheral attention. Whatever their exchange entailed, it concluded with Jarod's abrupt departure through his Portal back to Earth. The quick transition from heated debate to sudden exit left a lingering tension in the air.

Parallel to this, Kain's private discussion with Luke reached its own culmination. Observing from a distance, I saw Kain accompany Luke to his Portal, their conversation persisting until the very threshold. Luke's subsequent departure through the Portal, devoid of any acknowledgment towards Beatrix or me, added a layer of introspection to my search. His silent exit, without a customary gesture of farewell, underscored the transient, sometimes isolating nature of our current existence.

Beatrix's nonchalant response to my inquisitive look piqued my curiosity further. Her reluctance to depart, contrasting sharply with the other Guardians' swift exits, left me pondering the multitude of reasons behind her lingering presence. *Was it a lighter load of responsibilities today, or perhaps the aftermath of the previous night's exertions weighing on her?* My mind wandered through these possibilities, entertaining itself with speculations as I refocused on my primary mission – retrieving our family's cherished journals and photos.

The unexpected clatter of a dining chair colliding with a precarious stack of books snapped me out of my reverie, redirecting my attention to Beatrix's movements. Her unintentional disruption of the already chaotic setting was a stark reminder of our current state of disorder.

Beatrix's approach was cautious, almost hesitant, as if she was navigating the boundaries of our newfound acquaintanceship. "You appear to be on quite the search," she remarked, her voice tinged with a mix of curiosity and restraint, seemingly unsure of her place in this intimate quest of mine.

Her observation warranted a response, yet my own wariness mirrored hers. Engaging deeply with someone I barely knew, particularly in the midst of such a personal endeavour, felt daunting. "Yep," I replied, my answer brief yet not unfriendly, a guarded acknowledgment of her presence and observation.

Beatrix's inquiry, "What are you looking for?" narrowed the distance between us, her steps tentative yet driven by a genuine curiosity. The vulnerability of sharing the intimate contents of my journals with someone relatively unknown nudged me into a realm of cautious openness. With a measured motion, I extended the dark folder I clutched—a gatekeeper to a trove of personal history—towards her.

Her gaze, sharpened with intrigue, met the folder as she accepted it from my hands. "What's this?" she queried, her voice laced with a blend of curiosity and anticipation.

"It's one of my journal folders," I responded, a sense of pride unfurling within me as a grin etched itself across my face. The action of sharing this piece of my life felt unexpectedly liberating, a small bridge built in the midst of our shared uncertainty.

Beatrix's reaction was immediate and visceral as she delved into the contents of the folder. Her exclamation, "Oh my God!" resonated with a vibrancy that piqued my interest further. Her eyes danced over the photos, her attention caught by a particular image that prompted her to lean in closer.

"Is this Luke?" she inquired, pointing to the photo that had captured her attention.

I moved in to view the image over her shoulder, a nostalgic chuckle escaping me as I recognised the scene. The photograph depicted a young child, garbed in little shorts and delightfully engaged with the water from a garden hose. "No. That's actually Jerome," I clarified, the resemblance between the brothers in their youth a common source of mix-ups. "He and Luke looked quite similar when they were young kids."

Beatrix's laughter served as a warm echo in the midst of our scattered surroundings, her amusement brightening the moment. "What's he doing?" she asked.

"That's why I do a combination of photos and text on every page," I explained, guiding her attention to the descriptive text that accompanied the photo. It was my way of ensuring that the richness of our experiences wasn't lost to time, that each picture was more than just a visual snapshot but a story captured in its entirety.

Beatrix shifted her focus to the words, her curiosity piqued. Meanwhile, I took a moment to reflect on my endeavour, a labour of love that spanned years, a repository of memories crafted with care and dedication. "A picture may be worth a thousand words," I mused aloud, my voice tinged with a blend of nostalgia and pride, "but words help to tell an accurate story of the photo." It was a philosophy that had guided my efforts, a belief in the power of combined narratives to offer a fuller, richer recounting of our lives.

Her response, after lifting her eyes from the folder, was unexpected yet deeply affirming. "You are very wise, Mr. Smith," she remarked, her gaze conveying a newfound respect. The formal address caught me off guard, prompting a gentle correction, "Noah is fine," I replied, aiming to bridge any lingering formality between us.

As Beatrix continued to explore the folder, her interest seemed genuinely piqued, leading her to inquire about the extent of my project. "How many of these folders are there?" she asked, her curiosity palpable.

The question prompted a moment of introspection as I tallied the volumes in my mind. "I think I've just started volume twenty-three," I responded, a figure that even I found daunting when voiced aloud.

Her reaction, an expletive followed by an expression of astonishment, mirrored the magnitude of the endeavour. "Shit," she exclaimed, her eyes reflecting a mix of surprise and admiration. "That's amazing."

Her words, simple yet sincere, resonated with me, validating the years of effort poured into these journals. It was a reminder of the value of our shared histories, the importance of preserving our stories, and the unexpected connections that can arise from sharing them.

The weight of nostalgia and loss momentarily pressed heavy on my chest as I considered the breadth of our family's history, potentially scattered irretrievably across this unforgiving landscape. The depth of what could be lost – the memories, the laughter, the struggles captured in those journals – surged through me, prompting a deep, steadying breath.

"I just hope I can find them all here," I voiced out to Beatrix, an admission laced with a blend of hope and underlying concern. It was a moment of vulnerability, a rare acknowledgment of the potential permanence of our displacement.

Beatrix's inquiry, "Do all the folders look like this?" snapped me back to the immediate task at hand. "Yep," I responded, the simplicity of my answer belying the complexity of emotions swirling within me.

Her offer to assist, "I'll help you look," delivered with a tone of determination and kindness, took me by surprise. The gesture was unexpected yet warmly appreciated, a sign of solidarity in the face of our shared upheaval. I nodded in gratitude, a silent acknowledgment of her support, while I swiftly averted my gaze to conceal the brief flicker of emotion her kindness had stirred in me.

In that moment, a reflective thought crossed my mind. Despite Luke's distancing from the church and the nuanced estrangement that had evolved within our family, he had, perhaps inadvertently, woven a network of caring individuals around him. Beatrix's readiness to aid in my search was a testament to that, a silver lining that Luke, in his own unconventional way, was not alone – nor were we.

Kain's voice, clear and curious, cut through the quiet concentration of our search, "What are you searching for, Beatrix?" The question, while simple, opened a window into the dynamics at play among the group, revealing layers of familiarity and camaraderie that I was only just beginning to discern.

Given my limited interactions with Kain, and his direct engagement with Beatrix, it was evident that their acquaintance was more established than mine with either of them. I chose to step back, allowing the interaction to unfold, using the moment to glean insights into their relationship and perhaps understand the social fabric of our group a bit better.

Observing Beatrix as she engaged with Kain was enlightening. Her demeanour, bright and eager, as she shared the purpose of our endeavour, painted her in a light I hadn't fully appreciated before – not just as a Guardian but as a person willing to lend her strength to others' causes.

Kain's subsequent glance towards me, a bridge of acknowledgment, prompted a subtle nod from my end, a gesture of mutual recognition. Despite the initial awkwardness that followed, his offer to join the search felt like a small but significant step toward building a sense of community among us.

The search unfolded in a concentrated hush, each of us absorbed in the task at hand, rifling through the remnants of a life once lived. My focus briefly wavered as I nearly tripped over a formidable pile of towels, their plushness a stark reminder of the comforts of home now out of place in this dusty setting. As I set some aside, considering their practical utility for our motorhome, a thought occurred to me.

"Kain," my voice emerged softer than expected in the stillness, yet it sufficed to draw his attention. Clutching the towels to emphasise my point, I extended an offer, a gesture of communal support amid our shared displacement. "As long as it doesn't look too personal, you're welcome to help yourself to anything you need. Sheets, towels—" I indicated, the fabrics in my hands serving as tangible examples of the resources at our disposal.

His response, marked by a cautious narrowing of eyes, reflected a consideration of the offer's implications. "But won't you need them?" he inquired, his voice laced with a hint of concern, perhaps unaccustomed to such open sharing amidst scarcity.

My gesture towards the vast array of our possessions scattered about us aimed to assuage his hesitance. "With Greta's hoarding, I'm certain that we could single-handedly cater for the entire settlement," I half-joked, acknowledging my wife's penchant for preparedness that, in this moment, transformed from a quaint quirk to a fortuitous boon.

In the backdrop of our exchange, Beatrix's soft chuckle resonated, a light-hearted acknowledgement of the humour woven into our predicament.

Kain's cautious inquiry, "Are you sure Mrs. Smith won't mind?" elicited a genuine laugh from me, an unguarded response that seemed to startle him slightly. His reaction, a mixture of surprise and curiosity, reflected the nuances of our budding interactions. "Oh, she'll definitely mind," I confessed, my humour transparent in the admission, while Kain's expression tightened, uncertain how to gauge my jesting tone. Beatrix, too, seemed intrigued by the unfolding dialogue, her attention fixed on our exchange.

Internally, I weighed the possible repercussions of my offer against the practical reality of our situation. The realisation that much of what we owned had lain unused for years fortified my decision. "What Greta isn't reminded exists, she'll never miss," I quipped, a lighthearted encapsulation of my rationale, hoping to convey a sense of levity to Kain and Beatrix.

My attempt at humour resonated, as evidenced by their laughter, a shared moment that seemed to further bridge the gaps between us. Kain's formal acknowledgment, "Thank you,

Mr. Smith," prompted a friendly correction from me, "Just Noah is fine," aiming to foster a more relaxed rapport.

Kain's offer to assist with transporting items back to camp or the Drop Zone was met with my gratitude, "Thanks, Kain," even though I harboured no immediate plans to enlist his help. His life, like ours, was undoubtedly filled with its own set of priorities and challenges.

However, a palpable shift in Kain's demeanour caught my attention. The lightness that had momentarily surrounded us seemed to dissipate as he delved back into the sea of belongings, his actions tinged with a newfound intensity. Observing him, a part of me was drawn to the complexity of his character, to the layers and stories yet untold. It was a poignant reminder of the individual journeys interwoven with our collective struggle for adaptation and survival, each person a mosaic of experiences and emotions, now part of the broader tapestry of our shared existence.

Beatrix's voice broke through the focused silence, her call infused with a hint of excitement that instantly piqued my interest. "Hey, Noah," she beckoned, her gesture inviting me to join her discovery. "I think I've found them," she announced, her voice laced with enthusiasm.

The sense of relief that surged through me was palpable as I navigated my way toward her. The prospect of reclaiming more of our cherished journals ignited a spark of hope amidst the disarray. As I reached her side and began to gather the precious folders into my arms, my eagerness got the better of me. One folder, slippery from the wear of time or perhaps the dust of our new environment, escaped my grasp and tumbled toward the ground, a reminder of the need for careful handling of these irreplaceable treasures.

Beatrix's suggestion, "Perhaps you should grab a shopping trolley," was delivered with a playful smile, a light-hearted nudge to temper my enthusiasm with a bit of practicality.

"Now look who is the wise one," I responded, my tone rich with a mix of admiration and gentle jest, acknowledging her pragmatic advice.

Beatrix's response, a blush coupled with a broad smile, added a touch of human warmth to the moment.

The shift in our conversation to Kain's background prompted a more subdued tone from me. "How does Kain fit in?" I inquired, my voice hushed, hinting at the layers of family dynamics I was just beginning to uncover. "He seems quite young."

Beatrix's response illuminated the connection: "That's Jamie's nephew."

"Jamie," I echoed, the name sparking a flicker of recognition. "That's Luke's partner, isn't it?" My query was more a confirmation of the scattered details I held about Luke's life, a life that had, over time, drifted into a realm of unanswered questions and unshared experiences.

Beatrix's affirmation, "Yes," was accompanied by a look that seemed to pierce through the layers of my façade. It was clear she understood the disconnect, the unspoken admissions that hung heavily between my words.

Compelled by a sudden need for honesty, I shared, "I haven't paid as much attention to Luke and his situation as I should have over the years." The admission was painful, an acknowledgment of the distance that had grown between Luke and our family.

Beatrix's lack of surprise at my confession was a silent confirmation of what I already knew. The realisation, stark and jarring, that I had allowed my relationship with Luke to fray, sent a sharp pang of regret through me, a poignant reminder of lost time and neglected connections.

Her next words offered a glimmer of unexpected insight. "He talks about you often," she revealed, a statement that stirred a mix of hope and sorrow within me. "He does?" My response was instinctive, a mixture of astonishment and a budding sense of loss for the conversations and moments we had not shared.

Her nod was empathetic, her subsequent words cautious yet candid, "It's not really my place to gossip, but I know that he misses talking to you." Then, with a hint of humour that barely masked the underlying seriousness, she added, "Even if the two of you don't seem to agree on much anymore."

The impact of her words was profound, slicing through the veneer of stoicism I had maintained. In that moment, the weight of missed opportunities and unspoken words settled heavily upon me, a poignant realisation of the distance that had grown, not just in miles but in the very fabric of our relationship. Beatrix's insights, unintended as they may have been, served as a reminder of the fragile threads that connect us to those we love, urging a reflection on the choices and actions that shape those bonds.

The relative calm of our poignant conversation was abruptly shattered by the cacophony of chickens squawking and flapping their wings in distress. The cause of the commotion quickly became apparent: Lois, the golden retriever, had taken a keen interest in the hens that had, until that moment, been quietly perched amidst our belongings.

Jerome's voice cut through the chaos, a mix of command and desperation, as he called out to Lois, attempting to rein in her newfound enthusiasm for poultry. Watching him chase after the dog among the disarray, a part of me was caught between concern and amusement at the spectacle unfolding before us.

The scene, while chaotic, was a simple reminder of the life we were navigating—a blend of the familiar and the utterly unexpected. Jerome's efforts to corral Lois, coupled with his affectionate approach to her misbehaviour, spoke volumes about the dynamics of our group and the connections that remained steadfast despite the upheaval.

When Jerome and Lois finally made their way over to us, Lois panting and Jerome displaying a mix of relief and exasperation, I couldn't help but offer a piece of advice, albeit with a hint of humour. "You might need to put her on a lead," I suggested, recognising the blend of order and freedom we were all trying to balance.

Jerome's assertion that Lois was fine, coupled with his affectionate gesture, painted a scene of gentle normality amidst our disarrayed backdrop. As Beatrix joined him, kneeling to lavish Lois with attention, there was an unmistakable warmth that radiated from the trio. Their laughter and smiles, sparked by the simple joy of interacting with the dog, brought a sense of lightness to the atmosphere.

Observing Jerome and Beatrix together with Lois, a realisation dawned on me. My approach to new individuals was typically one of cautious optimism, a balance of open-heartedness and a protective reserve. Yet, Beatrix, through her actions and demeanour, had swiftly navigated the barriers I often unconsciously erected. Her ease with Jerome, and her willingness to assist in my personal quest for the journals had impressed upon me her genuine nature.

The warmth in my smile deepened as I watched them, acknowledging internally that Beatrix's integration into our family might not just be inevitable but also beneficial. Her rapport with Jerome was effortless, indicative of a broader potential to mesh well with the rest of us. It was an intriguing prospect, the idea of expanding our circle, of weaving new threads into the fabric of our family's collective narrative.

In this moment of shared laughter and mutual care for Lois, the lines between acquaintance and friend, outsider and insider, began to blur. Beatrix, with her kind gestures and empathetic presence, was subtly reshaping my perception of what it meant to be part of a community beyond church. It was an insight into the power of genuine connections, a suggestion that even in the most unexpected circumstances, we have the capacity to find kinship, understanding, and perhaps, a new sense of family.

Jerome's question, laden with a mix of wonder and disbelief, echoed the magnitude of what we were confronting: the entirety of our home's contents seemingly uprooted and strewn before us. "Is this really everything from our house?" he pondered aloud, pulling himself up from the ground, his gaze sweeping over the scattered relics of our past life.

"It seems that way," I confirmed, my voice tinged with a mix of resignation and humour as I surveyed the scene. "Curtains, and carpet, and all," I added, the absurdity of it all coaxing a wry grin onto my face, a grin that seemed to mirror on Beatrix's face as a blush crept into her cheeks.

"What about Millie?" Jerome's voice broke the brief respite, his concern evident as he mentioned the Border Collie, the fondness for the pet shining through his words.

Beatrix's expression shifted to one of confusion, her gaze moving from Jerome to me. "Who's Millie?" she inquired, her voice laced with an odd defensive note.

"She's a Border Collie," Jerome explained, a hint of a smile breaking through his worry as he spoke of Millie. "She was a rescue dog," I added, feeling a surge of warmth at the memory of Millie's playful spirit. "All Jerome's doing."

Jerome's eyes held a spark of pride as he addressed Beatrix, "You'd love her," he said, his face flushing with a mixture of emotion and bashfulness at his own openness.

Beatrix looked around, as if expecting the dog to emerge from the landscape, then back at us with a furrowed brow. "I don't recall seeing any dogs at the house," she replied, her voice tinged with concern and confusion.

"You wouldn't," I interjected, my tone gentle yet firm.

Beatrix's eyes met mine, filled with questions and the dawning realisation of the depth of our family's history, now scattered like our belongings in the dust of this unfamiliar world.

"Millie was actually staying the night at the vets," Jerome clarified, his voice steady yet carrying an undercurrent of concern. "She has a few health issues. But nothing that isn't easily managed." His eyes held a mix of hope and worry

A look of concern flitted across Beatrix's face, her brows knitting together in a frown. The morning sun cast a gentle light on her, accentuating the worry in her eyes. "I'm not sure that it's a good idea to bring her here if she's not well," she cautioned, her voice laced with apprehension. Her gaze shifted between Jerome and me, seeking reassurance in an uncertain situation.

Jerome, however, stood resolute, his determination shining through. "With Sarah and Grant's expertise here, I'm sure that Millie will be perfectly fine." His confidence was palpable, a beacon of hope in the vast, desolate landscape that surrounded us.

Beatrix's expression remained tinged with doubt, her skepticism a silent shadow in the conversation.

"Besides, you can get any medical supplies we need," Jerome directed at Beatrix, trying to bridge her concerns with a touch of practical levity.

The emergence of Paul approaching the scene caught the corner of my eye, his figure gradually becoming more distinct against the backdrop of the dusty landscape.

Jerome, sensing the shift, looked to me for support, his eyes seeking an ally in the unfolding debate. "Jerome knows what's best," I stated simply, vaguely aligning myself with his judgment. Yet, I quickly excused myself to intercept Paul, hoping to manage whatever concerns he brought with him.

As I turned to leave, the dynamics of the conversation shifted. Jerome, emboldened by my endorsement, launched into another attempt to persuade Beatrix. However, she cut him off sharply, her voice slicing through the tension as she called out for me. Stopping abruptly, I pivoted, my curiosity piqued by her sudden urgency.

Beatrix, with a slight stammer that betrayed her confidence, shared her plans about the Drop Zone. "If you're going to be the manager of the Drop Zone, just thought I'd let you know that I plan on delivering several additional motorhomes today."

I fought to control my expression, striving not to let my grin spread too broadly. It was heartening to see one of the Guardians showing a willingness to adapt and communicate. "Thank you for letting me know, Beatrix," I responded, my tone appreciative. "I'll make sure we have the space cleared at the Portal to receive them."

Beatrix's demeanour shifted slightly, a hint of vulnerability showing. "I know that I can be a little impulsive sometimes," she confessed, her hands fidgeting nervously, a glimpse into her inner turmoil. "But I'll do my best to keep you informed."

I offered her a smile, a gesture of solidarity and understanding. "It's the least I can do," she added, her voice a mix of determination and humility. With that, she turned her focus back to Jerome and the ongoing discussion about the acquisition of Millie.

Departing the conversation, my mind churned with thoughts about Beatrix's commitment. Skepticism lingered like a stubborn shadow, yet a part of me clung to the slender thread of hope that her promise marked a turning point, a new chapter in her approach to collaboration and communication.

As I walked, I found myself reflecting on the conversations between Beatrix and myself, particularly as they pertained to

Luke. The broader implications of my role in this new environment began to take shape in my mind. The Drop Zone wasn't just a physical space; it was a crucible for learning and understanding, a vantage point from which I could observe and engage with the intricate web of relationships and events that defined our community. The thought that I might glean valuable insights here, especially about individuals and their roles in our collective narrative, was both intriguing and daunting.

A sense of satisfaction began to bloom within me, despite the uncertainty that lay ahead. The unfamiliar terrain, the challenges of building a new life from the remnants of the old, the complexities of navigating a community in flux—somehow, these elements combined to ignite a spark of enthusiasm within me. I felt a connection to this place, an unexpected affinity for the rugged beauty and raw potential it represented.

With a smile of quiet contentment, I acknowledged this newfound appreciation for my surroundings. The journey was filled with unknowns, but in that moment, I felt a surge of optimism. Perhaps this strange, barren world could indeed become a home, a place where growth and discovery went hand in hand with survival. As I neared Paul, ready to engage in yet another interaction that would shape our shared future, I held onto this flicker of hope, determined to nurture it into a lasting flame.

PREGNANT DILEMMA

4338.214.4

Paul arrived at the Drop Zone before me, his silhouette etched against the chaotic backdrop of scattered goods. I watched him from a distance, a curious silence enveloping me as he navigated through the disorder. Around him lay the aftermath of a frenzied scavenging spree—clothing tangled with bedding, kitchen utensils peeking out from under a mishmash of personal items, all spilling haphazardly from overflowing shopping trolleys. These were the spoils of a midnight store heist, a clandestine operation led by Luke and Beatrix just a few nights ago, or so Paul had mentioned in passing.

An overwhelming array of items littered the ground, with trolleys—perhaps fifty, maybe even a hundred—scattered around like fallen soldiers after a battle. It was a sight beyond my comprehension, a reminder of the sheer scale of our operations. As I surveyed the Drop Zone, my gaze inadvertently drifted to the Portals, where the remnants of our once-cohesive family home lay strewn about. A pang of realisation washed over me—the task of organising the Guardians' actions was going to be monumentally challenging.

Turning my focus back to Paul, I observed him meandering aimlessly among the debris. He wasn't searching for anything specific; his actions seemed more reflective, almost hesitant. It dawned on me that Paul's unexpected return might be rooted in his struggle to relinquish control over the Portals and the Drop Zone to me. His attachment to this place, to the responsibilities it entailed, seemed to weigh heavily on him, casting a shadow of reluctance that contrasted starkly with the physical chaos around us.

As I approached Paul, navigating through the scattered relics of their scavenging endeavours, I pondered on the most effective way to anchor his wandering attention back to the immediacy of our situation.

I figured a gentle, fatherly nudge might help steer Paul's focus toward the pressing needs of our burgeoning settlement. After all, the success of our community hinged on the efficient management of these resources. And there I was, the newly appointed Drop Zone manager, bearing the weight of ensuring our supplies didn't just languish under the open sky, vulnerable to the capricious whims of nature.

"This is quite the haul, Paul," I remarked, my voice a mix of admiration and concern, aiming to snap him out of his reverie. The sheer volume of goods amassed was a testament to their audacity and skill, yet it posed a logistical challenge that couldn't be ignored. "But where are we going to store all of this?" It was a question meant to prod him, gently yet firmly, towards contemplating a tangible solution, grounding his thoughts back to the practicalities that our settlement hinged upon.

Paul rubbed the back of his neck with an intensity that spoke volumes. His brow furrowed, eyes scanning the chaotic landscape of provisions, a visual representation of the dilemma we faced. "That's the problem," he confessed, his voice laced with the strain of impending logistical hurdles. "We're running out of space. The Food Shed can only hold so much, and the Tool Shed will be full soon enough with the construction gear."

I nodded, my mind whirring with the possibilities that sprawled before us, a vast expanse of resources awaiting deployment. My role as the Drop Zone manager suddenly felt more significant, a pivotal force in the transformation of this nascent settlement. The sight before me was not merely a collection of items but the building blocks of a community, each piece a potential cornerstone in the edifice we aspired to erect from the desolation that surrounded us.

As I stood there, enveloped in the dusty air, a vision began to crystallise. The notion of mere sheds seemed suddenly inadequate, too small for the grandeur of what we could achieve. "We need more than just simple sheds. We need a full storage solution. Something bigger, grander," I mused aloud, my voice echoing the breadth of the vision that unfurled in my mind's eye.

The glint of shared understanding in Paul's eyes was heartening as he pivoted to align with my gaze, his stance shifting from contemplation to resolve. "I've been thinking the same. We might need to consider building a warehouse or something similar. A central place to store and organise everything," he echoed.

A smile, genuine and hopeful, spread across my face. Paul's response was the spark I had hoped to ignite, a sign that my nudging had borne fruit. "Makes sense," I concurred, eager to nurture the momentum of our shared vision. "It would make managing supplies a lot easier. Plus, it could serve as a distribution centre for the camp."

Paul's momentary lapse into contemplation painted a vivid picture of the daunting task that lay ahead. His words, "Yeah, a warehouse could be the solution. But it's going to be a big project. We'll need to plan it carefully," hung in the air, heavy with the weight of the responsibility that we were about to shoulder. I watched as his gaze drifted, perhaps envisioning the scale of the project, the myriad of complexities it entailed.

Feeling a surge of paternal instinct, I reached out, placing my hand on my son's shoulder—a gesture laden with silent reassurance. "Well, if anyone can manage it, it's you. You've got a good head on your shoulders for this sort of thing," I offered, hoping my words would bolster his confidence. It was a tightrope walk of encouragement, aiming to uplift without overburdening him with the expectation that he had to have all the answers.

The reality was that while I could conjure grand visions of what could be, actualising those visions was another matter entirely. It demanded a specific set of skills, a detailed understanding of logistics and construction—skills that Paul was better equipped with, especially when donning his Settlement development hat.

"Thanks, Dad," Paul's words, infused with warmth and gratitude, momentarily lifted the weight from my shoulders. His smile, sincere and filled with resolve, reflected his readiness to tackle the task at hand. "I'll start drawing up some plans," he announced, his determination evident in his tone.

However, his declaration ignited a flicker of alarm within me. Paul's enthusiasm, while commendable, stirred a wave of concern. His 'go get 'em' attitude was a trait I deeply admired, but the thought of him embarking on the intricate journey of drafting technical plans on his own seemed daunting. My mind raced with images of complex architectural designs and logistical schematics, far beyond the realm of layman's expertise.

"In the meantime," Paul's voice sliced through my spiralling thoughts, pulling me back to the present. My heart skipped a beat, bracing for what he might propose next. "We need to categorise everything and find temporary storage solutions until this warehouse is up." His words floated in the air, a blend of pragmatism and foresight.

A wave of relief washed over me as I processed his words. This interim plan, focused on organisation and immediate solutions, was indeed a sensible approach. It grounded his ambitious vision in tangible, manageable steps, providing a much-needed anchor to the whirlwind of tasks that lay ahead.

Kain's brisk arrival abruptly shifted the atmosphere, drawing our collective focus away from our immediate concerns about storage and plans. His presence, always tinged with an aura of privacy, piqued my curiosity. I couldn't help but speculate if he sought a one-on-one dialogue with Paul, given his apparent preference for discreet conversations. Yet, our prior engagement left me hopeful that the ice had thawed sufficiently, allowing me to remain included in this unfolding scenario.

"Paul, I've got news," Kain announced, his voice carrying a blend of excitement and tension that immediately set my senses on alert. The array of emotions playing across his face added layers of complexity to his announcement, sparking a flurry of possibilities in my mind about the nature of his news.

Paul responded with a measured casualness, "What's up?" though his quick, wary glance in my direction betrayed his expectation of significant news. It was a subtle acknowledgment of our shared understanding that Kain's interjection was far from trivial.

"It's about Brianne, my fiancée," Kain revealed, his voice brimming with a mixture of thrill and a hint of nervousness, an emotional cocktail that seemed to thicken the air around us. "She's coming to Clivilius. Today!" The weight of his words hung in the air, charged with implications and unforeseen consequences.

The news took me aback, and by the looks of it, Paul was equally surprised. Brianne's imminent arrival to Clivilius wasn't just a personal matter for Kain; it had broader ramifications, introducing a new dynamic to our already complex web of interpersonal relationships and responsibilities within the settlement.

"Wait, Brianne's coming here? Today?" Paul's repetition of the news echoed around us, his tone imbued with a mix of surprise and concern. There was a brief, heavy pause as he processed the information, before he added, "But she's pregnant, right? How far along is she?"

"Yeah, she's in her third trimester," Kain responded, his voice laden with an unmistakable worry that seemed to cast a shadow over his features.

From my vantage point, I watched the exchange with a deepening sense of apprehension. The thought of Brianne, in her delicate condition, venturing into our rudimentary settlement stirred a maelstrom of concerns within me. Our community, though resilient and resourceful, was hardly the ideal place for prenatal care or childbirth, lacking the fundamental medical facilities and expertise such a situation demanded.

"Kain, we're not equipped for this," Paul stated, voicing the very concerns that churned in my mind. His straightforwardness was necessary, albeit harsh, a reflection of the raw reality of our limitations. "We don't even have a doctor here," he pointed out, underscoring the critical gap in our preparedness for such a significant event.

I observed Kain's reaction closely, noting the distress that washed over him as he ran his fingers through his hair. There was a part of me that silently urged him to reconsider, to see the practicality in Paul's words.

"I know, I know," Kain admitted, his acknowledgment tinged with a resignation that tugged at my empathy. "I've already talked to Luke about it. He thinks we can manage." His reliance on Luke's optimism did little to assuage my concerns, leaving me to grapple with a mix of hope and realism.

The revelation that Luke had sanctioned this plan without considering the glaring logistical and health concerns was typical of his sometimes overly optimistic nature. I fought to keep my skepticism in check, knowing all too well the kind of risks such decisions entailed. The settlement, with its makeshift infrastructure, was hardly a sanctuary for anyone, let alone a pregnant woman in her final trimester.

"Manage?" Paul's incredulity mirrored my own, his voice tinged with a rising alarm. "Kain, this is serious. We need to think about prenatal care, a place for her to stay..." His voice faded into the charged silence, leaving his unfinished thoughts hanging like a heavy cloud over us.

Kain's nod, though resigned, signalled a mix of understanding and a trace of defensiveness. "I get it, Paul. But it's happening. Luke's bringing her through the Portal today." His words settled with a finality that left little room for further debate, marking the impending arrival of Brianne as a new chapter, one fraught with unknowns and challenges.

As I exhaled a breath laden with concern, my thoughts drifted to Greta, a beacon of maternal experience within our family. Her history of raising six children sparked a glimmer of hope in my mind. Perhaps she could be a guiding presence for Brianne, offering wisdom and support in an environment where conventional medical care was a luxury we couldn't afford.

Paul's deep inhalation marked a shift in his demeanour, a transition from hesitancy to a resolute acceptance of the situation at hand, a situation orchestrated by the ever-unpredictable Luke. "Okay, first things first," he declared, locking eyes with me, a clear signal that the conversation had moved into the realm of immediate action. "We need to clear the area near the Portals. Luke seems to have a habit of accompanying the people he brings, with a vehicle. So, we'll need the space."

I found myself nodding in agreement, not just in acknowledgment of Paul's words but also as an affirmation of my own mental preparations. Beatrix's update, now crucially relevant, had already set a course of action in my mind, one that was now being vocalised and set into motion.

"And Beatrix is bringing us more motorhomes, right?" Kain chimed in, having also been privy to Beatrix's update.

"Ah, that's right. I forgot about that aspect," Paul confessed, his expression mirroring the flurry of considerations now racing through his mind. "We'll definitely need the space near the Portal's cleared, then."

"Alright," I responded, signalling my readiness to tackle the immediate task at hand while harbouring a lingering question about our larger logistical dilemma. "But where do you want us to put all of our house belongings?" I inquired, sweeping my hand toward the Drop Zone, a visual testament to our ongoing struggle against the clutter of survival. The question, initially poised to jog Paul back into his role as our logistical anchor, echoed oddly in my ears, almost mocking in its naivety. The Drop Zone, after all, was merely a defined patch amidst an endless stretch of barren land, its boundaries arbitrarily marked by stones—a reminder that our constraints were, in some sense, self-imposed.

Paul's contemplative gaze swept over the area, his mind seemingly untangling the web of immediate necessities and future contingencies. "For now, just move everything to the side. We need to keep the space directly in front of the Portals clear. It's crucial for safety, especially with the Guardian's driving vehicles through." His instructions cut through the complexity of our situation with a clarity that grounded me back in the present. The importance of maintaining a clear path for the vehicles, a seemingly simple directive, was a beacon of practicality.

I found a quiet admiration for Paul's ability to distill our immediate actions down to their essence, preventing us from getting lost in the mire of 'what-ifs' and 'how-abouts.' His guidance was a reminder of the importance of tackling one challenge at a time, a principle that seemed increasingly vital in our precarious existence.

Internally, I acknowledged that our possessions, scattered and piled between the Portals and the Drop Zone, would soon find their way back to their owners—Greta, Jerome, Charles, Kain, and others—each reclaiming bits and pieces of their old lives, piecing together a semblance of normality in our shared, transient home.

"I'll get right on it," I affirmed, eager to show Paul that his directives wouldn't go unheeded. My words were an acknowledgment of his leadership but also a subtle reminder of the broader challenges we faced. "But, Paul, we really need to think about long-term storage solutions," I emphasised, not wanting the urgency of the immediate to overshadow the necessity of planning for our future stability. My experience had taught me the importance of balancing the now with the next, and I hoped to instil this perspective in Paul.

"I know, Dad," Paul's reply came with a detectable undercurrent of stress. "We're working on it. The construction of the sheds is just the beginning," he assured me, his words offering a glimpse into the broader strategy he had in mind.

Curious about the tangible progress we had made, I inquired, "And speaking of sheds, what about the one that was finished yesterday? What's its purpose?"

"It's a Food Shed," Paul clarified, the response bringing a sense of relief but also raising further questions about our logistical capabilities. "But we need another one for tools, especially with all the construction going on."

My nod was an acknowledgment of his plan, a gesture of support for his thoughtfulness in ensuring our resources were well managed. Yet, internally, I chastised myself for the lapse in my memory about the Food Shed. "Good thinking. That'll help keep things organised," I commended, masking my momentary embarrassment with a veneer of paternal approval.

"Until we have specific places for everything, like the Food Shed, just keep moving stuff to the Drop Zone. We'll sort it out from there," Paul reiterated, emphasising a step-by-step approach to our sprawling logistical challenges.

Despite the practicality of his advice, my mind was already racing ahead to the next concern: manpower. Specifically, Jerome and Charles' involvement. "You know I'm happy to manage affairs here," I started, making sure to capture Paul's full attention. "But, I don't really want to put my back out moving all of this. Last thing we need is me laid up in bed for days." The mention of my back wasn't just a bid for sympathy —it was a strategic play to remind Paul of the necessity of distributing the workload, ensuring that everyone contributed to our communal effort.

Paul's response came with an understanding nod. "Don't worry. I'll send Jerome and Charles to help you out," he assured me, immediately grasping the underlying message about the importance of shared responsibilities.

"Jerome is already here," I informed Paul, nodding toward where Jerome remained immersed in conversation with Beatrix. Observing Jerome's easy demeanour and his ability to adapt to his surroundings brought a fleeting moment of happy reflection. It was a small, personal victory to see one of my children transition so seamlessly into our new life.

"I'll fetch Charles, then," Paul declared, ready to mobilise the additional hands I sorely needed.

"Thank you, Paul," I expressed my gratitude, not just for his immediate solution but also for his overall leadership.

As Kain began to drift away from our conversation, his movements caught my attention. His indecision was palpable, reflected in the way he alternated his weight from one foot to the other. I observed him intently, noting the direction he was heading—to the camp. Sensing an opportunity to further involve him in, I raised my voice to halt his retreat. He paused, a look of mild surprise crossing his features before he pivoted back towards me. With a beckoning gesture, I encouraged his return. Meanwhile, Paul offered a quick, supportive smile before he set off towards the camp, his departure carrying with it the task of bringing Charles to assist me.

"Are you able to stay for a while and help us clear a space at the Portals?" I asked Kain, eager not only for his assistance but also to find opportunities to engage further with him. It was crucial that he felt a sense of responsibility, especially given the imminent arrival of his fiancée, which would undeniably impact us all.

"Of course," Kain responded, his readiness to help easing some of my concerns about his commitment. "Where would you like me to start?"

The warmth of my smile was as much for his willingness as it was to bolster my own spirits. As I placed a hand on Kain's shoulder, guiding us toward the Portals, I felt a surge of camaraderie. Yet, as we neared the cluttered area, the magnitude of the task ahead became starkly apparent. I inhaled deeply, a subtle stalling tactic, as the disarray before us loomed large, demanding a swift, yet thoughtful, strategy.

"Great," I replied, my voice a mix of gratitude and determination. The brief pause allowed me to gather my thoughts, to transition from the theoretical planning to the tangible action required. The mess at the Portals wasn't just a physical challenge; it was a symbol of the ongoing struggle to impose order on the chaos that defined our new existence.

HELPMEET

4338.214.5

Approaching the jumbled mess that once belonged in our family home, I gestured to the haphazard mix of furniture, boxes, and personal effects scattered in front of the Portals. The sight was almost overwhelming. But even amidst the disorder, I knew that we had to press on, to find a way to create order from the chaos.

"I need you to clear a space here," I told Kain, my voice steady and calm despite the growing turmoil that stirred within me. "Move everything to the side, and if you can, try to sort it into rooms. Kitchen items together, bedrooms, living room, that sort of thing."

Kain's face split into a grin, his enthusiasm infectious, even in the face of such a daunting task. "You got it, Noah. I'll have this area looking ship-shape in no time," he declared, his eyes sparkling with determination.

As he set to work, I couldn't help but notice the slight limp that still plagued him, a reminder of the injury he had sustained in the nighttime attack of the black shadow creatures. It was a reminder that Greta still wanted me to organise getting the gruesome head that remained staked to the ground at the camp's entrance gate, removed. But even with the pain that must have been coursing through his leg, Kain moved with a sense of purpose, his strong arms making quick work of the assortment of items that littered his path.

Watching him eye-off the dining room table, concerned for his well-being, I called out to him, my voice cutting through the din of his labours. "Kain!" I shouted, waiting for him to pause and turn back to me.

When he did, I fixed him with a stern gaze, my eyes filled with a mix of worry and authority. "Make sure you ask Jerome and Charles to help you move the heavier furniture," I instructed, unwilling to let his stubborn pride lead him to further injury.

For a moment, I could see the internal struggle playing out in Kain's eyes, the desire to prove himself warring with the wisdom of accepting help. But finally, he nodded his agreement, his shoulders slumping slightly in acquiescence. "Sure thing," he called back, his voice tinged with a hint of reluctance.

Satisfied that I had done my due diligence, I turned my attention elsewhere, my mind struggling to build a clear plan of action amidst the disorder that surrounded me. The Portal area and the Drop Zone were in shambles, a haphazard collection of belongings and supplies that seemed to stretch out as far as the eye could see, merging with the rolling dusty dunes.

Like a magpie, my gaze was drawn to a glint of metal in the harsh sunlight, the gleam of an empty trolley beckoning to me like a beacon in the night. I made my way over to it, my steps slow and measured, as an idea sparked in my mind.

With a grunt of effort, I wheeled the trolley through the thick layers of dust that coated the ground, the metal frame clattering and rattling as it moved. And then, with a sense of reverence that bordered on the sacred, I began to place my journal folders into the trolley, each one a precious record of our family's journey, from the emigration of my parents from England to Australia, my marriage to Greta, and the birth of Paul right down to the birth of Charles.

The older folders were battered and worn, their edges frayed and their covers scuffed from years of use. But as I flipped through the pages, the memories contained within remained as clear and vibrant as the day I had printed them, the photos and descriptions a memory to the life we had lived, to the moments that had shaped us and brought us to this point. Reflecting on the history of our lives, I felt a soft voice stirring inside me, whispering to me that I needed to continue the habit, that I needed to document our journey and life here in Clivilius.

As I worked, lost in the pages of our past, the sound of panicked footsteps and frantic voices began to filter through my concentration, pulling me back to the present with a jolt. I looked up, my brow furrowing with concern, to see Charles racing towards me, his face a mask of fear and excitement.

"Dad!" he cried out, his voice high and breathless, the words tumbling from his lips in a rush. "Have you seen Nibbles?"

My heart sank, a wave of dread washing over me at the thought of my son's beloved pet lost and alone in this shambled landscape. Nibbles, the tiny hamster that had been a constant companion to Charles for the last few years, was more than just a pet – he was a symbol of the life we had left behind, of the innocence that would never be again.

I opened my mouth to reply, to offer some words of comfort and reassurance, but before I could speak, Jerome appeared at Charles's side, his face flushed with exertion and triumph. In his hands, he held a small cage, and there, nestled inside, was the tiny form of Nibbles, his fur ruffled and his eyes wide with confusion.

Charles's face broke into a grin, his eyes shining with relief and joy as he took the cage from Jerome, his fingers curling around the bars as he cooed and murmured to his pet. "Beatrix brought him here," Jerome explained, his voice filled with a mixture of amusement and affection.

At the mention of Beatrix's name, Charles's head snapped up, his eyes scanning the area for any sign of the woman who had become such an integral part of our lives. But she was nowhere to be seen.

Noticing our searching gazes, Jerome offered a brief explanation, his words coming in short, clipped bursts. "She's gone back to Earth. She's going to get another motorhome or two," he said, his eyes sparkling with excitement at the prospect of more comfortable accommodations.

I smiled warmly, my heart swelling with gratitude for Beatrix's tireless efforts on our behalf. Accommodation was definitely a needed and valuable resource, and I knew that her contributions would go a long way towards making our transition to this new world a little bit easier.

"And she's going to collect Millie from the vet," Jerome added, his voice softening with a mixture of concern and anticipation.

I felt a slight frown cross my face, my brow furrowing with worry. "Are you sure that's a good idea?" I asked. "With her health troubles and the limited resources we have here, it might be difficult to care for her properly."

But Jerome nodded determinedly, his jaw set with a stubborn resolve that I recognised all too well. "Yeah. Beatrix and I have a plan in place," he said, his words filled with a confidence that I hoped wasn't misplaced.

I hesitated for a moment, torn between my desire to protect my son and my trust in his judgment. But finally, I nodded, my face softening with understanding. "Okay," I replied simply, allowing Jerome to maintain his autonomy. "You'll need to look after her," I added, my voice gentle but firm.

Jerome's brow furrowed, his eyes flashing with a hint of annoyance. "I already do," he stated flatly.

I felt a twinge of guilt at my poor choice of words, my heart aching with the knowledge that I had unintentionally caused my son pain. "I know you do," I told him, my voice soft and reassuring. "I didn't mean to imply otherwise. I'm just worried about Millie, and about you."

Jerome's face softened, the tension draining from his shoulders as he nodded in understanding. "I know, Dad," he said, his voice filled with a quiet strength that never ceased to amaze me. "But we'll be okay. Millie's tough, and so am I."

I smiled, my heart swelling with pride at the young man my son had become. And then, with a sense of purpose that belied the disorder that surrounded us, I turned to the task at hand, my mind beginning to race with plans and possibilities.

"Can the two of you please help Kain clear the space from around the Portals?" I asked, my voice filled with a quiet authority. "Especially with his injured leg, make sure you help Kain with the furniture."

"Of course," Jerome replied, his eyes sparkling with a newfound sense of purpose. "I want to stay close by for Millie's arrival anyway."

I nodded, grateful for my son's willingness to help, and for the distraction that the work would provide from the anxiety of waiting for Millie's return.

I turned to Charles, my gaze firm with expectation for his response.

But Charles, his face still split with a grin, held up Nibbles' cage, his eyes shining with excitement. "I'm going to take Nibbles back to camp first," he declared, his voice filled with a childlike glee that was impossible to ignore.

I hesitated for a moment, knowing that Charles's idea of taking Nibbles back to camp would likely involve playing with him and getting distracted from the work at hand. Yet, it was hard to argue with the logic of ensuring that Nibbles was secured in a safe environment, especially if it was going to be another warm day in the sun. Sitting around exposed would not fare well for the small furry creature.

"Make it quick, then," I told Charles, my voice firm but not unkind. "And then come straight back to help your brother and Kain."

Charles nodded, his face still split with a grin as he hurried off towards the camp, Nibbles' cage clutched tightly in his hands. As I watched him go, I felt a sense of warmth and love wash over me, a reminder of the bonds that tied us together, even in this strange and unfamiliar place.

And then with Jerome making his way over to where Kain was sizing up the couch, I turned my attention back to my trolley of journals. These were perhaps my most prized possessions, and for a moment, I considered following after Charles, taking the folders to the safety and security of the motorhome. But as I looked at the piles of belongings and supplies that littered the area, I knew that I couldn't afford to waste even a moment.

There was work to be done. I had no idea when Beatrix might return with her first motorhome, and there was a lot of work ahead of us to make space in front of her Portal. And so, with a deep breath and a sense of resolve that burned bright within me, I turned back to the daunting task at hand.

BREWING STORMS

4338.214.6

The wind whipped through the air, sending tendrils of dust dancing across the barren landscape. I stood near the Portals and Drop Zone, watching as Clivilians gathered, their faces etched with a mix of anticipation and unease. The atmosphere was charged with a palpable tension, a sense that something momentous was about to unfold.

Amidst the hustle and bustle, my gaze settled on Kain, his eyes fixed on the shimmering Portal with an intensity that spoke volumes about his emotional state. I knew he was waiting for the arrival of his fiancee Brianne and their beloved dog, Hudson. The love and devotion he held for them were evident in every line of his body, every flicker of his expression.

Nearby, Jerome and Charles busied themselves with moving house items, their faces flushed with exertion. Despite the remaining effort surrounding them, they worked with a determined focus, their movements coordinated and purposeful. I couldn't help but feel a surge of pride as I watched my sons tackle the daunting task with such resilience and adaptability.

Greta, ever the diligent wife and mother, moved through the scene with a quiet efficiency, collecting essentials for our motorhome. Her actions were a testament to her unwavering commitment to our family's well-being, a constant reminder of the strength and support she provided in the face of adversity.

As I surveyed the scene, taking in the myriad of emotions and activities playing out before me, I couldn't shake the feeling of unease that crept up my spine. The wind seemed to be picking up, growing stronger with each passing moment. It whipped around me, tugging at my clothes and sending shivers down my back.

There was something almost otherworldly about the way the wind moved, as if it carried with it a foreboding presence, an unseen force that set my nerves on edge. It was a familiar sensation, one that I had experienced during my time in Broken Hill, a place where the elements seemed to hold a strange power over the land and its inhabitants.

I remembered the way the wind had howled through the streets of Broken Hill, carrying with it a sense of unease that permeated every corner of the town. It was a feeling that had never quite left me, a lingering reminder of the unpredictability of nature.

As I stood there, lost in my thoughts, I couldn't help but wonder what this wind might bring to our new home in Clivilius. Would it be a harbinger of change, a force that would shape our lives in ways we couldn't yet imagine? Or would it simply be another challenge to overcome, another obstacle in the path of our journey?

I shook my head, trying to clear my mind of the unsettling thoughts. There was no use in dwelling on the unknown, in letting fear and uncertainty cloud my judgment. We had come too far, survived too much, to let the wind or any other force break our resolve.

With a deep breath, I squared my shoulders and turned my attention back to the task at hand. There was work to be done, people to support, and a future to build. Whatever the wind might bring, we would face it together, as a family and as a community.

❖

Suddenly, a commotion erupted near the Portal, shattering the tenuous calm that had settled over the area. Luke emerged from the swirling vortex, driving a car at a breakneck speed that seemed to defy the laws of physics. The tires kicked up plumes of dust as he slammed on the brakes, the force of the sudden stop nearly sending him through the windshield. Without a moment's hesitation, he leapt from the vehicle, leaving the door wide open, and sprinted towards the Portal with a desperation I had never seen before. He vanished once more into its swirling depths, leaving us all stunned and confused.

"You bastard!" Brianne's voice cut through the confusion like a knife, raw and filled with a potent mix of anger and betrayal. She clambered out of the car, her movements jerky and uncoordinated, as if she were moving through a nightmare. Her eyes, wide and haunted, remained fixed on the spot where Luke had disappeared, as if she could will him back into existence through sheer force of will.

Kain, who had been waiting anxiously near the Portal, rushed forward to embrace Brianne, his relief palpable. They clung to each other, tears streaming down their faces as they whispered fervent words of love and reassurance. For a moment, the world around them seemed to fade away, and I couldn't help but feel a twinge of sympathy at their unbreakable bond.

The Portal burst to life again, its shimmering surface rippling with an otherworldly energy that set my teeth on edge. But instead of Luke, it was Hudson, Kain's faithful companion, who emerged from the shimmering gateway, alone and disoriented. The dog stumbled forward, his legs trembling beneath him, as if he had witnessed horrors beyond imagining. Kain and Brianne, still locked in their embrace, reached out to comfort the distressed animal, their love extending to their beloved pet.

As they stepped away from the Portal, their reunion complete, I couldn't shake the feeling that something was amiss. The air seemed to crackle with tension, and I found myself holding my breath, waiting for the other shoe to drop.

Suddenly, the Portal flared to life once more, its surface shimmering with an intensity that seared my retinas. I shielded my eyes, squinting against the blinding light, as a cacophony of sounds echoed from the depths of the vortex. The ground shook beneath my feet, and I stumbled backward, my heart pounding in my chest.

Through the shimmering portal, a scene of utter chaos emerged. Luke and a policeman tumbled through, locked in a fierce struggle, their bodies intertwined in a deadly embrace. They crashed to the ground in a tangle of limbs, grunting and cursing as they grappled for dominance. But that wasn't all. A torrent of objects followed in their wake, spilling out of the Portal like a flood of debris. Tools, boxes, and various pieces of equipment, all seemingly from a shed, clattered to the ground around them, adding to the confusion and mayhem.

I watched in stunned disbelief as the two men fought, rolling in the dust and debris, their faces contorted with rage and desperation. The policeman seemed to have the advantage, his training giving him an edge over Luke's raw fury. He pinned Luke to the ground, his knee pressing into his back, as he reached for his handcuffs.

But Luke wasn't going down without a fight. With a roar of defiance, he bucked and twisted, throwing the officer off balance. They rolled again, exchanging curses, as the contents of the shed lay scattered around them like the aftermath of a tornado.

I glanced at Greta, seeing my own shock and confusion mirrored in her eyes. This was beyond anything we had ever witnessed, a scene straight out of a nightmare. The Portal had brought chaos and violence to our doorstep.

Luke and the policeman rolled through the dust, grappling with each other like wild animals, their movements a blur of flailing limbs and grunts of exertion. The officer finally gained the upper hand, pinning Luke beneath him with a force that made me wince. He held Luke's hands firmly above his head, his fingers digging into his wrists with a brutal intensity. I couldn't hear the words exchanged between them, but I could see the fury etched into the policeman's features, the vein pulsing in his temple as he stared into Luke's face.

With a swift, hard punch to the head that made my own skull throb in sympathy, the officer rendered Luke unconscious, his body going limp in the dust like a discarded rag doll. "Fuck you!" the policeman yelled, his voice thick with rage and frustration, the words tearing from his throat like a primal scream.

As Kain and Paul ran towards the scene, their faces etched with a mix of concern and determination, the officer scrambled to his feet, drawing his gun with a speed that left me breathless. He waved it wildly at the approaching crowd, his eyes wide and feverish, as if he were seeing demons in every shadow. "Stay back!" he warned, his voice trembling with an adrenaline-fuelled intensity that made my heart race. "I'll shoot!"

Instinctively, I sought cover behind some nearby boxes, my heart pounding in my chest like a trapped bird. The adrenaline coursing through my veins heightened my senses, making every sound and movement seem amplified. I knew that any sudden actions could attract unwanted attention from the armed officer, potentially escalating the already tense situation.

My eyes darted around the area, searching for Greta amidst the chaos. The need to ensure her safety was a primal instinct. When our gazes finally locked, I felt a momentary wave of relief wash over me, seeing that she was unharmed.

With a subtle nod and a firm look, I signalled for her to stay put, to avoid drawing any focus to herself. The last thing I wanted was for Greta to become a target, to find herself in the crosshairs of a panicked or trigger-happy officer. She met my gaze with a mix of understanding and trepidation, her own fear evident in the tightness of her expression.

The thought of losing her, of watching her fall victim to a stray bullet or a panicked reaction, was a nightmare I couldn't bear to contemplate. The mere idea sent a chill down my spine, a horror that threatened to overwhelm me. I had to trust that she would understand my silent plea, that she would remain still and out of harm's way until the danger had passed.

With a deep breath, I forced myself to stay calm and focused, ready to react if the situation demanded it, but determined not to be the catalyst for any further escalation. I knew that the slightest misstep could have dire consequences, and I refused to be the one to tip the scales towards tragedy. All I could do was watch, wait, and pray that the officer would come to his senses before it was too late.

"Karl!" Beatrix's voice rang out from the group, cutting through the chaos like a beacon of hope. Her tone was steady and calm, despite the tension that hung thick in the air, threatening to suffocate us all. The officer, Karl, seemed to hesitate for a moment, as if considering lowering his weapon. But he didn't. He kept it trained on Beatrix, his finger twitching on the trigger.

"What the fuck is Clivilius?" Karl demanded, his words laced with a fear and confusion that bordered on hysteria. His gun remained pointed directly at Beatrix's chest, the barrel trembling slightly as he fought to keep it steady. In that moment, I saw the depths of his terror, the realisation that he had stumbled into a world beyond his understanding or control.

"This place is Clivilius," Beatrix replied, her voice soft and soothing, her hands gesturing to the world around them. "Karl, it's okay. You're safe here."

Karl's breathing grew deep and ragged, his chest heaving as he struggled to make sense of his surroundings. I could see the war raging behind his eyes, the desperate need to cling to some semblance of recognition in a world turned upside down. Slowly, the gun slipped from his grasp, falling to the ground with a soft thud that seemed to echo in the stillness that followed.

I let out a breath I hadn't realised I'd been holding, relief washing over me like a cool breeze on a sweltering day. As Paul stepped forward, his hand outstretched in greeting, I watched with bated breath, wondering how the officer would react. Would he lash out, driven by fear and confusion, or would he accept the offered hand of friendship?

"Hi. I'm Paul Smith," Paul said cheerfully, his voice cutting through the tense silence like a ray of sunshine through storm clouds. "Luke's brother," he added, glancing over at Luke's still form, now stirring with signs of life.

Karl blinked rapidly, his eyes wide with disbelief and terror, as if he were seeing ghosts in every shadow. "Shit!" he cried out, his voice cracking with emotion, the weight of his realisation crushing him like a physical force. "I'm dead!"

With those words, Karl collapsed into the soft dust, his body going limp as the weight of his fear crashed down upon him like a tidal wave. He lay there, motionless, as if the very life had been drained from his body.

I caught sight of Beatrix approaching Karl as he began to regain consciousness, her movements slow and cautious, as if she were approaching a wounded animal. There seemed to be a flicker of recognition in their eyes, a shared understanding that went beyond words, as if they had known each other in another life.

I maintained my distance, watching the scene unfold with a growing sense of unease that twisted in my gut like a knife. The wind continued to pick up, whipping the dust into frenzied eddies that danced around us, obscuring my vision and filling my lungs with grit that tasted of despair and desolation.

Suddenly, a cry rang out from the top of the closest hill, a warning that sent a chill down my spine and turned my blood to ice. "Dust storm!" someone shouted, their words carried away on the swirling currents of air.

I turned, my eyes widening in horror as I saw the sky darkening in the distance, a massive wall of dust approaching with terrifying speed. It was a sight straight out of a nightmare, a roiling mass of darkness that seemed to swallow the very light itself. It was coming from the direction of the camp, from across the other side of the river, and I knew in that moment that we were in grave danger, that our very lives hung in the balance.

Glancing around at the chaos near the Portals, at the scattered belongings and the makeshift structures of the Drop Zone, I realised with a sinking feeling that there was no cover, no protection from the impending storm. We were exposed, vulnerable, like ants caught in the path of a raging flood. It was too late to salvage anything now.

Paul's voice rose above the din, urgency lacing his words, each syllable a desperate plea for survival. "Everyone, back to camp! Now!"

I reached for Greta, my heart pounding in my chest with a ferocity that threatened to tear it from my ribcage. I saw the fear in her eyes, the raw, primal terror that comes from staring death in the face. She screeched for Charles and

Jerome, her voice raw and ragged, the sound of a mother's love and desperation given voice.

The storm was moving rapidly, the wall of dust growing closer with each passing second, a relentless juggernaut that would crush us beneath its weight. As Greta and I reached the peak of the first dune, our lungs burning with the effort, we realised with a sickening feeling that the dust would have already reached the camp by now. It was a devastating realisation, a blow that struck me with an almost physical force, threatening to bring me to my knees.

"Noah, what do we do?" Greta asked, her voice trembling with a fear that bordered on hysteria. Her hand gripped mine so tightly that I could feel the bones of her fingers pressing into my skin, as if she were trying to anchor herself to me, to hold on to some shred of hope in the face of annihilation.

I looked out at the approaching storm, at the swirling mass of dust and debris that threatened to engulf us, to consume us whole. The wind howled like a tortured beast, its voice a deafening roar that filled my ears and shook me to my core. The air was thick with the scent of fear and desperation, a cloying, suffocating odour that clung to the back of my throat like a living thing.

In that moment, I felt a terror unlike anything I had ever known, a soul-crushing, mind-numbing fear that threatened to paralyse me where I stood. It was the fear of the unknown, of the horrors that lurked within the heart of the storm, waiting to tear us apart with merciless fury. It was the fear of losing everything I held dear, of watching my family, my very reason for living, be ripped away from me by the uncaring brutality of nature.

But even as the fear threatened to consume me, to drag me down into the depths of despair, I knew that I couldn't let it win. I had to be strong, for Greta, for our sons, for the slim hope of survival that still flickered within me like a dying ember. I had to find the courage to face the storm, to defy the odds and fight for the chance to see another day.

I looked out at the approaching storm once more, at the swirling mass of dust and debris that threatened to engulf us, to consume us whole. In that moment, I knew that there was only one thing we could do, one slim chance at survival.

"We run," I told her, my voice steady and determined despite the fear that gripped my heart like a vice. "We run like hell and pray to God that we make it."

TO BE CONTINUED...

Printed and bound by CPI Group (UK) Ltd, Croydon, CR0 4YY
29/04/2024
01005952-0002